The Featherbed

For my late grandmothers,
Chip Kellermann and Claire Miller

The Featherbed

~ *a novel* ~

John Miller

SIMON & PIERRE FICTION
A MEMBER OF THE DUNDURN GROUP
TORONTO · OXFORD

Editor: Barry Jowett
Copy-Editor: Andrea Pruss
Design: Jennifer Scott
Printer: Transcontinental

National Library of Canada Cataloguing in Publication Data

Miller, John, 1968-
    The featherbed / by John Miller.

ISBN 1-55002-401-9

I. Title.

PS8576.I53885F43 2002   C813'.6   C2002-904331-X   PR9199.4.M555F43 2002

1   2   3   4   5   06   05   04   03   02

 Canada

THE CANADA COUNCIL | LE CONSEIL DES ARTS
FOR THE ARTS | DU CANADA
SINCE 1957 | DEPUIS 1957

ONTARIO ARTS COUNCIL
CONSEIL DES ARTS DE L'ONTARIO

We acknowledge the support of the **Canada Council for the Arts** and the **Ontario Arts Council** for our publishing program. We also acknowledge the financial support of the **Government of Canada** through the **Book Publishing Industry Development Program** and **The Association for the Export of Canadian Books**, and the **Government of Ontario** through the **Ontario Book Publishers Tax Credit** program.

Printed and bound in Canada.⊕
Printed on recycled paper.
www.dundurn.com

Dundurn Press
8 Market Street
Suite 200
Toronto, Ontario, Canada
M5E 1M6

Dundurn Press
73 Lime Walk
Headington, Oxford,
England
OX3 7AD

Dundurn Press
2250 Military Road
Tonawanda NY
U.S.A. 14150

Acknowledgements

My uncle, Bob Kellermann, surely could not have predicted five years ago that a simple birthday gift would lead to all of this. The gift was a book about Jewish immigrants in North America, and reading it sparked my imagination. David Mayerovitch, holding up Shakespeare and *Buffy the Vampire Slayer* as examples, taught me the importance of building a story good enough to tell. My deepest gratitude goes to novelist Cary Fagan, both for his thoughtful editing and review of early drafts and for helping me to find Rebecca's voice. Zoe Kende, a talented midwife and good friend, educated me about the wonders, risks, and logistics of pregnancy and childbirth.

Throughout my life, I have been lucky that so many sensitive, powerful, and intelligent women have taken me into their confidence. In writing in the female voice, I hope that I have done them justice. Some of these women read my work critically and offered the kindest encouragement: Linda Bradbeer, Jeanette Browne, Kathryn Drummond, June Galbraith, Judy Godfrey, Sophia Ikura-MacMillan, Janet Killoran, Edda Kirleis, Myra Lefkowitz, Heidi Maroney, Vanessa Russell, Debra Shime,

John Miller

Pam Shime, Carol Toller, Hilary Trapp, Ellen Waxman, Dubravka Zarkov, and especially my mother, Ruth Miller.

Thanks also go to those who, in spite of their Y-chromosomes, offered similar advice and support: my father, Eric, my brothers Daniel and Tony, and friends David Adkin, Adam Arshinoff, Tim Clarkin, Scott Henderson, Onindo Khan, Bryan Patchett and Wolfram Walbrach.

The curators and staff of the Lower East Side Tenement Museum in New York are to be commended for their meticulously reconstructed apartments, which helped me to imagine the possibilities and limitations of tenement life. For bibliographical research, I consulted numerous sources, of which the most influential were: Abraham Cahan's *Yekl and the Imported Bridegroom*; Kathy Friedman-Kasaba's *Memories of Migration*; Susan Glenn's *Daughters of the Shtetl*; Emma Goldman's *Living My Life*; Irving Howe's *World of Our Fathers*; C.W. Hunt's *Booze, Boats and Billions: Smuggling Liquid Gold*; *A Bintel Brief*, edited by Isaac Metzker; Kathy Preiss's *Cheap Amusements: Working Women and Leisure in Turn of the Century New York*; Jacob A. Riis's *How The Other Half Lives*; Barbara A. Schreier's *Becoming American Women*; Kate Simon's *Bronx Primitive*; Sydney Stahl Weinberg's *The World of Our Mothers*; Lillian Wald's *House on Henry Street*; and the novels of Anzia Yezierska.

I am grateful to Dundurn for taking a chance on an unknown author, in particular to my editor, Barry Jowett, for his enthusiasm and his careful stewardship of my final draft, and to Andrea Pruss, for her meticulous copy-editing.

Finally, I must thank novelists Chaim Potok, Amy Tan, Barbara Kingsolver, and Ann-Marie MacDonald, whose exquisite prose and beautifully crafted stories inspired me to become a writer.

6

Chapter One

Four days before she died, Anna Cooperman's mother made a banal and seemingly pointless confession from her hospital bed, a non sequitur in the middle of grumbling about the dirty linen in her apartment.

"Objects hold meaning," she said, as though this were an important and novel idea.

Anna had decided not to pursue it. After all, every few hours her mother said something baffling. Just a short while before, she had muttered in her sleep something about a chicken.

Rebecca became agitated when her daughter did not acknowledge the remark.

"Listen!" She struggled to sit up in her bed, propped herself precariously against the headboard. Her face turned grave, the wrinkles in her skin seemed deeper than usual.

"Sometimes, you have to look at an object like a special doorway," she said, holding up her hands as though to cup a crystal ball, "a doorway to the heart. And if you can find the key to the door, what you see on the other side might surprise you. For instance, Anna dear, an object might reveal a person's hopes and dreams. Hopes and dreams you maybe didn't know about. Or —" she threw the crystal ball to the ground "— it might reveal all of her follies and her heartache. And sometimes, the same object might represent all of those things. All of them."

"That's very true," Anna said, to humour her, and then she settled the old woman back into her bed. When her mother became emotional, her descriptions were often elaborate metaphors, but they usually weren't riddles, and so she dismissed the remark as another demented outburst caused by the stroke.

But today, hurrying around the corner onto Eldridge and catching sight of the old synagogue's rose windows, it occurred to her that the building might tell her something about her mother, if only because she had loved it so much. She remembered the story she had been told as a child about how the temple came to be built, and suddenly she wondered if there was more to the hospital outburst than she had allowed.

Anna had been seven years old when she first learned the temple's history.

"The Eldridge Street Synagogue was the first great house of worship for Eastern European Jews in America," her mother had begun, pulling her two daughters along the street toward the building. Their father was walking ahead.

"This shul was built for us by our own people." She said this proudly, and her finger went up and waved in the air. She knew her mother meant, of course, not that Jews had actually built it with their own hands, but that they had footed the bill.

"They hired the same boys who decorated the homes of the Vanderbilts! That's America for you girls; we go to a fancy shul even though we live in a poor neighbourhood. Did you know that over in Europe, Bubbe and Zayde have to worship in a nearby storefront?"

Anna understood perfectly well when a question was rhetorical. Her mother might be lecturing, but she wasn't giving a test — not yet. Nevertheless, she was intrigued.

"You mean like the three synagogues on our street?"

"That's right, Anneleh, like the ones on our street. Some people still like to worship in those cramped and dark places, and we don't judge them for that even though we don't understand why, except that maybe it reminds them of the past. But just look at the place we go to! The architects made sure we had the best. Look at those beautiful doors! So simple and stately. And inside? They made an ark from a tree all the way from Italy. Even that wasn't grand enough, so they put red velvet lining inside to make sure the Torah had a proper place to rest. And then they built windows so high up they were almost in the ceiling!"

Her arms reached to the sky, and her shirt pulled out a little at the sides, revealing cream-coloured underpants.

"The sun was so bright the day the synagogue opened its doors that people rubbed their eyes to get used to the light pouring in. That was before your mama was born, kinderen, wasn't it?"

Her mother looked from Anna to her sister and back again. This question wasn't rhetorical, but how were they to know the answer?

"I dunno." Anna shrugged, and she looked at Sadie, who did the same.

"Of course it was! That was long before I was born. I'm not *that* old, you know!" she laughed and gave them both taps on the bum. Then when she looked up again at the street, Anna and Sadie craned their heads back behind their mother and rolled their eyes.

Her mother yanked them forward to continue the story. "This synagogue is a gift — a gift to all of us, and I'll tell you why. There has never been a shul with a sanctuary that so deserved its name. Doesn't it feel, girls, that when we breathe in the air inside that hall and feel the warmth from the sun coming in through the windows, and when our ears — oy! — for once in the week, our ears can rest from all the shouting and the haggling — doesn't it *feel* like we're in a sanctuary, girls?"

She pulled them toward her, the end of her story punctuated by the squashing of their faces into her stomach.

Anna observed the building now as she stopped to catch her breath. The doors needed a varnish, and the brickwork was pocked. It was ignored by the crowds of people who crisscrossed in front. She looked up at the awnings on the Chinese storefronts that surrounded it. An old man had set up a rickety table in front of a shop and was sitting behind it on a low stool hawking ties for two dollars apiece. Despair immobilized her for a second — this man could be her father sixty years ago. The same struggle, the same hope, undiminished by any evidence of how seldom America fulfilled her promise.

She pushed aside her cynicism, deciding that it was unsuitable on the day of her mother's funeral to be thinking of anything but her. She stopped at the foot of the synagogue's stairs and took a moment, while she caught her breath and smoothed her hair, to admire the height and width of the great wooden doors. Even faded, the deep earthen-brown panels conveyed a feeling of sturdy dignity.

The sweat on her back made her blouse cling to her skin. She had only come a few blocks, but this was July in New York, and she had been rushing. At almost seventy, she should know by now to forget about saving money and just take a cab. She cursed the Manhattan summer, worse than Los Angeles, where at least they had the sense to plant a few trees for shade.

A few deep breaths calmed her before she went down the stairs to the basement. It did not please her that they had to perform the service in the basement, but the main sanctuary had not been used since the '50s.

The synagogue no longer had a resident rabbi, but her mother wanted to have her funeral in the place where she had worshipped her whole life. Anna had tried to honour her wishes as much as she could stomach them, so she made sure to find someone who could perform the necessary rites, but she had drawn the line at an Orthodox service. She offered to make a donation to the synagogue in exchange for their allowing her to bring in a Conservative rabbi. It was a gamble, but the cash-strapped members let their pragmatism overrule tradition, and agreed.

When she entered the room, she tried to ignore the heating ducts that clung to the ceiling on both sides. Now that she surveyed the room with people in it, she was sure that it would be more than large enough to hold everyone. Pews were set up facing three sides of a raised oak bimah. Her mother's coffin sat up front, and there was an ancient man sitting beside it reading a tattered paperback.

That Sadie would be coming at all had come as a surprise. For many years now, Anna had wondered if her sister was still alive. When she received the call, it was the first time Anna had heard her voice in over fifty years. Was she somewhere in the room now?

She looked around to see whom she recognized. Her mother's landlady, Mrs. Huang, gave her a weak smile and then looked away in embarrassment. Mrs. Gutstein, an old neighbour of her mother's, was being helped by her daughter Danielle to settle into the bench. Her neighbours the Teitelbaums were at the back to the left talking to one another. Other friends sat in the first pew, as she had asked them, to give her support.

She looked around again in case she'd missed her. No, it would be the same old story, Sadie would not show.

For years she had constructed dialogue to prepare herself just in case Sadie ever did reappear, but today, when she had real reason to believe she would finally see her, she could not think of a thing to say. What words could bridge a gulf as wide as half a century? She tried to imagine what Sadie would look like today, but the picture that came to mind was her eighteen-year-old self, a tall girl with a flapper hairstyle. And the way her cheeks were so smooth and tight, especially when she used to smile with her mouth wide open. But that was silly, her face would be quite different now. She pictured someone much older, maybe like Katherine Hepburn. But she shook that image away too, self-consciously snorting to herself.

Sadie would be seventy-two years old, but the voice that played on the answering machine did not sound like the voice of a feeble old woman, and so it complicated her imagination. The message was simple and cold as it echoed against the brick walls in her Jersey City brownstone. She had heard their mother had died and wanted to know if it would be all right to come to the funeral. She left a phone number in Toronto.

Toronto? She had gone to Toronto? For some reason, she had always imagined Sadie in Chicago or San Francisco. Why on earth would she have gone to Canada?

Anna had obsessed before returning the call, and even though she was relieved to get a machine, she was nevertheless so nervous by the time the beep came that before she could catch herself she let out the huge breath that she had been holding in. She cringed, afraid that on the message tape it would sound strangely like a sigh. Never mind, she left simple instructions regarding the service and was grateful not to have to engage in a conversation like that long distance. She did not invite her sister to stay.

Now, here in the synagogue basement, she regretted not extending the invitation, because she found herself twisting in her seat, as she had at her father's funeral, when she was seventeen years old. As she had at every funeral and every wedding throughout her life.

Then she saw her.

When Sadie stepped through the doorway, Anna recognized her instantly for her height. From her seat, she watched her sister scan the room. She had steel-grey hair, cut shoulder length, and it was parted at the side. Anna forced a smile as they locked eyes for a few seconds, but as soon as Sadie averted her gaze, she was mortified that she had even tried to be civil, sure that her face had betrayed her true feelings — a mixture of terror, guilt, and anger. Nevertheless, she was transfixed as Sadie moved into the room to walk down the aisle.

She walked with controlled steps and tugged at the hem of her black jacket. The olive skin on her face was taut against high cheekbones, making her wrinkles almost imperceptible at a distance. Sadie held her mouth tightly shut, but Anna could see that her chest was heaving considerably. Perhaps her lateness wasn't intentional after all.

Her sister picked at the sides of her white blouse, smoothed out her skirt, and, as predicted, chose a seat on another bench to the left of the bimah. Anna felt the room's eyes going back and forth, from Sadie to her, back to Sadie, watching for any reaction.

People began talking in low whispers. When Sadie raised her eyes, Anna saw in them a brief flicker of surprise, quickly suppressed. The whole room was looking at her. Without losing her composure, Sadie caught old Ida Gutstein's stare and returned it almost without blinking, until the woman became visibly shaken and was forced to look away, and then finally down into her lap.

"Yit-gadal v'yit-kadash sh'may raba b'alma dee-v'ra che-ru-tay..."

Anna looked across the grave. Sadie stood alone at the back of the grounds, a few steps behind the other mourners, and looked away as soon as the rabbi said the Kaddish. There was only one row of tombstones behind her sister, and then the cemetery ended with a wire fence that separated it from the noisy street. A few of the tombstones had stones and pebbles on top.

Anna looked at the people gathered around the grave. She wondered how many of them their mother had really cared about. In her experience, there were always a few at any funeral crying more out of guilt than out of grief. She clasped her chest with one hand and grabbed her friend's hand with the other. A light rain began to fall. She looked back at her sister. Sadie looked old now that the rain was wiping away the shine from her grey hair.

The Kaddish over, Anna approached the pit, picked up the spade, and shovelled some earth into the grave. She looked up and saw the surprise in the rabbi's face. The others followed discreetly one by one, and she stood back to listen to the slicing sound of the spade going into the mound of earth, and then the thump of the dirt clods as they fell on top of the coffin. When the last mourner had put down the shovel, people started filing away, and Anna realized Sadie was not going to approach the grave. Her sister was still turned the other way, looking at the cemetery fence.

Anna cleared her throat and picked her head up. "Excuse me for a moment, everyone."

People stopped and turned. She paused and looked down at her mud-covered shoes. The rain had begun to make the ground slick under their feet.

"Thank you for coming today. I know it's raining; I won't be long." She took a tissue out of her purse to blow her nose.

"My mother was truly blessed to have such caring people in her life. It would have made her very happy knowing that you came all this way to pay your respects.

"As you may know from the announcement in the paper, the shivah will be held at my mother's place in Manhattan. When she and I talked about her funeral, she was adamant the shivah be held there, even though I tried to convince her it would be more comfortable at my house. But you all know how she was, there was no point in arguing, and I want to respect her last wishes. In any case, anyone who has been there knows that her apartment is very small, so my sister and I would ask that you give us a few hours to prepare the place and to clear it out properly so that you can all visit more comfortably."

She watched people look at each other in confusion. Perhaps some wondered who the sister was; more likely it was the delay that caused the murmur. They were probably wondering why the apartment wasn't prepared ahead of time. Her request was unusual, but she didn't care; she had her reasons for lying.

"We will be pleased to see you all, if you can make it, from four o'clock onwards." Anna smiled, and when people realized she had nothing else to say, they began to move again.

As the group drew back to wash their hands in the basin at the edge of the cemetery, Sadie was left staring at her. Anna stepped forward to close the gap between them.

"Hi, Annie. It's good to see you."

"You can come with me to Mama's place if you like," she said, and they started toward the basin. "I have one of my neighbours' cars today. They've been very good to me since Mama got sick."

"Of course."

Anna shook her hands dry, then led the way to the car.

The apartment building was five stories high and stood out garishly from its neighbours because of its red-painted brick walls. But Anna felt that the black fire escape that hung down from the fifth floor to the second was the giveaway to the interior decor. As they approached the building, she looked back at Sadie, who was trailing behind her, looking around at the old neighbourhood. Her sister stopped on the opposite curb and took in the street as a whole.

"The fire escapes didn't used to be here," Anna said. "That's why it looks different, if you were wondering. And of course the building used to be painted brown, remember? And that school across the street went up in the sixties. At least Mama's had a better view since then."

The street was almost empty of people, and the air barely moved. Anna waited for Sadie to cross to her side, but now she was staring up at the third floor, to the window of the old apartment.

"Looks different, doesn't it?" she called out.

"Not so different."

Anna shrugged, moving on without her and opening the front door with her key. She turned once again to wait and saw that Sadie was following her.

"We'll have to prop the door open later so people can get up," Anna said, shutting it behind her. "There's no buzzer to open the door. Besides, it'll give more light to the hallway too."

The entranceway was dominated by the coconut scent of a curry being cooked in one of the apartments, but it couldn't quite conceal the mustiness underneath. An old veneer was wearing off of the stairs, revealing a dull, darkened oak.

Climbing ahead of her sister, Anna pulled her weight up the first few steps by grasping the banister. It was also made of solid oak, and it had always been the sturdiest thing in the building — an aberration in the poorly constructed tenement.

The walls of the stairwell were papered with a dusty floral print, which was peeling where it met the ceiling, revealing pressed tin. Flickering electric lamps shone weakly at the landings, in a style that imitated the gas lanterns from the turn of the century. Anna could hear that climbing the stairs was not easy for Sadie either, and they were both wheezing by the second flight. It never ceased to amaze her how their ninety-year-old mother had managed this every day.

When she reached the top of the stairs on the third floor, she stopped to wait for Sadie and to catch her breath. She looked at the carpeting and saw that it was threadbare, beginning to expose thin wooden floorboards. She made a mental note to tell the landlady. Sadie reached the landing and looked at the door to the broom closet. It was ajar, and she pulled it open. There were a few brooms and pails and rags thrown in any which way.

"They took the toilet out years ago," Anna explained, "and thank God. It stank to high heaven, do you remember?"

Sadie nodded.

"The landlady's made improvements, but it's the bare minimum, believe me. It's still very shabby, as you can see." She wiped her finger against the wall and showed her the dust.

Sadie grunted. "The sad thing is how much worse it used to be. Compared to then, this seems *fancy*."

Anna went to the end of the hall and unlocked the apartment door. Sadie followed her over the threshold and they stood for a second, contemplating the room. Anna was used to how small and cramped it was, how economically it was furnished for its many functions. She wondered what her sister must be feeling.

Next to the front door there was a rectangular wood-framed mirror and some hooks on the wall to compensate for the lack of a vestibule. On the left, beside the door to her mother's bedroom, a mauve loveseat and a round pine side table were set off against the wall for when her mother used the room for reading. The side table displayed a tall lamp with a blue columnar shade and some old framed photographs. There was one of her and Sadie as children, an even older one of her mother and grandparents, another of Anna's son when he was a teenager, being crushed in a sandwich hug by his parents.

Anna removed her jacket, put it on the arm of the loveseat, and went to run some water to cool herself off. The sink was against the back wall, a deep old white porcelain tub with a gooseneck faucet and daisy-handled taps. Cupboards and drawers above and below were painted blue to match the lampshade, and to the left of them was a pink stove and refrigerator set from General Electric. She closed her eyes while the water soothed her hands, then wet a cloth to dab at her forehead, careful not to wipe away her make-up. She knew one wasn't supposed to wear make-up, but she would anyhow. A touch-up would be required before they covered the mirrors.

A narrow kitchen table and two wicker-backed chairs hugged the right wall between the door to the back bedroom and the door to the toilet. In the middle of the table a bowl of sugar, a napkin holder, and salt and pepper shakers huddled together atop a stack of pink and green plastic placemats.

Anna looked back at Sadie. She was looking in the front bedroom, but she turned around, hung her coat on a hook, and went to sit at the table.

"How does it look?"

"Pretty much the same, some new appliances. I think I'd forgotten how small this place is. Did we ever know how big it was?"

"Five hundred square feet."

"It's shocking. It feels even smaller now that there's the toilet over there where the pantry was."

"I know — I wish Mama had moved out of here, but I could never convince her."

"Do you remember the old stove that used to be here?" She pointed to the electric oven.

They were interrupted by a knock on the door.

"Halloo!" came a voice from the other side.

"It's the landlady. Just a minute."

Sadie left her chair to retreat into the back bedroom while Anna opened the door. Mrs. Huang thrust a plate of almond cakes into the opening.

"Don't want to bother you, I'll just give this to you now. So you can get ready."

"Oh, how lovely, Mrs. Huang. They look delicious. What a sweetheart you are. Come in for a second."

Mrs. Huang adjusted the shoulder of her sleeveless cotton dress and stepped into the apartment. "It's nothing. Least of what I could do. You need anything else?"

"Actually, some extra chairs if you have any. Perhaps my sister and I can come down to get some."

"I have a long bench. Only needs two of us to carry. You come, leave your sister to prepare things."

"All right. Sadie, we're going down to get a bench. There's a box here beside the oven that I took out. There are some pictures in it, maybe you can arrange them on Mama's dresser in her bedroom. And there's a broom beside the fridge if you have time to sweep up. Oh, and don't forget to cover the mirrors and set out the bowl of water."

"Yes, yes. Go, it's okay," she called from the bedroom.

"I'm sure I'll be back to help you by the time you get to that."

"It's fine. Go ahead."

Anna set off down the stairs, following the landlady.

They reached the ground floor and went to the back of the building to Mrs. Huang's apartment. The curry smell had died down somewhat. Mrs. Huang let Anna into her apartment and squeezed past her to move from her hallway into the kitchen. The apartment was much bigger than her mother's, but no less cluttered. Stacks of newspapers were piled on both sides of the hallway, framing shelves crammed with knick-knacks and photographs. The air in the apartment made Anna's nostrils curl. It was tangy, probably some cleaning solution, but it made her think of formaldehyde.

Mrs. Huang's husband called from the bedroom. "Daisy?"

"It's me. Just getting a bench for Mrs. Cooperman. For her ma's shee-va."

Anna waited in the hallway until she heard the bench being scraped along the floor in the kitchen. She rushed in to help Mrs. Huang pick it up, and they set off up the stairs.

Mrs. Huang chattered all the way up, appearing to be only mildly out of breath.

"Your ma, she was a special person. Always paid her rent on time, always greeted me with news, how much fruit cost that day, or fish and vegetables. Was always polite even when she was a little melancholy. Never complained about anything. I hope I'll be like that when I'm ninety."

"Yes," said Anna. It was all she could manage to say through her heavy breathing. Sweat was beading her forehead.

"My Donnie says you could set your clock by the woman, and it was true. I notice everybody who comes and goes in this building, but with your ma, you knew the day of the week just by where she was going. On Mondays, to the market on Canal Street. On Tuesdays, the library. Wednesdays, her Mah Jong game at the Bialystoker Home. Thursdays, the book club, and Fridays she worked in the back garden in the morning, then her constitutional in the afternoon. Always wearing that nice beige jump suit you bought her, Mrs. Cooperman. You remember?"

"I...," Anna gasped and yanked the bench up another step, "remember."

"And your ma, she was wise, knew the ways of the world, like me. She knew when you were suffering. Sometimes, just when Donnie was driving me crazy, there would be a knock on the door and there would be your ma with some chicken soup or a piece of spice cake. She would come in, and I'd put out some tea and almond cakes. Your ma — such a sweet woman, Mrs. Cooperman. So good to my husband, you know?"

Anna smiled with jaw clenched as she pulled the bench up to the second floor landing. Mrs. Huang pushed from underneath, almost knocking her off balance. Still hardly breaking a sweat.

Anna sat on the bench and waited to catch her breath before continuing. Perspiration was now pouring down her forehead. Mrs. Huang sat next to her and put her hand on Anna's knee.

"Ha ha! You need exercise, Mrs. Cooperman! Your ma, she hardly got out of breath even with ninety years old." She chuckled and pulled a tissue out of her brassiere, offered it to Anna.

"Is that so?" Anna nodded politely. She was less than thrilled at the idea of wiping her face with something that had been stuffed down Mrs. Huang's chest, but she took her offering so as not to offend and dabbed lightly at her brow.

"Ya-siree! Only the day before the stroke, from my apartment I heard her go up and down the stairs many times that day."

People were always telling Anna about her mother's physical fitness. They talked about how she carried her groceries effortlessly up to the third floor. Since they shopped together, she knew it was an exaggeration, but it was true that her mother was in better shape than most people thirty years her junior.

"That day I remember — three times up and down. The last time, I came out of my apartment and said, 'Mrs. Kalish, do you keep forgetting something?' but she paid no attention, just moved out to the backyard. 'You'll pick me some vegetables to make a nice soup, Mrs. Kalish?' I joked with her. Then she laughed. Said she would make me some soup in the morning, but not from her garden. Too bad."

Mrs. Huang got up to rub a spot on the wall with a rag she pulled out of her pocket. Anna was thinking about calling Sadie down to help when she heard the stairs creaking and her sister appeared around the corner.

"Thank you, Mrs. Huang. My sister and I will take the bench from here. We'll see you at four. You've been a dear."

They heaved the bench up the next flight, Sadie pulling from the top, Anna pushing from underneath. Inside the apartment, they sat side by side to catch their breath and looked straight ahead at the wall. Anna noticed that the hall mirror was still uncovered. Sadie followed her stare, and then there was a moment when they realized that they were looking at one another in the mirror. It was only an instant, hardly enough time to even fix an image in the mind's eye, and then they both looked away.

"I forgot the mirror," Sadie said.

"I'll go get something." Anna stood abruptly and left the room, returning a moment later with a brown and ochre embroidered scarf. Arranging it carefully over the mirror, she waited to make sure it would not slip off. On the bench again, she listened to her own breath subside. When her chest calmed itself, she heard Sadie clear her throat.

"Well, Annie?"

"Anna."

"Anna. Shit, I'm sorry — Anna. I keep forgetting." She gave a few seconds to show she meant it. "So, what are we going to do now for the next two hours? The place is ready."

"I thought we could take the time to go through some of Mama's things in her bedroom and in the closet in the back room. There are a few boxes in the bedrooms with some old clothes and stuff."

"Fine. I'll do her bedroom." Sadie picked herself up and marched into their mother's room. Anna got up to follow her, but Sadie closed the door. Anna sighed, then sat back down, sloped her shoulders forward, put her palms to her forehead.

She sat still and listened until she heard Sadie rustling about, then got up and went into the back room. Beside the bed was a small wooden night table. A dresser stood against the side wall, displaying a comb, a brush, and a faded doily. A throw rug lay on the floor beside the bed. On the other side of the bed was the closet. Opening the closet door, she reached her hand in to push aside a few dresses and pant suits hanging in front.

At the back of the closet on the floor she saw two boxes. She leaned over and pulled one out. It was filled with books. *Mila 18. Uncle Tom's Cabin. The Urban Gardener. Jane Fonda's Workout Book. The Treasure of Sierra Madre. Roots.* A hardcover copy of *The Mosquito Coast*... She tugged at the second box and sat down, her knees to the side. Folded on top was the purple dress of a small child.

She recognized it at once. Her mother had made it for Sadie on her seventh birthday, with lace ruffles on the sleeves and a sash at the back. She remembered that Sadie had resisted wearing it to shul that day, and that she could not understand why. Anna was four, and she thought it was the most beautiful dress she had ever seen, so fancy and special. But her sister complained that it made her look ugly. Anna had cried because she wanted one too, and when Sadie tried to take it off in shul so that she could try it on, her mother had become angry with them, saying one did not undress in shul. It had caused a commotion in the upper gallery, so that their mother had to pull them both down the stairs and into the street to sit on the steps of the synagogue until the service was over. Later, their father had slapped them both across the face.

Anna pulled the dress up to her cheek and breathed in the smell of the fabric. There was a faint odour of perfume, but mostly it smelled of must. After a moment, she pulled it away and smoothed it against her lap. Her eyes were moist, and she blinked the box back into focus. There were more books at the bottom, peeking out from under some other clothes.

Reaching inside, she pulled out a plain, brown volume with no title on it. Opening the cover to the first page, she saw, inscribed in the top corner, in curlicued handwriting:

Rebecca Ignatow, Ludlow Street, New York.
November 12th, 1909

and underneath,

My very own personal diary — Do not read!!

Chapter Two

November 12th, 1909

Dear Diary,

Papa has found me someone to marry. He told me so tonight. He said I was already sixteen and that being married would be better than working in the factory. But I am not ready to get married, and I told him so. Yes, this apartment is cramped, dark, and awful, and maybe factory work is exhausting and dangerous. But I still don't want to get married. Not yet.

When Papa told me this, I argued with him and managed to buy myself some time, but now I can't sleep because I am overflowing with thoughts and feelings.

Mrs. Pearson, my night school teacher, says that when one wants to make sense of something upsetting, sitting back and writing about it helps to sort out one's feelings and clears one's mind to think more objective-

ly and more creatively. She says, "First write about what
happened, write about it fully, then write about how
you feel about it." So that is what I will try to do. I am
not sure I will be able to do this every night, especially
since I have to do it by the light of a single candle if I
don't want to disturb Ida (she is so sensitive to light
when she is sleeping) and try to keep as quiet as possible afterwards when I grope my way under the covers.

Nevertheless here I am, it is well past eleven,
and I am sitting on the floor against the bed with my
candle beside me barely illuminating the page. It is
so low on the ground that if I move it any closer I
might set my nightgown on fire. Now that would
certainly wake up Ida!

My friend Hattie gave me this diary some
months ago as a birthday present. Hattie wants to be
a writer, and perhaps her diary will become a published book some day. She says even if it doesn't get
published, it will be a record of her life that she can
show to her children when they grow up. Mrs.
Pearson says I should think of being a writer too, but
I don't think that will ever happen. But then again,
who can tell everything that life will bring? She says
I am at the top of my class, and that I should be
proud of that, even if it is only because Hattie graduated and is now in college.

One thing seems certain: since Papa wants me to
marry, I will one day be a mother. But unlike Hattie, I
would never show my children what I write in a diary.
It's not that I disagree with Hattie that it will be
important for my children to know some day who I

am. But unlike her, I will probably only use this diary as a record from which to select the important things that I shall tell them myself. That is because I wish to follow Mrs. Pearson's advice and write from my heart, and matters of the heart are not shared just like that, except with one's diary. Not like events. Events happen and children need to know about them. They are history. But the two should remain separate — emotions and history, that is.

I wish Mama thought this way. I have today discovered only for the first time an important piece of my parents' past. I do not understand why parents do not just tell children about the events in their lives, plain and simple. To me this is entirely different from telling them about secrets of the heart.

Mama says that because I am only sixteen, I do not understand that one's history is connected to one's heart, and she tells me that when I have some history of my own I shall understand. But I do understand. The difference between me and Mama is that I believe history should be separated from the feelings that get in the way of the telling, if at all possible. I want to know the story of people's lives, but I also believe that what lies in their hearts should not necessarily be discussed.

Mama cannot fully separate her emotions like this, but in her case I believe it is partly intentional. That is to say that she uses the emotion to make me feel ashamed. I do not want to be the kind of mother who inflicts this unpleasant effect on my children. Mama has a special gift for making me feel just awful, and sometimes I believe she is happy to make me feel that way.

Tonight was a perfect example of why I believe this to be true. On the way back from work today, the heel of my shoe came unstuck again. I trussed up the sole to the upper with some strong thread that I pinched from work, but the solution was makeshift and didn't really hold things together very well. The shoe was flip-flopping all the way home. I only mention the shoe because I have been wishing this week that I could buy a newer, better pair of shoes, and Mama's story of course made me feel grateful to have any shoes at all. It was all about how she used to have to walk barefoot through the snow back in Russia. It was quite maddening. Sometimes I would swear she can hear all my selfish thoughts, and even that she has discovered my guilty secret.

Of course I must confess my secret to my diary, and here it is: Instead of taking the train, I walk home from work. It does not sound so bad when one looks at the words on the page, but I will explain. Every day, after we are let out of work, I walk partway with my friends, to Prince and Broadway, and then I say goodbye to them and continue on to my regular stop at the Cristobaldi Family Bakery. For my secret daily ritual. And although it is wrong, I cannot give it up.

Ever since I started at the factory two years ago, the meals Mama prepares do not fill me up. So, I save on the cost of the ticket for the El, and stop for a bun before dinner. The only way to truly avoid feeling terrible about this is to stop buying the bread, but I simply cannot do it. I am so hungry all the time.

It is wrong for me to be spending money when I am not sharing it with my family. It is not that I feel

bad for Papa; Mama always gives him more food anyway. I do, however, feel guilty about Mama. The problem is that she would never simply take extra food if I
brought it for her; she is far too dutiful a wife and
mother not to share it with the family. And of course
sharing with the family would mean a big piece for
Papa, two tiny pieces for me and Ida (our boarder), and
only after we all had, she would take the tiniest piece
of all for herself.

This would never happen anyway, because I am
supposed to turn over all of my wages, except for my
train fare, to Papa, and they would consider buying the
bread wasteful. So, walking home instead of taking the
train is really the only way I can save money. I have
tried to convince myself, in order to soothe my guilt,
that Mama is not actually as hungry as I myself am,
and that because I am only sixteen and still young I
need more food than she does. But because I know this
to be a lie, it does not work, of course.

Also, I see the way she eats. She raises her fork to
her mouth so slowly it is almost shaking. She is trying
with all her might not to tear at her food. She only
restrains herself out of pride, and so as not to set a bad
example with table manners. But whenever we finish
a meal, such a look of sadness comes over her face, and
she tries to hide it by looking down at her plate, and
then she fidgets by wiping the plate repeatedly with
her last morsel, making sure no drop of sauce or kernel
of kasha is wasted. When this happens, I turn my eyes
downward too. Seeing her do this gives me a lump in
my throat exactly the size of my pre-dinner bun.

What is worse is when Mama announces that she will not be eating with us, and she tells us to go on without her because she wants to get a head start cleaning the pots. When she does this, I know it is because she is extra hungry and cannot bear to slow down her eating that day. I know this because on occasion I have caught a glimpse of her crouched over the wash basin either before or after we have all eaten, rapidly shovelling food into her mouth as though she should hide the fact that she eats at all.

I don't know what my own children's lives will be like, but I most sincerely hope that they are never trapped in circumstances like these. It is a terrible thing when a person cannot escape her trap except to deceive, and then that deception does not really make her feel any better, because she is sick with guilt.

But as I wrote at the beginning, if I had children of my own, I would not necessarily share these thoughts with them. They would be told our history plain and simple: at age fourteen I quit day school to work in a shirtwaist factory, food was scarce in our house, and my mother made great sacrifices for her family.

I have just re-read what I have written and do not feel at all that my thoughts are sorted out. But then I suppose that I am not properly following Mrs. Pearson's advice. Perhaps I am jumping about too much, not waiting until I have finished telling the story before leaping in with how I am feeling about it. So let me begin again, maybe starting from the scene of my crime, and continuing on from there.

1909

The foreman let the Jewish workers out early on Friday afternoons, but he expected them to make up for it by working overtime and on Sundays. So when Rebecca stopped at the bakery, there were so many reasons to feel shameful. On the eve of the Sabbath, when she should have been rushing to help her mother prepare dinner, she was wasting time walking home, secretly spending her train money on food, and, to make matters even worse, was about to eat food from a bakery that didn't keep kosher. The bakery's air was thick and pungent and warm, and she could feel the heat sink through her hair and warm her nape. Afraid that the smell of bread would linger on her if she stayed too long in the shop, she quickly approached the counter and pointed to a bun.

Mrs. Cristobaldi smiled, wiping her hands on her white smock just below her ample bosom. "You wanna try some different bun today, bambina? You always have the same thing."

"No, thank you, Mrs. Cristobaldi. I love this kind." Rebecca took it with one hand and poured her pennies into the woman's palm with her other.

"You have a nice evening. We will see you tomorrow?" The old woman nodded, prompting Rebecca for the answer.

"Perhaps Sunday. Thank you. You have a nice evening too." Rebecca tore a piece off of the bread as she walked out the door of the bakery.

She still had several blocks until she reached the Jewish part of the neighbourhood, but she took her time, walking slowly. As she passed by a storefront, a bearded grocer tried desperately to bait her by catching her eye and calling out to her, waving her in with his fleshy palm. Above him, a woman stirred a huge pot near an open window. She could just smell the sweet aroma of some soup the woman must have had on the boil, but it was quickly overpowered by the tang of dill pickles floating in two barrels standing like gateposts in front of the grocer.

At the next shop, a pot- and skillet-maker leaned over his table, placed tantalizingly in front of his shop, and accentuated the appeal of his wares by opening his arms at her as if to invite an embrace. He smiled at her, and she smiled back, but his fickle attention shifted to the next passerby when Rebecca failed to stop at his table.

Pushcart vendors vied for space on the sidewalks and on the streets. Taking a more aggressive approach, they shouted out their prices to her, almost angrily. Rebecca wondered how they could think she would choose to buy from someone simply because he was the loudest. Besides, was it not clear she wasn't shopping? She was walking far too quickly, and she had no shopping bag. She supposed anyone was fair game, there always being a possibility one could remember suddenly that one needed something after all.

She avoided their gaze and looked up at the tall buildings, erected shoulder to shoulder so they shared one shadow. Her eyes followed the shadow outwards. In the late afternoon sun it was held out over the street, the ragged rooftops forming the ruffled edges of a cape that draped partially over the backs of a pair of horses standing up ahead. The animals were harnessed to their carriage and scuffing their hooves against the ground to pass the time while they waited for their master to finish a transaction with a woman selling potatoes.

Beside the horses, she saw a boy try in vain to find a space in which to play in the midst of the chaos. He was balancing a top on the lid of a carton, but each time he spun it, someone would jostle the carton, sending the top flying into the street and the boy diving after it. On his third attempt, the child's top rolled under the legs of the horses. Recklessly, he scuttled crab-like under their bellies, grabbed the errant top with his left hand, and rolled out the other side. He picked himself up again just in time for Rebecca to avoid stepping on him and jumped out of her way.

Despite the frenzied activity surrounding her, and despite her guilt, Rebecca enjoyed this part of the day the most, because it was the only time that she had to herself. Her teeth cut through the bun's crunchy, powdery crust, and her tongue savoured the reward of the sweet-soft doughy centre. On evenings like these, when the November wind blew through the streets, pulling her skin taut, Rebecca liked to heighten her senses by drawing the cold air through her nostrils as she chewed and walked, grateful just to be outside, and alone.

It was not that she was antisocial, but it did always seem to her that now that she was grown up, there were expectations that came with being in the company of others. She should help her mother with the morning chores, bring her father her wages. She should listen to the troubles of her friends and remain cheerful, no matter how tiresome the complaint. At the factory, she must be dependable to her co-workers, and a diligent employee. Only her friend Hattie didn't demand much of her, because she was so independent, but Hattie was going to college now and so she hardly saw her.

During her walks home, Rebecca could breathe. If at other times she found the noise of the streets distracting and upsetting, at this time of the day she could shut it out. The sounds faded into the background, and, once the nagging hunger in her gut was sated by a nice piece of bread, she would retreat into her thoughts.

It was six-thirty when Rebecca rounded the corner to Ludlow Street, the earliest she had been home all week. The sun had already dipped behind the tops of the buildings when she had left the factory, and now it was almost dark. Rebecca snapped to attention in time to avoid running into the pushcart that was blocking the front stoop of her building.

"Good evening, Ribecceh!" said Mr. Zussel. He was closing up his herring cart. "Careful, kinderleh! Ein bissel fish for your papa?"

"Good evening, Mr. Zussel. No, thank you."

Mr. Zussel looked down from his considerable height, squinting one eye and frowning at her. In two giant steps he rounded the corner of his cart, his lanky torso following after in syncopation. Because of the way he moved, and also the way his lower jaw jutted out, he reminded her of a pelican. She tried to picture him holding his fish in his teeth.

"Such a good tochter like you, and no herring for your father? Nu, they don't give you money for this hard work such you do at the factory?"

Rebecca's face burned. "You know very well that if I'm to be a good daughter I have to give all of my wages to my father. My mother didn't come buy from you today?"

"Aach! Two weeks, your mother goes to Sender on East Broadway. A good woman she is, sure. Always the bargains for her family, she finds. So good, she's killing me!" He brought his hands up to his throat.

"I'm sorry, Mr. Zussel. But maybe if you lowered your prices a penny or two every so often..."

"Ayy! Exactly like her mother she is. A shark! A shark!" His hands made teeth marks in the air. "All the Ignatow women — beautiful and smart, yes, but so heartless. Like sharks. And I should live from what, lowering my prices — a thank you from your mother and a blessing from God?" He waved her away.

"Good evening, Mr. Zussel," she chuckled, and left him still muttering as she pivoted on the stoop and ran in the front door. When she heard the doorknob click behind her, she leaned against the wall and fished a box of matches out of her coat pocket. Her eyes blinked several times, but it was futile. The darkness fell damp and cold upon her face, sending shivers down her spine as it seeped through her.

Sometimes, but rarely, a person opened a door to an apartment and an oil lamp spilled some weak rays onto the floorboards. Not today. Today it was heavy and pitch, making it an effort to keep her eyes open. She struck a match against the wall and held her palm around it to shield it from the draft she felt biting at her ankles.

Her family lived on the top floor, because her parents took the cheapest apartment they could find when they came to New York and then never moved. When they got off the boat from Poland, someone in line at the Castle Clinton processing centre introduced them to his cousin, who showed them the building at number fifty-five. According to her mother, her father believed at first that they had outsmarted the landlord in that the rent on the top floor was cheaper and there was less noise from the street. But her mother knew they were getting what they paid for because every day she had to carry groceries and a small child five flights up the dark stairwell.

Rebecca was used to the apartment, having known nothing else, but when she thought of her future she wanted more than to live like old Zussel's herring, packed together in cloudy brine. Not too much more, maybe a room of her own someday, instead of sharing with a boarder. Some privacy and a toilet in the apartment. Some air and a bit of light coming in.

Some light. Every time she climbed the stairs, day or night, Rebecca thought of nothing else. She had been climbing them on her own since she was three years old and started carrying small packages of matzoh meal up the stairs for her mother. By seven, she was running errands alone. But instead of getting used to it as she got older, the stairwell began to frighten her more and more. Partly it was because she heard ghost stories from the girls in the factory, but mostly it was because she simply knew more about the world, and more about the things men could do to women.

So she lit matches. It was the only other thing that she spent her wages on, except that in this case, her mother and father knew about it. It took her three matches to get to the top floor, if she was good and didn't stumble. One she lit right after closing the front door, the second on the landing to the second floor, and the third on the landing to the fourth.

To take her mind off her fear, she made it into a game: to see if she could make it up to the fifth floor with only two matches. She had not yet succeeded, but she was determined. It was an unusual game in that speed and slowness were equal opponents: too fast and the match would be blown out by air currents, too slow and it would burn out on its own. Rebecca believed that her agility and concentration would eventually beat these worthy adversaries. If she was lucky and didn't have parcels to carry, the trick was to get her legs moving fast but isolate her upper body so that her hand could remain steady to shield the match.

Today, she made it to the middle of the fifth flight before her second match blew out. The closest yet. She struck another one against the wall and continued up to the apartment. Outside the door, she blew it out, quietly turned the handle, and slipped inside. Once she stepped in from the hallway, she was already in the tiny kitchen. Her mother was at the wash basin making a loud scratching noise with a scouring pad and didn't immediately turn around. But then the smoke from the match must have reached her nostrils because she craned her neck over her shoulder and looked Rebecca up and down, standing there at the door all sweaty and out of breath. She raised an eyebrow, shook her head, and turned back to the dishes.

Rebecca opened an eye and peeked at her mother as she lit the shabbus candles and said the benediction. Her eyes were closed, her chin tilted down, and the corners of the lace kerchief that she had placed on her head hung down in points over her cheeks. The hair from her black wig could be seen through the holes of the creamy cloth, and Rebecca thought that this made her look like those floppy-eared dogs on fire trucks.

When her father blessed the wine, Rebecca again glanced up but caught her mother staring at her, so she quickly turned her gaze down to her plate. When she noticed her watching her again during the blessing for the bread, Rebecca looked down at her dress to see if it was unbuttoned, but it was not. Her mother completed the blessings by burning a very small piece of challah as an offering to God, which she blew out immediately, vigorously waving away the smoke.

Her mother brought a pot to the table and served lentil soup. She seemed distracted as she ladled some into a bowl, looking to Rebecca's father, then to her. She began to pick her head up as though to say something, but a subtle shake of her father's head stopped her.

"What is it, Mama?"

"It's nothing darling. Later, after dinner, there's something we want to talk to you about."

Rebecca was about to press for information, but her mother spilled a drop of soup onto the sleeve of her black dress. "Ach, the one day I buy some shmaltz to add a little flavour, and I get it on my dress. As if God were punishing me for being extravagant." She sucked the material quickly into her mouth, then rushed off to blot it with a cloth.

Everyone stared at the spot on her sleeve while her mother resumed her task and, starting with her father, skimmed most of the fat from the top of the pot into his tin bowl. Next she served Ida, the boarder who shared a room with Rebecca. After Ida, she divided what was left between Rebecca and herself. This was exactly why Rebecca didn't feel bad about not bringing any bread for her father. He always got the tastiest piece of food: the fat from the soup, the skin from the chicken, the crust from the noodle kugel.

Thank God her mother chose to eat with them today. She watched her father and Ida tear at their piece of challah and dip it deeply into the soup. Her mother brushed again at the spot on her sleeve, then adjusted her wig before beginning.

"Mama, is it bothering you?"

"No, it's nothing. You know sometimes it's a little scratchy."

"Why don't you take it off for a while? We can pretend we're a modern American family tonight. There's no company, it's just us here."

"Pfaa!" her mother replied. "In Poland, a fine they could give if they caught you wearing the sheitel, because the czars made laws. Here there are no such laws. This I wear not only because I respect God — not that you would understand such a thing, mind you — I wear this also because it is a symbol of liberation!" she said, her voice rising in agitation.

Rebecca chided herself. Usually if she made any reference to the old country, it was turned into a lesson. Nevertheless, she found she couldn't resist pursuing her point, even if she might be stepping further into the trap.

"Well, I know it was terrible in Poland. But that's exactly the thing. We have more freedom here in every respect, and that also means in religious matters. In America, lots of women *choose* not to wear the sheitel, even though they can. Isn't that liberation?"

"America, shmerica. Sure, here in America, they don't fine you, but they still yell at you and call at you 'filthy Jew.' It's as bad as in Russia, frankly."

Russia? Wasn't it Poland? She could never figure this out. When her parents talked about the old country, they spoke in cryptic references and confusing contradictory recollections, one praising, the next damning. And the two country names appeared to be interchangeable.

"Oh, forget it, I can't win," said Rebecca.

"You're right, you can't," her father said.

"Yesterday when you complained about the price of bread, I tried to sympathize, and you told me that here at least there was food to buy, even if we can't pay. You switch allegiance so quickly, I can't tell which country you hate more. Poland-Russia or America."

"Don't be ridiculous, Rebecca," her mother said sharply. "I don't hate it here. But does that mean I have to stupidly smile and remain cheerful if something is not just?"

"No, of course not, Mama."

"What are you getting all bothered and hot for? Because I wear the sheitel? This does not mean you will have to, we have never said so. That will be between you and your husband." Again, she glanced to her father.

Rebecca tried hard not to appear foolish in these conversations, but there was no steadfast rule she could follow. Whether or not she said a word, her mother was just as likely to hold a perfectly depressing debate with herself. If Rebecca stayed out of it, the difference was that she was less likely to be accused, in the course of that debate, of being naive or too young to understand. But one could not always rely on this strategy; her mother sometimes presumed opinions or attitudes in her silence and scolded her anyway.

Her mother adjusted her wig again, making it a little lop-sided. Rebecca suppressed a giggle. She had to admit that though her mother looked old-fashioned, it took courage to wear it, and that was to be admired. Also, even though she would never tell her this, it made her look sweet.

"So Ida, how is your job in the office today?" her father segued.

"Fine, thank you, Mr. Ignatow. There were quite a few accounts to type up this afternoon."

Rebecca rolled her eyes.

"Don't you make your eyes like that, Rebecca. You could be earning the better wages too if you took that secretarial course like Ida did. Get a job in a nice accounting firm."

The previous fall, a week after Mr. Vanderholtz increased their rent, Ida Eisenstein announced at synagogue that she had graduated from a course given by the Henry Street Settlement and was looking for a family with whom to board. Rebecca's parents took her in the following Monday, and by Sabbath dinner, Rebecca was already hating her. Ida was a wispy, bird-like creature with long, reedy arms, high cheekbones, and wide, bony shoulders. Her hair was a dull, mousy brown, but Rebecca was jealous of how straight it was, of how easily she could tie it into a bun. And she had to admit that Ida had beautiful skin. Her own hair had an unmanageable wave to it, not curly enough to be considered beautiful, and her skin still suffered from frequent blemishes. Ida was a year younger, but acted as though she knew the world inside out. And when they were alone, she never shut up.

"That's a good job you have, Ida," her father continued. "Be careful, work hard, and they could promote you!"

Her mother looked amused. "To what, Sholem?" she asked. "*Senior* typist?" Then turning to Ida, "I don't mean offence, dear — it is only that my husband thinks if we simply worked a little harder, we would all be rich as the Astors by Pesach." Ida gave her a weak smile.

Her father slurped his soup, then said, "Maybe that boss of hers needs a personal secretary some day. Maybe *that's* what." He tapped his piece of bread on the table for emphasis. Now Ida's smile broadened, and she beamed it in Rebecca's direction.

"Yes, Ida," countered Rebecca, "I'm sure you could find a way to prove to him that you're right for the job..." She got up to bring her bowl to the wash basin. When she turned around again, Ida still had that stupid smile on her face, but it soon faded as she grasped Rebecca's meaning.

"Sure! Of course you will! Such a smart girl, that Ida!" her father shouted to his daughter. Then to his wife, "Fania, more soup!"

She poured the last ladle-full into her husband's bowl, then put the ladle down and squeezed her daughter's arm.

"And how was *your* work today, Beckeleh?"

"The same."

"Oh, Beckeleh, come now. Always I ask you, always you say the same. Nu, what's this same? Same good? Or same bad?"

"I go to work, I sit on a bench, I sew shirtwaists, I come home. What do you want to know, Mama? I bring home my wages, don't I?"

"Oh, such a long face. You have been lucky to have such a job." She wagged her finger.

"Did I say I wasn't lucky? I'm glad to help out. I'm glad to have a job so we can eat. It doesn't mean I have to love my work."

Her father pointed his piece of challah at her. "You're glad to have a job so you can have a dowry and not be an old maid." He raised his eyebrows to her mother and nodded.

Her mother shrugged. "That's what this country does to our young people, Papa. Never they are happy with what they do. Too much fanciness right in front of them in the store window. Everyone thinking like a millionaire."

He grunted. He was busy chewing.

"Mama, you raised the subject and now you're making me feel guilty about it. You have no idea what it's like at the factory."

She saw Ida look nervously around herself to find dishes she could clear, obviously sensing there was a family argument brewing. She wanted to go to the bedroom, where she would overhear but not have to participate, no doubt. "May I be excused, Mrs. Ignatow?" she said meekly, and then left at her mother's nod.

"Coward," Rebecca whispered to her under her breath. Ida took a plate to the wash basin, turned around, and smiled at her from behind her mother's back. Rebecca glowered back at her and waited for her mother's onslaught.

"So." Her mother's eyebrows joined to form a single line. "I don't know what it's like at the factory, do I? I have it so easy, do I?"

"No, Mama, I didn't say that..."

"I sit around eating poppy-seed cakes all day, do I?"

"Oh Mama, you asked me good or bad — I said bad, and you think I'm saying your life is easy. All I meant is that it's different, and you're not there with me in the factory."

"You think it was for nothing we came to this country? You think I would let my own daughter suffer in a factory if I thought a life in Poland or in Russia was so good?" Her open palm slapped the table. "You think I don't wish we were millionaires that you could sit around in a fur coat or go shopping all day? You think it is easy running a household? Well, you will soon know different."

"What is that supposed to mean, Mama? I don't think your life is easy. I know how hard your life is here."

"So hard here. Do I complain like you do? Compared to back home, compared to what we left, this place is Paradise. You children have no idea..."

Her mother paused, her face hard, her lips pursed together. When eventually she spoke, she switched to Yiddish, and her voice became very soft.

"When I left Kovel, I was nineteen years old..." She breathed in and out several times through her nose, opened her mouth and made a noise to begin to speak, but then closed it. Her eyes opened wide, calling to her husband for help. Sholem stopped his chewing and smiled encouragement to her.

"My parents, your bubbe and zayde, they had moved from Poland to Bechcin, in Bohemia, when they were young. They had seven children already when the pogrom came through in sixty-six. The village was devastated, and they lost their eldest child to the knife of a crazy soldier. After that, they decided to move back to Kovel. My parents decided to have another child to replace the one who was lost. But my parents still had six children. So you see, Beckeleh, I was a replacement for a dead brother."

Rebecca leaned over to touch her mother. "Oh, Mama, I'm sure that's not true."

"It *is* true. It didn't mean they didn't love me, though I thought, until I got older and understood, that this was exactly what it meant. In such a village of poverty I grew up, you can't imagine. My mother and father had potatoes, bread, and cabbage, sometimes only potatoes to eat. And we had more than most people because my older brothers and sisters worked. When I was very young I didn't know any different, and I laughed and laughed with the other children my age. But as I got older, then I knew.

"I worked in the summertime from the age of eleven years old, bringing in six cents a day. Work in the fields, weeding, digging potatoes, planting. In the winter, I helped my mama with some sewing for a tailor. This work we had because there was nothing else. But because we all worked in the family, between us, we just had enough to eat. Most of the time. Sometimes, if one of my brothers lost work, we went hungry."

Rebecca looked down at her empty plate, at her mother's empty bowl. She felt a little sick.

"Your bubbe, my mother, I hardly saw her. She was up before me, baking bread and peeling the potatoes. When I came home from work, she was always in a bad mood. She spoke to my sister Rivkeh sometimes, and some to another sister, but not to me. Me, I was the baby, and another mouth to feed. And I was the last one she thought of with six older and louder children.

"We didn't dare complain too much, because my mother wouldn't hear of it. I remember once Rivkeh complained about her work, and my mother, whose father was a rabbi, told her a story about another rabbi who suffered from ailments known to involve great pain. He suffered without a word. When his doctor asked how he could be so strong, he said he thought of pain as the scrubbing and soaking of the soul in a strong solution. And since he thought of pain in this way, he could not do otherwise than to accept such pain with love and not grumble."

Rebecca shook her head. "That's crazy. Who would think like that?"

Her mother swatted her. "My mother, that's who. This was my mother's crazy philosophy too. Except that I would not say she accepted her pain with love. More like resignation. Once she said to a neighbour, 'Everyone has his pack of troubles. Sure. But if everyone laid those troubles out in a row, and each person had to choose whose troubles to take, each of us would choose his or her own. At least they would be ours!'

"Your zayde, he was another story. He complained all the time. He made caps, like your papa, but he was gone a lot to other villages, peddling his wares. When I was eleven years old, your zayde went away to another village and never came back. We all said it must have been a pogrom, or an accident of some kind, but I know my mother wondered if he just ran off to a better life.

"Sometimes even now when I walk through the streets here in New York, I see someone who looks like him, and I stop in my tracks. It seems crazy, I know, but he could be here as much as he could be anywhere."

She stopped talking for a moment. Her eyes were misty. Rebecca looked at her and said softly, "Do you really think Zayde could be alive?"

Her mother blew her nose with a handkerchief and composed herself. "Who knows?! What does it matter anyway? It was so long ago. Anyway, after he left, that's when I started working. Until I was fourteen, I went to work without shoes. Everywhere I went it was with bare feet. In the winter, I ran from one house to another with my bare feet in the snow. Finally, at thirteen, I begged my mother for shoes. It took me six months to convince her, but at last I got my first pair.

"I wanted squeaky shoes with sugar in the soles, so they would make lots of noise like the shoes of some fancy adults in the village. But the shoes with sugar soles cost more, so I got the kind without any noise — not as good, but to me they were like gold anyway. I felt so big, wearing those shoes. My sister said they made me look like a lady.

"Because I felt big, so I started thinking like a big person. I started thinking I might soon be a woman. And within a few months of that, I was. My mama and papa, they had promised me as a baby to a boy in the village, but he got conscripted into the Russian army when I was five years old and was sent to the Turkish front. Like all the Jews who were sent to the front, he was killed, of course. If you were a Jew in the Russian army, it was a death sentence. Everyone knew that.

"So you see, Beckeleh, there I was, a child whose parents didn't want her, whose father disappeared, and who now found herself a woman with no real marriage prospects. I'm not saying my childhood was without happiness. We did laugh and play. Maybe you would say we were too stupid to have the sense to be miserable all the time, I don't know. But you see, kinderleh, at least I was smart enough to realize that my future was not in that Russian village."

Her mother got up from the table and got a log for the stove. She went through to the front bedroom and made sure the window was shut tightly. Then she placed another piece of wood on the floor to hold open the door between the bedroom and the kitchen, so that the heat from the stove would reach the other rooms.

Rebecca looked at her father, and said, "Russian village? I thought you and Mama were from Poland."

"I will explain, sweetheart," her mother said, sitting back down at the table. "Your papa and I met in Poland, but my village was on the other side of the Russian border. What does it matter anyway? The czars rule Poland. Poland, Russia, it is all the same for the Jews. We spoke Jewish at home, and learned Russian at school. So did your father. Polish, he learned from the villagers where he grew up.

"When I met your father, at first I spoke Russian to him, because I was ashamed of my Jewish, and I was afraid I wouldn't understand his — it was full of Polish words and expressions. Later, we taught each other the missing words from each other's dialect and got used to the different accent.

"In those days, everyone had a story about someone who had a relative in America. In Kovel, my friend Ilana had an uncle who went to Chicago ten years before, and who wrote back about how a poor Jew could make a fortune in America. Now I realize he never actually said that he made a fortune himself, but then what were we thinking? Our lives were hunger and hardship, we were not so critical. We wanted to believe it was the Golden Land."

"When I was eighteen years old, I told my mama that I was going to America. I had no plan, only that I would go first to Kiev, then to Krakow, and find my way from there. When I told my mama, it was the first time I saw her cry. She didn't try to convince me not to go; she simply got up, and went to the bedroom.

"She brought out two featherbeds that she had made and gave them to me. She said I would need them for a dowry, so that I could attract a rich husband in America. I knew I could not take them both, and I tried to refuse, but she persuaded me to take one with me.

"I never thought before that she would care if I gave her a thought after I left, and I certainly never thought she would miss me at all, but when she offered me the featherbeds, I realized that she did as best she could, but when she finished with all her duties, she had nothing left for me.

"The day I left for Kiev, my mama packed the featherbed, along with my clothes, in a bundle of cloth that she tied to my back. She made a criss-cross with the four corners over my shoulders and under my arms, and tied the knot between my bosoms. Then she turned me around, adjusting the bundle so that it would carry properly and wouldn't give me a sore back. When I turned to hug her goodbye, I saw she had already started down the road. She walked quickly away, and I could see her shoulders heaving up and down. That was the last time I saw my mother."

Rebecca squirmed uncomfortably in her chair, trying to think of what to say. Her mother was breathing deeply with her eyes closed, and her father was stroking her forearm.

"Beckeleh," she continued once she had composed herself, "I went to Krakow the day after my nineteenth birthday. It seemed that everybody was on the move. It took me four weeks to get there what with the poor transportation, all the people going here and there, and my stopping to earn some money. When I got to Krakow, I took the money I had saved, and I looked up a man about whom my friend Ilana had told me.

"I paid him some money to arrange for immigration to America. He took my papers and then took me in a buggy and said we needed to go to the settlement office, but after an hour, when we arrived outside of the city at a big fancy house, I felt something was wrong. He took me by the arm, and we went in the door.

"Inside, there were other women standing and sitting just here and there, some of them in only underclothing. I remember one of them looked at me with the saddest eyes. Another also looked at me, but she looked at me with worry — from my eyes to the door, and back to my eyes. I asked the man what was this place. What were we doing there? He laughed, and said not to worry, that everything would be all right. I looked back at the woman, and her eyes went wide and flickered a little to the left.

"I don't know how I knew to do this, or how I did it, but I pulled my arm away from his and ran out the front door. I shot off to the side of the house and into some bushes. I ran and ran, my bundle flopping about on my back, until I was sure they could not follow me anymore. I ran until I found a farmer who took me to a police station. It turned out this man was selling girls into white slavery in Argentina. Now, whenever I am feeling sorry for myself, I think of that girl who saved my life with her eyes."

Rebecca couldn't believe what she was hearing. Her mother had been a moment's hesitation away from being a prostitute in Argentina. "Mama! You were so brave!"

She dismissed the comment with a wave. "Not so brave. Just scared to death. The important thing is that I got away, and that I met your papa at the police station. He was there with his friend Yekl, you know, the same Yekl with whom he does business here. They were complaining about a business associate who had cheated them.

"Your father saw me there crying. When I heard him turn to his friend and speak in Jewish, I was so relieved. What did I know from his character; I only saw in him someone who could help. And he did help. He helped me find a place to stay, and he helped me find some work. Eventually, he asked me to marry him. Your papa was a cap-maker then, same as here, but there he had his own shop. Someday here you will too, won't you, Papa?"

Her father grunted.

"I convinced your papa to come to America with me. It took us two years to earn the money for the passage and to arrange the details. The second year we saved more money because we were married by then, and we lived together. You were born, Beckeleh, four weeks before we left. I bundled you on my back wrapped in your bubbe's featherbed — you were warmer than any of us on that boat!"

"Mama, Papa, I didn't know. You never told me any of this before. I had no idea..."

"Well now maybe you will have some — what is the word?" Her mother scratched at her wig.

"Guilt?"

"Don't be smart. The word meaning better way of looking."

"Perspective?"

"Something like that."

Her father interceded. "You're not happy in the factory, Rebecca?" he said, looking at her sweetly. His eyes were squinting, and he smiled faintly. "Your mama and I have been talking. Yekl knows a boy, a good boy who has been doing work for him. Hard worker, observes the Sabbath. His father is from Poland, from a village next to where I come from. I knew his father's cousin back home."

"Oh, Papa, I don't think..."

"I talked to them, and he's willing to take what we've saved for you. Considering who he is, with no business of his own, I think this is fair."

Rebecca's heart started racing. "Papa, no. I don't want to marry someone I haven't seen. I want to marry for love, like you and Mama."

He harrumphed, then looked at Rebecca. "This way is much better — a boy we know, who works hard. You will like him, Beckeleh. Anyway, it's all agreed. The arrangements are made. You will get to meet him before the wedding. We have arranged that too."

She began to panic. "Arranged? You talked to him without asking me? How could you do that? No, Papa! I won't marry him. I won't!"

Her father's voice boomed. "Don't you raise your voice like that to your father, little girl! This is arranged, and you will marry him!"

"I am not a little girl anymore, Papa!" Then realizing the danger of what she said, added, "But I'm also not as old as Mama was when she married. I'm sixteen! You were both much older when you were wed."

Her mother came over and stroked Rebecca's hair. "Sweetheart. That is only because we didn't have parents to look after our interests. Other girls are married younger than you. There is nothing to worry about, my darling. Everything will be fine."

Rebecca's mind raced. She knew that she needed to change strategy, because she could see her father getting angry, and when her father got angry, there was no hope for reason. He had already begun to speak when she said suddenly, "Okay, I'll marry him."

Her father was obviously taken off guard by his daughter's rapid capitulation because he had started to say something, but stopped in the middle of his sentence.

"But Papa, please don't make me marry him yet. Not just yet. Let me first finish my classes at the night school. Didn't you always say education is the key to getting ahead in this country?" She looked into her father's eyes for some hope of concession.

"For boys, yes. For girls, more important you should get married, and to someone who can put bread on your table."

"Please, I'm begging you, Papa! Put off the wedding. At least until I'm nineteen."

She looked at her parents' faces. They were tight and silent. Then her mother turned to her father. His eyes were bugging out, but she raised an eyebrow at him. In the nuance of this gesture, her family always knew what she was thinking.

"One year," he said, still looking at his wife.

"Two." Rebecca's heart beat faster.

"Two?! I should have you marry him tomorrow!"

"Sholem," her mother tilted her head to the side.

Silence. Then he said, "Eighteen months," and got up from the table. Under his breath, he muttered, "She should bargain so well with the pushcart vendors." He retreated into the bedroom and shut the door behind him.

Rebecca smiled at her mother, but she frowned back, got up, and went to the wash basin. Alone at the table, Rebecca heard her speaking softly into her scrub pot. She only faintly made out the words. "I hope you're happy at your factory now."

Rebecca couldn't sleep. Her mind swam with the possibilities of what might have occurred had the conversation gone the other way. Married? She couldn't imagine it. Not yet. Still, she had agreed to the wedding, and only delayed it a year and a half. Perhaps there would be another time to convince her father to postpone for longer.

After an hour of tossing in bed, listening to Ida snoring beside her, Rebecca needed to relieve herself. She hated when this happened. If she had only had to urinate, she could have used the chamber pot, but her stomach was twisted and jumping. The pit toilets were down in the yard behind the tenement, and all the residents from three buildings used four stalls.

Rebecca got up and lit a candle, which she took with her into the stairwell. She heard noises as she reached the bottom flight. As she approached the back door, she could make out the sound of men talking. Opening the back door and stepping outside, her nostrils were assaulted with the terrible odour of human feces.

The toilets always stank, but this was worse. The structures that usually covered the pits had been lined up at the back of the yard, and four men stood down in the uncovered holes.

Night-soilers.

They had shovelled most of the contents into crates placed on the ground. Rebecca had never seen the men do their work; she had only heard stories. It was no wonder that they waited until the fall to do this. In spite of the cold, the stench was nauseating.

One man caught sight of her staring.

"Coming in here with us, missy?" he chuckled.

The others started laughing.

"See you got a candle there. Now all's we need is some wine, boys, don't we? Too bad we finished it all earlier. Don't matter none, come on down in here, we'll find another way to warm ourselves up!"

The men hooted and laughed and grabbed at their loins. The one who had spoken to her climbed out of the pit and started wiping his boots with a rag.

Rebecca jumped back inside the door and shot up the stairs. Her candle blew out on the first flight. She wasn't sure, but she thought she heard someone come in behind her. She put the candle inside her sleeve and ignored the wax scalding her wrist as she grabbed hold of the banister and pulled herself up. The stairs creaked a flight below. The man was following. Faster and faster, she threw her body forward, pulling her legs up beneath her with great strides, clearing two stairs at a time.

As she ran up the last flight, she could hear him getting closer. She grabbed the top of the banister and used her momentum to fling herself around the corner. Her leg muscles screamed. She reached the apartment and slipped inside, shutting the door behind her. She pressed her back against the wall and tried not to make any noise. She didn't want to wake anyone up. She fought back tears and stifled her gasps for air. She heard the man breathing on the other side of the door. After a few seconds, she heard him chuckle, and then his footsteps retreated down the hall.

She went into her room and shut the door. Ida stirred awake.

"What's wrong, Rebecca?" she mumbled.

"Nothing, go back to sleep."

Ida turned over and pulled the covers over her head.

Rebecca knew now that there would be no falling asleep, even though she no longer needed to use the toilet. She lit her candle again, got an ink bottle, a pen, and a dirty cloth from the dresser, and set them all down beside the bed. She sat down on the floor beside them and leaned back against the bed frame. Reaching behind herself, her fingers searched out a hardcover book under the bed and drew it out. Her friend Hattie had given it to her over a month ago for her birthday, but she had never opened it.

She dipped the pen into the bottle and blotted the excess ink on the cloth. Opening the brown cover and turning to the first page, she steadied her hand and, with utmost care, began her first entry.

Chapter Three

Today was Tuesday, and that usually meant an extra heavy workload. Rebecca sewed leaning into her machine, struggling to focus on her work. She looked up and squinted to see the clock on the wall across from her and then began to pump more vigorously with her foot. She was behind. Straight lines, she told her herself, it was important to concentrate on the straight lines. Keeping her fingertips as close to the guide as she dared, she watched the needle flying up and down, so quickly it was a blur. But the chug-chug of the wheel and the hazy grey of its swirling spokes soon lulled her back into a reverie.

A high-pitched scream came from across the floor and jolted her back to attention. Stopping her wheel, she swivelled in her chair to look. The room was long and wide, with fifteen rows, and she could just make out her friend Elsie standing up, ten aisles over by the windows, waving her arms. It was difficult to see her clearly at first, not so much because of the distance as the sun's glare, casting her body in shadow.

Elsie shouted for a foreman to come. Rebecca's eyes adjusted to the light, and she saw that a woman beside Elsie, it looked like Gertie Reznikoff, had one hand pressed flat on the sewing table, the other clutching at Elsie's hair. Because her hand was so close to the guide, it looked like she had a finger trapped under the needle. The row where her friends sat erupted into chaos. Elsie extracted Gertie's hand from her hair and put it on her forearm. She grabbed a piece of material and pressed it down against the trapped finger.

She called again, this time for Lev Sklawer, the floor supervisor, but Rebecca saw that he was near her side of the floor trying to make his way over to them. Many of the workers stood up from their chairs and watched, as Elsie shouted for everyone to be quiet. The noise slowly died down to a low hum, and people waited for her next move.

Then Rebecca heard her friend speak, calmly and steadily. "Gertie, honey. Take a deep breath. I'm gonna turn the wheel at the count of three and pull out the needle. Be a brave girl now, okay?"

Gertie was now crying in a series of short sobs that were cut off when she ran out of air, followed by a gasp, a staccato of whimpers, and then another sob.

Elsie had her hand on Gertie's arm. "Okay, honey, are you ready?"

Gertie nodded, her eyes closed, her face red and pinched.

"One, two. . ." Elsie turned the crank in a sudden movement, and Gertie screamed.

Gertie grasped her freed finger in her other hand, squeezing it tight, and rocked back and forth in her chair. Lev motioned to one of the foremen, who came and carried Gertie off into a room at the back.

Elsie crumpled back down into her chair, and Rebecca could see her other friend, Dora, crouching down to comfort her. Thank God for Elsie; Gertie had been lucky to be sitting next to her. From where she sat, it looked like Dora was now helping her to fix her hair. Together they drew it up and pinned it into her usual pompadour. Dora took a piece of excess cloth and mopped Elsie's brow. Elsie had a stout, round face, and when she took the cloth to mop the back of her neck, Rebecca noticed that it was unusually long for someone so short.

It was a good thing that Elsie was always so coolheaded and sensible, and not like one of the flighty girls in the adjacent row. She looked for solutions to whatever troubles came her way, no matter how terrible. The world was a horrible place, Elsie claimed, but there was no point in waiting around with your head up your tuchus, or up in the clouds, when there was usually something to be done to make things a little less bad. That was Elsie — so pragmatic it was depressing.

A murmur rippled through the crowd and eventually reached Rebecca's table. One of the women across from her received the whispered news and leaned across the table to share it with Rebecca.

"The needle go straight through that bone." She wagged her index finger. "They will take it off," she said. Her curled lips conveyed both revulsion and disapproval. Which was the more dominant emotion, or what exactly she disapproved of, Rebecca couldn't tell.

"Poor Gertie," she said.

"She is schlemozel, that girl," the woman answered. "This is third accident this year."

"Well, that's true, but still…"

"Yes, of course true. First, with her hand in that wheel, with all blood everywhere. After, remember? Finger again with hole, but not in that bone. Not so bad like this. This, they must take off." Again, she wagged her finger and curled her lips.

"I know she's careless, but don't you feel sorry for her?" she protested. "She'll probably be fired now, finger or no finger."

"Yes, of course I'm sorry." But the woman's tone spoke more of ambivalence than sympathy. She turned her head, disengaged from their conversation to begin a new one in Czech, with her neighbour.

Rebecca missed her friends in the other row. There on the other side of the floor, the conversation had been more lively. Or at least more compassionate. Also, she had assembled and pleated the main bodice, which struck her as a much more important part of the shirtwaist, closer to the shape of the final product. Here in her exile for the last year, she was stuck with sewing the sleeves. The Czech woman only rarely spoke to her, preferring to speak to her neighbour and countrywoman who hardly spoke any English at all. The woman at Rebecca's back could be chatty at times, but she had an unpleasant and disturbing odour that was somehow easier to ignore if they weren't engaged in conversation.

Rebecca settled back into her work. She could see Lev coming toward her.

That vulgar little man, she thought. I wish I could wring his pimply little neck.

He approached her table. "Rebecca, you stupid animal! Your time here should be *waist*-ing time — not time to be wasted!" He snorted, "Get it?" and then explained his joke, as though she were not bright enough to figure it out. "'Waist'-ing? Like shirt-'waist'? Get it, Becky?"

She cringed. Normally, it was best to just ignore him and hope that he would go away. Today, she felt she couldn't bear it anymore.

"Lev, please, I'd almost rather you dock my wages than tell those awful jokes. I should take it up with the union!"

"Sure, I guess that would be a 'strike' against me, wouldn't it? Get it? 'Strike' — against me? Get it, Becky, sweetheart?"

She leaned forward and pressed her forehead against her sewing machine. Lev was now right behind her. He put his hand on her shoulder, and she flinched, bracing herself for whatever.

"Anyway, today's your lucky day, Becky. You get to go back with the old gaggle there on the other side of the room. I switched you with Gertie thinking you'd both be more productive, but it looks like she's not gonna be doin' much of anything for a while. So I'm chopping off your arms, and giving you back your torso!"

"What?"

"You saw — Gertie Reznikoff — gone. We need you there again."

He poked her in the back. "This is poor little Gertie's finger I got here poking you right back over there to the other section, Becky my dear. Of course, I'm sure Gertie'd be much happier if this bloody thing were still attached to her and not here with me carrying it about, huh Becky?"

She jumped around to look, her face twisted with disgust. And maybe a flicker of ghoulish curiosity. But there was nothing, of course, only Lev's own index finger, which poked her on the nose.

"Gotcha! Ha ha! God, Becky, you're such an easy mark."

She closed her eyes. "Should I go right now, or shall I finish this sleeve?"

"Yeah, right now! Your friends here can finish up that sleeve. What are ya waiting for? Go!"

She handed her unfinished work to the Czech woman, who nodded politely to her and smiled, and she stood up to leave. Lev was intentionally blocking her path so that she had to force her way past, brushing against him.

Crossing the floor, she zigzagged her way up through the aisles, clicking sounds assaulting her from all around. Two hundred needle pistons going at once made it sound like a downpour on a metal roof. Each person had his or her pile of fabric to one side on the table, and then a pile of finished or semi-finished garments draped over a chair in front of it to the worker's right. A little girl of eight loped by with a handful of buttons to deliver to one of the tables. She deposited her buttons beside a surly woman, who took the child's hand, held it tight, and slapped it. "I've been waiting five minutes for those buttons!"

Rebecca caught up with the girl, pulled her tiny hand out of the woman's grasp, and smacked the woman across the back of her head.

"Leave her alone! My God, you should be ashamed! Does it makes you feel big and important to yell at a little kid?" Rebecca and the woman locked themselves in a stare-down, and Rebecca won. She turned to the girl and bent down to comfort her, but the child's eyes were filled with terror, and she darted past her and shot back across the room. The woman muttered after Rebecca as she continued on toward the window aisle.

When she reached her old table, her friends smiled, and Dora pulled out her chair to welcome her.

"I can't tell you how glad I am that I'm back working with you all! Only God, poor Gertie! Elsie, I saw almost everything, you were so terrific with her."

Elsie stopped her pedal for a moment. "There's no chance of her keeping her job now. Three times in a year? Forget it. Lucky her mama does piecework. Maybe there'll be some extra work for her there."

Dora unfolded some cloth and began measuring out the unpleated waistline. "Yeah, poor thing. I hate to say it, but that finger looked real bad. Makes us all think twice about jumpin' every time Lev gets on our backs to pick up the pace, don't it? I'm sure she'll lose the finger. The needle went through above the second joint."

Rebecca grimaced. "What do you mean? Was Lev rushing her?"

"He was at her this morning," answered Dora. "That creepy little pisher — someone oughta chop off *his* finger — or better yet, some other teeny tiny dangling thing!"

The girls broke into laughter, and then tried immediately to stifle it with held breath and hands over mouths. They could see Lev approaching.

"Don't make me send ya back over to the other side, Rebecca!" he bellowed from three rows over.

Rebecca grabbed a piece of fabric, turned her eyes down, and smoothed the cloth purposefully on the table. She settled into a steady rhythm but was distracted by Dora's frequent stops to pat at her hair. A strand of it hung down at the back.

"Dora, you're fidgeting. Let me help you with that."

"It's this new hairdo that I saw in the *American Magazine*. It's a bit complicated, I had to have my roommate help pin in the extras. I got them from that lady on Mott Street. She's got all the nice stuff — fringes, switches, braids, everything."

Today's hairpieces were not exactly matched to the light brown of her hair, producing an odd effect. Rebecca knew better than to ask if it was intentional, she just pulled up the strand of fake hair and fixed it in place with a pin that was already there.

Elsie nudged her under the table. Lev was cycling back to their side of the room again and approaching their row. He rarely spoke to Dora, so they were surprised when he leaned over her, putting his mouth near her ear. He whispered loudly, on purpose so that others could hear.

"Be sure to leave lots of room in the bust, Dora Segal, so that big girls like you, who fills out their shirts nicely, will want to buy our merchandise."

"Lucky whoever made your trousers didn't have to worry about that, Lev Sklawer."

Dora's razor-sharp tongue was legendary. She fixed her brown eyes on him, producing a withering look, and glanced down to his crotch.

Lev turned red. "Very funny, very funny."

Lenny and Carlo, sitting on the other side of Dora, were virtually suffocating, they were laughing so hard.

"Get back to work everyone, before I decide to keep you here 'till midnight," Lev said, moving away again to attend to a disturbance on the other side of the room.

Dora raised her head in victory. As she did so, a beautiful pendant peeked out above her high collar. It was a burnished silver-grey and was intricately carved.

"Dora, that necklace is beautiful. Is it new?"

"Yeah, isn't it adorable? Elsie and I found it in a shop on Allen Street."

"Allen Street? You were shopping there?"

"Yeah, look here." She tilted her head down and pushed her chin into her chest. "I also got this pin for my hair. Isn't it gorgeous? I'm gonna wear it to my next audition. There's a show having tryouts next Sunday."

"Allen Street? Isn't Allen a little — you know — a little bit on the shady side?"

"Whaddya mean, shady?" answered Elsie. "For God's sake, it's practically next door to where you live. It's where all the craftsmen have their shops. The rabbis even shop there!"

"Yeah, and besides, we were tryin' to find a present for my poor old mama. I wanted to give her somethin' nice, 'cause she just had another baby. Can you believe it? Poor woman — I move out to give them more room, and she pops out another one not a year later. Makes you feel like a goddamned weed. Pull me out, and another one shoots up to fill my spot."

"Okay, Dora, but isn't Allen Street also where they have all the — what do they call them — those bawdy houses?"

"Yeah, and?"

"Well, I don't know ... I guess I don't think I'd like to be shopping in that neighbourhood, that's all."

"Ya know, Rebecca, those girls, they aren't so different from us, really."

"What do you mean, no different? Of course they are! They're nothing like you and me." Maybe in Elsie's gloomy version of the world they weren't, thought Rebecca.

"How would you know? Have you ever met anyone who worked as a whore?"

"Shhhh! Keep your voice down ... Of course not. Have *you?*" She looked back and forth between them.

Elsie didn't answer. Dora picked her fingers, looked at her nails, then spoke lightly, for effect. "Yes, as a matter of fact." Rebecca saw Elsie shoot an angry glance at Dora, who waved her hand dismissively.

"You have?"

"Yeah, I have."

"Who is it?" Rebecca's eyes lit up.

"No one you know. Let's just leave it at that."

"Well, howdya meet her?"

"Through a friend."

"And what was she like?"

"It's like Elsie said, she's not so different from you and me."

"How could you say that, Dora? I would never do something like that. I just couldn't. And neither could you."

"Sure I could."

"Could not."

"I'm not saying I *would* do it, but I could if I had to."

"What could possibly be so bad you couldn't earn money with a regular job?"

"Oh, come on, Rebecca," Elsie said, "Think about it a bit. Not everyone comes from a family like yours, with parents that care about them. You never know what choice ya might make if your situation was different." Elsie never talked about her family, other than to say that they made artificial flowers in a crowded tenement, and that she and her sister had left as soon as they could afford to. When Elsie got her job at the factory, she rented a room by herself from a landlord on Baxter Street.

Rebecca giggled. "Oh my God! Can you imagine if I was doing that? I can't even *think* what my parents would do. I sometimes feel like they're gonna disown me just for going to the dance hall on Saturday nights. Or to union meetings."

"Well, they'd most definitely sit shivah for you for this one, sweetheart," said Dora.

"Oh absolutely they would. 'Cause of my papa — for sure."

"You don't think your mama would feel the same way?"

"Probably. But she just told me back in Poland once she was almost kidnapped and sent to Argentina into white slavery. So I don't know ... I'd think she might have some sympathy."

"How charitable." Elsie breathed in and out through her nose. Her voice was icy.

"Trust me," said Dora. "If it was her own daughter, I'm sure she'd object."

"Yeah, you're probably right. And anyway, that was different. Those girls — it sounded like they had no choice. Lotsa the girls on Allen Street — they choose it. At least I heard that's how it is. No one's forcing them. If my mama and papa thought I'd chosen to be a whore, for sure they would sit shivah for me."

Rebecca could see Elsie shifting again in her seat adjusting herself to sit stiffly upright. "Lotsa people make choices for lotsa reasons, Rebecca."

"What kind of reason would make a person choose to lie down with all those men who they don't even know, and take money for it? I can't imagine it. Even if their parents didn't love them."

Elsie's fists tightened on her bunch of cloth. Rebecca saw her exchange a look with Dora, who turned to Rebecca and placed a hand on her shoulder. "Don't worry about it sweetheart. Concentrate on your fabric there. You're getting sloppy, and you're also getting behind. We don't want another accident."

Rebecca hated when her friends treated her like a child. Disagreeing was no reason to tell her to calm down. After all, it was Elsie who was obviously upset. It was more than clear she knew someone. But, even though she was dying to find out who it was, if Elsie didn't want to talk about it, she wouldn't press the matter.

She quickened the pace of her sewing for a few minutes, and stewed for a while as the machines buzzed away.

Carlo broke the silence, whispering a welcome change of topic.

"You girls going to Cooper Union on Sunday?"

"Uh huh." Elsie glanced at her friends when nobody else answered. She seemed to brighten up at the thought of it. "Aren't we?"

Rebecca nodded. "I am."

Carlo reached behind Lenny and poked Dora in the ribs. "You too, right?"

"I dunno..." Dora's voice trailed off.

"Whaddya mean, ya don't know?"

"Well, okay, here it is: I wanna know why aren't we asking for better wages? This rally — as far as I can tell — it's just for better conditions, isn't it? Not for wages. I think it's a waste o' time."

"You think we've got it so great here?" asked Lenny. "You like Lev breathin' down your neck?"

"I can handle Lev."

"Yeah, we all saw that. But I'm not talkin' about him *actually* breathin' down your neck, I'm talkin' about the rules here."

"Yeah, I know, I know. But still, you can sorta understand some of the things they do... I mean the owners, you know, lookin' at it from their point of view."

Elsie frowned at her. "We're not owners, Dora. In case you forgot?"

"I know! But imagine if you were. How would you do things? Some of these girls would be off in a second to meet their boyfriends in the middle of the day, if those doors over there weren't locked. They'd say they're goin' for a bathroom break, and off they'd be smoochin' for a good ten to fifteen, a coupla blocks over."

"Oh come on, Dora," said Rebecca. "What about that fire downstairs last month. Thank God they got it out in time. What if there's another one, and we're locked in? You don't think Lev does a good enough job keeping us in line?"

Elsie snorted. "Really, Dora. You'd think you were the company spokesman. What good is an extra buck a week if I'm gonna be trapped in here and end up like a piece of charcoal?"

"And plus," added Lenny, "this strike is as much against the city as it is against the factories. Damned inspectors are so stupid. Or more likely someone's paying them off. They gotta know that as soon as they come in, those guys are unlocking the doors and shuttling the kids out the back. Have ya ever seen this place get a fine? Have ya? That's 'cause they're all patsies."

"I know you're right, but I just wish we were gettin' up for a better wage is all, as long as we're talkin' about a strike. For Pete's sake, I'm still gettin' eight dollars a week after three years here!"

"Just be there," said Carlo. "I hear there's gonna be some good speeches. And you never know, Dora. Maybe you'll meet the man o' your dreams."

Dora stopped sewing for a second and raised her hands in defeat. "I'll be there, I'll be there! But I'm not gonna be pickin' out my wedding dress just yet."

Neither am I, thought Rebecca, and she hunkered down into her machine, trying to focus on her pleats, which were being pulled just a bit too fast under the pistoning needle.

Chapter Four

November 20th 1909

Today I met the man who will be my husband. That is, he will be my husband if I cannot find of a way out of it, and I must confess I'm losing some hope.

It is not him that I find objectionable. He wasn't so bad, really. I just wish I could think of a better way to convince Papa that I should be able to pick the man I marry. I have not dared raise the subject since last Friday, for fear that Papa would change his mind about the delay and arrange the wedding for sooner. All the perfectly reasonable arguments he will not believe are valid ones, so as a result I am condemned to hours of unproductive plotting. No, if I am to convince him to cancel the arrangement it will have to be something very very good. Especially now, after the meeting.

But here I go again, not telling the story first, before my reaction bubbles up like soup at a raging boil. Mrs. Pearson would be most displeased. Story, reflection. Story, reflection, she'd say. I should write it out five hundred times on a slate for punishment. Then maybe I'd get it right.

The meeting with Isaac and his father took place in our kitchen. It was just moments after Mama sprang the news on me as we walked in the door. Mr. Kalish and his son would be arriving for tea, she said.

No sooner had she said it than they arrived at our door, quite the sight the two of them. The father was wrinkled and tiny with a wispy, tangled grey beard and a big, dark hat. He was walking with a cane and looked old enough to be his son's grandfather. His face was sunken in at the cheekbones, but he was pink-faced and had a sweet smile and a sparkle in his eyes. He seemed confused but lighthearted, as though he had no idea where he was but trusted it was somewhere nice.

The son was tall and broad shouldered, but his physique was contradicted by his unhealthy skin tone and his breathlessness. He also had a scraggly beard, but to be fair it was a lot less scraggly than the father's, and it was also thicker and dark brown. He wore no hat or yarmulke at all, perhaps he is not so religious, I don't know. A bouquet of daffodils dangled from one hand until he offered them to my mother like he was trying to get rid of a burden. It did not really seem rude, I'm sure it was because of his lack of air and his preoccupation with his father. But whatever his senti- ment, it was certainly strange.

I couldn't smell the daffodils at all until later in the day because as soon as my mother took them, he took off his coat, and a waft of stale pipe smoke emanated from the fabric. Maybe even from his beard, G-d forbid. The thin strip of exposed skin between his facial hair and his brown eyes was shiny and smooth, but it was a strange color — a blotchy patchwork of turnips and ash.

We were introduced, Isaac, Rebecca, Rebecca, Isaac, pleased to make your acquaintance, he said. "Make your acquaintance?" I thought. This is the man to whom I'm to be married! Perhaps he was more nervous than I, I thought.

He led his father into our apartment and to a chair at the table. Mama went to the wash basin to put some water in our one chipped, ceramic vase, and then Isaac asked her for a glass of water for some medicine. At first I think we all assumed it was for his father. But then he fished an ampoule out of his pocket, broke off the tip, poured the liquid into it, stirred the mixture with his pinky, and gulped it all down. My mother was too slow to hide her worry, but when she saw me looking at her, she smiled as though there was nothing of concern at all, and wasn't Isaac's display quite endearing.

After that we quickly assembled around the table and sat sipping tea. Occasionally, we talked about nothing. Eventually, my parents suggested they and Mr. Kalish take a walk in the neighbourhood to discuss some details about the wedding. I assume this was their way of informing him of the postponement, but it was also a rather unsubtle way to leave us together to promote some conversation.

So there they left me, at the mercy of awkwardness, feeling quite naked but for the meagre protection of a tiny teacup and a long piece of mandelbroyt, quickly vanishing as I gnawed at it instead of my own finger.

The door latch clicked loudly behind their parents, and all Rebecca could think of was prison bars being locked shut. To hide her face, she brought her cup to her lips and sipped, but to her embarrassment it sounded more like a slurp. To make matters worse, some tea escaped and dribbled down her chin.

"Excuse me," she said, and hurried over to the wash basin to get a cloth, her cheeks flushing. She sat down again, but felt his eyes resting on her. She wiped again with the cloth and then leaned down to fuss over the cookies. Their nutty smell, usually a comfort to her, seemed a bit off.

"Would you like another one?"

She lifted the plate while still crouched down, wiping at an imaginary spot on the table. He declined her offer, putting his cup down and joining his hands in his lap, looking like he was preparing to leave. She wondered how she could have offended him so easily and so soon, but instead of announcing his departure, he looked about the room and smiled. The greyish walls were almost bare, revealing numerous scratches in the paint and nicks at the plaster, but he looked at them as though he were admiring an art gallery. Surely he was trying to avoid looking at her.

"Is that your bubbe and zayde?" He pointed to a tiny, pine-framed photograph hanging beside the door to her parents' bedroom. A man and a woman sat stiffly side by side dressed in dark clothing with startled, almost frightened, expressions on their faces.

"Yes. On my father's side. They live in Poland. I understand they know your family there too."

"Yes, or so my father tells me. But I don't remember them." He scratched at his cheek with his pinky.

"I didn't realize you ever met them at all. How old were you when you left?"

"Seven."

"Then I suppose you wouldn't."

"No."

He picked up his cup and sipped a little. An amber drop of tea clung to a hair just below his lip. She tried not to look.

"I understand you live here with a boarder," he said. "It must be quite cramped."

"It is. Her name's Ida, and we share a bed. I barely get any sleep because she chatters incessantly. But then it's the same everywhere, isn't it?"

"Yes, where we are, too."

"I shouldn't really complain."

"No, it's quite all right. I know what it's like. We don't have a boarder, but cousin Sophie takes care of us, and we only have two rooms. So that means I share a bed with my father."

"Ugh. As bad as it is with Ida, I can't imagine sharing a room with my parents."

"It's not the best situation, obviously, but then none of us is rich people."

"We should only be so lucky."

"Yes."

"Indeed."

Silence swooped in, exposing the creaking of her chair.

"Excuse me for a second," she said; she got up and slammed a fist down on the seat, locking the loose leg into place. When she sat back down, she noticed that Isaac seemed startled, and realized that what she had just done was probably considered unladylike. She decided it best to move the conversation along.

"I hope you don't think I'm being rude," she said, "but may I ask when your mother passed away?"

"It's okay to ask. It was four years ago. After that, cousin Sophie came from Poland to be with us."

"I'm sorry."

"Thank you. It's been hard on my father."

"He doesn't seem so well, if you don't mind my saying." She wanted to say neither do you, though at least now his cheeks were flushing a little bit.

"He hasn't been the same since she died. He was beginning to get a little confused beforehand, but it's been worse since then."

"It's lucky your cousin could come, then."

"Yes, it is."

Rebecca got up to put more cookies on the plate. She thought she would die if the conversation didn't get more interesting. At least it was moving, but more like a hunchback dragging a lame foot. When she sat down she was aware of Isaac staring at her face again.

"What is it? Do I have a crumb?"

"No, no, that's not it. I was just noticing you're quite pretty."

She felt her neck get hot. "Thank you, but you don't have to say that."

"I know."

"These situations ... These arrangements are so outside of our control. It doesn't really matter what we think, does it?"

"But it doesn't hurt when you find a person pleasing."

Rebecca turned her face away. She wondered if she should say something about him; it was the polite thing to do, but it didn't feel right. He wasn't bad looking, really, but to say he was attractive would seem forced. She picked up the teapot and felt its weight. It was almost full.

"Should I make more tea?" she said.

"No, don't, let's go for a walk. I want to show you the street I was thinking we could move to when we're married."

"Are you sure? What if our parents come back, shouldn't we wait?"

"Don't worry — we won't be gone long."

"Okay," she said, removing the tray from the table. Actually she was relieved that they would be getting outdoors. At least walking with him the silences would be less uncomfortable. They wouldn't have to look at one another.

Isaac helped her on with her coat, and they left the apartment. When they reached the street, the cold air slapped her face, and the sweet-sickly smell of burning garbage tickled her nostrils. She looked left and right to see who was outside. Thank God she didn't see Mr. Zussel. Thank God it was the Sabbath and he took the day off. She couldn't have faced an encounter with him right now, it would surely have involved embarrassing questions and very probably some teasing.

The street traffic was sparse, but not enough for her liking. People she recognized from the neighbourhood were still returning from services, walking briskly along to get out of the cold as quickly as possible. A family that lived a few buildings down and to whom they had been introduced once at shul nodded at her as they passed, then slowed down and stared as she walked by. It might have been her imagination, but she felt their eyes following her, as if her body, flanked by Isaac's, were exerting some magnetic pull on their faces.

The wind picked up as she moved around the corner, intensified by the tunnel effect of the buildings. A cloud of dust picked up, and she squeezed her eyes shut until it passed. It hadn't rained in a few days, so the usually swamp-like street had dried up, leaving a shifting layer of grime on top of dry, cracked earth. In this state, their boots were temporarily safe from mud and sog, but now the rest of their clothes would acquire a fine, brown coating. A scarf pulled from her pocket and wrapped around her face protected her from the next lashing.

Isaac pulled a cap out from under his coat. "This is one of mine. Do you like it?"

She looked it over. It was grey wool, smooth and neatly made, but she could find no features that distinguished it from hundreds of her father's that she had seen.

"It's very nice."

"Look at the stitching. Yekl taught me that."

She looked at the seam near the brim, but still could not notice anything special. She decided it would be best to steer the conversation elsewhere.

"You work with him, my father told me. He seems like a good man."

"Yes, he's been very kind. He's taught me everything I know. He says when he dies I can have his part in the business."

"That's lucky for you."

"For us, you mean."

"Yes, of course. For us."

"I think by that time, I'll be better at the money part of the business. As opposed to the cap-making part. That's the part I really like."

"The money part?"

"No the other. The cap-making."

"Well it sure is nice to have something you like doing."

"It sure is." He scratched his cheek with his pinky again.

"I'm going to night school," she offered. "That's what I love to do."

"Your father told me you worked in one of the factories."

"I do. But that's just work. When I go to school, that's when I feel alive."

"I know what you mean. It's like when I make a great cap, when the stitching is absolutely perfect, and the material I've chosen is just right... smooth, nice texture, and then someone buys it. It's the greatest feeling. Pure satisfaction."

They walked in silence for about ten minutes, while Rebecca searched desperately for something else to talk about. When they got to Seward Park, Isaac was out of breath again and suggested they sit on a bench for a moment.

"Are you all right?" she asked. His face was looking sickly again.

"I'm fine, I just have to be careful not to overexert myself."

"Do you mind if I ask what's wrong? You took some medicine when you arrived at the apartment."

"It's digitalis. For my heart. I have to take it if my heart gets going too much. It slows it down."

"It sounds serious." She didn't want to pry, but this was the man she was supposed to marry. Would he become an invalid? Would she have to take care of him? Mrs. Bryant, two floors down, had a husband with a bad heart, and haggard would be a kind description of her.

"It's not, really. It's a problem I've had since I was a kid."

Since he was a kid? What was not serious about that?

"How old are you now, if you don't mind my asking?"

"Twenty-four. Anyway, don't worry about my heart. I feel fine, mostly. It's really nothing, I just have to be careful. You won't have to worry about my health, I promise. We just have to get an apartment on the second or third floor and we'll be fine. I think the five flights to your place is a bit too much to do every day."

His words didn't inspire much confidence, coming as they did from his ghost-like face.

"Look, Isaac, I have to tell you something."

"What is it?"

"It's about the wedding."

"I want you to feel like you can tell me anything."

"Yes, well, you know how you love cap-making? Well, I really do feel that way about my classes."

"Yes I know, you said that."

"Yes, but the reason I mention it again is that my papa is right now telling your papa that the wedding's to be delayed."

"What?"

"For a year and a half. It's nothing personal, I just wanted some time to finish my studies and get my diploma."

"Oh." He turned away from her. He seemed hurt.

"And I didn't think it would be possible once we were married."

"Well, no, I don't suppose it would be," he said, "what with your household duties and all. And then when the children start coming..."

She didn't like the turn this conversation was taking. "Even though that may not be for some time," she added.

"Yes, but you never know. And I want us to start right away, don't you? I want to have a big family."

"Well, you might feel different after the first one, and we're up all night with the baby crying."

"I doubt it."

His face was serious, her attempt to lighten things had failed.

"Even still, I wanted you to know. It's not about you. I just want to graduate."

"Well, you're right, once we're married it won't be possible."

She wished he hadn't repeated that. She looked up at the trees. A brown leaf clung desperately to a branch just above her.

Suddenly he turned and smiled at her, and his eyes brightened; their steeliness caught the light and glinted a little, making them seem more liquid. A flush of pink rushed into his cheeks.

"If you were at school at night I'd never get to see you, would I?"

She smiled, but looked down. "No, I guess you wouldn't."

He stood up and held out his hand to help her up. "Let's go see the tenement I wanted to show you. Although now I guess there might not be anything available by the time we're ready to move in. Still, you never know."

"It's only a matter of months, if you think of it that way."

They walked on in silence for a few blocks, side by side but not touching, until he took her arm and hooked it underneath his, pinning it there.

Chapter Five

"Hattie, maybe I *should* get married."

"Shhhhhhh! I'm trying to watch!"

"If I do, at least I won't have to work in the factory anymore..."

Hattie took her finger away from her lips, simultaneously tilt-ed her head, and pointed with both toward Mary Pickford. She furrowed her brow and jutted her chin forward in concentration.

The piano player at the front of the theatre pounded the keyboard dramatically as Billy Quirk emerged from behind a tree; Mary Pickford recoiled and drew her open palms up beside her face in defence. Her mascaraed eyes widened with terror, and her mouth opened wide in a mute scream. Hattie jolted ever so slightly.

Rebecca rolled her eyes. "Sorry." She fidgeted on the hard wooden bench and shoved back against the man on her left, who was taking too much room with his elbows. "I didn't realize that the story was so complicated that it required this much attention."

She looked around. The theatre was choked with people, men and women overstuffed into row after row, some also leaning against the plain, brown, panelled walls, the occasional one crouching under the too-low sconces, even a few sitting cross-legged on the floor in the aisles. Their body shapes rippled with the changing light, becoming murky when the actors passed under a dark bridge, dancing and animated when the actors were bathed in sunlight. It seemed that everyone except her was mesmerized by the screen, and most of them looked like their brains had dribbled out through their open mouths.

Hattie had a different expression. She looked as though she were studying something under a microscope. Ever since she won her scholarship to college, suddenly culture needed to be analyzed. Later, she would no doubt want to have a serious conversation about the merits and failures of the production. Rebecca was no longer allowed just to *enjoy* the moving pictures, she now had to *appreciate* them. She was starting to find their trips to the nickelodeon tiresome.

Other things preoccupied her these days. She bounced her knees up and down and drummed her fingers against her calves, and when that had no effect, she let out a loud sigh.

"Rebecca, the picture is no more than fifteen minutes long. Can't it wait?"

"Okay, okay." She backed off. Twirling a strand of hair, she looked back up at the screen. The scene took place in Central Park, and several people in the audience murmured excitedly, recognizing a fountain that they had seen in person. Rebecca also turned to voice her recognition, then stopped, remembering her promise.

She sat still for the next few minutes, until "THE END" appeared on the screen. The piano player stood up for his bow, and the audience cheered.

Hattie turned to Rebecca as they began to file out of the theatre. "It's ridiculous and unrealistic, all that mugging, and that stuff they do with their eyebrows and the wide-open eyes. Why can't they just *act*, like in the theatre? Just because there's no sound it doesn't mean they have to scrunch their faces into unrecognizable shapes. I'll betcha if you put that Mary Pickford on the stage she wouldn't last one night before they closed the show down. Billy Quirk neither."

They helped each other on with their hats. Her friend was several inches taller, a young woman of much bigger features who seemed always to buy hats the wrong size for her disproportionately small head. Hattie's hat was a rich navy blue, and this one was a little too big. Rebecca adjusted it for her, reaching up to try tucking in a few strands of curly jet-black hair. She thought the hair's volume might keep the hat from sliding to the side.

"Didn't Mary Pickford start out on the stage?" she asked, giving up on a few frizzy strands at the back, where they could bounce about freely without Hattie's knowing it.

"Well, she obviously didn't last that long at it."

"Hattie, I don't wanna talk about the picture. I've been trying to tell you all evening about my papa and how he's trying to marry me off, and you're not paying attention!"

"I'm sorry, Rebecca. I'm listening now."

They had emerged onto a busy section of 3rd Avenue and headed toward 8th Street. Her friend was walking very quickly, with her eyes trained straight ahead. They were late for the rally. The scent of roasting chestnuts filled the air, coming from the outdoor oven of a blind man, crouched over his low coal fire at the side of the road. Rebecca scuttled ahead of Hattie, turned so that she could face her friend as she spoke, and walked backwards for a few steps. She had to shout because they were walking under the train tracks, and a car rattled by overhead.

"I was saying, maybe I *should* get married. I mean, I don't want to, and I've been trying to figure out ways to get out of it, but then, today, I was thinking..." The train passed, and she lowered her voice. "I was thinking that I just don't know how much longer I can stand it in that factory. I'm not very fast. It's probably only a matter of time before I get fired."

Hattie was visibly bored, her eyes rolling here and there in their sockets, and Rebecca's pouting lips seemed to have no impact on her level of interest.

"You have to make some choices about your life, Rebecca. You're the smartest student in the whole school. You could get a scholarship if you wanted to."

"No, I couldn't, Hattie. I'm not smart like you."

"Yes, you are. You have the highest grades in your class now."

"That's only because you left."

"And because you started to apply yourself a little more. You always got higher grades in English composition anyway. Even better than me. The problem is you can never make up your mind about anything."

Rebecca pondered this a second, but she was getting annoyed at her friend because, maddeningly, she couldn't decide how to respond. It wasn't fair — Hattie had planted the seed of indecision in her mind. She pulled her wits together.

"So what would it do if I got a scholarship? My papa would still want me to get married."

"You could come live with me — that's what it would do. We would make a go of it together."

"But Hattie, I do want to get married someday. Just not now. And not to a stranger. Besides, I can't leave my parents, if it's not to get married. That would be so selfish. I just can't. They need my wages."

"I know you can't. So stop complaining. Either do something or stop complaining. It's simple, Rebecca."

"It's not so simple."

"Yes it is. I'm not saying it's easy. I'm just saying it's simple."

Rebecca pondered the difference as they emerged from out under the tracks and headed toward the Cooper Union. The building was an imposing brownstone with five stories, capped by a wide rectangular section housing a gleaming white clock.

As they approached the entrance, Rebecca caught sight of Dora and Elsie waiting for them outside, and her stomach knotted. There was no telling how this would play out. She presented them to Hattie, reminding them they had met once before, and hoped to usher them all quickly inside to avoid any awkwardness. Unfortunately, Elsie's politeness thwarted her plan when she stepped forward to shake Hattie's hand.

"So nice to see you again, Hattie, how's college going?"

"It's wonderful, thank you. The program I'm in is so stimulating."

"Tell me again what you're studying?"

"It's Theatre and English Literature."

"Did you say Theatre?" said Dora. Oh God, thought Rebecca, here it comes.

"Yes, it's a terrific program; we study a play, analyze its structure and meaning, then we put on an amateur production."

"Isn't that nice!" Dora commented, her sticky-sweet voice a dead giveaway. "Amateur productions are so important! I started out in those too, back in Chicago. Of course, now that I have professional experience, I'm told it wouldn't look good to focus on amateur productions anymore."

Rebecca closed her eyes, wishing this would all go away. It was exactly what she had hoped to prevent. Dora had come to New York just over a year ago to see if she could make it in vaudeville. While the rest of them went to school, Dora spent what extra money she had on singing and dancing lessons and on clothes. Sometimes on the weekends, she would go to auditions, but since Rebecca had known her, there had been no "professional experience."

"Well, that's great, Dora. What shows have you been in?" Hattie asked. Rebecca turned to Elsie, and they exchanged a look of despair.

"Oh, little productions here and there. No long runs yet."

"Well, keep at it. It's tough breaking in."

"You too," Dora answered, her face still smiling, but looking like it had been pricked and drained of air. It might have been her imagination, but Rebecca thought she heard her teeth gritting.

"C'mon gals, let's go inside, we're already late for the rally," she urged.

They went down the stairs and into the Great Hall. The rally had already begun, and they could hear a man's voice getting louder as they approached the room. The hall was surprisingly small for its name, with an arched ceiling and stone pillars lining the two sides and blocking the view from many angles. People were seated where they could, and others were packed into the empty spaces.

From the podium at the front of the stage came the now-booming voice of a man speaking in Italian. As he spoke, the crowd broke into cheers, half of them understanding his words, the other half catching his intent. The man stood on a long and narrow stage behind a dark brown podium. Some chairs were lined up in a row tucked behind and to the left of the podium, occupied by three young men, an old, stout-figured woman, and a slender young girl. A large banner was draped overhead across the back: *International Ladies Garment Worker's Union, Local 25*.

Rebecca and her friends joined hands and wormed single file through the bodies. They stopped partway down the aisle and stood in a close huddle just next to the seats. They opened their coats, as it was getting hot. The hall smelled of cigarettes and damp wool. A thick cloud of smoke hung in the air above people's heads. Some women in front of them shouted.

"Viva il sindicato!" The man's voice rose, his fists began to punctuate the air above his head. The hall erupted into applause again, and the man, obviously finished, was greeted at the podium by the moderator and led off the stage to hugs and pats on the back.

Rebecca saw the young girl rise from her seat to approach the podium. From where she stood, the girl looked no more than eighteen, perhaps younger. She was quite tall, and her face looked pale and her eyes large. She tugged at her blouse, closed her eyes, and took a deep breath. Colour filled her cheeks, and she smoothed the surface of the podium with her palms, straightened her back, stuck out her chest, and picked up her head.

The noise of the crowd hardly died down, but Rebecca stared straight at her. For a moment, she thought the girl seemed to be looking back. But then her eyes shifted, and she fixed on a point above Rebecca's head.

"My name is Sarah," her voice was loud and strong, and more people turned to the front of the hall, "and I am here today to demand that we not be treated like animals."

The crowd hushed. Rebecca looked intently at the girl. Her brow was shiny — perhaps she was perspiring. It made her skin look like buttermilk. She seemed familiar somehow, but Rebecca couldn't put her finger on it. She had never heard someone so young speak with such confidence.

"I am not a great unionist. And I have never spoken in public before. I am a simple factory girl, who works hard and tries to earn a living for my family." She paused. "Like so many of you."

People clapped. The girl pulled a strand of hair out of her face, and tucked it behind her ear. Rebecca noticed that her nails were red.

"When I started working at my factory, I was fifteen years old. Now I am seventeen. Like many girls my age, I must work to bring food to my parents' table. I started at six dollars per week. Two years later, I only earn seven."

A shout. "Criminals!"

"This is unacceptable!" was Sarah's answer.

"That's right, sister!" Some men in the front row held up some signs and shook them vigorously. One of them blocked Rebecca's view so that she had to move a little to her left to see properly.

"I work, and yet with my wages, I have to pay rent on the chair I sit on. I must buy my needles. They even make me pay for a clothes locker at work!"

A hissing began from the right of the stage. And also, Rebecca realized, from Hattie, who was standing beside her.

"But I am not so badly off as the girl next to me — she's a so-called helper, hired by one of the men — you know — so he can get more pay. Do you know how much he pays her? Three dollars! And she's been 'learning' for a year now!"

Someone from the front called out, "Maybe someone dropped her on her head when she was a baby!"

Laughter. How could people laugh at such a thing?

"Yes, I know, we all need to laugh sometimes in order to handle these terrible conditions. But this is no joke. Exploitation is not something to laugh at."

Dora leapt up in the air beside her. "That's the stuff, kid! You tell 'em!"

Rebecca elbowed Hattie, and they exchanged an amused look. This girl had reached past even Dora's cynicism.

"Yesterday," she continued gravely, "a little boy of seven years old, no bigger than this," she stepped beside the podium and illustrated the boy's height by cutting her hand sharply inwards against her hip, "his name is Angelo. He was trapped under five bolts of cloth when they fell off a table. Were these bolts secured? No, of course not. Had they fallen off before? Yes, many times. Had we complained? Yes, of course we had. Many times. What did the owners say to us? They said we were negligent in how we piled up the bolts of cloth!"

Boos and hisses.

"What do you think happened to that boy?"

The din lowered again.

"I'll tell you what happened. His legs were crushed like matchsticks!"

People gasped. A woman in front put her hand over her mouth.

"That boy, he may never walk again. His mother has six other children. She speaks no English. Has no husband to help her with her children. How will she take care of that boy, I ask?! How?!"

The hall was now completely quiet except for the sound of a few chairs scraping the wood floor. Rebecca held her breath.

"Do you think the factory will compensate her for her lost wages?"

"*No!*" The shout came from some women down in front.

"Do you think they even paid for his hospital bill?"

"*No!*" This time, it came from all around them.

"Do you *know* what they told his *mother* when they brought his crushed little body to her?"

Silence. The crowd was rapt.

"They told her ... that she owed them money! On account of his count of buttons at the end of the day. It was off. By *ten* buttons!"

"Bastards!" Hattie cried, so loud that Rebecca flinched. She saw Elsie close her eyes and shake her head. She seemed strangely unmoved, almost amused.

"Never mind that it is not even legal to employ that child. Never mind that their disregard for safety may have cost him any chance in life but to be a beggar on the street corner. Never mind that someone else probably took those buttons. If indeed they were taken at all!"

The girl's voice rose in anger with every sentence. Rebecca's heart beat faster and faster. People throughout the hall began to murmur to one another. A few got up from their seats.

"Never mind ... that his mother ... and his brothers and sisters ... will have to work even *harder* to put bread on their table. Do the owners even *care?*"

"No!"

"Do they even have *hearts?*"

"No!"

By now, almost everyone was standing.

"I began by saying they treat us like animals. But now, I ask you, who are the real animals? Who, I ask you?"

"They are!" a man off to the left screamed out.

"Well, if they are heartless animals, then how can we get them to listen?!"

"Striiiiiiike!" came a chorus from the back.

"What's that? I can't hear you!"

"Strike! Strike! Strike! Strike!"

The chanting became a steady, rhythmic pounding, and it shook Rebecca to her bones. Before she even realized it, she heard her own voice rise. People stomped their heels on the floor, the reverberations ran through the soles of her shoes. Her face was flushed. That girl, she was so good at making an argument, so forceful. Who could disagree with her? Rebecca wanted to tell her how well she had spoken, how brave she was, ask her a thousand questions.

She turned around to watch the crowd. Fists and placards were slicing the air above their heads, cutting at the cloud of smoke, disturbing its rest, whipping it up so that it seemed a storm might break out indoors. She heard some benches scraping the floor behind her and turned to look at the doorway. Ten policemen had come in. Some of the people at the back were standing toe to toe with them, shouting into their faces.

She turned back to the stage and saw Sarah descend the stairs to the side, then walk back in front of the stage toward their aisle. Rebecca caught a glimpse or two through the crowd, and now that she was closer could make out her features more clearly. She had an angular face with smooth skin, darker than she had thought. Some freckles above the cheeks. Her curly, red hair was pressed flat and wet at the temples. She walked proudly past some people who patted her on the back. Rebecca stepped forward timidly.

"Miss, I wanted to tell you how…"

A scream behind them. Rebecca turned to see a man on the floor near the entrance, his forehead slick with blood. One of the policemen was standing over him with a billy club raised above his head.

"No!" shouted Sarah, and she pushed past Rebecca to get to the back. "This is a peaceful rally!"

Hattie and Elsie came up to Rebecca and held her arm. Sarah rushed forward to try to stop the officer, but he was already striking the man on the floor. As she approached him, her arms outstretched to grab hold of his club, another officer swung a wide arc and struck her shins. She crumpled to the ground.

Two men who had accompanied her from the stage reached her and helped her up, putting an arm on each shoulder. One of them was tugged on the arm by a man who pointed to another commotion happening near the front. Elsie pulled away from Dora and moved to where Sarah was being helped.

"Elsie, no!" Dora called out after them. More police charged into the hall. Near the other doors, fights were breaking out, and someone threw a chair at a group of three policemen. A crush of protesters pushed toward the exits. Rebecca pulled free of Dora's arm and followed Elsie. She saw Elsie reach Sarah and take the place of the man who had left.

Hattie had followed Rebecca and pulled Dora with her.

"Let's get her out of here!" she cried.

"There's no way out!" said Elsie. "The exits are blocked!"

They pulled Sarah the other way. They struggled to get to a chair, but there was another line of police officers in the direction that they were moving. There was a crowd of people now pushing them in the direction of the police line.

"Get back!" one of the officers yelled. His eyes were wide, and he was looking rapidly from one side to the other, taking steps slowly backward as the crowd advanced. "Get back *now*, ya crazy kikes! I'm warning you!" The crowd pressed harder against Rebecca's back. She was being jostled dangerously close to the officer. She took Elsie's free elbow and tried to manoeuvre them sideways and backwards through the crowd.

Suddenly, a push sent Rebecca tumbling forward. Her hand slipped from Elsie's elbow and Rebecca fell against a policeman.

A blow struck her on the left temple, and her head snapped to the side, her hat falling away. She felt the club connect with her left arm, knocking her off balance in the other direction. The pain shot through her arm and reached the back of her neck.

She fell to the ground. Hattie screamed. She heard Elsie yell, "Stop it! It wasn't her fault!"

Rebecca felt warmth seep into her hair. Out of the corner of her eye, she saw Hattie and Dora rushing toward her. Dora moved out of her line of sight. She saw the officer's arm raise above his head, then bring his club down on Hattie's back. Hattie splayed forward onto her stomach, beside her on the floor.

Some blood dripped into her eyes, and she was forced to close them for a few seconds. When she reopened them, Elsie and Sarah were at her side, with Dora standing above them, her hands over her mouth, muttering "No, no, no..."

Rebecca's cheek was pressed against the wooden floorboard, and she could see Hattie pull herself up and begin to crawl over her way.

She felt dizzy. Hattie's face dissolved into a blur of pink and red. Dora's voice, chanting *no, no, no*, began to fade, until it sounded a thousand miles away. The warmth of someone's chest against her back felt wet and hot like her brow.

She saw Sarah's face come into her field of vision and then blur again. Someone's hand pressed her temple where the wetness was. Stinging. She felt a thumb in her palm. Reflexively, her hand engulfed it and held tight, until her eyelids, heavy as molasses, flowed shut, and the room went dark.

When she awoke, her father was standing above her. His beard was grey and scraggly, his eyebrows a tangle of worry. She felt something cold on her forehead. A hand slipped off of the cloth and slid down the side of her face. Rebecca tilted her head back to see her mother, but a sharp pain at the back of her neck made her seize her shoulders.

"It's all right, kinderleh, I'm here."

Her mother was sitting at the head of the bed and leaned over her to show herself. She kissed Rebecca's forehead. "You have a fever, I think." She got up, wrung out the cloth in a bowl, and then placed it back on Rebecca's forehead. It tingled. Rebecca became aware of her arm throbbing.

"Rebecca, we need to have a talk," said her father.

"Sholem, leave us alone, please. Not now. She needs some rest."

He was about to say something, but instead turned to leave. But he stopped, turned around again, and reached down to press his daughter's hand. Rebecca thought his eyes might be glassy, but he turned away too quickly for her to tell and left the room.

"What time is it?"

"It's four in the morning."

"How did I get here?"

"Those two boys from your factory. The Italian boys. They brought you here. It's been five hours. We were worried sick."

"Where's Hattie? And..." She tried to sit up. "Ooh!"

"Stop with the moving and lie down! Hattie was with the boys."

Rebecca eased back down on the bed. Her voice was weak. "What happened to Elsie and Dora? And the other girl?"

"What girl?"

"Sarah, the girl from the rally."

"Shush now, don't agitate yourself, Rebecca. You have such a bump on your head." She wiped her daughter's brow again. "I don't know who you're talking about. Your friends are fine. They were all together when they dropped you off. You are a lucky girl."

"What were you thinking, Beckeleh, going to such a rally, fighting with policemen?"

"I wasn't fighting with policemen, Mama. They hit us. And we were there to fight injustice. You of all people should know about that. People have to stand up for themselves — you taught me that."

"Other people. Not my daughter."

Rebecca paused for a moment, waiting for her head to throb a little less. "Mama, don't you read about what's happening in Russia these days?"

"Yes, of course I do."

"And don't you always say if there was a revolution you'd want to go back home?"

"Sometimes, I say that. Then I think to myself: my daughter will have a better chance here, and there will never be such a revolution anyway."

Her mother tilted her head back and spoke to the ceiling, as if God were peeking at her through the slats. "Gevuld. Never forgets a word I say. If only she could distinguish fancy from advice, and then really listen to me, I wouldn't have so many wrinkles..."

"Of course you could go, Mama. It was your country. And if it were a better place, you'd go. Well, try to understand. This is *my* country Mama. Don't you see? All around, there are people trying to make a better life for themselves. And while they're making a living, they just want to be treated like human beings."

A shadow fell over Rebecca's face. She looked up to see her father. His face looked grim.

"Papa. I didn't hear you come back in. Mama and I were just talking..."

"I heard the talking. And I've heard enough." He moved over to the window, rubbed at the glass, and looked out. His body blocked the oil lamp so that his shadow cast itself over the bed. When he spoke his voice was clear.

"You won't be working in that place where people are treated like animals anymore, Rebecca. I'm arranging the wedding for next month."

"Papa!"

"There will be no more discussion. I have made my decision. Only foolishness allowed me to sway from it for a moment last week. This night — this ... thing that happened — I won't see it happen again. Not to my daughter. Not while you are in my house. That factory, and all that goes with it, it is too dangerous.

It is time for you to be married, and then you can have these arguments with your husband, if he is as lenient as I am, you should be so lucky."

Rebecca looked at her mother. Tears welled in her eyes so that she could barely see. Her mother stroked her forehead, leaning and speaking softly now, tears in her eyes too.

"You will be happy, Rebecca. It's a good match." Her voice was wet and raspy, like gravel being moved by a stream.

Rebecca pushed her mother's hand away and pulled the sheet over her head to muffle her sobs.

Chapter Six

1983

Anna stood leaning against the wall, staring out at the people gathered for her mother's shivah. Danielle Gutstein stood beside her, her arm linked with hers, planted in its crook. Beyond Danielle, through the crowd of people, she could just see the back of Sadie's head in their mother's bedroom.

"You should be sitting, Anna," said Danielle.

"It's okay, I've been sitting long enough."

Danielle's mother, Ida, was occupying the chair next to them, and she was squinting at the spines of the books on the shelf opposite her and stirring her tea very slowly. There was barely a ripple in the cup.

"What does that one over there say?" she asked.

"The little one?" asked Danielle.

"No, the big one beside it, the one that looks like it might fall off the shelf."

"It's a cookbook, Mama. Julia Child."

"Julia Child. She's that big, fat woman you can barely understand when she talks, right?"

"That's right, Mama." Danielle rolled her eyes at Anna.

"I don't know why I'm even trying to read the titles. From here they're all just a blur anyway, even with this new prescription."

Anna squeezed Ida's shoulder.

"Ay, such a strong grip! *That* you get from your mother. Was she ever strong, I tell you. I couldn't believe it. Maybe because she was so strong it also made her a little meshuga too, mind you. And I say that out of love and kindness. Anna, did you know the day Sadie was born, your mama, as big as a house, was down in the backyard in the noon-hour sun burying her cutlery? I was remembering that just now stirring my teacup. This spoon might even have been one of the ones she buried."

"Burying her cutlery? What do you mean?"

"What do I mean? Just what I said, burying cutlery. God only knows why. I guess she mixed the milk with the meat by accident. That's what the Orthodox do to purify it afterwards — you know that. Your mama was much more observant back then, when your father was still alive. We all did what we were supposed to in order to keep a good kosher home."

"You mean she was actually out digging in the backyard the day Sadie was born?" The corners of Anna's mouth curled a little upwards as she pictured it.

"Only a few hours before. It was so long ago, I don't remember the details. But I remember her, still big with Sadie in her belly, down on all fours covering up the earth. I said, 'Rebecca, what are you, meshuga? What are you doing there?' And she told me she was burying the cutlery, that's all. As if it were the most normal thing a pregnant woman could do. And then later that day she gave birth — all by herself. She delivered the baby all by herself. I must have gone out in the afternoon, I don't remember why I wasn't there to help. Like I told you, we were very close."

"What on earth was she thinking? Where was Papa?" Anna said.

"Who knows? Out working, probably." She put her hands up in the air. "That mama of yours. It was a crazy thing to do when she was that pregnant, and it was a miracle that Sadie was okay, that's all I can say. God smiled down upon both of them that day. That was just one example of how your mama was strong like an ox. With her tiny body — you wouldn't have thought so, but she was. Your mama, she was such an angel. We will all miss her very much."

The old woman finished her story and turned to examining her own hands. A pink, frosted nail traced an intricate pattern of veins, like fat cobwebs, from the cuticle of her other index finger up to her ruffled, white sleeves. She clenched and unclenched her fists, perhaps trying to work out some aching in her knuckles. She picked her head up again.

"It doesn't seem like your sister is going to come say hello, does it, Anna dear? You and your mother always had better manners than her. I see fifty years hasn't made one bit of difference."

"I think she feels awkward, Ida. Wouldn't you if you were with a bunch of people you hadn't seen in all this time?"

"Hmmph. Still, I'm your mother's oldest friend. How does it look? She 's trying to reacquaint herself with all these people — well she's not making such a good first impression by ignoring me. And look, she's not too shy to be over there talking with that man in the dark blue suit.

Anna, tell me something, is he single?" Her pink nail poked her daughter in the ribs. "Danielle, you could use a little company already, it's been over a year now since your Morty left you for that floozy."

"Mother!"

"What? He's nice looking, even with the chicken neck. Can't I wish for some happiness for my own daughter?"

Anna looked over at the man she was talking about. It was the son of one of her mother's Mah Jong friends.

"Honestly mother, you amaze me. This isn't exactly the time..."

"Oh, piffle. Rebecca would be pleased if I fixed you up at her shivah. He's eating a little too much food, but that's all right, better than not eating. A man with an appetite is easier to hold onto. Especially since you're such a good cook. That Morty never had an appetite anyway. I warned you about him when you got married, but did you listen to me? No, of course not. Remember? I told you — a man with no appetite can't be counted on. He'll eat your food, but only because it keeps him alive, no other reason. Other than for that, he doesn't give a damn."

"Ida, I think he's married," said Anna, trying to save her friend.

"Oh, well. I can't see the wedding ring from here. Maybe it's under the plate. And I see our Sadie isn't holding back too much either. You know, it's not so dignified to eat that much in front of visitors at your own mother's shivah."

Danielle laughed. "But it is dignified to be combing the mourners for a potential husband?"

"It's different, Danielle. Sadie is Rebecca's daughter, everyone is looking at her. I only say this, Anna dear, because I'm like family. Someone should tell her. Is she trying to make up for fifty years of not eating at home? Enough already with the kugel and the desserts already!"

"Mother, do you want another cup of tea?" said Danielle, moving in front of her.

Anna shifted too, so that they were both now in a path blocking Ida's view. "A mun cookie, perhaps?" she offered.

Ida craned her neck around to keep looking. "Thank you, dear, tea would be lovely." She relinquished her cup, and Danielle went to the counter to fill it.

"Anna, look at how tall your sister is, I can't get over it. She doesn't look a thing like your mother, she took after your father in that way — tall and gangly, even his same nose. It's hard to believe she was so tiny when she was born. Barely as big as a minute."

Anna slipped a cookie onto Ida's saucer. She noticed the woman had closed her eyes and put a hand up to her cheek. Her teacup listed dangerously.

"Help me up, Anna dear, I need to stretch my legs."

Danielle took her mother's teacup, and Anna extended her hands. Ida grasped them to lift herself out of the chair and waddled over to the oven. She placed a wrinkled hand on the metal door handle and rubbed her palm over it, buffing it to a shine.

She opened the oven door. "This is a fancier stove than you had back then," her voice echoed from its depths.

"Mother, what are you doing? Is there something in there?"

"It's another funny story about Rebecca and Sadie. When she was just a baby."

Anna smiled at Danielle as they gently pulled Ida out of the oven. "The inside of the stove made you think of it, Ida?"

They sat the old woman down on the bench at the table, and Anna sat with her, putting her hand on Ida's knee.

Danielle rubbed her mother's shoulders from behind. "When Sadie was born. That's what I was remembering. I had this image of a baby, lying on an oven door. And then I remembered — it was Sadie. Tiny, weak, sickly Sadie. I'm trying to remember when it was, exactly. Sadie, put down that plate a second and come here, dear! I want to tell you something, a story about you — from when you were a baby."

Anna beckoned to her sister to show it was safe, and Sadie broke away from a woman who seemed to have trapped her in the corner of the front room. She approached the kitchen, plate still in hand, to lean against the door frame. Others stopped their conversations too, gathering behind and in front of her so they could listen in."Your mama," Ida began. "She was such a funny woman. And so smart! I was just remembering you, Sadie, when you were a little baby, lying on an oven door to keep warm. Did you know about that?"

"What do you mean, Mother?" Danielle asked. "Rebecca had allowed me to go out to get some fish heads and some green vegetables for a soup — she needed something healthy, and she barely got out in those days. When I returned to the apartment, I walked in the door, and there she was sitting on a chair, and there you were Sadie, wrapped in a soft cloth, lying flat on the inside of the oven door, heat seeping into the room.

"You weren't moving at all. She had bound you up like a papoose, and your little cheeks were glistening and pink. I thought: Has Rebecca gone out of her mind? Is she planning to roast the baby for Shabbus? So I dropped the groceries and ran to snatch you from the oven door.

"You know how mothers sometimes go a little crazy after their babies are born. I had heard that. When God finally gave me my own daughter, I found it hard to believe that such a thing happened to anyone, so much joy I felt in the weeks after my Danielle was born," she pinched her daughter, her fingernails two pink pincers, "but back then, long before my own blessing arrived, it seemed that going crazy with a child was quite possible at any time, let alone just after a birth. So I felt it was the role of a mother's friend to keep a watch out and make sure her children didn't get hurt. Later when Danielle was a teenager, *then* I could understand a mother going crazy. Then, I was grateful for help from others. Then, I could have..."

"Yes, Mother. Moving right along?"

People in the room chuckled, and Ida seemed pleased she was holding their attention. She gave the room a broad smile before continuing, and had a sip of her seltzer water.

"Sorry, dear. So what happened after that? Sadie was on the oven door, I dropped my groceries, and then? Oh yes, I grabbed the baby, and little Sadie started crying. Rebecca came over to calm me down and take her baby back. She said there was only a low fire in the oven, and that she was being careful.

"I remembered saying to her that the baby could roll into the oven on her own, and wasn't she worried about such a thing? But Rebecca explained that the women from the old country did this to keep babies like Sadie warm. It was a cold February, and Sadie had come early. Did you know that, Sadie?"

"No, I didn't."

"Well it doesn't surprise me, Rebecca never talked much about anything. But the thing is, you seemed to be sweating there all wrapped up. I asked if maybe the oven was too hot, but she said the shininess on your cheeks was from the butter she spread on them to keep your skin moist. And that she had wrapped you in a blanket to keep in the heat. So you can imagine why I thought she was making a roast of you — she had even basted your cheeks!"

"That's amazing, Ida," said Sadie. "I never knew any of that."

Ida shrugged her shoulders. "I know it sounds crazy now. But it's not necessarily any more crazy than what they do these days. Now they put premature babies in an incubator in a hospital and barely let their mothers near them. It's so sad, all those little darling babies lying there all alone just like in their own little controlled oven. Everything is taken out of a mother's hands these days and placed in the doctor's. It's not like it was back then — in those days, women had to improvise, not just with this, but with a lot of things."

Anna saw Sadie smile. Her sister approached the table and knelt down to take Ida's hands. "Thank you for telling me that story, Ida. It's wonderful."

"It's nothing, dear. What good is an eighty-nine-year-old woman if she can't tell a story or two about the past?" She brushed Sadie's cheek. "I can hardly believe you grew to be so tall and big, from such a tiny little shrimp. It's only because you were always such a *chazer*, that's why. God gave you an appetite to make sure you'd live, and that's good."

Danielle used the moment to tactfully point out how late it was, and wouldn't it be better to get a jump on the rush-hour traffic into Brooklyn.

While Anna and her sister said their goodbyes to Danielle, she noticed Mrs. Gutstein fussing with the buttons on her coat and trundling off to the sink to wash up. They waited while she ran her hands under the water, but when she started doing some dishes, Anna interceded.

"Ida, please. Leave the cutlery. We'll do it later."

Sadie also came over to her.

"I'm just doing a few. It's no trouble." She put them on the dish rack and was led back to the door. Danielle leaned in to give Anna a hug.

"You know," Mrs. Gutstein grasped Anna's arm and then pulled Sadie toward her as well. She had a tear in her eye. "Your mother — she was a fine woman. A woman like her you won't find again for a long time."

Sadie nodded and avoided Ida's stare, but Anna leaned in to give her a kiss. "We know."

With a wave of the hand to mark the end of their little moment, Mrs. Gutstein gave them each a peck on the cheek and turned to go. Danielle steered her mother down the hallway, around the corner, and eased her down the first step.

Others took their departure as a cue that the evening was wearing on. Within twenty minutes, most were gone. Mrs. Huang was the last to leave, bearing a container of soup that Anna insisted she take for her husband. When the door shut behind the landlady, Anna was alone once again with her sister.

Sadie was already busy doing the dishes in the kitchen, finishing the job Mrs. Gutstein had started before she left. Anna went up to the sink and grabbed a dishtowel to begin drying. Staring at the fading tiles on the backsplash, she focussed on their swirl pattern. She towelled off two casseroles and four plates before she noticed that Sadie had tears running down her cheeks. She went to put her hand on her back, but then drew it away.

She went instead to the drawer and handed her sister a dry towel for her eyes. Sadie took it and dabbed gingerly under the lids. The gesture struck Anna as odd, because she wasn't wearing any make-up.

"It's nothing," Sadie said, "I was just thinking about Mama's diary, what you told me she wrote. The whole thing about the rally, her marriage, and then that story Ida told us. Here was this bright girl, so full of hope. And then she was shunted into some... some stupid arranged marriage. Did you know any of that? I don't feel like we knew her at all."

Anna slowly rubbed the plate she was holding, unaware that it was already dry. She thought it funny Sadie should be surprised she didn't know their mother, since she had missed the last fifty-four years of the woman's life. Why should the first sixteen be any different? She resisted the temptation to make a bitter joke.

"No, I didn't know much, maybe bits and pieces. Of course, you remember her friend Hattie. After she left, Mama would talk to me all the time about her, how she was a writer, how much I was like her. It used to drive me crazy. It was like she was trying to make more of this friend she lost contact with by keeping her alive in me. Just because I wrote too. But the similarities ended there — it was so obvious I wasn't like her at all. I felt quite sad for Mama really."

Anna put the plate into the dish rack. "Did you know? I mean, did she ever talk to *you* about those things? You know — when we were growing up?"

Sadie took out a kerchief and blew her nose.

"No. I knew Bubbe and Zayde lived on Ludlow Street. Before they went back to Russia. That much she told us both. The rest — I don't know ... I can't say I thought much about Mama's life before she met Papa. Too caught up in my own stuff, I guess." She paused. "You know, what I can't get over is that she was actually involved with the unions. I mean, can you really imagine Mama at a rally? I can't picture her getting that excited about anything, let alone about worker's rights... Well, what am I saying? I guess I can't really say she didn't get excited, can I? She sure as hell did whenever I did something that she didn't approve of. At least most of the time she did."

Anna bunched up her eyebrows. "You? What are you talking about? You were her favourite. I was the one who could never do anything right. I was the stupid younger daughter."

"Stupid? Oh come on," Sadie said. "It was obvious she favoured you. Why else were you allowed to go out and work, and I had to stay at home."

"That was different. That had nothing to do with who was smarter or stupider, Sadie, and you know it."

"Maybe not, but you were still the favourite."

"No. You're wrong. You stayed home because you were the older daughter, and the older daughter stayed home to help — Papa's old-fashioned rules. And it's true you always did better in school than I did. Teachers always compared me to you. 'Good, but not quite as good as your big sister Sadie!' they'd say."

"Well, it doesn't matter because I had to *leave* school — that's my point. Mama always was harder on me than she was on you, Anna."

"She was not! Sadie, I can't believe you would say such a thing!"

"Absolutely she was. Who would she always make do all the chores, even when you were home? Who caught hell if she even saw me talking to a boy? It was always me. Never you. You were Papa's little girl, petite and pretty, not some tall, freakish thing. Mama didn't dare scold you."

"Now I was Papa's favourite too?" Anna jerked her head back in astonishment. "Sure Mama didn't scold me as much, but that's because she didn't give a damn about me. She was hard on you, but she had high expectations for you. And she loved you. I should have been so lucky. She had absolutely no expectations for me, except that I should find someone better than Papa."

"Mama had such high expectations for me, eh? How come she kept me trapped in that house if she had such high expectations for me? Some way to show it. You'd think she'd at least have wanted me to get a job, or something. Or stay in school, maybe. *Anything* for chrissake!"

"You know why she didn't encourage it, Sadie — it's because she would have had to stand up to Papa, and she barely ever stood up to him. And besides, you could have up and left. Oh yeah," she put her hand up to her mouth in mock recall, "how could I forget?! You did! You *did* up and leave!" Her eyes bugged out, and she stuck her chest forward in defiance. "For *fifty-four goddamned years*, you left! And *then* who was left trapped in that house, I wonder? Who, Sadie? Who?"

"I had no choice!"

"Of course you had a choice. You left me alone in that god-forsaken madhouse! Do you have *any* idea what it was like? Do you have *any* idea what I went through? No, of course you don't. Because you never called. You never wrote. Do you have any idea how it felt to have my older sister just abandon me there without an explanation? Just 'cause it was easier to leave than to stay? Do you?"

Sadie stared straight ahead, her face bright red. Her hands shook at her side.

Anna waited, spitting mad, until her sister turned to her and, in a steady voice, said, "You're right, Anna. I was wrong. You really are stupid."

And then she walked out of the apartment and slammed the door behind her.

Anna stared at the door for a moment and then slid down against the cupboard in front of the sink, until she was sitting on the ground, her skirt stretched tight by her legs spread out in front of her. Her mascara stung her eyes and spread its emotional effluent on her cheeks.

She listened to see if Sadie would come back, but after ten minutes, she could still hear no sound in the hallway, and so she picked herself up, straightened her skirt, and started to tidy the apartment. She pushed in a chair here, smoothed off a tablecloth there, looked at her watch. It was only eight-thirty.

She contemplated leaving to go back to New Jersey, but noticed Sadie's purse sitting on the counter as she prepared to go. The catch was open, but she resisted the temptation to look inside. Still, she needed to see if Sadie had left her hotel key. She stuck her hand in, and felt a key attached to a plastic tear-shaped holder. She pulled it out. It read "The Columbus."

It would serve Sadie right, she thought, if she just left, and forced her to deal with the hotel to get another key. No, she couldn't leave, it wouldn't be right. She would wait for her to come back.

She went into the back bedroom and lay down on the old mattress. It was lumpy, and it felt like the wire coils would eventually dig right through her skin. She closed her eyes to see if she could get some rest, breathed in deeply to calm herself.

The argument replayed itself over and over in her mind. Each time, she revised her part of the exchange. In some versions, she retaliated with a more cutting comeback to Sadie's departing blow. In others, she averted the fight altogether, but none of the revised versions left her satisfied.

After some time, she accepted that she would not fall asleep, and got up from the bed. She looked at the closet and sighed. She opened the door, took out the box.

She had left her mother's diary on top, splayed open at the page she left off before the guests arrived. She picked it up and leafed through the parts she had read. The creamy pages were neatly cut at their outer edges, the heaviness of the paper softened by the uneven edges. Her mother's handwriting was rounder than it was in recent years, with more loops in it, less cramped.

She snapped it closed, but then opened it again and skimmed ahead a few years until a sentence caught her eye. Ironically, it was a sentence about an argument.

Chapter Seven

March 18th, 1911

Dear Diary,

We had another quarrel tonight.

Isaac said, You don't want to have children, and your thoughts fly up to G-d's ears and tell him you're not fit to be a mother!

Of all the days of the week, why did I have to bleed on the Sabbath? Isaac of course took this as a sign from G-d, and I must admit that I am beginning to wonder myself. What is it that I am doing wrong?

I said that I do want to have children, but I don't believe I was very convincing, because then he said, It's your duty Rebecca, as a woman, to be the mother of my children. G-d is watching you — you should try harder.

I protested. There are no degrees of trying, I said, when it comes to making children. There is only doing and hoping.

He said I could hope more, and maybe in that he has a point. I do want to have children, but I am not sure whether I want it because it is expected of me, or because I actually do want them. In any case, Isaac accused me of being barren again. Look at Nussbaum's wife, he said. Three children in three years. Two of them boys, he said, as though that were evidence she tried even harder than usual those years.

I said, Isaac, that's not fair, I don't compare you to others in how well you provide. Well, that was a mistake. He raised his voice and shouted that I should be grateful that he was such a good husband, not like Blum, who was off all the time with other women.

I told him he missed my point. I made my voice very low and calm, to try to bring the level of tension down a little. I only meant that a comparison like that wasn't fair, I said. But did he really miss my point? Hadn't I wanted to get a little dig in where I knew it would hurt?

I talked about this the other day with Hattie, about how I feel I am letting him down. Hattie told me it isn't my fault, but I think it might be. I must admit I am less enthusiastic than I should be.

I know it is a woman's duty to lie with her husband when he wants, and particularly for this purpose, but it seems unfair that the pleasure should be all his. Wouldn't it make things much easier if women enjoyed this more, if it were a little less rough? I understand that some women do, or so says Dora, but she's very coy about the whole thing. She won't tell me exactly what it is that they like, so personally, I can't imagine what it would be. It would be nice to be able to talk to Mama about this, but can you just picture that conversation? No, intimate relations between couples is not a conversation one has with one's mother.

Hattie has been quite smitten with a man she met at college, but they are not married yet, so I can't really ask her these questions either. Hattie is lucky. She has everything. Brains, independence, and now a man. She even has dreams of her own career. Last month she published her first story. I read it, and thought it grand. The story was about a girl from the tenements who gets a job as a domestic in a rich family that believes itself to be compassionate to the plight of the poor. The girl is treated like she is dirty and inferior, and eventually quits, but not before shaming her employers by giving them a piece of her mind.

Hattie is doing some work now for a small publishing company, and they can barely afford to pay her. As a result, she has almost no money, but she seems happy nonetheless. I hardly see her anymore. Perhaps she thinks I am too boring a person, now that she has met all those educated people from college, like Marty Ruben, the young man who is courting her. Or maybe she doesn't like Isaac. It is probably a bit of both.

She and Isaac never got along. Hattie came for dinner last week, and they got into an argument about interpretations of the Torah. Of course, the fact that Hattie would even dare to argue with Isaac about such a thing — imagine a woman arguing about the Torah, he said — it drove him wild. I can't even remember what they argued about, only that when they did, Hattie was winning. Because Hattie is so smart, she has the ability to trap Isaac into the corner of his argument and then block all exits. Isaac's face got red as a beet, and his voice louder and louder, until he started telling her she was a stupid woman. I felt embarrassed for him, because it was so obvious that she was not stupid, that calling her so only made him look more foolish.

It was a little insensitive of Hattie, though, to go at him so when she was invited to our new apartment for dinner.

Nevertheless, I couldn't help but find a little pleasure in it. There have been enough times that Isaac has told me I'm stupid, and there has been nobody around to see how unfair it is. When that happens, you can't help but feel deep down that you really are stupid. Funny how what one is sure one knows in one's heart can be worn down, chipped away by insults, until knowing it in one's head isn't enough anymore.

It isn't really Isaac's fault that he gets in such bad moods. He works very hard, and now he has all the pressures of taking over Papa and Yekl's business, because after Yekl died last year, Mama and Papa decided they will go back to Russia.

And I was so sure that they wouldn't go unless there was a revolution.

When Yekl died, I saw the change in Papa. His business never did well. Then they took on Isaac as a full partner, thinking he would bring in more business. But since Isaac hasn't really begun to excel at it yet, that has just meant more wages, same amount of money.

Of course, they have only kept him on because of the marriage. What else could Papa do? Fire his own son-in-law after he made such a big deal about how he would be a good provider, and how he was in the same business, such a good match for his daughter?

Well, now Isaac has at last begun to work a little harder, because I convinced him to move into this bigger apartment instead of staying in Mama and Papa's less expensive one after they are gone. He is also working harder because the business is about to rest on his shoulders. I'm only sorry Yekl had to die for this to happen. He was such a kind, good man, a friend to Papa. The only person, other than Mama, who knew him from the old country. Maybe that's why Papa became so obsessed with going back. In any case, as for Isaac, I think this is exactly what he needs to give himself a kick in the pants.

It's not really that he hasn't been working hard, I shouldn't say that. It's just that he isn't aggressive enough in getting business. Or maybe it's not that, but that his pride doesn't let him meet the customers on their terms. Isaac always has to show that he's right, that he's better than his customers. That doesn't work in business. Also, he has let Papa and Yekl run things, and that was maybe Papa's fault. It drives Mama crazy. She knows Isaac has to learn for himself, and he is getting better, but now she's so worried about us because they are leaving.

Mama came and visited me yesterday. She said not
to complain so much about Isaac, that he was my husband and that I should respect him a bit more. I found
this surprising since I can't remember a day growing up
that she did not complain of something about my father,
and she had only half of the reasons to do so that I have.
Of course when I said this to her, she shushed me and
denied that she has ever complained at all.

We danced around the topic of her leaving for
Russia, talking as if it were an interesting story we read
in the newspaper. They will go to live just outside of St.
Petersburg, because one of Mama's sisters moved there
with her husband, and so they will have a place to stay.
They leave in two weeks. Perhaps they will find happiness and comfort in the familiarity of the old country.

I am quite desolate imagining what it will be like to
have them so far away, across the ocean. I have never
gone more than two days without seeing them. And
now we will probably never see one another again.

I don't want them to go, but I can't bring myself to
say it. It is too painful for Mama as it is — she doesn't
need to feel that I am pulling her back with sorrow and
guilt. Still, I am terrified of being left alone.

Rebecca opened her eyes and looked at the clock. How could
it be six-thirty already? She could swear it was only a minute
ago she had put her head down on the pillow. Her piecework
had kept her up late, and she was holding to a strict schedule,
realizing how tight money was going to be in this new place,
especially if she was to resist Isaac's requests for them to get a

boarder. She knew they would eventually have to find some-one, but she wanted to experience just a few months of luxury. Just the two of them, even if that had drawbacks of its own. She would have a memory of adequate living space to cherish in the years to come, even if she starved in the process.

But how could she bear this exhaustion every morning, this early morning fatigue, the kind that made even breathing a chore? She lay on her back staring at the ceiling, waiting for it to pass. Was that a new crack? She wondered how many it would take before she woke up one day with a pile of plaster burying her in her bed.

Isaac snorted beside her, and she wiggled a little to shift under the weight of his heavy arm. His head faced hers, and the ends of his long, brown beard were crushed upwards and sideways by his hand, which was tucked inwards like a chick-en wing. He had a slight grin on his face, and she wondered what he was dreaming about.

His expression and his every-which-way beard made her smile. What a relief it was to see him looking so funny after last night's argument. She stared at the ceiling a moment longer before she figured out how to wiggle out from beneath him without his waking. She needed to change her cloth; it was beginning again to get moist. She had been up already twice during the night, and if she wasn't careful it would stain the bed like last month, and Isaac would be mad again.

She changed her cloth and washed the old one out in the sink, hanging it up behind the stove. When she was finished, she continued the rest of her washing up in silence until Isaac appeared in the door frame rubbing his eyes. She pretended not to notice him, moving some dishes about to prepare a lit-tle something for breakfast.

"I'm sorry I was so cross with you last night, Rebecca. You know ... It's just that I want us to have a child so badly. You would be such a good mother."

When she didn't answer him, he came up behind her, put his arms around her waist, and nuzzled her neck with his beard. It tickled her. She tried not to smile.

"Go get ready for work, Isaac," she said, wriggling herself away from him.

"Will you be taking those sleeves to Kirshbaum today?" he said, shuffling back to the bedroom wash basin.

"Later. I'm going to do some shopping with Elsie and Dora."

"The sooner you give those pieces back, the sooner we have money."

"I know, Isaac, but I saved some money for groceries, and we're almost out of food. I've been planning this shopping since last Monday. I'll take the pieces with. I promise."

He left the apartment to use the closet near the landing, and his voice echoed in the hallway. "Don't forget."

Rebecca fixed them some tea and a piece of bread with jam. They ate in silence. She finished hers quickly, then began to clean up while waiting for Isaac to leave for work. In the bedroom, she piled up the sleeves she had been working on last night. Only ten. Still, they would bring them a little extra for food.

Although the moodiness was a recent phenomenon, her worry about his temperament was not. Rebecca had posed questions about it from the day they met. He was shy and courteous and complimentary, but she had found that little comfort. After all, why should a strong jaw line, a honeyed compliment, or a held-open door mean anything at all? She was shrewd enough to know this was just courtship.

It was what she did *not* know about his character that bothered her, at first. He was an unsettling mystery, cloaked by dashing appearances and sweet, carefully chosen words. His unknown defects swam like sea monsters in the ocean depths, lurking just below the calm, reflective surface of his smile. Did that same smile fool her parents? In that first year, she comforted herself with the notion that it was only a matter of knowing a man, and then one was far less likely to be nervous about him, no matter how unpleasant he might turn out to be.

But as the months passed, Isaac slowly revealed himself to her, and Rebecca realized she had got it all wrong. First, she had not anticipated how difficult it would be to ignore or avoid a husband in a tiny living space, or that sharing a bed with a man would make it so much more difficult to really get away. But for their first marital year they lived with her parents, and though she had rejoiced at Ida's departure, that joy was dampened when she found that Isaac took up twice as much room in the bed. And though they had recently moved into their own place, things had not improved any. Ida had married Sydney Weiss, a landlord on Henry Street, and she found them a place in her building. While Rebecca enjoyed the increase in square footage and the slightly bigger bed, without her parents for distraction there was now nowhere to look but at each other.

Her second mistake was thinking that she could work on his shortcomings. She discovered that this was seriously thwarted by Isaac's belief that his flaws were in fact virtues. For instance, he pestered her constantly about managing money. Although it had been demonstrated to him early in their marriage that Rebecca was good at arithmetic and skilled at handling finances, he continued to supervise. He believed it was prudent, rather than insulting.

True, it was only recently that she had been put to the test since, until the move, she and her mother had managed things together. But when she gently pointed out that he needn't monitor her activities — that it was in her best interest as well as his to make sure they made ends meet — he dismissed her objection out of hand. It only made good business sense for him to keep a handle on things, he said. What kind of a husband would he be if he lost control of the household finances?

Rebecca's worst discovery of all came when she realized that knowing someone's character did not always give one the ability to predict behaviour. In night school she was taught that "forewarned is forearmed." It had not occurred to her that knowing a person's character might provide little comfort, that sometimes knowledge was even more troubling than ignorance.

It surprised her, when she thought of it now, that she could be so blind. She felt so strongly that knowledge of a person's *emotions* could indeed be troubling, especially as those emotions related to a painful past. How, then, did she miss that what would apply to emotion might equally apply to temperament? Temperament, a person's intrinsic character, was the constant from which emotions spring. The connection was so blatantly obvious that she couldn't explain how she had missed it.

The soapy water swished and licked at the dishes, smelled syrupy. The trickling sound and pleasant scent encouraged her introspection, held her there until she felt Isaac's hand on her shoulder. She flinched at the intrusion.

"I'm taking the cart over to Broome Street today," he smiled at her hopefully. "Sidney Weiss told me he was there on Friday, and there was only one cap-maker per block. Or was it

Ida? She was nattering on about something anyway, I can't remember what. Anyway, maybe with some luck, I'll find a block where I'm the only one."

"Best of luck then, Izzy. And remember to speak up a little when people go by. Remember how Papa does it."

The smile quickly drained from his face, and for a moment he looked hurt. Then almost instantly the hurt was smeared away by a brush stroke of anger.

"Now you're telling me how to do business? Suddenly you've studied with J.P. Morgan?" He turned his back to her and took his cap from the hook beside the door.

"I'm only saying. You have to be a little more aggressive. Of course you already know this, I'm only saying it out loud for myself, more to make myself feel good."

"Well, while you're making yourself feel good, you don't have to treat me like I'm a dimwit."

"I'm sorry, Izzy, of course you know how to sell. Now go on, and leave me to wash up."

He murmured something into the fabric of his coat, pulling the sleeve on with his teeth, and left without saying goodbye. From the hall, Rebecca heard his booming voice.

"Don't forget to bring the sleeves to Kirshbaum!"

Her fingers tightened over the edge of the washbasin, and she took a few deep breaths with her eyes closed.

Rebecca got dressed, pulling on a dark skirt and a beige top. She brushed at the fabric on the front of the skirt, dismayed at how threadbare it seemed. She had hemmed it again recently, but the outer edge of the fold was worn and tattered in several spots where it folded under. No amount of mending could fix that. Her shirtwaist was not much better, but at least it was clean looking. She brushed her hair out and pulled it up into a bun, high atop her head.

The apartment needed very little tidying, so she decided she would spend another half-hour sewing some more sleeves. She was finishing the last stitches on a cuff when a knock came at the door.

"Hell-ooo!" Dora's bright voice pushed its way through the spaces in the walls.

Rebecca opened the latch and let her in. As per usual, her friend was wearing some awful outfit with mismatched colours, drawing attention to herself in the worst possible way. It so distracted Rebecca that it took her a moment to realize that Dora was alone.

"Where's Elsie?" she asked. The three of them were to do their shopping together.

"I don't know. I thought she might have come here first. I said I'd meet her at the corner, but I waited fifteen minutes, and she didn't show up."

They went into the bedroom to look at the clock. It sat on a very small, ornately decorated tin chest. Both were wedding presents from Isaac's parents. It was eight-twenty.

"Well, she didn't come here ... I don't know." Rebecca went to get her coat in the other room.

"It's not like Elsie. She's always on time. She teases me that I'm always fifteen minutes late wherever we go. What do you think Rebecca, should we wait for her here? Maybe she's been delayed fixing up her new place."

Rebecca gathered her piecework into a sheet, tied the corners of the bundle into a knot, and threaded her arm through the opening of her makeshift basket. "Let's go — we'll follow your steps back to the corner and then make our way back to her apartment — we'll probably run into her. It's on the way to where we're going anyway."

They left the building and hurried along the street, in case Elsie was late arriving at the corner and wondering where Dora had gone. The sidewalk bubbled with activity — two children hawking eggs while their mother oversaw their activity from the curb, some women discussing the quality of cloth being sold from a pushcart, holding sheets up to the sun to see the tightness of the weave, or maybe if there were any spots.

At the corner, a game of cards was underway. Four men sat around a cheese crate with blankets around their shoulders. As the men held up their hands, they took the opportunity to blow on their fingers to keep them warm, the evaporation of their breath a visible counterpoint to their puffing. One of them caught the man to his left leaning over to cheat, and so he let out a huge breath in his neighbour's direction that quickly clouded the view of the cards. The cheater retreated to his spot with a sour look, and Rebecca wondered whether it was because he was caught or simply because his friend had bad breath. She thought she could smell his breath herself, but then she realized it was the acrid smell of pickles from the shop next to them.

"Have you seen a girl about my height waiting here, maybe looking lost?" she asked the card players.

"Sorry, miss." They must be assuming she was unmarried because she did not wear a wig, she thought. This also happened on occasion when she was with Isaac, another sore spot for him, but in this matter Rebecca stood her ground.

Dora's face was creasing with concern. "I think we should go to her apartment, Rebecca. Maybe she's sick. She hasn't been feeling so good this last week. Friday was the birthday of her friend Celie who died in the Triangle fire."

"Oh God. That's so sad."

"Let's get a pickle," Dora said, her face brightening a bit, "and bring one for Elsie, to cheer her up." She dug some money out of a pocket in her skirt. She handed the coins to the pickle woman, who plunged an enormous arm into the barrel of brine and emerged with three fat ones to wrap in some paper.

They crunched on their treat as they walked. When they turned onto Baxter Street, Rebecca squinted into the sun.

"Which one is it?" she asked.

The week before, Elsie had moved into a new building on the same street. One with gas lamps in the halls, she said, and a much bigger room.

"Here it is." Dora pulled her in the entrance and tugged her quickly up the stairs to the second floor.

They knocked on Elsie's door. There was no answer.

They knocked again. Dora pressed her ear against the wood.

"I can't hear anything. Elsie! Are ya there?" She knocked more loudly. Rebecca turned around to look down the hall.

"Something's not right, Dora. I can feel it. Do you hear anything?"

"No, I don't hear a thing."

"Exactly. There's no sound at all. It's Sunday morning. How come nobody's making any noise? Is Elsie's building Italian? Maybe they've all gone to church."

"No. I think her neighbours are mostly Jewish."

Rebecca had begun to run down the stairs. "Where does the landlord live?"

Dora ran after her. "It's a landlady. She's on the first floor. First door to the left."

Rebecca was there already, and she banged loudly. There was no answer. She kept at it, until a minute later, the door unlatched and a small grey-haired woman poked her head out, her eyes half-closed.

"Wha' time izit?," she slurred.

"It's eight-thirty!" Rebecca said. "Are you the landlady?"

The woman rubbed her eyes. Her face was mottled and puffy. "Yes. Ohhh. I don feel righd."

Suddenly, the woman convulsed and put her hand over her mouth. She lurched from the door and spewed vomit onto the floor, getting the last of it on an upholstered armchair in her attempt to get to the wash basin.

"Oh my goodness! Are you all right?" Dora went in and helped seat the woman on a wooden chair.

Rebecca got a cloth and wiped the woman's mouth. "What's going on in here today? Where is everyone?"

The woman looked at them as if she wasn't sure where she was.

Dora held the woman's face in her hands to look into her eyes. "Have you seen Elsie Dawidowicz? From the second floor?"

"I hava see anywa. I mussa oversllep." She closed her eyes.

Rebecca went to open the window to let in some air. She shouted from the front room. "Can you give us the key to Elsie's apartment? We're worried about her."

The woman had her hand on her forehead. She waved her other arm at the wall. "Iz there — hangn there — nummer thirdy wa."

Rebecca helped her to the bedroom and lay her down with a wet cloth on her head.

"Stay here with her," Dora shouted. "I'll go upstairs and check the apartment," she said, rushing out the door.

The woman moaned on the bed. Rebecca looked around. The apartment was unkempt, clothes strung over chairs and lying in piles on the floor. The woman seemed drunk, but there was no smell of anything on her breath. She looked around for the empty bottle, but couldn't find any. Leaving the bedside for a moment, she went to the window to close it again — the apartment had become cold very quickly.

From above her a muffled scream pierced the ceiling.

She sprinted out the door of the apartment and leaped up the stairs. Tumbling into Elsie's apartment, she saw Dora crouched over the bed, shaking their friend by the shoulders. Elsie's body jiggled like a rag doll. Her eyes were closed as if she were in a deep sleep, her skin the pink-purple colour of magnolia blossoms. At first, she thought Elsie was wearing some strange make-up, but then something in her mind shifted into place, and the room began to swirl around her.

"There's no pulse! She's not breathing!" cried Dora.

Rebecca shook off her dizziness and turned on her heel to look into the hall through the open door. There was an unlit gas lamp bolted to the pressed tin wall. She ran out the door and reached her hand up to unscrew the glass fixture, then felt the top of the opening. A cool breeze tickled her fingertips.

"Dora! We have to get out of here. Now. It's gas. Come on!"

Dora didn't respond.

"It's too late — Elsie's gone. Leave her. We have to help the others get out of here."

Dora let out a moan and rocked back and forth over Elsie's body. Rebecca grabbed the collar of her friend's shirt and pulled her to her feet. A lump was forming in her throat, but she pushed through it and found a scratchy voice.

"Dora. Please — come now. It's dangerous. There's gas everywhere. You've got to help me."

Dora stumbled, pulled backwards away from the bed. "Oh my God. Oh my God."

Rebecca took her hand and pulled her out of the apartment.

"Start knocking on those doors. I'm going to get the rest of the keys."

Dora moved to the next door and started shouting. "Hello? Hello? Please, you've got to get out! Do you hear me?" She began to knock loudly, then shouted up at a small window vent above. "You've go to get out! Do you hear me? Is there anybody there? Please! Open up!"

Rebecca was back in a moment, fumbling with keys. Number thirty. They opened the door. An entire family of five lay in their beds, peaceful and glowing, their skin the same strange, pinkish hue. Dora shook them violently but there was no response.

"C'mon, Dora. Let's go." Rebecca pulled at her arm.

"We should take them out of here, Rebecca!"

"They're dead, Dora."

"You don't know that."

"It's too late. And we're not strong enough."

"What about the kids?"

"C'mon! Leave them, there may be others we can help!" she shouted.

They left the apartment and rushed to number thirty-two. An old couple lay motionless, asleep forever, the man's arm draped over his wife. There were two boarders in the other room. Number thirty-three: a young woman lay alone, with blankets clutched tightly into the folds of her stomach. Her two children shared a crib in the same room. Completely still, the room looked like a photographic portrait, painted in with the wrong colour.

Tears stung Rebecca's face as she tried to hold her breath to ward off as much of the odourless menace as her lungs would permit. No time to linger, there was always the risk of an explosion. Upstairs, just above Elsie, Dora roused a woman and helped her down the stairs. Her husband was already dead. The woman was too groggy to understand what was going on. Another apartment on the floor was empty. Perhaps, through a stroke of luck, Rebecca thought, the family had gone away for the weekend.

Most of the first floor was awakened and helped to stumble onto the street, looking like sleep had stolen their souls. A young man with a red beard walked crookedly about in front of the building. He was looking up to the other side of the street with a strange, misplaced curiosity. His eyes squinted defensively at the bright day, but his hands remained at his sides. He was wearing nothing but an undershirt and skivvies and was not covering himself in any way, neither out of modesty nor to protect himself from the cold.

A woman with wild, long, black hair walked out in her nightgown carrying a limp child. She rubbed her eyes with her free hand, then shook her daughter. As she took in the chaos about her and realized her daughter was not responding, her countenance melted and changed shape, a sculpture of anguish defined more by each new layer of understanding.

By now, police officers had arrived. They corralled the survivors to a safe distance then scrambled to secure the building, barring a few dazed or hysterical tenants from re-entering the front door.

Rebecca held Dora's shaking body close to hers, and they sat down on some steps across the street. They rocked forward and back, looking up at the clear, blue sky. Above the rooftops, the air rippled and distorted, and a few wisps of smoke swirled into a curlicued border, then dissipated in the morning sun.

Chapter Eight

March 30th, 1911

Dear Diary,

Mama and Papa are gone. Today I saw them off on
their journey back to Russia. There I was, my toes
practically dipping into the Atlantic, my hand waving
in the air, and if you hadn't known what was happening, I'm sure it would have seemed like they were off
on a grand adventure, as if I were waving my parents
off to a holiday on the first-class deck of a great ship.

But I caught sight of Mama bringing her handkerchief up to her nose, standing there in her dark brown
cloak, Papa beside her in his old, worn-out winter
coat, and I knew this was no grand holiday. They are
not going first class, but steerage, not on a holiday, but
on a long and terrible voyage back to a country in tur-
moil. And it is possible I will never see them again.

Yesterday, Mama came to my door. She was holding the featherbed that my bubbe gave to her before Mama left her village. She reminded me of the story then started to cry and said, "Beckeleh, I'll say this to you now as my mama once said it to me. Please take this, and remember your old mother." She heaped the featherbed into my arms, I don't remember who was crying more, and I dropped it so that I could hug her tight.

She let go before I did, and when I finally released her, she turned quickly to leave.

Today, as I stood on the pier, the cold wind blew up my long skirt and sent shivers up my spine. I had to fight to keep a cheery face for Mama, even though I could see plainly from the shape of my parents' bodies that they were not hugging one another for warmth, but for consolation.

Now there is no denying it — I am alone in New York, without family to rely on. I know that I still have Dora and Hattie, and that they love me and show their support, but I feel nevertheless a biting, stinging ache of loneliness deep in my chest. It seems to have leapt up out of the darkness so quickly in the last month, with Elsie gone, her shivah barely over, and now Mama and Papa off to the old country.

I wish I could talk with Isaac. He is not able to show comfort as I'm sure he wishes he could. Things seem to be getting worse and worse with money, and so he has his own worries. I don't know how we can survive if Isaac doesn't sell more caps. I feel swamped under the weight of my piecework, but still it is not enough. Well, that is not exactly accurate; there are only two of us to feed, and so far we have always had enough to eat — just enough if we don't eat any meat.

Isaac tells me that I am not very pleasant to be around these days, and I'm sure it is true.

March 31st, 1911

Dear Diary,

The strangest thing happened today. I was just finished preparing breakfast, deep in thought, when a knock at the door sent the dish slipping out of my hand.

Rebecca moved to see who was there, swallowing her pounding heart back down to the depths of her chest where it belonged. This happened too often, jumping out of her skin whenever a repetitive task was interrupted by a noise. She resolved to find a way to lower her agitation level while washing dishes, because it was getting absurd.

"Rebecca, come open up. What's taking you?" Dora's voice chirped. "I brought someone with me."

She squeezed her hands into her apron and then unlatched the door. Dora had on a new hat with a purple sash at the back that, surprisingly, did not clash with the rest of her outfit. She stood foot to foot with a woman who was bent over, using a long, red fingernail to scratch some dirt off of a shoe. The woman picked herself up quickly and lifted her head, revealing a handsome face framed by wisps of red hair. She looked familiar enough that Rebecca thought maybe she should recognize her.

"Rebecca, I'd like to introduce you to Sylvia Dawidowicz. Sylvia, Rebecca Kalish."

Sylvia's handshake was solid, and it seemed strange that a person with red nails should have such a firm grip.

"Did you say Dawidowicz?" Rebecca asked.

"She's Elsie's little sister."

Rebecca's smile fell a second, and her mouth hung open until she realized she was still holding the woman's hand, and should let it go and invite her in.

"Oh my God! How are you? Where are my manners? Come inside! Come inside! I'm so pleased to meet you, Sylvia. Little sister! You're about a foot taller than her! You weren't at the shivah. Have you come in from out of town? Your sister was a dear, dear friend of mine. You can't imagine how much I miss her. Well, of course you can — what a stupid thing to say. I'm so sorry, I'm babbling. It's just..."

"It's okay. I know." Sylvia pulled her lips tight against her teeth and looked at Rebecca, tilting her head a bit. "You don't remember me, do you?"

Rebecca squinted her eyes. "I feel like we've met before, but I don't think we have. Have we?"

"Well, I wouldn't say we really met. It was at Cooper Union a few years back. At that rally. When you tried to help me after that cop socked me with his club."

"That was you? The girl on the podium? It was you? *You're* Elsie's sister?"

"But why wouldn't Elsie have said so? Here — give me your coat, Sylvia. You know — that speech at the rally was so wonderful — I'll never forget. Elsie must have been very proud of you. I just don't understand why..."

"Actually, I don't think she was that proud of me."

Sylvia looked to Dora for help.

"Sylvia's... Well, you see Rebecca, Sylvia's..."

"It's okay, Dora. You can say it." She turned and looked Rebecca in the eye, smiled sweetly. "I'm a prostitute, Rebecca."

Rebecca blinked. "What do you mean, you're a prostitute?"

"That's what I do. I'm a prostitute. Although we usually call ourselves whores. You know, among ourselves. I live and work at one of Rosie Fine's bordellos on Allen Street. I'm sure you've heard of her, she's in the papers all the time."

Rebecca's face went scarlet. She turned around to put a dish in the cupboard. "I don't understand. You said you worked in a factory. In that speech, you said you..."

"I'm sorry if I've embarrassed you. I wanted to be honest. That speech, at the rally, it was all made up."

Rebecca turned back to her and stared, saucer-eyed. She thought about the speech, remembered the story about the boy with the crushed legs.

"It's true," Dora said, walking up to Rebecca and pressing her arm against her shoulder. "She made the whole thing up — isn't that a laugh? You know how Elsie was always working hard for the cause, right? Well, you see, she asked Sylvia to do it because they needed someone who was a good speaker to get the crowd all worked up. Elsie said her sister was a good speaker, and a good actor too."

"You kind of have to be with what I do, kiddo."

"You know, I *believed* you. I believed that story about the little boy. I believed the whole thing. It's very cruel to deceive people like that. People believed what you said, Sylvia."

"Oh, come on — that was the whole point. They believed it because it wasn't that far from a million stories they could have told themselves. I only made it more dramatic-sounding. There's nothing wrong with that, is there?"

"Yes, there is." Rebecca's voice got very soft. "You lied, and people got hurt because of it."

"Well, yes. I was one of them, but as I recall, it was a policeman's club that hit my shins, not my words bouncing back at me."

"Well, I was hurt too." Rebecca chewed her lower lip, and looked down at her fingers.

"I know. And I *am* sorry you were caught up in all of that. You know, I was very worried about you, but Elsie assured me there were no long-lasting effects."

Rebecca sat down at the table, and she whispered downward into her chest. "Not unless you count my marriage, that is." She wasn't sure if anyone heard her.

Sylvia looked at Dora, and then down at her shoes. "I'm sorry Rebecca. Um, listen Dora, maybe we should go. I don't know if this was such a good idea." She started toward the door.

Dora grabbed her arm. "No, stay. Rebecca, look. We didn't come here to talk about the rally. We actually came here for another reason. An important reason." She pulled Sylvia close. "Sylvia's pregnant."

Rebecca interlocked her fingers and looked up. "What does that have to do with me?"

Dora was shocked into silence for a moment by the callousness of her remark, but she recovered and said, boring her eyes into Rebecca's, "She needs a place to stay."

"Don't you have a place of your own, Sylvia? I remember Elsie saying her sister had a place of her own."

Dora approached Rebecca, and leaned in to whisper in her ear. "Rebecca..."

Sylvia took a step forward. "Look. I'm not asking for charity. I can pay. I just don't want to have the baby at Mrs. Fine's. There's always noise, from the carrying on inside, from the rattling of the damned El... Dora said you and your husband were having trouble," Rebecca picked her head up and glared at her friend, "and I thought since you were a friend of Elsie's I might stay as a boarder. Just until a few months after the baby's born, and then I can start working again."

Dora sat down at the table and took her hands. She gave her a pleading look.

"How will you pay?" Rebecca's voice didn't give an inch.

"I have money saved. Plus I figure I can still work for another six weeks until it starts to show."

Rebecca got up and walked into the front bedroom. She looked out of the open window onto the street. She needed fresh air to make a decision. She turned around to look back at Sylvia.

The woman was completely unconcerned with the immorality of her profession, confident to the point of being patronizing. On the other hand, she was clearly in trouble. Pregnant, looking for a place to stay after her sister's death ... But she didn't seem at all desperate, that was the strange thing. It was as if she couldn't care less what Rebecca decided. In fact, Dora seemed more worried than Sylvia. And why did that bother her so much? But then, sometimes people put on a show of pride when they were trying to hide shame.

And she had money, however ill-gotten. She and Isaac sure could use the extra income. It was clear they couldn't afford to live alone for much longer. But if Sylvia had money, couldn't she easily find a place to board? She could make up a story about being a widow, or something like that. Probably

Dora had convinced her it would be better to be with friends. And maybe she really wasn't as confident as she made herself out to be.

She looked back at her again, trying to picture how she had looked at the rally. Hadn't she told the audience her name was Sarah? Oh, what did it matter, it was all a pack of lies anyway. Sarah was a fraud, that little child with the crushed legs was made up, and she didn't care what Sylvia said, her speech had riled up the crowd and incited a riot. If that had not happened, she might have had another eighteen months of freedom before getting married. Might have even convinced her papa...

Suddenly a wave of shame washed over her, and she felt sickened by her own pettiness. What difference did it make who the woman was, Sarah, Sylvia, a seamstress, a prostitute? Here was someone who needed her help, the sister of a dear friend. She could deal with her uneasiness later.

She turned to the window again to compose herself, then quickly twirled around and walked out to the kitchen.

"Okay — you can stay in the back room. And I want four dollars and fifty cents per week for room and board. But I'll have to ask Isaac first. And we can't tell him what you do, Sylvia."

"Why not?"

"Isn't it obvious? You're unmarried, you're a prostitute, and you're pregnant. He's not going to want someone like that living with him. No offence."

"None taken. But ... um. You see, Rebecca, this is the thing. I understand what you're saying, don't get me wrong. And I am very grateful for your offer. But I would prefer it if things were out in the open. I don't think I would be comfortable keeping that a secret."

Dora jumped in. "Listen, Sylvia, we have a good situation here. Why stir things up? Why don't you just see how it goes? Maybe Mr. Kalish won't even ask."

Rebecca shook her head. "No, Dora, he'll want to know who she is and what she does. And he'll probably want to know who the father was. I'd have to make up a story."

"And I don't want you to have to do that. Dora, I understand that telling the truth might mean I have to look elsewhere. But I don't want to bring my baby into a house of lies. I don' t have a problem with what I do. If Mr. Kalish does, I'll look elsewhere."

Dora shook her head at Sylvia in exasperation, but Rebecca interceded. "It's okay, Dora. I'll think of a way to ask him."

"Thank you, Rebecca." Sylvia tilted her head and smiled a little. Rebecca wondered if the smile meant she was unexpectedly impressed.

"You're welcome. Just do me a favour. The less you mention about your work in front of my husband the better, okay?"

"Understood." She extended her hand, and Rebecca shook it.

Dora rushed up to Rebecca and gave her a hug. "Thanks, Rebecca. You're the best. I'm gonna go with Sylvia, help her get her things ready. Is tomorrow too soon?"

The question didn't register for a few seconds because she was busy thinking about her strategy for dealing with Isaac. "Hmm .... what? Tomorrow? No, wait a minute, wait a minute, hold on. Give me tonight and tomorrow to prepare Isaac, and to get the room ready."

Sylvia smiled broadly. "Prepare him, huh? Before you said you would ask him — now I see you're gonna prepare?"

Rebecca looked at her and smiled back. "Let's see how it goes."

Chapter Nine

Isaac slouched in the door at the end of the day, and for the first time Rebecca was grateful that he was so glum. She could use this. She noticed he did not have his coat on. Armed with a bowl of hot soup, she put on her most sympathetic smile. "Come in, you poor thing. You look like you could use something hot. I have some nice barley soup to start with."

"Oy, Rebecca, it was terrible today. I had such a day I can't tell you. There was a fire on Canal Street."

"A fire? What happened?"

"I was pushing the cart along, and I saw smoke coming from around a corner. When I followed it, I saw that there was a rooming house that caught fire. People were already being dragged out, although thank God almost nobody was home. I don't think anybody died, but..."

Rebecca shuddered and put her hands to her mouth. "It makes me think of poor Elsie."

"Yes, I was thinking the same thing. But wait until you hear what happened. In all the hubbub, I noticed this old man, he must have been a hundred if he was a day, and he was just wandering around with soot all over his face and his clothes. He looked completely and utterly lost. And nobody was paying him any attention."

Her fingertips padded her lips. "Oh my God — the poor man."

"So I went up to him and asked him if he needed some help, but his mind must have been somewhere else. Who knows if it was because of the fire, or just because he was so old. Remember Zayde Leo, before he died? It reminded me of him."

Rebecca tilted her head in sympathy. "I remember."

"Anyway, I held the man's hands and made him look me in the eye, and I told him he would be okay. He couldn't tell me anything about himself, not a thing. Not if he had family, his name, nothing."

"Maybe he didn't speak English."

"Yes, you're right, his English was very poor, and I don't know what other language he spoke because he certainly didn't understand when I tried speaking with him in Jewish. The poor fellow started to cry like a baby on my shoulder."

Rebecca went to rub Isaac's neck. "Terrible. What did you do?"

His eyes looked off into the corner of the room. "What could I do? I decided I would take him to the settlement house down the street. I lifted him onto my cart and wrapped him in my coat. He was shivering like a cat after a rain storm."

"Isaac." She stopped her neck massage and squeezed his shoulders. "What a mitzvah you did. Think what would have happened to that man if you hadn't been there. So what did they say at the settlement?"

"They thanked me, and a nice nurse took my name down. They brought him inside for some soup and assured me they would take care of him."

"You know, thank God for that place. What would this neighbourhood do without it? I keep meaning to go there and see if there's anything I can do to help."

"Yes, that would be a nice thing to do."

"Anyway, come now. Don't worry about that man anymore, he'll be fine. Now sit, it's time for you to have some soup. All of this is not good for your heart. The doctor said you shouldn't get too excited."

"Mmmm. Your soup never smelled so good."

"So when did this happen? On your way there, or on your way back?"

"On my way to work. Then I went all the way back to see if I could do some business. It was useless, I only sold two hats. All day, there were two other vendors on the same block. I don't know where Weiss gets these stupid tips — I wandered for five blocks and couldn't find a place to myself."

"Shush. First soup. Then we'll talk about work."

Isaac hung his hat up, wiping his beard to clean the day away. He shuffled to the basin to soap up his hands. Rebecca poured him a glass of water and pushed him down into his chair. She watched in silence as he said a prayer then slurped his soup. She sat down with him with her own bowl and, while she ate, examined his face to consider when she should begin. After a minute or two, he came up for air and let out a sigh.

"How can I compete when every person goes to every single cart before buying? And one of the fellows, he always goes too low with his prices. So low he's barely making back his costs. Just because he thinks the fellow who bought from him will be loyal and buy from him the next time." He dipped some bread that she gave him into his bowl, and sucked out the soup before biting off a piece. Through his chewing, he said, "The fool doesn't realize that they'll only come back to buy at the same price that lost him money in the first place!" His hands flew up, and he shook his face so that his cheeks jiggled.

"Oh, I'm so sorry, Izzy. What a day for you." She got up and rubbed his back, let out a deep breath. "Things are never easy, are they? We work *so* hard and the money is *so* tight. And here we are in this place, paying so much in rent."

"Don't get me started on that one, you with your kvetching since we got married, 'I need a place to *breathe* or I'll die.' This place is too big, you know I think so."

"Not if we got a boarder, it wouldn't be."

His head corked back, pigeon-like. "So now you want to get a boarder? I've been saying this from the beginning, and suddenly it comes from your head like a newborn thought?"

"No, no. What I mean is that I realize you've been right all along. Maybe I'm only seeing it now because Mama and Papa are gone, and I'm seeing lots of things differently lately."

Isaac tucked into his soup again, pushing her hand off of his shoulder. "Hmph. Well, good. When can I let it be known that we're looking already?"

"Actually, I know someone who needs a place very badly. A very sad situation really. You'd be doing another mitzvah taking her in."

"So who is this person, what does she do?"

"Well... she's a prostitute. But before you..."

He twirled around in his chair to face her. "What? A prostitute?"

"Now, before you go crazy, Izzy, let me explain. It's Elsie Dawidowicz's baby sister." She put her palms up toward him to hold back the torrent. "I know, I know. The sad story of that family never seems to end. I myself never even knew what her sister did until today because it seems Elsie was too ashamed to tell me. But now with Elsie dead, and Sylvia pregnant..."

His mouth fell open. "A pregnant prostitute? And you want a pregnant prostitute to come live with us in this house? Are you crazy?"

Anticipating the timing of her next move, Rebecca had already moved to the counter to prepare the next part of the meal. She had arranged a roast chicken leg on his plate, next to a generous serving of tsimmes, and passed the plate by his nose as she moved it down to his place setting. The sweet smell of the brown-sugar seasoning in the carrots wafted over the table.

"Oh, Isaac, please, it's Elsie's sister. She was so good to me. I owe it to her. To honour her memory. And think of poor Sylvia! Shunned by her parents because of her profession, left alone in the world after her beloved sister dies horribly from a gas leak. Pregnant by some filthy good-for-nothing whose name she probably doesn't even know, and her only option, unless we help, is to have that baby in a brothel. What kind of place is that to have a child?"

"It serves her right."

"You don't mean that, Isaac. At least think of the poor baby. Whatever we might think of the mother, it's not fair to the baby. She was all set to go and live with Elsie. Elsie even moved into a bigger place so that there would be room for all three of them. And it was because of that move into that building with the faulty gas lamps that Elsie is dead. Think of the guilt that poor woman must be feeling!"

He was looking at her, arms crossed, exuding impatience with his gaze.

"Plus, Isaac, she can pay decently, don't think I didn't already consider that. She earns a fair bit of money doing what she does. I guess through high volume, though I don't really want to think about it too much, quite frankly. And if you're worried about where the money comes from, just think of it this way: the deed's already done, and Sylvia has money to spend. We need it, and we have the extra space."

He had returned to his chicken, and was tearing into it as she spoke. A couple of swallows bought him time to brood.

"How much did you say we'd charge?"

"Four dollars and fifty cents per week room and board."

A flicker in his eyebrows betrayed his interest. He chewed silently for a couple of minutes while Rebecca sat down and fussed in her chair.

Isaac swallowed loudly. "We couldn't tell people what she does. We'd have to think of a story, and she'd have to be willing to go along. And she'd have to agree to dress decently, though God only knows if she even owns decent clothes. Well, you'll tell her she'll have to get some if she doesn't. Tell her those are my conditions."

Rebecca smiled. It had worked. She gave him a kiss on the cheek.

"Thank you, Izzy. You won't regret this. She's really a very nice person, considering everything. I'll tell her she can move in as soon as she's ready. Things won't be so difficult anymore, I just know it!" She looked at the chicken shavings on her plate and scooped some up with her fork, imagining the meagre portion to be two huge thighs twice as plump as the one she had given to Isaac.

"And one more thing, Rebecca."

"What's that?" she said through a mouthful.

"Maybe now that we'll have some more money coming in, you won't wait until you want something from me before I get a decent piece of meat for supper?"

Chapter Ten

For three weeks after she moved in, Sylvia left every day for "errands." Rebecca was positive she was going to work; she had told her when Dora first brought her to visit that she could still work for a little while longer. Why, then, was Sylvia lying to her? Hadn't she been the one to say she didn't want to live in a house of lies? Isaac wasn't even awake when she made her daily announcement, during their breakfast preparations, though it was true that sound carried to the other room, and one could never be sure he wasn't listening in. Perhaps she would have discussed it later if Rebecca had been able to muster the courage to ask, but she couldn't dredge up the question. It seemed like an invasion of privacy.

She was gone for four hours, usually, but not always, in the afternoon. Every day Rebecca's curiosity grew cat-like inside her until she thought she might have to padlock herself to the kitchen table to keep from following her down the street to her secret lair. She imagined it in ways she knew were not at all realistic, a snake or two slithering by on the floor, the occasional working girl hanging upside down from a chandelier in the main parlour, men grabbing at her wrists to try to pull her down. A large woman, dressed in the most ostentatious fashion, worse even than Dora, would be at the back of the room laughing at the whole scene, red feather boas hanging from her neck, her fingers heavy with fake jewel-encrusted rings. Occasionally she would bring a fleshy arm up to wipe sweat off of her partially exposed bosom.

"Rebecca, I'd like to be some use to you occasionally if I'm going to be living here. Is there anything you'd like to assign me as a chore? Some shopping? Some cleaning so that you don't have to do it?" Sylvia had been following after her, wiping counters she had already dusted, lining up Mason jars in perfect rows, all chores Rebecca considered a waste of time. The question came as a relief. She hadn't known how to broach the subject. Was it all right to ask Sylvia for some help when she was already charging her rent? Plus she didn't know how to tell Sylvia that she was being helpful in the most annoying possible way.

"Actually, to tell you the truth, I really need to get some work done on some sewing I've taken in for extra money. It's been coming in steady since I offered to help out after the Triangle fire."

"Oh, I could help you with that!" she said, and finished turning the little glass spice jars label out.

"I feel quite guilty about it because it just gives them an excuse not to hire back other girls in their new factory, but then we need the money too. If you still know anyone in the union, please don't tell them."

"Don't worry, I won't. Though I'm sure they'd understand."

"I'm not so sure. Anyway, would you mind giving me a hand moving the machine over to the table? It's there, tucked into the corner beside the counter."

"I can do better than that, I can help you with some cutting. Or even do some sewing if you're patient with me while I remember how."

"You know how to sew?"

"My mother taught all of us how to sew. I'm just a little rusty. And you'll have to show me the pattern, of course."

Rebecca grabbed the sewing machine, a stand-alone model, with black iron fixed to a chestnut base crowning elaborately curved iron legs and a latticed foot peddle. It was second-hand; the varnish on the table was peeling and gouged, the gold Singer logo already half scratched off. Sylvia held on to the cloth and the bobbins of blue and white thread lying on top.

They centred it at one end of the table and put chairs in front and beside so they could work together. Sylvia cut the fabric according to Rebecca's instructions, following the pattern with an impressive deftness. Rebecca hummed away with her task, and they talked very little for some time.

Once they had settled into a certain rhythm, Rebecca lifted her head to ask Sylvia a question that had been bothering her since the week before. Not the question she most wanted to ask, but another.

"Sylvia?"

"Hmmmm?"

"Why weren't you at Elsie's funeral?"

"Well, first of all let me say that my family is ashamed of me, Rebecca. Elsie was ashamed too. It's the sad truth of the matter."

"But she was the one who went at me, about prostitutes being not much different from her and me, about how people make choices, etcetera, etcetera..."

"Well, she may have talked a good line, but look at how she behaved. She was too ashamed to introduce me to her friends. The only one of her friends I met was Dora, who, by the way, does not in the least bit have a problem with it, and I met her by complete coincidence one day when I was hanging out on the stoop of our building with some of the girls."

"When was that?"

"A few years ago. I saw Elsie across the street shopping and called out to her. I thought she was alone. I didn't see that she was with someone 'cause I think Dora was turned the other way, looking at something in a shop window. Or something like that. Anyway, Elsie was forced to introduce me to her. And of course she was great, it was all Elsie's worrying for nothing. So don't be mad at Dora; if she'd had it her way, I'm sure they would have told you."

"I guess Elsie didn't tell you who I was or where I lived. That's why you never came by after I was hurt at the rally, isn't it?"

"What did you want me to do? I made a choice to respect Elsie's feelings on the matter. Don't get me wrong, it's not that it didn't burn me up. But I swallowed my pride, even though it meant doing things like being rude and not coming by to see how you were doing, and even though it made me feel pretty damn cheap. But she was my sister, Rebecca. Things are difficult enough between sisters as it is. So I just decided to let her be when it came to her personal life. The alternative would've been not to have her in my life, and I had lost enough family."

"Well then what about the shivah? Surely she would've wanted you to be there for that."

"That was my parents. They're... well, they're not very nice people. They disowned me when I was sixteen. No. They did-n't just disown me. They said the Kaddish and sat shivah for me, like I had died. You know how it is."

Rebecca thought to ask what she'd done that her parents would sit shivah, but decided it would be rude. And besides, she had a fairly good idea. She brought the conversation back to the present.

"But your own sister's funeral! I can't believe parents would be so cruel as to prevent you from being there."

"What can I say? I get on without them. And I find my own way to mourn my sister. I didn't need to be at the syna-gogue or at the shivah house."

"Everyone there said you were too sick to come. I ... I don't understand how people..." She looked up from her sewing. Sylvia was biting her lip and looking down at her fidgeting hands. "I'm sorry. I don't know much about these things; I don't have any sisters or brothers, but my parents aren't so bad, so it always surprises me." Her eyes fogged up at the thought of them. "They just left for Russia, you know. Or did I tell you that already?"

Sylvia breathed in deeply through her nose. "Look. Don't feel sorry for me. Now I don't have any sisters or brothers either. And my parents may as well be in Russia, even though they live about five blocks from here. So we can be only chil-dren together, both of us with our parents far away. The only difference is with me it's because of death and cruelty. You? Well I guess it's through bad luck on both counts."

Rebecca nodded. There was nothing much she could say to that. Sylvia seemed to let go of traumatic events as though they were fish she was throwing back into a stream.

"Sylvia," she said, "I have another question. I don't mean to be rude, prying so much, but I'm still a little curious — why exactly did they ask you to pretend to be a factory worker at that rally?"

"That really bothers you, doesn't it?"

"No, it doesn't bother me! I mean not personally at least. It's more an intellectual question. I just don't understand why everyone seems to brush off so lightly deceiving a crowd of people who are supposed to be your sisters and brothers in the struggle. You, I can understand, 'cause you're not part of the struggle, so what does it matter to you? But the rally organizers? It just seems unnecessary. And not in the spirit of what they're trying to do."

"And I suppose you never conceal the truth, tell a little story to get what you want?"

"No, I don't think I do," she said defiantly.

"What about in your marriage?"

"I most certainly don't lie to my husband!"

"Oh?" Sylvia looked at her, bemused. "Not even a little?"

Rebecca quickened the pace of her sewing. "Certainly not in the way we're talking about."

"So in what way is it then?"

Rebecca shook her head, dismissing the question, but Sylvia was obviously not giving up so easily.

"Oh, come on, Rebecca. It's all a matter of degrees, isn't it? Haven't you ever pretended to be cheerful so that you can keep peace in the house? Don't you ever pretend to enjoy yourself when he lies down with you at night? If you don't, I can tell you one thing: you're not like most married women I've met."

Rebecca's face flushed. "That's not an appropriate question to ask."

"I'm sorry. I know I lied at the rally, but the thing is, I've gotten used to speaking candidly when I talk to women one on one. Because, you see, I tell lies to men all the time. So I don't want to have to pretend with women."

"Why do you lie to men?"

"Lying to men just sort of goes with the territory in my business. It's the only way to *survive* doing what I do. I live in a really different world than you do, Rebecca. But you know what? At the same time I think Elsie was right. There *are* similarities in how all women cope. And the sad reality is that being honest with men usually doesn't lead to happiness."

Rebecca had kept her head down while Sylvia was talking. Sylvia might think she was the wise woman of the world, but she refused to play into it. She didn't want to seem too enthralled by what she was saying. Besides, she needed time to think of a way to let her know that she was not some naive, sheltered little child.

She halted the spinning of the wheel suddenly and looked Sylvia straight in the eye.

"You're pretty sure you know what my life is like, aren't you? It must be nice being so knowledgeable about everything."

Sylvia turned red. "I've offended you. I'm sorry. I didn't mean to get us off on a bad foot. My sister always said I speak too freely. It's always been one of my worst faults."

Rebecca pulled the sleeve out from under the needle and handed it to Sylvia. "Don't worry about it. Here, this can be the last one. I think we've probably had enough for today. We should probably quit before my stitches start getting crooked. Don't you think?"

Sylvia took the sleeve and looked at Rebecca with a conciliatory expression.

"I like crooked lines," she said.

Well, how nice for you, Rebecca thought, and then she yanked the thread out of the machine.

Chapter Eleven

May 4th, 1911

Dear Diary,

Sylvia and I ran into Gert Reznikoff today. I couldn't believe it, there she was flogging herring and such from behind a stand. I haven't seen her since they carried her off the shop floor with a big hole through her finger.

We were out shopping, just surveying all the tables in sight for a nice carp for supper or some heads for a soup. Different shapes and sizes and colors shingled the angled surfaces, and if it weren't for the powerful stench in the air, you could almost have called the experience lovely.

As we stood crouched over one table, Sylvia picking at the scales of one fish with one of her long, red nails, the man behind the counter asked which one we wanted, he would give us a good price. He was built like an ox standing on his hind hooves, and he had coal-black hair greased back and parted at the left.

Could he show me that one, I asked, but when he went to reach for the fish, another customer came up, so he called into the store. His wife came out and picked up the one he pointed out to her. When she held it up for me to see, I noticed that the woman's index finger was missing.

I looked up into her face and recognized Gertie immediately.

We hooted and hollered, well will you look at you, and so on. She declared the obvious, that she was a fishmonger's wife now, a Mrs. O'Leary now thank you very much, she said proudly. And she had heard that I was married too. I told her about Isaac and the quick marriage, and I introduced her to Sylvia, but I was anxious to hear what had happened to her and I said so.

She told me that after they took off her finger her parents became insufferable. They were certain she would never work again and that she could never find a husband on her own, and since Gertie couldn't tell them she was dating Jimmy (his being Irish Catholic and all), her parents spent every waking moment trying to find her a man. Two weeks before her supposed wedding to Paul Kamen, she and Jimmy eloped. When she told us that, she smiled, but it looked more like a pained grimace. Then she admitted her parents haven't spoken to her since.

But her face brightened a little bit, and she went inside to the shop. She came out with the most adorable little boy, her Frankie. She smothered him in her arms. He was just under a year old, had cute little freckles on his cheeks and a tiny little wisp of black hair sitting on top of a huge head. Frankie struggled a little in his mother's arms until she went to put him down again in the back of the shop.

She patted her stomach and told us she had another on the way, and then of course she asked me about whether I had any, and all I could do was make light of it. Sylvia didn't mention her baby at all. I wonder if she was trying to spare me the awkward moment or if she was just being private. Well, she won't be able to hide it for all that much longer. Maybe another month if she's lucky and wears loose clothing.

I changed the subject and told Gertie that Sylvia was Elsie's kid sister. Well, what a surprise she had when I said that. She went on at length about how Elsie had helped her out that day of the accident, kept repeating how much she could see the resemblance now that it was pointed out to her.

I wonder what Sylvia is thinking when people tell her about her sister, speak about her the way they do. She looks proud, but there's something behind her eyes that I can't put my finger on, and I wish I knew if it was jealousy or just plain grief. We were still talking about Elsie when Gertie's husband called her back to work, and so she quickly sold us a fish so we could be on our way.

Sylvia and I walked back toward Henry Street with our groceries in hand, not talking much. Sometimes I don't know how to start a conversation with her. When

we talk, it often ends with me in a huff about something or other, and Sylvia trying to make it all better.
But she is truly maddening sometimes! Nobody but she
can take a conversation about a simple thing and twist
it all around so that before you know it you are engaged
in a full scale debate. I didn't even know that I had
such strong opinions until I met her.

What aggravates me is that she never seems to get
worked up in any way. She just says something that's
flat out contrary with the most bland expression on
her face, as if she were commenting that the price of
oatmeal had gone up. It has occurred to me that perhaps she doesn't think herself contrary at all, that
maybe she thinks I'm the perverse one. Well if that's
the case, it must be that I'm the first person she's ever
met who does not swallow every little thing she says
whole and say yum-yum, give me some more.

Take, for instance, the conversation we had just
before we met Gertie, about Oriental Jews. We bought
some eggs from a Turkish woman who spoke to me in
Ladino, perhaps because my coloring suggested I might
be part of her community. I, of course, didn't understand a word, and the woman quickly changed to
English, but after we left, Sylvia mentioned she had
heard they were all strike breakers.

Where did she get this information, I asked her,
already exasperated. I mean, who would say such a
thing? She said she had heard it from one of her customers, a union organizer. He said every time they try to
organize a strike, the Oriental Jews get intimidated by
the bosses and they go back to work while their sisters

walk the line. I told her that wasn't true, that there were lots of Oriental girls who were part of the union when I was in the factory and she shouldn't say those things.

Sylvia said I was getting all worked up over nothing, that she was only repeating what she heard, not saying she necessarily believed it, but that the man clearly had said that it was very difficult to organize them, especially the Turkinas, that's what they call themselves, she said, and she wondered why that would be. I told her it sounded very much like she believed what she was saying, but she insisted she was only asking a question.

Just like that. She barely raised her voice, and already I was flapping my arms about looking like a fool, I'm sure. I don't know anyone else who can get me so worked up as that woman, even Hattie when she goes on about theatre criticism. And over what? When I think back on the argument, I was the only one arguing. Sylvia was acting like it was just a conversation.

It's not as if Sylvia and I never have any fun together, obviously. She takes an interest in me, and I in her, and we have moments. And she isn't completely a know-it-all. She seems impressed that I keep a diary, for instance. The other day she told me so, and said she has no talent for writing, but that she wants to write something sometime, she just isn't sure what. I suggested she start with writing down what happened during the day, or just write anything, if all she wants to do is practice, but she said she needs to feel inspired, and she'll know what to write about when that happens. She'll surprise me, she said.

In any case, there we were going to the settlement house, barely saying a word after the Oriental Jews incident, because I didn't want to get into another quarrel to which she would be oblivious.

We arrived at the settlement house at about four o'clock, and when we told them I was here to see how I could help, they told us to have a seat because they were busy and we'd have to wait for someone to talk to us.

We sat there for at least an hour and a half. The front hallway of the main house was a hustle-bustle that didn't let up for a moment from the second we stepped in the door to the second we left. It was painted bright white and had very nice oak benches to sit on, and every doorway and banister was embossed with some form of carving.

While we waited, I got up four times to let them know we were still there, so unsure was I that we would be remembered in the midst of all that activity. I'm sure they found this a little annoying, since the bench we were sitting on faced the long front counter, and they could plainly see us every time the crowds parted.

A small, stout woman directed traffic for most of the time we sat there. She wore a nurse's cap and a dark petticoat covering hospital whites and had small, round eyeglasses that perched at the tip of her nose. She seemed barely to use them because she was always peering over top of them to speak to this person or that. She spoke at least four languages that I could make out, and though her physical demeanor seemed austere, everything she said was conveyed in the most soothing tones.

Families straggled in and out looking stunned and helpless, mothers frequently bursting into tears as soon as they got a few words out. They were whisked away by an army of helpers, mostly women but also a few men, who appeared from upstairs or the room off to the side or generally out of nowhere to spirit people away, presumably to get some medical attention or some form of shelter. A stream of young women came down the stairs at one point laughing and talking, and I remembered that Ida took her secretarial course here.

Just when I thought we couldn't wait any longer, because we were running late, the woman behind the counter had a break in activity and called us over to ask how she could help us. When I explained our purpose, after all that waiting it took about five minutes before we were done and out the door. I explained that I could mend clothes for them if they needed that, the woman took my name and address, went into another room, came back with some shirts and pants that she heaped into our arms, and said the sooner I could have them fixed up the better. That was it. Her last words to us as we walked out the door were that she had our address and would be in touch if she didn't hear back from us in two weeks. I suppose that was her way of warning us not to run off with the clothes. I felt sad that they would feel the need to say that, sad that anyone might abuse their charity when it was freely available by just walking in the front door.

As we left the settlement house, I thought how fortunate it was that we live just down the street, not only because it was warming up outside and we were weighed down with clothes, but because it was getting late and we hadn't started dinner. When we walked in the front door, Ida Weiss was just coming out of Mr. Gutstein's apartment. We tried to get quickly by, but she chattered on about how she had been to see the landlord to ask about the clog in the closet on the second floor. Sidney is frequently out at work, leaving Ida to pester anyone who will listen. Today, we were her prey and it took us a full ten minutes to escape the trap, though we tried valiantly several times before managing to get up the stairs. Sylvia can barely hide her impatience when Ida is talking, but fortunately Ida seems oblivious.

The problem is that she is lonely, doesn't have very many friends yet, and is also very young for her age. She fills any silence with an endless stream of conversation, leaving very few opportunities to interject or gracefully exit. It's unfortunate, because she is really quite a sweet person — I can see that more now that we don't share a bedroom. Perhaps she will settle down a little bit when she gets older. She is only a year younger than me, but she seems like a child.

In any case, when at last we made it upstairs, we had to hurry to get dinner prepared. Isaac was not yet home, but we knew he would be arriving shortly, expecting his meal to be ready. Things were thrown quickly out of shopping bags, and the knives and bowls were flying about in hasty confusion. Amazingly, Sylvia and I have come to quite a routine in the few weeks she has been here, and things were progressing quite quickly.

Unfortunately, we were not quick enough, because we had only just lit the stove when Isaac came in the door. He did not say anything right away, but I could see in his eyes, the way he looked at us and at the stove and then paused before taking off his coat, that he was upset.

It took us half an hour to finish cooking, and Isaac pretty much stayed in our room until it was time to sit down at the table. We all ate without speaking until he finished his soup and I made the mistake of asking how it was. His answer was that it was all right, not up to my usual standards, but what could I expect when a meal is thrown together out of disorganization.

What Isaac said didn't upset me so much — it's what I have come to expect from him, and personally I would have just left the comment alone, but before I could say anything, Sylvia interjected. She said, we're sorry, Mr. Kalish, but Rebecca went to volunteer at the settlement house and they kept us waiting a long time — we didn't expect it to take so long.

Isaac grunted and said that even so, it was not good planning to do that so late in the day. I was about to just agree with him, but before I could say anything Sylvia responded again. She was smiling but there was a bit of an edge to her voice. She said, well, fortunately it all worked out in the end and we didn't get delayed too much, did we?

I thought Isaac was choking on a chicken bone, his face was so red. He didn't say anything at all, just continued eating until he had scraped his plate clean and announced he was leaving to go to a lodge meeting, that he would have to hurry because of the delay. Then he said the kicker — "But not too much, I've only been slightly delayed."

By the time he left, I was fuming. Sylvia was shaking her head as if to say isn't he something, but I wasn't mad at Isaac, I was mad at her. I said to her, you have no business stirring things up like that, Sylvia. Now she was the one who looked like she was choking on a chicken bone.

Stirring things up? What are you talking about, she said. He was being insulting to you — I was only sticking up for you, she said.

I told her I did not need someone to stick up for me, I know how to handle my own husband. To that she said, what, by lying down on the floor and letting him stomp all over you? I could feel the temperature rising in my cheeks. How dare she, I said, how dare she stand in judgement of me about how I choose to deal with my own husband? You move in here, I said, and in less than three weeks, you think you know everything about me and how I should live my life.

I didn't say that, she answered. I just think he's unfair to you, and I thought I was helping by being on your side.

We just stood there for a few seconds, eyes locked, and then I said, as icy as could be, I didn't ask for your help, I can defend myself. And when I said that, I turned around to face the wall.

It took her a few seconds, but she said she was sorry, and so I said it's okay, let's forget it, and then we just stood there dumbly for a while, my back still turned. I hated that I had tears in my eyes, and I was certainly not going to let her see that. Discreetly, I dried them, and then I moved to the counter to clear some dishes. She joined in and together we tidied the kitchen in silence.

When we were done, Sylvia went into her room and came out with a book in her hand. She said, I really just meant this to be a simple present, but now I hope you'll take it as a peace offering too.

I took the book and looked at the cover. It was a novel by Abraham Cahan, the editor of the Forward, called "Yekl, A Tale of the New York Ghetto." My night school teacher had told me about it a few years ago, but I had never read it. I was only five when it was first published in the newspaper.

I was stunned, overwhelmed. Here was a woman I had just berated for what she believed was a kindness, giving me a present. I must have looked quite spoiled and ungrateful just standing there leafing through the pages, mute. But I felt ashamed. And maybe just a little miffed that she had made me feel so. I took a deep breath to look the situation head on. How could I accept such a gift from my boarder? I thought about how much she must have spent on it. And yes, I admit I even thought about where that money had come from.

But on the other hand, she would be terribly insulted if I refused, and it would make a bad situation worse. The book would go to waste — it didn't seem to me that Sylvia herself read all that much. And oh, how badly I wanted it!

I recovered from my stupor and clasped the book to my chest. It's extremely generous, I said. She said something about the shopkeeper who recommended it, and I thanked her again, told her I would begin reading it right away. I think I even talked over her as I said it, I can't remember. But I know that I was already halfway to my room by the time I heard her say you're welcome.

Honestly, I couldn't bear the awkwardness even one second longer.

Chapter Twelve

Sylvia shuffled her feet as they walked, wiping streaks on the ground as her shoes disturbed a carpet of tiny, greenish-yellow flowers. The leaves on the elm trees in Seward Park were poking tendrils out from their buds, the first awakening of colour after a dreary early May.

The park was hemmed into a short city block, a busy concentration of play areas and pavilions with a large fountain and a tall maypole near the centre. The fountain was not yet working, and Rebecca picked up a pebble to toss into it as they passed at a brisk pace. She listened behind them for the pitter-pat as it rolled to the bottom. The rising mist of a mid-afternoon rain carried the fragrance of the fallen leaf blossoms up into their nostrils. Two children were hanging lazily on the maypole's colourful streamers, their bottoms swinging just above the ground, looking around for a few others to join them so they could start a dance. A trio of elderly men sat on a bench by the footpath.

As they emerged on the other side of the park, they made their way west along Hester Street. Passing a couple of women on the sidewalk, Rebecca noticed their eyes turning to follow them. Sylvia had her hair done up in an unusual style, an arrangement worthy of Dora, with strands of her red curls hanging out every which way. And she had put a lot of rouge on her cheeks this morning.

Rebecca turned her head back at the women and glared at them until they looked away.

"I hate it when people are so rude. Do you see how everyone stares at us as they pass? It makes me so mad."

Sylvia dismissed them with a wave of her hand, flopping her empty canvas shopping bag upside down.

"Ah, it's nothing, don't let it get to you. If they start yelling and throwing things, then we can start to worry. Personally, I think it's kind of funny that people are so shocked by anything the least bit different."

Rebecca poked Sylvia in the waist. "I don't suppose you could just for once dress normally so we don't cause a commotion everywhere we go."

"Nope," Sylvia poked her back, and got a smile to bloom from Rebecca's exasperated pout. "Think of it as a public service. This city is changing fast, and I'm just preparing people for the changes to come. I'm doing them a favour."

"Yeah? Well, I'm not holding my breath waiting for the city to give you its key."

Rebecca hooked her arm under Sylvia's and steered her out of the way of a child running down the street with a sack of potatoes over his shoulder. Two fell out as they passed. A large man with furry mutton-chop sideburns huffed past a moment later, shouting, "Stop that kid! He stole those potatoes!" But the child was already out of sight. They stared as the man loped around the corner, and they shook their heads as his voice faded, drowned out by the noise of the street. Sylvia bent down and picked up the child's lost potatoes and threw them in her shopping bag.

"Sylvia!"

"What? The man won't be back here for ages. Someone else will pick them up if we don't. He certainly won't get them back."

Rebecca knew she was right. Several eyes had been watching them enviously.

"Hmph," was all she could manage to say.

Reaching the western stretch of Hester, they worked their way through the shopping list, poking their way from pushcart to shop. Lentils, kasha, butter, a few more potatoes, four eggs, some onions, a half pound of flour, and a little salt.

"We need a nice fish for Friday night dinner. Let's go to see Gertie again."

"There." Rebecca pointed to the O'Leary's shop across the street. But before they could cross, a voice called out.

"Ribecceh! So long I don't see you! A married woman now, let me look at you." It was Zussel, the old peddler from Ludlow Street.

Rebecca shot Sylvia a quick warning glance before engaging with a broad smile.

"Hi, Mr. Zussel, how are you?"

"Not so good. My knees, they hurt me all the time. And my back, from bending every minute over this cart. But I carry on, no? What to do otherwise? *Nu*, and your mother, how is she?"

"My parents left for Russia a few months ago. I haven't heard from them yet."

"Back to Russia, are they meshugah? Same thing my neighbour's cousin. First we sell everything to leave that misery, then time passes and all of a sudden? Poof!" his hands made little explosions. "The misery, she becomes so misty, and our memory, she plays tricks. Begins to mistake this for happiness. We are crazy animals, we are. Never mind, who is your lovely friend? I see you with her last week, but you don't stop to say hello."

"Sylvia Dawidowicz. Pleased to meet you." Sylvia stuck out her hand, much to Rebecca's horror, and shook Zussel's fishy palm, then pulled her arm back behind her back to wipe it discreetly on her canvas bag.

"Pleased to meet you too." Zussel too put his hands behind his back, and then he just stood there, smiling at the two of them, looking at Rebecca, then at Sylvia, then at Rebecca, as if waiting for them to say something.

God, what an odd little man, Rebecca thought. She always got the feeling that he thought he knew some secret about you that you didn't even know yourself.

"And so. You need some nice fish today?" he said, still smiling.

Rebecca hunched into a bargaining stance. "Depends on the price — what can you do for me for that nice carp there?"

"Twenty cents."

"Oh come on, Mr. Zussel. For an old friend, you won't give a more fair price?"

"Fair? That's a fair price! You know how much I pay for that fish?"

"It's not so great. Look at the colour around the head. You'll give it to me for fourteen cents?"

"Fourteen cents! Your mother, she was a heartless bargainer, but this! She would never be so heartless as this. I can't let it go for less than nineteen."

"We'll come back maybe. Come, Sylvia." She pulled them away.

Zussel called after them, "Eighteen! My final offer!"

Rebecca called back without turning around, "We'll come back — I'm just looking around."

"Ayyy!!" His cry followed after them, reverberating in her ears.

Sylvia looked at her in astonishment.

"That wasn't very nice, Rebecca. You started much too low, and you didn't even give him a chance."

Rebecca cast her eyes down.

"I know, I know. I didn't want to buy from him, but he saw us coming across the street. What could I do?"

Sylvia's mouth gaped. "Oh come on, you knew exactly what you were doing. You didn't have to say we were shopping for fish, but you did!"

"But did you see his face when I said fourteen? I can't help it. He's so long-suffering, it always gave me pleasure to drive him crazy. He makes me laugh. Oh, I'm a terrible person, aren't I?"

Sylvia chuckled. "Ah well, it's good to know you're not so perfect. I'll be able to use this the next time you start nagging me for tormenting that ridiculous Ida Weiss. Speaking of which, I caught her coming out of Mr. Gutstein's apartment again. Now I'm sure she's having an affair with him."

"Don't be ridiculous."

"I swear. Don't you see how often she visits him in the middle of the day? I'd bet ten bucks on it. Anyway, she saw me, and I think she was so nervous that I had seen her coming out of his door, she started talking endlessly about how she couldn't get the blackness out of the bottom of her pot, and I thought I would go crazy so I made up this whole thing about a special scrubber."

"You didn't!"

"You should have seen the look in her eyes as she ran off to find it."

They looked into one another's eyes and broke out in laughter. An onion spilled from Rebecca's bag, and she had to jump in front of a briskly walking woman to pick it up before it was crushed.

"Oh, it's clear. We're both awful people. What are we going to do? You're a terrible influence on me, Sylvia Dawidowicz. Terrible."

"Oh, don't blame this on me, kiddo. It's becoming quite obvious to me that you were just as bad before you even met me." She put her arm around Rebecca's waist and pulled her toward herself for a little hug. "Come on, let's go see Gertie. Maybe you can torment her too."

Gertie greeted them with a kiss, but her smile was half-hearted.

"How are things today, Gertie, we haven't seen you in a few weeks."

"They're okay," she said, but Rebecca thought her tone was more weary than she had intended; her eyes seemed a little glassy.

"Frankie's okay?" Sylvia asked.

She didn't respond. Her hands wiped vigorously on her apron. She looked over at her husband, who was just beginning to bargain with a customer.

"Jimmy, I'm just gonna take a minute with my friends. Are you okay?"

Mr. O'Leary grunted his permission, and they stepped away from the table to sit on the stoop next door.

Rebecca placed her hand in Gertie's.

"So tell us, what's wrong? Where's Frankie?"

Gertie started to cry. She and Sylvia looked at each other, and Sylvia leaned over Rebecca's lap to look in Gertie's eyes.

"Gertie?"

"It's nothing really. It's just that he..." She brought the four fingers from her right hand up to cover her mouth. "Um. Well ... it's Jimmy. He's not so good with children." She blinked quickly, then pressed her eyes shut for a few seconds. "Excuse me for a moment," she said.

Rebecca hugged her.

"What do you mean, he's not good with children? Come on honey, it's just us. You can tell us what's wrong."

"Oh, I'm so embarrassed. I didn't mean to talk about this. It's just that sometimes ... sometimes, when Frankie starts to cry, well he can't really help it, you know what I mean? He's just little, you know how kids are. He doesn't get what he wants, and has a little fit, and starts to whine or to cry."

Sylvia squeezed Gertie's hands.

"Of course he does. He's not even a year old. That's normal."

"That's what *I* think. But Jimmy, he gets so *angry*. And, well, sometimes..." She paused again. "You know, it's not so bad, really. This time he just grabbed him a bit too hard."

"Oh, Gertie, that's awful, honey." Rebecca pulled out a handkerchief from her sleeve and handed it to her. "I'm so sorry. I'm not sure what to say. How's Frankie now?"

"He's doing okay. Jimmy's sister Sheilagh is with him in the hospital. Everyone thinks it was just an accident, 'cause his wrist is in a cast. You're the only ones I've told." She took the handkerchief and blew her nose, wiped under her eyelids. "I don't know how we're gonna pay for the hospital bills."

"Life isn't fair, is it Gertie?" Sylvia offered. "Is there anything we can do?"

"I don't know. I don't know. The thing is, I love him. And anyway, I'd have nothing without him. What's better? For my kid to get hit every so often but be alive, or for him to starve to death without a father? I don't want him to end up like one of those kids on the street that you see collecting garbage from the alleys. I figure there's always a chance he'll change, isn't there? This time it was really bad. It's not usually this bad. I think this shook him up a bit."

Sylvia scuffed her shoe on the ground and mumbled, "I sure hope so."

Her tone betrayed anger, and by now Rebecca was used to how undiplomatic she could be. The three of them sat silently for a few uncomfortable seconds.

Gertie dried her eyes, then straightened her apron. She picked herself up, apologizing for burdening them.

"I have to get back to work. Thanks for listening. We'll be fine. I'm sure of it. We'll be just fine."

"Of course you will be." Rebecca felt sickened by the insincere sound of her words. "Just fine."

Gertie wrapped up a fish that she insisted they take free of charge, and they hugged her goodbye.

Walking silently for a few blocks back along Hester Street, every so often Rebecca would glance over at Sylvia to see if she could tell what she was thinking. Her face was inscrutable.

Rebecca switched her shopping bag from one arm to another to ease the ache in her shoulder. If Sylvia wouldn't say it she would.

"She should leave that man." She knew even as the words were coming out of her mouth that Sylvia would take the opposite position. She always did.

Sylvia snorted. "And do what? Where would she go? Her mother and father disowned her."

"I can't believe you're disagreeing. She could surely find the means... I don't know how she'd do it, but she should, that's all. You did, not that I'm suggesting she do what you do."

"No, of course not." Sylvia's annoyance was obvious. "Anyway, she has a child to think about, and I didn't have a child when I left home. And look what considerations I've had to make now that I'm about to have one."

"But it's horrible. That poor little boy." Rebecca stomped on a bug that was walking in front of them and crushed it into the dirt under her pointy-toed boot. "Arranged marriages. It all comes down to arranged marriages. If we were just free to choose who we married, these things wouldn't happen."

"How do you figure that, Rebecca? Gertie *did* choose the man she married."

"Yes, but not really. I think maybe she only chose him because she was under pressure from her parents to marry Paul Kamen. Maybe she had to make a quick decision in order to escape. If that's true, she probably thought she had no other choice. And how could she know her husband would turn out like that? *And,* even if she had an inkling, maybe she thought the devil she knew would be better than the devil she didn't. My mother had the freedom to choose her husband, and she ended up with someone good."

"Well, I might agree with you kiddo, except for one thing. My parents had no pressure from their parents, they married for love, and look what happened to me and Elsie. And your parents, who had your best intentions in mind, arranged for you to marry Mr. Kalish. Face it. Men are men, arranged marriage or not. And sometimes you can't tell what kind when they come courting."

Rebecca walked a few more steps without answering. She considered coming to Isaac's defence, but found she didn't have the heart. She had to admit that what Sylvia said was true. She still felt it was better to have some choice, but she couldn't deny that Sylvia was also right.

Usually, these conversations drove her crazy, her own observation coming out as childish emoting, Sylvia's rebuttal as the sensible correction. For almost two months, out of pride, she had been challenging Sylvia's words of wisdom, or had teased her, called her the female Maimonides. Something in Sylvia's past had given her a special lens through which she saw shapes in the world's fog. And this afternoon, for the first time, that clear thinking didn't threaten her. It was not quite comfortable yet, but it felt like a firm railing on which to steady oneself and keep moving forward. She didn't know why she felt different today, she just did.

Rebecca opened her mouth to say something else about Gertie, but Sylvia cut her off.

"Rebecca, I want you to keep my baby."

She stopped in her tracks. "What?" Her interlocked arm was tugged forward as Sylvia, who had still been moving, was also pulled to a halt.

Sylvia's voice betrayed no emotion. "I want you to keep my baby. I've been thinking about it for a while."

"I don't understand. Why would I..."

"I don't want to have that baby raised in a brothel. Or worse, in one of those baby farms some of my friends send their children to. Some old whore raising other whores' kids. It's not what I want for my baby."

"What are you talking about, Sylvia? You're not actually still thinking of going back there, are you?"

Sylvia ignored her question.

"You would be a wonderful mother, Rebecca. I could visit every so often, if you would let me."

"But... but you don't have to go back there." Rebecca grasped randomly for an out. "You can find a place! You can stay with us as long as you need to, you can get a job..."

"I have a job."

"I mean a real job."

Sylvia took her hands into her own and looked in her eyes. "I know you don't approve, but it's my work. I make decent money at it, and it suits me fine."

"Oh, Sylvia. I'm trying to understand your way of thinking, but you're not making it easy. You say one thing, and then you say the opposite! If you think it's so wonderful in that place, then how come you don't want your baby to live there with you?"

"I don't want to argue with you about this, Rebecca. If I don't always make sense to you, well then fine. It's not important that I do. But let me just say this. I'm not the only one who says one thing and then says another. Or maybe *does* another."

Rebecca bristled. "What are you implying?"

"I'm not implying. I'm asking. What makes you so sure you'd be able to leave if you were in Gertie's situation? No, forget it. Don't even answer that. I said I didn't want to get into an argument and here I am throwing out 'what ifs.' I just..."

She paused for a moment, and looked up at the sky while she gathered her thoughts.

"Look, Rebecca, I won't beg you; if you can't do it, I'll understand. I'll find someone else. I'll ask the midwives at the settlement house. They'll know someone. It's just that I think my baby would have a better chance with you. We might disagree on whether or not Mrs. Fine's place is good for adults, but we both know it's no place to raise a child."

Rebecca leaned against the wall of the building next to them. "I don't know what to say. I'm so overwhelmed you would even ask me. I'm honoured, really I am. But I don't get it, Sylvia. If you think my husband is so bad, then why would you want to leave your child with us? We hardly have any money..."

Sylvia took her hand and squeezed, pulling her forward again along the street. "Rebecca, it's true I think your husband doesn't treat you well. And it's true he and I don't get along. But none of that really matters. I look at it in terms of what my other choices are. You obviously have a lot of patience to put up with your husband. It takes patience to raise a child. Lord knows I certainly don't have any. My baby will be much better off with you."

Rebecca punched Sylvia in the arm. "You always have such a way of making a compliment into an insult. Or vice versa, I'm not sure which." She walked for a few more paces and then stopped again.

"But seriously, Sylvia. We've only known each other a few months. You don't even really know me. Why me?"

Sylvia narrowed her eyebrows and thought for a moment. Then she smiled.

"Because I trust you. It's as simple as that."

When they returned home, Isaac was waiting for them, sitting on a chair in the kitchen. Rebecca saw the tendons in his clenched jaw ripple. He looked at the clock, then back at them.

"Where have you two been? I've been waiting here a half-hour, and you two haven't even begun to get supper ready!"

Rebecca dropped her shopping bag, and stepped up to him, put her hand on his forearm. "Isaac, I'm sorry. We got delayed..."

He jerked his arm, dislodging her hand.

"I'm out all day trying to make a living, and all I ask is that I have a warm meal ready when I come home. Is that too much to ask? I would have thought that since there are two of you, it would be easier to accomplish such a simple task, but no, it seems that all this means is that two women together means more talking, less work."

Sylvia went to the counter and lifted her shopping bag, dropping it with a loud noise. Rebecca's heart pounded faster, hoping Isaac didn't notice. Her arm tightened around the back of a chair.

Fearing Sylvia would say something, she filled the silence. "You're right — it's not too much to ask. We should have paid attention to the time."

Sylvia turned around. She was seething.

"Why don't you tell him? Why are you apologizing to him? We haven't done anything wrong! Mr. Kalish, we ran into an old friend of Rebecca's. Her husband was beating her son. She cried on Rebecca's shoulder — what was she to do? Walk away, say, I'm sorry your baby is in the hospital, but I have to go home to cook for my husband who can't wait a half-hour, he should die from starvation?"

Isaac got up from his chair and stood face to face with Sylvia. Rebecca's heart raced so fast she thought it would burst from her rib cage. Isaac pointed his finger at Sylvia's nose so that it almost touched the tip of it, but she did not budge.

"I will not be spoken to like that in my home — not by my wife, not by any woman, and especially not by some ... whore! If you don't want to respect the rules we have in this house, you're free to leave any time you want, Miss Dawidowicz — the door is there!"

Sylvia kept her lips clamped, and Rebecca wondered what torrent of invectives would otherwise have escaped them. Isaac's finger was still pointing at the door, and Sylvia stared at him for a few seconds. Then she turned on her heel, walked into her bedroom, gathered some things, and, still stuffing them into her purse, opened the door and slammed it behind her.

Chapter Thirteen

June 8th, 1911

Dear Diary,

I never cease to be amazed at how sadness and joy can exist together in a person's heart, pulling in opposite directions like two children tugging on their mother's arms. But the heart is a resilient organ indeed, and I do believe G-d put it in the centre of our chest as an anchor, lest all that tugging should tear us apart.

So much has happened since I last had the time to write in my diary, so it is difficult to know where to begin. First Sylvia stormed out of the apartment a few weeks ago after she and Isaac had their big fight, and it took a lot of convincing of both of them to patch things up. In the end, she agreed to come back, and he to let her — probably because he became so used to the money coming in. But the strain of the first few days after she returned was unbearable. I waited almost a week before raising the subject of keeping Sylvia's baby, but it was too soon. Isaac refused.

Sylvia does not know what to do now, and I don't know how to advise her. She is not happy about letting a stranger found by the settlement house raise her child — she admitted this to me only after some days of putting on a brave face. Saying that she could ask other people was simply Sylvia's being prideful, as I suspected.

She is certainly now considering some difficult choices regarding her future. She did have the money to fix the situation before she ever came to live with me, but she did not want to do that. Certainly it is dangerous if one is not careful about who one finds to help, but it is not as if there is any shortage of mid-wives who know what to do, and a few doctors, I have also heard told. Isaac says such a thing is against G-d, but I hear that lots of women have done this, G-d notwithstanding.

I believe that deep down Sylvia wants to have a child, but she does not believe that she will be a good mother, and therefore is filled with dread at the thought of raising it. I think that she wants to be able to see her child grow up, but without the fear that she will ruin its life. Whatever her feelings about mother-hood, Isaac's decision has not improved matters in the way that he and Sylvia get along.

I wrote of sadness pulling me in one direction, and here is the reason for the sadness: Isaac is doing well at his business in the last two weeks. He has found a street with no other cap merchant, and it seems to have inspired him to be a little more aggressive with his sales approach.

I don't begrudge his success, but even though it is only recent, he is already suggesting that we won't need a boarder for much longer. If he continues with this way of thinking, it will only be his grudging sympathy for Sylvia's situation that will convince him to let her stay until her baby is born. The money she pays us is barely enough to offset his dislike of her. But I don't want Sylvia to leave.

However, there is wondrous news I am bursting to write about, the joy tugging me away from sadness — a new life I have inside of me. The realization leapt up at me so unexpectedly that I barely knew it until the signs were too obvious to ignore. In truth I don't think I wanted to believe it at first. This seems strange to write down, since I have written so often before about my frustrations.

I can't explain my hesitance, my unwillingness to recognize what was happening to me. All I can say is that now that my eyes and my heart have opened, I have felt the most tremendous sense of happiness. It is a sense that my life is being completed by another, one more precious than my own.

Chapter Fourteen

January 8th, 1912

~~Dear Diary,~~
Dear Sadie,

I have waited two months, and I must put something down on paper or I will go mad.

It seems fitting to write this entry directly to you, sweet little Sadie, since you are right here with me, more precious than I could ever have imagined. Yes, I will write to you, sitting here on my lap, curled up and snuffling away, warming my thighs when I should be warming you.

I will write to you because I know it is only pretend — I still do believe that matters of the heart should not be shared except with one's diary. But how can I address my thoughts to some inanimate object, when you are here? Nevertheless, though I write this down and address it to you, I will protect you from the full story of what I will be writing in these pages — too much of a burden to a child of any age.

I should begin with the day you were born, November 8th, two months ago today.

Sylvia and I had been staying together in the back bedroom — Isaac's snoring had been keeping me awake all night, and I convinced him that in my condition this arrangement would be preferable. Sylvia did not have an easy confinement and was so anxious that she would occasionally wake up in a sweat, her face asking a million questions about her life, her baby's future...

I would talk to her until she calmed down, sometimes for a few minutes, say, shhh, it will be okay, go back to sleep, and wipe her brow free of her damp wisps of hair. Sometimes we stayed up a full hour with reassurances and plans, other times she fell back to sleep quickly.

On occasion she would call out in her sleep for Elsie. Usually it was as though she were trying to find her, but a few times her cries sounded more like warnings.

Elsie — get out! Get out! she shouted once. I assumed she was having a nightmare about trying to wake her sister from the gas, but one night she muttered something different, and I began to question this. Elsie, please! Just come with me, she cried this time. Downstairs with me, it's safe there. Sadie can give us tea and cake... her voice would trail off. When she awoke, I asked who was Sadie. She said she didn't know, but her face told me she knew exactly who she was.

Sylvia didn't like to talk about her nightmares. She said it just made them worse because then you remembered them all day long. I guess there's no accounting for the crazy dreams people have when they're filled with worry, or when a woman is with child. Well, it's enough to say that it was better for me to be with Sylvia to calm her down, and that even with her occasional sleep-talking I got more rest than I ever did with Isaac.

And thank G-d for that, because, Sadie, you have just woken up again, which means no rest for me for a while. But it's okay — you've given me the excuse I needed to stop here, before it gets too difficult. Maybe I will continue tomorrow.

January 11th, 1912

Dear Diary,

The baby is sleeping in the next room, and though I have had a few days to gather myself, it hasn't helped. I have tried several times to think of a way to write about what happened that day, but I just can't do it.

I'll write about the next day instead. I can't remember it as well because I didn't sleep at all that night, but I do remember one part of it clearly.

Isaac came home at seven o'clock at night, and I knew from his face he had been wandering the city all day. I wonder was it out of shame? I hope so. He saw me sitting in the rocking chair, the baby suckling at my breast. I was trying to feed her, but she wasn't latching. She was crying and crying until I gave up and fed her some warm water with a small spoon. I told Isaac we were out of milk, and that he had to go get some right away, or to go get Ida to fetch some. He looked at me, and noticed my stomach.

He put his hand up to his mouth. There was a strong, terrible odour in the room — the smell of excrement and new life, all churned together. I had become used to it, but I could see that Isaac was close to gagging.

He went into the bedroom, perhaps to find Sylvia, but when he came back, he didn't even ask what happened to her. All he said was, What's going on here? I told him I had lost our child, that this was Sylvia's baby, and that Sylvia was gone.

When? he asked. It started a few hours after Sylvia gave birth, I said. It took almost five hours.

I had done this on my own, he asked? He didn't believe it. Why hadn't I called for help? Why hadn't I sent to fetch him? I laughed. You didn't want anyone to help when it was Sylvia, I said, but it would've been okay for me? Don't worry, I said. I had Sylvia with me. My voice was as flat and dry as parchment, filled with exhaustion, maybe. Definitely anger.

For once Isaac was speechless. I did it all on my own, I told him. I said, You told me I could do it, Isaac, and you were right, I delivered the baby. Unfortunately, I also lost our little boy in the process.

Isaac's eyes started to well up. It was only the second time I had seen him cry. The first was when I told him I was pregnant.

This little girl survived in spite of me, I said. She is a survivor. Say hello to our little survivor, Isaac, our little Sadie. She has her mother's eyes. And her spirit too, you'll be sorry to hear.

He went back in the bedroom. Where was our baby, he sobbed. Right here in my arms, I said. That's not our baby! he shouted. I want to know where the other one is — our real baby — my son! I felt his spittle on my face.

I buried him already, I answered. At noon. In the backyard, wrapped him in my mother's featherbed, soaking in my blood. I packed him inside the chest your parents gave us and buried him in that tiny little coffin.

I thought his eyes would pop out. You buried our son in the backyard? he shouted. In my parents' chest? Without letting me see him? His furious glare cut into me, but I didn't care. What could he do to me now? What could he possibly do to me now?

In case you never noticed, I am a strong person, I said, a tear escaping the corner of my eye. Stronger than I look. I never knew how strong until last night.

What's going on? he said. What on earth were you thinking? Didn't people help you? Or stop you?

I gathered myself, made sure I was not crying anymore, and then told him calmly, no, that the only person who saw me was Ida, who found me smoothing over the earth, crouched down with my belly still big so she thought I was still pregnant. I told him Ida asked what I was doing digging in the backyard in my condition, and who was upstairs with Sylvia and her baby.

And what did you tell her? Isaac asked. I could tell he was getting a little worried.

So I said to Isaac, well, I wasn't prepared to find her there, so I had to think fast. I told him that I gave her some story about tainting the milk cutlery and needing to bury it, and that also I told her another lie — that Sylvia's baby had died. She started to cry and said she knew she should've gone to get help, started blaming herself. She wanted to go visit with her then and there, but I told her Sylvia wanted to be alone.

Isaac was shaking his head. Why on earth, he said. I don't understand, he said. What made you say all those things? What were you thinking? I'm going to the backyard, he suddenly announced, and he started for the door.

It doesn't matter that I buried the child, Isaac, I called after him. Jewish law says that it doesn't need a proper burial. My words stopped him at the threshold.

He wasn't born alive. Isaac's shoulders slumped when I said that.

I'm not sure why I lied to Ida about which baby died, I said. But now that we have lost our child, it's lucky I did. We can raise this one as our own, I said.

What do you mean, we can raise it? he asked. That baby is not ours, we are not raising it, since when are you making decisions in this house... he went on and on, his voice getting louder and louder, and I was tired of it.

So I said, fine.

Just that. Fine.

My voice was now like iron. But here are the options, Isaac, I said, just so that you're clear what you're doing. And we'd better decide before people start asking questions, so tell me which one it will be. I could tell people that you refused to get help — that you abandoned two pregnant women and that because of your own cruelty, G-d has punished you and taken away your own son. The truth. I could tell people that I will never be able to have a child now, a result of your ruthlessness, that you and I are clearly now unable to ever have children. The truth. I made the word sound as vile as I knew he would find it.

Or, I said, and I softened my voice again because I looked down at my lap to see Sadie's funny little face, we could lie. I made that word sound sweet and benign and as gentle as could be.

We could pretend that this is our own daughter, I said. That Sylvia's child died. Then we could tell the neighbours that we are coping with our grief, but blessed by our own daughter's arrival. We would be just like most families, I said; a lie, which, if you say it often enough, becomes the truth. Which one will it be, Isaac?

He was still at the door, with his hand on the knob ready to turn it. But he took his hand off and stood still for a moment.

And one more thing, Isaac, I said, not waiting for an answer because there was never any question in my mind what his choice would be. You'll tell people I don't want to have any visitors for a while. This baby, if it is ours, is supposed to be early — almost two months early. She's tiny, so it won't be hard to convince people. But just the same, I don't want people schlepping in and out of here examining her, fussing over me. I want to be left alone.

He turned around and came to sit in the chair. I smiled down at Sadie and stroked her bumpy, tiny head. I had won.

So say hello to our daughter, I said. Little Sadie Kalish. Then go and get me some milk.

Chapter Fifteen

1983

Anna shifted on the mattress in the back room to make herself more comfortable. She looked at the box in the middle of the floor, a bound volume of the diaries open beside it. The mattress sagged under her weight and felt lumpy. Until now, she had remembered this bed as a refuge, a safe place she used to share with her sister. She brushed her hand over the coarse woolen blanket, smoothing out the lumps, and then snaked her hand under the covers. The sheet underneath felt cool to the touch. Her eyelids closed to better enjoy the flowery scent, and body memory guided her as it followed her arm under the silky layers. She wriggled herself into an old, familiar position, her breasts squashed against the soft bottom sheet, her head slightly tucked under the pillow, her arms up, forming a cradle for her head.

She used to dangle her left foot ever so slightly over the side, the only part of her she would let escape the warmth, her right leg pulled up under her so that her shin pressed firmly against her sister's thigh. Sadie would sleep on her back, she on her front, and they would stay that way, all night barely moving. Gently, playfully they tugged at the blankets, their subconscious ballet disturbed only by the occasional surfacing to wakefulness. It kept them linked, felt secure. Touching of legs, taut blankets and sheets, warm, and snug.

She tried to relish the memory, but it was suddenly wrenched aside; this bed was now blood and death, the screams of childbirth, red-soaked sheets, a lifeless baby. Distorted faces, the wrenching shock of life's cruel selection...

But her mother had cautioned her about beloved memories, about how fragile they can be. Memory, she once said, is like the class clown. When he's mocking the teacher, he's our hero, he's hilarious and invincible, and there's nothing else in our mind. But when the teacher turns around, our image of the clown dissolves, and all we see is a little boy's ear being tugged away by two fingers and his twisted face following close behind. So cherish your pleasant memories while you can, her mother had warned, for you could learn something next that might change their meaning forever.

Anna jerked herself upright, and the covers fell in a crumple of cloth at her waist. Who had that child been that her mother had lost? An older brother she never knew. Instead, there was Sadie, the child of a hooker and an unknown philanderer, her sister only through some terrible twist of fate. Suddenly, the boundaries of family had been redrawn, the landscape of kinship had re-formed under her feet, and for the moment it felt like quicksand. She could only imagine how Sadie would feel. How was she going to tell her?

She looked at the clock. It was ten-thirty, and Sadie had still not come back for her keys. She slid out of the bed, pushed herself up to her feet, straightened the sheets, and went to close the volume she had just read. She pulled the box out farther into the middle of the room and emptied its remaining contents. She sifted through to look for the next instalment. The first four volumes were piled in a heap, together with a bunch of other books, but that was all.

She crawled into the closet to look for another box, got up on her feet again, and pulled a chair in to reach the shelf above the clothes rack. There were a few hat boxes, a shoe box filled with jewellery and some cosmetics. Another small plastic milk crate filled with old bank books and tax returns. But no diaries.

She got down again and opened the last entry she had read. It was dated January 11th, 1912, and the rest of the pages were blank. But that couldn't be so. Or could it be possible that her mother had stopped writing? Forever? Certainly she must have been very busy taking care of babies in the first few years, but had she really never written another word, nothing about what happened to Sylvia after she left? About their childhood or about Sadie's running away? Nothing about their father's death? Nothing after it?

She couldn't believe it. It wasn't like her mother to just give up on anything.

Anna got up and stood with her hands on her thighs, thought harder about where they might be. She went into the kitchen and went to the hutch, opened the drawers. There was the pink sewing kit. Some photo albums lay underneath it. She pulled them out and leafed through them quickly — maybe there were no other bound volumes, but only loose sheets from another diary. Maybe they would be stuffed in among the pictures.

A photograph in the second album caught her attention. It was a portrait taken at a professional studio. Sadie looked about twelve years old, and she just eight or nine. It was 1924 or 1925, she wasn't sure which, but she knew that day was her birthday. Their father stood behind her on the left, their mother behind Sadie on the right, barely peeking over Sadie's head she was so tall already. They were wearing clothes borrowed from the studio, a lot fancier than they could ever have afforded to buy, and it made them seem like they were people of means.

She remembered the afternoon vividly. The photographer was a tall, handsome man with a trimmed brown moustache and round spectacles. Sadie had complained that it was silly to get all dressed up so that they could barely recognize themselves, that there was no shame in their real clothing, and that they should get photographed the way they really lived so that people could look at the picture and see that their lives were difficult, and so what if they were.

Their father had told her to be quiet and could she leave her socialist politics in her head for ten minutes, or did they always have to spill out from her lips at every moment? And where are you getting all these ideas, he had asked.

Socialist politics, Papa? Sadie's reply had been defiant. You don't even know what socialism is, if you think that's socialism. What I was saying is just about having a little dignity.

SaaaaDIEEEEE! their father's voice was a train bearing down on her, until their mother stepped in, putting a hand up like a stop sign in their father's direction, an upheld finger in Sadie's.

I agree with you, Sadie, she said calmly, but we want to send this picture to your bubbe in Russia, and it would break her heart to see us looking like we were still living hand-to-mouth. There's a time for making a point, and there's a time for protecting the people that you love from worry and heartache. This is not about being undignified, kinderleh, it's about kindness. Bubbe's life is hard enough. Her hands are tired and sore from hard work — does she need to be wringing them constantly with worry about us? Not if we can help it. So let it be, sweetheart, and stand up straight so that she'll see how tall you are getting. And Anna, stop picking your nose and fix your hair a little, it's coming undone.

The photographer had laughed, and her face had flashed red with shame — her nervous, childish habit might as well have been caught on film. But the photograph was taken a few minutes later, when all that was left of her humiliation was her miserable expression fixed there now in black and white.

She leafed now through the rest of the album's pages. There were a few more pages of photographs, some pictures at Anna's own wedding to Mel, some shots of them with Mama holding little Allan. A picture of Allan at nineteen, one of the last, in his uniform, taken somewhere in Korea.

No writing. She looked in their mother's room, opened all the drawers in her dresser. There were clothes in the bottom three, slacks and shawls folded neatly in one, sweaters in the next, bras and underwear in the second from the top. In the top drawer there were phone bills, jewellery boxes, some hard candy. A search through her mother's closet revealed nothing but some old dresses and shoes.

She went to the kitchen and rallied her strength to stand up on a chair. She had to see if there was anything on the tops of the cupboards. She swept her hand across the surface, but found only mouse pellets and dust balls and a cockroach trap. She opened the cupboards and pushed the dishes aside. A tin roasting pan. An old, scarred wooden cutting board.

She got down from the chair, feeling the ache in her knees, and went into the bedroom again to sit down on the bed. She pushed down on the mattress, her fingers curling over the edges. Of course — under the bed! she thought. I should have looked there in the first place.

She crouched down and peered underneath. There was some stuffing from the mattress lying in clumps on the floor. Interesting. She didn't remember its being there. Mice? She pulled the mattress up, trying to control her excitement, but there was nothing there either. Then, as she lowered it down, the sheet pulled up, and she saw the rough pattern of thread underneath the seam. This was not from mice. The last she had heard, mice did not sew.

Years of tidying up with her mother had made her familiar with the details of the furniture, and she knew the mattress had been sewn up before, but there was new thread now over the old. She could tell from its different colour. The mending job was hasty, sloppy, and it wasn't hers.

She didn't bother to get scissors. A tug at the end of the thread pulled it loose, and she separated the two sides with her hands. She reached inside and felt throughout the mattress, but there was nothing there.

Her heart was racing now, and it made her breath more laboured. She got up and went into her mother's bedroom, untucked the sheets, and saw the same thread, the same messy sewing job. A tear at the thread and a look inside again revealed nothing, but this time she was only confirming what she expected.

She knew where to go next. From the top drawer of her mother's dresser she grabbed a fistful of phone bills. She leafed through and found January. Scanning the list, she came to a number in Toronto. She looked at the February bill. The same number was called twice. March, April, May, June, the number was there on all the bills. It had to be Sadie's.

Just to be certain, she dialed the number, scratched nervously at her neck with her free hand. It rang twice, and then Sadie's voice picked up on the answering machine. *"Hello, this is Sadie. I'm not in right now, so if you could…"*

She slammed down the phone and pressed her eyelids together to squeeze back tears. All this time, and Sadie had been in touch with Mama? How long had it been? How could Mama not have *told* her that she and Sadie had made contact again? Why didn't Sadie call *her*? She had even been in the apartment. Did Mrs. Huang know all of this too? Was she the only one who was kept in the dark? Why would they do this?

She pushed her hurt deep down inside, and for a moment held her breath to keep it lodged there firmly. She couldn't let herself be distracted by sentiment. She had a more practical matter to consider: what had her mother told her sister, that Sadie had been here looking in those mattresses? What was she searching for? Did she know about the diaries? Did she know if there were any others?

Emotions churned in her gut and her tongue filled the back of her throat. She got herself a glass of water, unlatched the door, and sat still at the kitchen table, sipping, watching the door, breathing deeply in and out through her nose. Waiting.

It was half an hour before she heard her sister's footsteps thump slowly up the stairs and along the hall. Sadie walked in the door, her eyes trained on the floorboards. She was wheezing from the effort of the stairs.

Anna got up from the chair and stared until Sadie lifted her eyes up timidly to meet Anna's.

Anna's icy voice cracked the silence. "I see you came back for your purse. It's there on the counter."

Sadie moved wordlessly over to get it.

Anna's eyes followed her to the counter. "I read the last volumes of the diary, Sadie. Some revelation in there. Big. It seems you and I aren't sisters after all. Isn't that interesting? But of course you know all of this already..."

"What?"

Her stunned expression took Anna by surprise, but Sadie was bluffing, she had to be.

"Oh, come on. You knew! Don't give me that innocent look."

Sadie's voice lowered, took on a tremor of agitation. "What are you talking about, Anna?"

"I'm saying we're not sisters, and you knew it damn well. Maybe it explains why we're so different, actually. If you ask me, it explains a lot."

"You're lying!" The anger in her voice had an edge of uncertainty.

"I'm not lying, and you know it, because you read it yourself." She went to get the diary, opened it, pointed to the page. "Here. It's all here, so you can't deny it."

Sadie took the book, but didn't read. She appeared even more unsteady, her anger suddenly sucked out of her and leaving her weakened. She put her hand against the wall to stabilize herself. "I — I don't understand — what are you saying? That Mama and Papa weren't my parents?"

"Oh, come on, Sadie, you knew this." She looked into her sister's face. "Didn't you?"

Sadie's eyes were a mile wide and roaming back and forth, focussing on nothing. The wrinkles below her cheekbones quivered a little.

"Sadie?"

Now her sister just looked defeated. "I didn't know. I didn't know. This is ... so ... I don't really know what to ..."

Anna suddenly felt sorry she had been so brutal. But she had been so sure her sister had known. But if she hadn't, then what had she been doing with the mattresses? Had she been looking for the diaries but not found them?

"I'm going back to Toronto," Sadie declared softly. She took her hand off the wall and brushed off her skirt, extended the diary for Anna to take back. But she dropped her arm when Anna didn't take the book. "It was a mistake for me to come back here. Maybe I never belonged here in the first place."

"No wait, Sadie. I'm sorry. Oh my God, I really thought you knew. I can hardly believe it myself, I can't imagine what a shock it must be to you. I'm so sorry. I would never have said that if I'd known..."

But she stopped talking, because Sadie walked away in the middle of the sentence. She followed her sister into the back bedroom and stood at the door as Sadie went to the box and knelt down. She dropped the diary in the pile and dug out her childhood dress, tucked it under her arm.

"Why didn't she ever tell me? All my life, all that I went through, and they weren't even my parents."

"Of course they were your parents, Sadie."

"No. They weren't. You just said they weren't, and it makes perfect sense. Does she say who they were?"

"Mama and Papa had taken in a woman named Sylvia — she was Mama's friend Elsie's sister, you know, the one who died in the gas leak. Elsie, I mean. Sylvia was a..." she hesitated a second, but then knew she had to tell her, "she was a hooker. She was pregnant while Mama was pregnant, only Mama miscarried. They pretended you were their child."

Sadie took in the information without expression. "And my father?"

"It doesn't say. I don't think Mama ever knew."

"And what happened to her. This Sylvia?"

"I don't know. Mama says she left after you were born. I can't find anything else written about her. I can't find anything else, period. There aren't any other volumes of her diaries."

Sadie fiddled with the dress, took it from under her arm and refolded it. "I was never a part of this family. From the beginning, I always felt like someone plopped me down in the middle of it all. All these years of ..." her voice trailed off.

Anna remained at a distance, unable to find the right words.

Sadie stood up. "I never belonged here. Never." And she walked past her to the hall door.

"Yes, you did, Sadie. You were a part of this family as much as any of us. It just wasn't a very healthy family."

Sadie had her back turned and was shaking her head. She reached for the door handle. Anna had to ask her now, or she would be gone.

"If you really weren't a part of the family, then why did Mama get back in touch with you? Doesn't that tell you something?" She tried not to sound angry, but she wasn't sure how successful she was.

Sadie stood still a moment and then turned slowly around. "How did you know?" She looked embarrassed.

"I saw her phone bills. She called you. A lot."

"I see." She walked foot to toe over to the chair by the kitchen table, her head down to measure the steps, and carefully sat down. "Please believe me, Anna, I was going to tell you. I just ... I didn't know how."

"Well, that's obvious."

"The truth is, Mama tracked me down about six or seven months ago. I wanted to call you, but I was trying to figure out what I would say. Mama kept asking me if she could tell you — you shouldn't blame her." Sadie rubbed her eye sockets aggressively with her palms. "I was the one who kept begging her to wait. I said I wanted to make the call myself. I put her in a terrible position, and I meant to make it right, but then she died, and ... I knew you'd be upset I didn't call you." She shook her head back and forth.

"Damned right I'm upset, but don't flatter yourself, Sadie — I'm not upset that you didn't call. I'm upset that *she* called *you*. I work myself to the bone for that woman for fifty years, and in her old age who does she call for support? *You!* Goddamned right I'm upset!"

Sadie shook her head. "Support? What makes you think that she called me for support? Anna, maybe she just wanted to talk to her long-lost daughter. Or whatever I was to her. A minute ago you were trying to convince me I was part of the family, and now you can't believe she would call me instead of you. Your true colours are showing."

"It has nothing to do with your being adopted, Sadie. It's about the fact that you haven't been around. I just don't think she called just to reconnect with you. I don't believe it."

"How would you know? Not everything has to do with *you*, you know. Has it ever occurred to you that people might sometimes do things that have nothing to do with punishing or hurting you? People have their own hurt, and their own ghosts, and sometimes — sometimes when they're trying to heal, or get away, or whatever, they just do what they think they have to do."

"Oh, piss off, Sadie. And spare me the sanctimonious crap. Are you trying to make a point about how you ran off without a trace? Well, forget it, 'cause it's too late. The point is, we both know she told you about the diaries. She told you and not me, and it's as simple as that. *I* play the good daughter my whole life, *you* bugger off to Canada and disappear for half a century, and she calls you — *you* — to tell about the diaries."

"It's not what you think."

"I know you were here, Sadie. I saw those mattresses. You don't know this, but I helped Mama with her laundry. I came here and changed her sheets every week. When a person knows a place, a person notices when things are different. What, did Mrs. Huang let you into the apartment?"

"Yes. I told her who I was, and that I was going to drop off some things and tidy up a bit before the funeral."

"So then you *did* read them."

"No! ... No. Look. I *was* trying to find the damned diaries, I admit it. Well, I was trying to find *a* diary. I thought there was only one book. But I never found anything, I swear. It was stupid. I was afraid that there would be something in her diary that would be hurtful to you."

"You don't expect me to believe that do you? That you deceived me out of concern for me? Oh please, Sadie. Don't insult me, I'm not that dumb."

"Okay, you're right. That's not the whole truth. I didn't know for sure that Mama hadn't told you anything. And I was worried that if you did know, you'd find it first, and I'd never get a chance to see what it said."

Sadie looked to her for a response, but all Anna could do was shake her head.

"I'm sorry, Anna, I don't know what else I can say, except that it was wrong. I don't know what I was thinking. Especially since Mama was probably out of her mind these last few weeks."

When she still did not respond, Sadie slumped her shoulders and got up from the chair.

"I can't talk about this anymore, Anna. It's just too much right now. I have to go." She walked by Anna again to open the hall door.

Anna tried to move in front of her. "No, please, Sadie. I'm sorry. Please don't go back to Toronto. I shouldn't have pushed it." Sadie stared at her until Anna moved aside, wringing her hands in self-admonishment. Then she opened the door and began to walk down the hall toward the steps.

Anna called after her, her voice sounding more desperate this time.

"Sadie, I don't care if we're not blood relatives, I just don't want to lose you again."

Sadie stopped where she was, her back to her sister, her shoulders lifting and falling with her breathing. She shook her head. "I won't go home, I promise. I just need to be alone right now."

"But when will you come back?"

"Tomorrow night. I'll see you tomorrow night. After people leave the apartment. You'll make an excuse for why I'm not there. Tell people I'm feeling under the weather and I'm spending the day in bed. It probably won't be far from the truth."

Anna watched her until she was around the corner and out of sight, until all she could hear were heavy steps thumping slowly down the staircase.

When at last Sadie showed up the next night, Anna had been contemplating just how long a person could sit still without going completely insane. She had combed through the diaries again, looking for any details she might have missed the first time. There was nothing of importance.

She had considered leaving several times, but could not bring herself to do it. She had called the hotel; her sister was not answering the phone in her room. What if she was on her way? What if Sadie came back, and she missed her? They had barely been reacquainted, and she had driven her out the door twice in one day. Not smart. She had to get hold of herself and be more psychological about this. If there was to be one last chance to mend their relationship, she could not pass it up.

Sadie closed the door quietly.

"I'm sorry I'm so late."

"I tried your room, there was no answer."

"I've been sitting outside across the street. Wondering whether or not to come in."

"And what made you finally decide to?"

"My bladder. I had to pee."

Anna smiled. "Touching. Don't let me hold you up."

Sadie went to use the small toilet in the apartment. Anna withdrew into the back bedroom and sat on the edge of the bed while she waited. When Sadie emerged, she joined her on the bed and they both sat stiffly looking down at their toes. Anna pointed hers inwards to stretch out her ankles. Sadie bounced her feet slightly up and down.

"So."

"So."

Anna looked up at Sadie and examined her face, tried to size her up. She looked old — she couldn't get used to how old she looked. And right now she looked old and frail, deflated.

They remained there quietly for a while, and every so often Anna would look at her sister's face again, studying the features. Her patrician nose was more fleshy now, more bulbous at the tip. Her skin was greyish in tinge. It was as though someone had taken Sadie's eighteen-year-old face and soaked it too long.

"What? What is it?" Sadie asked.

"It's nothing. It's just ... I keep trying to remember how you looked when we were teenagers. All I've ever had to remember you by was one or two old photographs. It's so ... strange to have you sitting here now, when I haven't seen you in all these years, and see ..."

"How old I am?"

"Yeah. I mean ... don't take offence, look at me! It must be just as strange for you."

"It is. It's almost like ... I don't know, like it makes sense that I grew old, but I expected you still to be young. I mean, not *really*. Obviously I knew you'd be older. But how can my kid sister look like some grandmotherly woman? It's not that I didn't picture it in my mind — your clothes changing with the years, you know, that sort of thing. I even gave you a new hairstyle every so often, but it was always just a game. It never looked realistic in my mind. I couldn't really picture you."

"I know what you mean." Anna smiled. "I used to try to imagine you too, but you always ended up looking like Katherine Hepburn."

"Katherine Hepburn! Hmph. Well, at least you didn't say Barbara Stanwyck. People always say I look like Barbara Stanwyck, which drives me crazy, since she's about five foot nothing!"

"Hey, be careful what you say to the little people."

"No, no. I didn't mean ... There's nothing wrong with being short, it's just ... Oh boy, I think I've put my foot in it now."

"It's okay. 'Cause you know what? I've pictured you as Barbara Stanwyck too, so there, now we're even." She started to laugh but suppressed the outburst with her hand. "I'm sorry. But you know your cheeks and your nose sort of ..."

"Oy. Not you too."

"Sorry." She pulled out her blouse and reached under it to tug at her bra where the underwire was biting her skin.

They sat there again for a while, glancing over every so often at one another's faces.

"And so," Sadie said eventually, "you never said what's changed about me. I mean aside from the obvious, you know, that I look like movie stars."

She sat back a distance from her sister, hesitating.

"You look tired, Sadie."

"I am tired. It's almost eleven o'clock. This is late for me."

Anna tapped her arm playfully. "No, I mean you look like things have been tough."

Sadie tried to smile. "Yeah. Well, it's not so bad now. But you're right, it's been pretty up and down. Unfortunately, down more than up, I would say. A few pretty lonely years here and there."

"I'm sorry."

"No, it's nobody's fault but my own. I could've made an

effort to be in touch, but I had too much pride. And I was too ashamed."

Anna looked away from her sister's face, wondering if she could let it go, give her some time in light of her having discovered the day before that she was adopted. She decided she couldn't leave it, she had to know.

In the most gentle voice she could muster, she said, "Sadie, I need to ask why you left us. I know it probably doesn't make any difference now, but I need to know."

"They never told you, did they?"

"They told me next to nothing. Papa just said that you ran off with some guy and left them a note, that you had been selfish, and that I should never speak of it again. 'Anyone who can turn her back on God and family like this does not deserve to be mentioned,' I believe were his exact words. That was all that was said. Believe me, I tried to get more information, but it was no use."

Sadie shook her head. "Oh my God. It figures they would lie. No, Anna, I didn't run off with anyone. Papa threw me out."

"But why? Why would he do that if there was no guy?"

"There was a guy, but that wasn't really why."

"I don't understand."

"I'll try to explain, but I'm not sure where to start. Maybe at the dance hall. No, I think it pretty much started with my being stuck day in and day out in that apartment, Anna. Remember, after I finished the eighth grade? I had to stay at home and help out. As you pointed out, I was the 'older daughter,' and that's what the older daughter did. *You* got to go to night school *and* work. I would've *killed* to do either. But instead, I had to spend my days and nights helping Mama. Geez, what year would that have been, then? Twenty-eight? Twenty-nine?"

"You left in twenty-nine."

"Right. So you remember how a couple of years before that, I guess I had just turned sixteen at the time, so that would've made you thirteen, Dora Segal came to live with us for a few months? Remember Auntie Dora?"

"How could I forget? The three of us shared a bed when there was barely enough room for two of us."

"Well, Papa told me if I stayed with Mama and Dora all day long and helped them out, he'd allow me to go to the dances on Saturday night. So I'd go. Dora even came with me, supposedly as my chaperone, but it turned out that it was more the other way around, frankly. I'll tell you, that woman was no role model. At least not in the way that Papa and Mama expected her to be.

"You remember how she was this failed vaudeville performer. I don't know if she ever even performed in vaudeville, but she sure talked about it enough. She was always clinging to this hope of making it big, but you knew she didn't have one iota of talent. But boy could she dance in the way that boys liked it. She was about thirty-seven years old then, but she looked a lot younger. She was tall and had a terrific figure and was extremely outgoing, and she played it all up."

"I remember. She was nearly as tall as you."

"Yes, but she actually had curves, which made her seem exotic. I was just long and thin, and I had no bust at all." Sadie brought her hands to her chest and pressed them flat.

"You were beautiful, Sadie. You still are."

"Well, thank you for saying so, but I didn't feel very beautiful then. But that was the problem — I didn't feel beautiful until I started going to the dance halls, then that started to change. I don't know if Papa ever allowed you to go after I left, but in those days the dance halls were packed with boys and girls cutting loose on a Saturday night. Lots of half-lit hallways and dark spots where you could get into trouble, and Dora was the first to disappear into them. Sometimes she'd come back bragging about gifts she'd been given by this guy or that.

"At first I was quite shocked. And I was surprised she'd be carrying on like that in front of me. But then I suppose she considered herself a free spirit and didn't really care what anyone thought of her. And to tell you the truth, I admired that quality in her. Plus, as you can imagine, it was all very exciting for me — it was the only time of the week I was allowed out, except occasionally to go shopping with Mama.

"It was the only time I felt like I was growing up, so naturally I thought since Dora and I were there together, that all of what she was doing was very grown-up and sophisticated. Maybe even liberated, although I don't think any of us used that word then, at least not when we were talking about women.

"So remember when Dora moved out of the apartment because she met that big rum-runner? Shiny Parker. The guy was smuggling in contraband from all over the place, from England, from Canada, from the West Indies. Quite a character. His real name was Bud, but they called him Shiny because he always had his hair slicked back with a little bit too much pomade. Whenever you saw him, he was flipping a coin, just to show off that he had change in his pockets. He tried to pretend people called him Shiny because of the coins, but everyone knew the real reason.

"So Dora took up with him, and within a couple of months, she was moving out of our flat and in with him. She told Mama and Papa they'd married in a quick ceremony, but I don't think they actually did. I would still see her at the dance halls on Saturdays, only now she always had Shiny on her arm."

Sadie got up to stretch, put her hands in the small of her back to work out the tightness. "You must remember Shiny."

Anna pushed herself to the back of the bed so that her back could rest against the wall. If this was going to be a long story, she'd need to settle in.

"Only vaguely. Was he a redhead? She must not have brought him by much. And by the way, I never did get to go to the dance halls after you left. There was no way in hell Papa would let me go out after that."

"I wouldn't have thought so. Anyway, one Saturday night Dora introduced me to this fellow who was a friend of Shiny's — Bobby Thompson was his name. He was taller than me and had big, broad shoulders, and the way his dark moustache curled up with his lips when he smiled made me positively swoon. By then I'd already been into the back hallways a few times before, you know, just for some heavy petting or what-not, nothing big, but enough to consider myself some kind of woman of the world. I thought I could handle anything that came my way.

"Well, he danced his way into my heart. I remember his moustache would tickle the back of my neck as we swept across the dance floor. And I remember just feeling ... so wonderfully lost when I danced with him. Every so often I would open my eyes slightly and see other shapes swirling around us. They were just barely lit by the electric chandeliers — it really made it seem like a dream.

"Before long, we were cutting out of the dance early enough to go back to his place and to get home in time not to arouse suspicion. Dora and Shiny nudged me on with a wink and a smile, so I felt very safe with him, like if anything happened, Shiny would take care of it.

"We carried on like that for three months, and then I missed my period. By that time I was completely gone on him, and I was so naive I thought he would marry me right away. The only thing I was worried about was that he was Episcopalian. I thought we could get married quickly, and tell Mama and Papa we eloped. The quick pregnancy would be suspicious, but not inexplicable."

"You think they would've been fine if you'd eloped with an Episcopalian?"

"Don't ask for logic, I wasn't thinking straight. It just seemed better to be married and pregnant than alone and pregnant. It never occurred to me he might drop me like a hot potato. But of course, that's exactly what he did. It seems so predictable when I tell it now, but I was really stunned by it then." Sadie sat down again and shook her head.

Anna reached forward from where she sat against the wall and put her hand on her sister's back. "Lots of girls have made the same mistake. You weren't the first."

"I know, I know. It doesn't matter, you still feel like an idiot. Boy, I'll never forget the look on his face when I told him I was pregnant. Like he'd been waiting for it. Like it had happened to him so many times before, he expected it. It seemed like he even had his exit line rehearsed. He said, 'I'm not ready to settle down and be a family man, sweetheart. Hope you understand,' as if he expected I would say, 'Yeah, this baby was foolish, let me just nip out and deal with it, I'll be right back.' Honest, I think men back then thought you planned these things to trap them, as if we had some way to stop it from happening but chose to ignore it.

"I went to Dora and Shiny for help, and begged Dora not to say anything to Mama. She assured me she wouldn't, and I knew she would keep her word because Mama would've had her head for letting me get into the situation in the first place. But when I asked for money, they showed their true stripes. Shiny was all excuses about how his business wasn't doing so well and how he'd sunk everything into real estate, and so he couldn't spare anything right now. I don't know if that was true or not, but he and Dora had just moved into a house in Brooklyn Heights and owned a few rooming houses they were getting rent from on the same block.

"And our wonderful 'Auntie Dora' wasn't much better. It's not that she didn't want to help, but she was too much of a doormat to stand up to him. She would follow him around everywhere, and he would never have let her out of his sight even if she hadn't. There was a doctor I had heard of who travelled around the Lower East Side, helping out the Italian and Jewish women when they'd decided they had too many children, but I had nowhere near what I needed to pay for it. Dora slipped me a few coins here or there when Shiny wasn't looking, but it wasn't very much."

Anna could hardly believe what she was hearing. "How could she not help you?"

"She was selfish and self-absorbed, and she had no sense of what was right or wrong, that's how. For a while, she left me completely on my own. If I hadn't been so afraid that Mama and Papa would find out, I might've dared to go to the settlement house, to see if I could get a midwife to do it for free. But you remember by then Mama was volunteering there, so I didn't think I could risk it. So for a few weeks I sank further and further into despair, trying to pretend to everyone that I was fine."

Sadie pushed herself back to where Anna was sitting and folded her hands on her lap. "But I was not fine," she said. "I felt like a spinning dreidel, always wobbling off its centre and landing every single goddamned time on *shin*. But I had nothing left. And I kept thinking: for God's sake, haven't I already paid?"

Chapter Sixteen

August 1929

Sadie sat on the edge of her bed to buckle her shoe, but she paused a moment while she waited for the bed to stop shaking as her sister fussed and shifted on the other side. A knot in her stomach tightened. It had been distracting her all evening, and it wasn't the food and conversation at dinner — both had been quite bland. She fanned herself to cool off a bit, maybe it would help settle her stomach. A low hum came from her parents in the next room, and she could hear the thump thump thump of the neighbours moving about upstairs.

The bed shook again, so she turned to glower. Anna was lying on her back reading a book about aeroplanes, still fully dressed, her feet on the bed, ankles crossed carelessly. A very thin pillow protected her head from the wall and pressed her chin awkwardly forward. She had slid down a few inches, and as a result her hair was now pushed up in a peacock fan. The book was propped up on her chest, a library hardcover that Sadie knew she had already renewed twice.

Anna shifted her eyes when she realized she was being watched. "What?"

"Could you just be still for one second while I'm buckling my shoes? I feel like there's an earthquake happening."

"Sorry, I was just trying to get comfortable."

"And speaking of shoes, could you take yours off if you're going to lie on the bed? For God's sake, how many times do I have to ask you?"

Anna moved her legs only slightly so that her ankles were off the edge. Sadie fastened her buckles, then straightened up and grabbed a blue and white dress draped over the corner of the bed. She pulled it over her head and wriggled until there were no bunches anywhere. It was a one-piece, but sewn to look like a sailor's shirt tucked into a two-tiered skirt. A stitched-on sash wrapped around the waist and hung down to the hem, just below the knee.

"Sadie, can't I come with you? Auntie Dora'll be there..."

"You're too young. Mama and Papa said so."

"I am not too young. Marge Slonemsky goes, and she's two months younger than me."

"Don't look at me, I don't make the rules in this house."

"Well, they're not fair."

"Go down the street and dance on the corner if you're so restless. Or read another book on aeroplanes. Oh, and by the way, in case you didn't know, girls can't be pilots."

"Shut up! Girls can so be pilots. Amelia Earhart is."

"Oh, how could I forget for even a minute about Amelia Earhart? Her picture's only staring me in the face every damn morning when I get up. You know what? Her parents are rich. If you have money, you can do anything."

"Mama says if you work hard you can do anything."

"Mama doesn't seem to be a good example of that."

"I don't know what you're talking about. Boy, are you ever grumpy tonight, Sadie."

"Just read your stupid book, Fig-Face. I'm not in the mood to give you lessons about life that you should be able to figure out yourself."

"I didn't ask for any lessons. You don't have to treat me like a baby."

Sadie whipped her head around to face her sister. "You *are* a baby, with a spoiled little fig-face and your head in the clouds. Flying your imaginary aeroplane right through the clouds."

"You know what, Sadie? You're the spoiled one. Who's the one who gets to go to the dance hall every week? It's not fair. Not one bit."

"Oh, excuse me for taking advantage of the one thing Mama and Papa let me do that's fun. The rest of the time I'm trapped here, watching my life turn out even worse than Mama's."

Anna put her hand up to her forehead and arched her back. "Ya, well before your *life* becomes even *worse than hers*, you better just get to that dance, Miss Melodramatic."

"Stupid imbecile. See you later — unfortunately."

She threw on a long string of fake pearls and went into the kitchen. Her mother stood at the washbasin talking to her father. She was doing the dishes from dinner but stopped when she heard Sadie come out. Without a word, she made a twirling motion with her finger, and Sadie turned around for inspection.

Her mother squinted to see if Sadie was wearing any make-up. She made a grumbling noise, as if to say: I can't *see* any but

I'm not sure I can trust my own eyes. Her father was sitting on a chair in the bedroom, near the open door. He looked up from his newspaper and scanned her up and down. He looked displeased, but also said nothing. Taking this to be permission to leave, Sadie quickly announced she was off and hurried out the door.

"Tell your Auntie Dora I want you home by eleven," her mother called out to her, "and not a minute later."

When she reached the street, the thick, cloudy air hit her face and filled her nostrils with the pungent smell of burning garbage. By the first block she already felt sticky, and the stench wasn't helping her stomach one bit. She thought about the argument with Anna and had a twinge of regret, but then decided her sister was simply being her annoying self, and that tonight she really wasn't in any mood to care one way or another.

At the corner she stopped for a moment to watch the hurdy-gurdy player and a dozen or so *spielers* dancing in a semi-circle around him. The musician was a man of fifty or sixty dressed in bright red and green old-country clothing. He sat on a small box on the side of the road, his small instrument lying across his lap. One hand busily cranked the wheel while the fingers of the other fluttered up and down the keys. The spielers, girls between the ages of about eight and sixteen, strutted this way and that, performing for a small gathering of passers-by.

Their movements were unpolished, but the children were energetic, unhindered by the heat. The older ones waltzed in pairs, pretending to be with a fine suitor, the younger ones just flailed about on their own, ignoring the convention of the dance entirely. The man's smile and tapping foot encouraged them, and his chin directed them this way and that. A few coins lay in a box at his feet, watched over by a bored-looking woman of uncertain age, his wife or perhaps his mother.

Sadie knew Anna wouldn't be caught dead dancing on the street corner anymore, she had only been goading her. Anna was too old for all of that now, or so she felt. But to Sadie, it looked like fun, for sure more fun than she would be having tonight. A few children recognized her and called out as she went by, invited her to join in, but she declined, and rounded the corner. As she moved on, her step synchronized with the beat in spite of herself, until she was well down the street and couldn't hear the music anymore.

The Orchard Street Dance Academy was a few blocks away, and she reached it already in a full sweat. The entrance was undistinguished, a double door with a simple painted sign overtop. A few dozen people milled about in front of the entrance, some smoking or drinking a soda to cool off. As she approached the front, she scanned the crowd, but couldn't find Dora or Shiny.

She didn't expect them to be there, really. If they had been outside, it would have been a coincidence. For a long time now, they were chaperones in name only. They were always already inside when she arrived, and though they would pretend they had been looking for her, all evidence was to the contrary. A perfunctory remark would be made about being good, and then she was usually ushered off to fend for herself. And she hadn't done so well in that department, obviously.

Five or so people blocked the front entrance, and she had to push past them because they made no effort to move out of the way. She stood on her tiptoes to scan the long corridor. Crowds clumped around two narrow soda fountains against the right wall, and also near the back around a fortune teller's table. There was some movement in and out of a few smaller, darkened rooms on the right side, and a large crush blocked the doorways to the left of the corridor, going in and out of the main dance hall. Though the door to the street was open and electric fans thrummed overhead, the air blew heavily, in waves, and carried a strong spicy scent of perfume and sticky bodies.

Dora usually wasn't that hard to pick out. The rule was, look for the most ostentatious person in the room, the person wearing the brightest colour, or with the most clashing outfit, and that would be she. Shiny was the more difficult to spot, as he was much shorter than Dora and was usually buried in a flock of men anxious to curry favour.

They weren't in the main corridor. To move from the front entrance to the archway leading to the dance hall, Sadie had to get past three men leaning against the wall. Two of them politely pressed their bodies flat to allow her by, but the third didn't budge, so she glared at him until one of his friends elbowed his ribs, and he grudgingly let her by.

She moved into the hall and took in the dancers shuffling sluggishly on the floor. A small orchestra laboriously executed a slow waltz from the raised bandstand in the back corner. Couples moved in and around one another, their faces dripping with perspiration and glowing with refracted chandelier light.

Through a break in the dancing, she caught sight of Dora on the far side of the room leaning against a fat pillar. She was wearing a red, beaded, sleeveless dress with a ragged, purple-green fringe that barely covered her knees. Skirts had lengthened again in the last few years, but Dora hadn't paid any attention. Also, try as she did to conform to the fashion of the day, her bosom failed to be discreet under the clothes she wore. The huge corsage of white, bulky flowers pinned to her dress was an unsuccessful attempt to downplay the size of her breasts. On the contrary, it drew attention to them, the long, curly tendrils of the greenery finding their way under the neckline and into her cleavage in several places. A very long string of pearls, wrapped twice around her neck and hanging down well below her waist, jiggled back and forth as she gesticulated wildly to some friends.

Sadie made her way across the floor. She had no intention of dancing tonight and did not want to waste time with chit-chat. Dora spotted her coming and pushed a woman aside to give Sadie an embrace.

"Auntie Dora, I need to talk to you."

"Of course, dear. Let's have a chat after the next dance."

"Um, I need to talk to you now. It's important."

"What is it, darling?"

"You know..."

Dora blinked a few times but never lost her smile. "Yes, dear. Of course. Let's go right away. Shall we go outside?"

She took Sadie's hand, made apologies to her entourage, and led Sadie back across the room, clearing a path through the waltzers. Once outside, she was about to sit down, but Sadie shook her head and urged them down the street and out of earshot. They found a closed storefront about a block away.

Their behinds had barely met the steps when Sadie said, "Auntie Dora, you've gotta help me find a way to make some money. I don't know what to do."

"Look, you know I wish I could help, darling, but I asked Shiny, and he won't cough up the cash."

"I know, I'm not asking for that. But there's gotta be a way."

"Sadie, honey, we talked about this already. There's no way to do it without your mother and father knowing. Your schedule doesn't allow it."

"But if I don't start earning some money, I'll be showing before long. I need to get this taken care of soon. I figured out my schedule. I have twelve clear hours a week when Mama and Papa are both out. Maybe I can do some piecework."

"No offence, honey, but sewing is not your strong suit. Remember that skirt you made me a few years ago? It was a sweet present to get from a kid, but I don't know if it's of the quality they look for..."

"But I've gotten better since then!"

"Maybe so, but I don't think you can waste time with the risk it won't work out. Then you'll have done all that work for nothing."

"Then what? What?" She started crying in deep sobs into Dora's lap. "Oh, Auntie Dora, what am I gonna do? I'm eighteen years old, and I'm gonna have a baby. And I haven't seen Bobby since I told him, except for the back of his stupid head."

"Honey, honey, shush, we'll think of a way." She took Sadie's head and pressed it against her bosom, crushing the corsage.

"Tell me about your mama's schedule. When does she go out?"

Sadie pulled a handkerchief out and blew her nose. "Twice a week. To do some shopping. And once a week to do her volunteer work. Oh, and also once a week to visit with her friend Hattie."

"Jeez, the only thing you could do with that kind of schedule I hardly dare to suggest."

"What? What could I do? Tell me, Auntie Dora."

"No, honey, not that. I was only thinking out loud."

"Auntie Dora, tell me, please! Let me decide if I can do it or not."

"Honey, I was just thinking about this place I know. A brothel where I used to know someone who worked years ago. Now do you see why I didn't want to mention it?"

"Oh." Sadie lowered her head and fiddled with the sash on her dress. "Well, I guess it's not so much worse than what I've already done, is it."

"Honey, you know I've never thought that way. I know most people would — your parents for instance — but I consider myself a more modern woman. Lots of people make judgements about other people's business without knowing a damned thing about what they're talking about. Besides, if you did that, and I'm not saying you should, it would only be temporary anyway. It wouldn't be like you'd *be* a whore. You'd just look at it as a way out. A temporary way to an out. Things are always easier if you think of them as temporary."

"I guess so."

"Anyway, I only thought of it because it's work in concentrated, short stretches, if you know what I mean. But you'd still have to get out of your place for long enough ... It's too risky."

"I suppose ..."

"No, you can't. There's no way. You don't have enough time to get there, do the deed, and get back in time."

"But what other option do we have? None."

"I don't know what to say, Sadie honey. I don't see how it could work."

Sadie started to cry again, so Dora stroked her hair. "Now, now, Sadie honey. Darling, sweetheart, hush now."

But Sadie was not comforted. Her crying became louder and louder, and Dora tried in vain to calm her down. When the wails were nearing hysterical and attracting attention, Dora said, "Honey, honey, okay. Shush now, let's try this: The only thing I can think to do is to introduce you to the owner and see if she'll send people over to your place. But that would be risky in another way."

Sadie gasped for air, and choked out, "B-but Auntie Dora, if you s-stayed there and kept watch..."

"Yes, I suppose. Let me just figure this out." Dora drew figures in the air, mathematically deducing the profits. "Yes, in a few weeks you'd have enough money saved up. It just might work."

"What about the neighbours, seeing all those guys coming and going?"

"That's the least of your worries. If *I'm* there, they'll think nothing of it. I already have a reputation anyway. If I showed up at your place with a new guy on my arm every time, they'd just think it was par for the course. I'd tell Shiny just in case, so if it gets back to him he won't be jealous. But think hard, honey. Do you really think you could do it?"

She wiped her face on her sleeve. "What choice do I have?"

"Okay then." Dora handed her a handkerchief and stroked her hair. "Honey, on the positive side, you'd feel good that you'd righted the situation yourself, instead of just having the solution handed to you in an envelope. Isn't that so?"

"Yes, I guess so."

"Of course it is, darling. And like you said, as for the means to the end, well, the horse is already out of the barn, now isn't it? There's no use locking the door now."

Chapter Seventeen

Sadie removed her apron and sat down on the covered toilet seat, still fully clothed, in the cramped little room at the top of the staircase on the third floor of the apartment building. She wiped her hands roughly on her brown cotton skirt and pulled out from her pocket the article she had cut out of the paper.

The article read:

Mrs. Sanger Unrepentant — Birth Control Advocate Continues Work

Story by Mr. Andrew Bryson

The Daughters of the American Revolution are outraged that Mrs. Margaret Sanger's Birth Control Clinical Research Center continues to operate four months after charges laid by the New York City Police were thrown out of court.

"There is no excuse for this flagrant disregard for justice and decency," said Mrs. Van Helsen, speaking to the press yesterday on behalf of fellow DOAR members. Mrs. Van Helsen, who laid the original complaint leading to the charges against Mrs. Sanger's clinic, has on numerous occasions publicly criticized the New York City Police for refusing to lay further charges.

A spokesman for the police force, however, shifted the blame squarely to the shoulders of the judiciary, and said Mrs. Sanger and her research center were being closely watched. Indeed, citizens of this city could be forgiven for wondering: how or why can the courts see fit to plainly disregard common immorality in our midst? Furthermore, should the police force abdicate responsibility for enforcing the law, allowing clearly illegal activities to propagate?

When asked how she felt about the opposition to her so-called research, Mrs. Sanger said that she and her supporters were adamant that their "family planning" work would continue.

"Sadie?! How long are you going to be in there?"

Her mother called from the apartment down the hall.

"Coming, Mama!" she answered, folding up the article to stuff into her apron pocket. As she emerged from the toilet, she heard footsteps from below and saw a woman appear on the landing. Climbing the stairs, the woman struggled to adjust a white cloche hat that hid her face, until she looked up, whereupon Sadie could see the problem: the woman's head seemed trapped inside of it. Sadie recognized her mother's friend Hattie, as much by her face as the fuss with the hat. Since she could afford them now, Hattie had recently begun wearing the latest fashions, but she always seemed ill at ease in them.

"My word, Sadie, let me look at you. Are you getting taller?" Her hands fluttered upwards.

"Oh Auntie Hattie, don't be ridiculous. I haven't grown an inch since I was thirteen, and you see me every week. It's just that you keep forgetting that I'm a beanpole. Plus, you're looking up at me from the bottom of a staircase."

Hattie reached the landing and leaned in to embrace her. She was wearing a two-layered, pleated cotton dress, the top layer coming down just below her hips, the bottom layer emerging from underneath the first and reaching just below the knee. On top she wore a marine-blue, five-button jacket with a round, white-trimmed collar. The jacket was done up at the neck button and then hung open, except for where a buckle cinched the hem tightly around her hips. The outfit was elegant, and it made Sadie feel conspicuously drab in her beige, sleeveless shift.

"Mama! Auntie Hattie is here!" she shouted, and then led the woman by the hand down the hall.

"Damned hat. Hold on a second dear, let me just fix this. Sadie, you're not a beanpole. You're tall and elegant. And I don't know where you get your height from, your mama being such a pipsqueak."

"Just my luck I take after my papa, I guess. You know how popular us giant-girls are."

"Oh, come now. You're stunning and regal-looking. And you're not so tall a nice boy won't turn his eye your way. Just be patient, it doesn't always happen for everyone at the same time. Not that I would rush you into anything. To be frank, you're better off free as bird for the time being."

Sadie followed Hattie into the apartment, and hearing them enter, Rebecca poked her head around the corner of the door frame from her bedroom.

"Hattie, where's your little Bobby? I thought he was coming shopping with us."

"He says he's too big to be wasting his Sunday shopping with his mother. I couldn't even bribe him with the promise of a pickle, that's how grown up he thinks he is."

"Oh, what a shame. It's just you and me then."

"Sadie, you're not coming?"

"No, Auntie Hattie, I have some things to do around here, and a few errands of my own if I have some time."

"Oh no, here it starts, Rebecca. Our children — abandoning us already. Soon we'll be stuck with only our boring husbands."

"So what's your complaint now?" asked Rebecca.

"Well, Marty's a nice guy, and I do love him, don't get me wrong. But he's very traditional in his own way. It's a hard thing to shake when your father was a rabbi, I guess. Yes, it's true I have some time to write, but I still feel like ... I don't know ... like I'm his. I think it inhibits the quality of my work."

"Auntie Hattie, your writing is marvellous!" Sadie interjected.

"Thank you, sweetheart, you're a doll." Rebecca grabbed her coat and put it on, and gave Hattie's hat back to her, indicating they wouldn't be lingering.

"See you in a few hours, sweetheart. I'll be coming back with your papa — I'm picking him up from the doctor; he's getting his heart checked again for the pains, and they're giving him some more medicine. Unless of course he drops dead beside me on the way home."

"Rebecca!"

"It's just a joke."

"Some joke." Hattie pulled her out into the hall, and the door clacked shut behind them.

Sadie looked at the clock as she listened to their conversation fade down the stairs. It was four o'clock. There was a full half-hour to fill before they would arrive. If she had known her mother would leave so soon, she would have said three forty-five, and not cut it so close at the other end. She went about the apartment to find things to tidy up, making herself busy for a while before going to change.

In the bedroom she shared with her sister, she put on another pair of underwear and chose a waist-length, sleeveless, striped cotton brassiere with a low, rounded neckline and front-button opening, and a matching pair of knickers with a drawstring waist. Then she went into her parents' room and untied a bow from one of her mother's hats. She unwound it from the hat's bulbous crown and tied it loosely about her hips in the current style. Using her mother's vanity, she applied some rouge and some lipstick, a little too quickly, she realized, then spent a few minutes touching up her mistakes.

A knock at the door caused her to jump. "Coming!" she called, then thought to check, "Who is it?" and waited until Dora whispered harshly to let her in.

Dora tumbled in and looked at the clock. She brought her hand to her chest to indicate her lack of air.

"I told him to come exactly on time, not a minute later, not a second sooner, and I think I saw him downstairs lurking about as I ran in."

"Why didn't you come up with him like you're supposed to?"

"Oh don't worry, honey, he'll be up any minute. I was a little early and I didn't want to stay outside in the sun. It's not good for my complexion. Are you ready?"

"As I'll ever be."

"You look fine, honey. Isn't it getting any easier?"

"No. But I'll be okay. I just have three more to go, and then I'll have as much as I need. Two more after today. Is he young or old this time, Auntie Dora?"

"You're lucky this time. He's young. Not bad looking, I think, though I didn't get that good a look at him."

"Thank God."

"I hear him coming. Go into the other room."

Sadie moved stiffly into the bedroom, willing her shoulders to drop to a more relaxed level. She heard the door open and listened for Dora's greeting, a sudden drop in pitch to a level of sultriness that reminded her of melted chocolate.

"Well, hello. Come on in, handsome." One could almost hear her eyebrow lifting.

Sadie felt the bile rising in her stomach. Her face felt clammy, and when she glanced in the mirror, she saw that it was a white mask with rouge and lipstick sitting on top, hideous, garish streaks that traitorously accentuated her pallor instead of hiding it. She swallowed and held her breath to settle the queasiness.

This was the hardest part. Figuring out how to push through the nausea to dissemble interest, never mind attraction. But she had the necessary images already fixed in her mind. She was almost ready. First an exhale, then a few deep breaths. She closed her eyes.

"Camille! Come on out! You have company, dear!" Dora's voice cut into her meditation.

She got up, smoothed out the wrinkles in her under-clothes. The smile she mustered felt like a hollow attempt at excitement. When she opened the door, she grabbed hold of both sides of the frame and canted her hips slightly. The puzzled look on Dora's face confirmed how awkwardly she had executed her entrance.

"Hello. How are you? My name's Camille." She extended her hand, but remembered halfway up that she should be offer-ing her knuckles for a kiss, not her palm for a shake. The resulting movement was confusing, looking as it did more like an intricate greeting from some secret society. The man who stood there, more a boy it seemed, hesitated a moment, leav-ing Sadie's hand hovering, waiting for its kiss.

He looked no older than sixteen, and Sadie could see immediately this was his first time. She wondered if his father was waiting downstairs in the street. He was clean shaven, and his hair was reddish brown and combed back with a part down the side, slick and perfect from the assis-tance, by the looks of it, of some petroleum jelly. The tip of his nose was pug-like, and his nostrils twitched a little with his attempt to smile. His youth showed its freshness in the skin of his hands, in their smoothness, and in the elasticity of his cheeks.

With a jerky motion, he realized what to do and took Sadie's fingers, pecking her knuckles quickly, perhaps afraid he might be scolded if he didn't do as was expected.

"Pleased to meet you, I'm Cecil."

He was dressed neatly, but in clothes that were somewhat ragged. His jacket had frayed pockets and his shirt collar was threadbare, but they were both well pressed. The black shoes had recently been polished, but not enough to cover some deep scoring in the toe. The sole on the right shoe was peeling back slightly.

Sadie glanced quickly at Dora, who smiled and said, "You two kids have a good time, now!" as she ushered them into the bedroom and closed the door before they could say whether or not they would.

Sadie and Cecil stood smiling weakly at one another, until she took matters in hand and moved him toward the bed. Best to get this over with, was her thought, no point in prolonging the torture. By the panicked look on the boy's face, it appeared his sentiments were much the same.

She stood beside him, still holding his hand. She towered over him by at least four inches, and so she could see the dandruff flakes on his scalp where his hair parted. She closed her eyes again briefly. Her stomach was still jumpy.

"Let me take off your clothes," she offered.

"Um, no, that's okay. I can do it myself." He pulled away quickly, and turned around shyly to remove his jacket. Sadie pulled off her top as he fumbled with his buttons.

Once they were both undressed, she looked him over. Thank God, hairless, she thought. Much cleaner. He stood there, scrawny and tense, waiting. Sadie lay down and pulled him over top of her. He draped himself clumsily over her body and groped mechanically at her breasts. She could feel his hardness already searching. Because of the height difference, he was too far up. Then she felt his hips pull down below hers to try a different angle. She adjusted them to offer some help, braced herself, and closed her eyes.

As he entered her, Sadie compelled herself to push off, lift up and out of herself, to journey far from the tiny room. She controlled her breathing, until the up and down of him became only the up and down of her chest, synchronized with the tides of the air, until there was only up and up, pushing and pulling the currents of her imagination.

She was light as dust, free to settle here a moment, then be blown there the next. No, even better, she was the wind itself, going where she pleased and carrying with her what she needed, what she wanted, leaving behind the rest to swirl in eddies just above the ground.

She saw her building from up high above, helped a bird fly by overhead by blowing upward under its wings. She did this in mid-glide, causing the delighted creature to suddenly rise to a new plane. She reached into a chimney-top and pulled out some smoke, then twisted it into a swirl between her fingers.

The tenements sparkled in the glow of the August sun, the streets were a lattice-work of human activity, lively and exciting, the uneven rows of pushcarts were the vines snaking here and there. She swooped down and blew on the face of Mr. Zussel, the kind old fish merchant she had known since she was a child, cooling his forehead where sweat beaded. He was standing outside his new shop across the street.

He looked up and winked at her. My little Sadeleh, he smiled, recognizing her despite her disembodiment. So big now you think you're the wind? I knew you when you were not so much bigger than a chicken leg, so don't be thinking you're so high and mighty now.

She blew on his cheek again and flew off, over to Greenwich Village, to the literary café she had read about in the *Daily Forward*, breezed in the window to sit cross-legged on the floor. Why couldn't she be the wind and also sit cross-legged if she wanted?

Little tables dotted the room, barely big enough to hold a few teacups and a candle. Men and women sat and sipped quietly, their attention turned to the words of an undiscovered poet. His words floated to her ears and filled her heart with gladness, inspired sighs from the cultured crowd. They were enchanted with the simple pleasure of contemplation.

She drifted out of the café, pulled herself free of Manhattan to the hills and valleys of Pennsylvania, wafted down to the grass below, became human again. She pressed her face softly against the skin of a calf as his lips puckered onto his mother's teat. She could feel the sun warm her hair and she breathed in wildflower sweetness, forget-me-nots, lobelia, clover.

Dandelion made her chin butter.

Some spores fluttered by and tickled her eyelids, and a light rain began to fall. It cooled her skin. She stuck out her tongue to capture its refreshing mist...

"Miss Camille?"

She opened her eyes slowly.

The boy was lying beside her on the bed, looking at her strangely.

"Um, I'm ... well, done. I guess."

"Yes, of course. I'm sorry. I was just letting the moment last."

"Miss Camille, can I ask you a question?"

"Of course," she said, gathering the sheets about her.

"My friend says you girls aren't afraid to talk about these things, so I thought I could ask you ..."

"It's okay. Go on."

"Is it always ... Do people get to, after a while ... Um, I guess what I'm trying to say is, it's no offence to you, you're real pretty and everything, but ... My dad told me it's real different when you're with a real girl. That it's much better. He says it's the best feeling a guy can have. Only, it didn't really feel much different to me."

"How did it feel?"

"More like, I don't know ... I felt pretty nervous I guess, all except my peter, which was sorta off on its own down there, and that sure was pretty great." He laughed nervously, then sat and thought for a second. " I guess what I'm saying is, it was nice and everything, but ... it wasn't the way I expected, is all." He looked away from her. "You're the first gal I been with."

Sadie started to laugh. "I think it gets easier, if that's what you're asking."

He smiled shyly and looked down. "You're making fun of me."

"No, not at all. It's just, to tell you the truth, I don't know what it's supposed to feel like for boys." She looked at him. His eyes were still on the bed sheets. "Also, maybe I'm not the right girl for you. You know, maybe I'm not your type."

"I don't know what my type is."

"Well, give yourself time. I'm sure you'll figure it out."

"Yeah, I guess so." He looked at her. "You're nice. Can I ask you another question?"

"Sure, go ahead."

"Is your name really Camille?"

"No. But I'd rather not say my real name, if you don't mind. Is your name really Cecil?"

He giggled. "Yeah, it's Cecil. You live here?"

"Yes I do."

"Is that the gal who just crossed the Atlantic up there on the wall? What does it say there?"

"It says, 'The Lady Lindy, the female Charles Lindberg, gives speaking tour: 20 hours. 40 minutes, Our Flight in the Friendship'. That's my kid sister's. She's been collecting stuff about her. She says Miss Earhart is going to be the first woman to cross the Atlantic some day, not just be the first woman passenger. My sister wants to be a pilot too. Or a writer. She can't decide which."

"Where's your sister now?"

"At work. She has a job uptown, and she goes to night school still."

"She must be smart."

"Yeah, she is."

"I'd like to be a pilot too," he looked down, embarrassed, "or a train conductor, but my dad says I can't do that. So I'm going to study hard and see if I can go to college to be an engineer."

"An engineer? Why?"

"It's what my father tells me I have to do 'cause I'm real good in math. That and marry Kathleen McCardle."

"Is she that difficult to figure out?" She made him blush. "I'm sorry. Is she nice?"

"Nice enough, I guess. We all grew up together. Her brother Dexter and me are friends. But I don't really love her. Maybe she's just not my type. I prefer this other girl, from my class at school."

"Oh. I'm sorry."

"Yeah. Well, I guess I should get dressed and not waste any more of your time."

"It's okay, really."

They got up from the bed and wordlessly pulled on their clothes, their backs to one another. Sadie buttoned up her shirt and fixed her hair.

Cecil turned around, and held out some money. "Here. Thanks a lot."

She took it quickly, counted it, then stuffed it into a small wooden box that she pulled out of the dresser.

"Good luck with everything, Cecil. I hope you figure things out."

"Camille?"

"Yes?"

"Can we get together again sometime? Not to do this. But just to talk ... maybe?"

She smiled at him. "We'll see."

He turned the knob and opened the door to the kitchen. "I kept you too long. I see your next appointment is already here waiting."

"What? No, no, that's just ..." She stepped into the doo frame, and the rest of her sentence caught in her throat.

She was staring at her parents.

Her father's left hand squeezed the chair back so tightly that she heard it creak. She had never seen a look like that on her father's face before, though she had not been a stranger to his temper. Perhaps the complication of pain mixed with anger was momentarily diluting the pure vermilion of blind fury. Perhaps her own horror was being reflected in her father's face, a primal mimicking being his most immediate response in the absence of any emotional compass.

Whatever its meaning, the look only lasted a few seconds, until her mother drew her hands to her mouth, covering all but her eyes. By the time Sadie looked back at her father, his face was already changing to the more familiar one, the colour rising in his jowls. Rebecca reached out to his arm, but her hand was slapped away.

"I don't know who you are," he said to Cecil, his sentence a spring being coiled ever tighter with each word, "but you have five seconds to get out of this apartment."

"Papa, Mama, I ..."

Her father slammed his hand down on the table, causing them to gasp. Cecil bolted out the door.

"I don't want to hear. I don't need to hear! You are a filthy whore!" He turned to Rebecca, and said in a low voice, "Just like your mother."

Rebecca jerked back and stood off against the wall. Sadie looked to her mother, but her expression had changed. Her eyes were fixed on a point somewhere in the corner of the room. The look of terror retreated to somewhere else, leaving her mother's face rigid and glassy, her jaw slightly slack. A polished turtle shell. Her hands clenched and unclenched, tugging and releasing some material at her thighs.

"You won't find support from your mother on this, Sadie. She knows there's nothing to say now. You were a daughter to us, but no more." Tears streamed down his face. "You do not exist any more for this family. Pack your things and get out of this apartment, and never set foot here again."

"Mama?" Sadie's voice was a faint echo, barely reaching her own ears.

Rebecca didn't move. Her father went to hold the door open. "Take some things, and go!"

Sadie jumped and went quickly into her bedroom. She gathered some clothes and stuffed them into a small, canvas bag. She retrieved the wooden box, emptied her earnings into her jacket pocket, and pulled the jacket on clumsily. She saw in the mirror that her collar was twisted, but she didn't stop to straighten it. There was no time to write her sister a note, and no paper anyhow. Surely her mother would tell Anna what had happened. She would write later maybe. There was no time to figure all of this out, there would be time later. Where was Dora anyway? Why on earth had she left the apartment?

She emerged from the bedroom again. Her mother was still standing there, scrunching up and releasing the front of her dress, her eyes turned away. Sadie moved to hug her, but Rebecca's body shuddered slightly as she approached, just perceptible enough to cause her to pull back. Her father was standing at the door holding it open.

She looked down at the floor as she walked by him, afraid to catch his eye.

Once outside the apartment, she stood still and heard the door close behind her. Her legs buckled, and her body fell back against it, sliding down to the floor in the hallway.

From inside, she could just make out the sound of her father's voice. High and plaintive, it was chanting the rhythmic cadences of the prayer for the dead.

Chapter Eighteen

1983

Anna stroked her sister's hair while she fumbled to pull a hand-kerchief out of her purse. But when she went to wipe Sadie's cheeks she was surprised to find them dry.

"Oh," she said, withdrawing it to rub against her own face. "I guess I'm the one who needs this."

Sadie looked up at her. "Now do you know why I never came back? And why I never wrote you after those first few let-ters? I never heard back from you."

"I never got your letters, Sadie."

"I suspected as much."

"You thought I got your letters and didn't write back?"

"It was a possibility."

"Sadie, I hope you believe me — I would've written if I'd known where to write. I swear. It would've been an angry let-ter, but I swear I would've written."

"Angry?"

"I thought you'd run off. Selfishly, without even offering to take me with you. And to not even tell me you were leaving? Not even leave me an address to reach you at? It made me feel like ... like I was ... an annoyance. I thought maybe I was part of what you were running away from."

"Running away from you? Why on earth would I do that?"

"I don't know. Because I was a part of your past. I was your kid sister — who wants their kid sister around when they're running off to a life of freedom?"

"Some life of freedom."

"Whatever happened, it couldn't have been worse than staying."

"What makes you so sure?"

"With what happened to you here, it would've been worse to stay."

"Well, you're right, it wasn't worse, but it could've been. My life here was awful. Even before any of that stuff with Bobby happened. Remember how Mama was always nagging you that you could be just like her friend Hattie if you applied yourself more, a big writer just like her? Well, she never even thought to mention anything like that to me. It never once occurred to her that I might have had some aspirations of my own. No, for me, she was happy enough that I should just be there with her keeping her company."

"You see, it just goes to show you — I was jealous that you got to spend so much time with her," Anna said. It was an envy so strong she was ashamed of how long its bitter aftertaste lingered in her mouth. Even now, knowing what had happened to Sadie didn't seem to wash it out.

"You wouldn't have been if you'd known what it was like. You know, I can't say I blame her for wanting me there when I think of how her life was. It was pretty miserable and lonely, so I must have been company to her, and some kind of protection from being alone with Papa. But did you know she used to use me as a sounding board to plan strategies to deal with him? It was just too much of a burden. Even though I wholeheartedly played along with it because I couldn't stand Papa. But it was inappropriate. Mama had no sense of what was appropriate and what wasn't. Maybe under normal circumstances she would have, but when it affected her directly, her perspective was completely skewed by her own predicament."

"Well, can you blame her? Think of what she put up with."

"You know what? I blame her. Not for her own situation, but for not thinking past herself to what *I* might have wanted from *my* life, to how she could help me a little bit. Like maybe allow me a little freedom to prepare myself for something more than just marriage! And the fact that her own marriage was so terrible only made it more obvious how selfish she was in keeping me trapped there, you know? Unable to prepare for anything else? Maybe she didn't know to what lengths I would have been willing to go to help us find a way out, all of us together, if only she'd asked me."

"I'm not defending her. I'm just saying, she probably thought showing her love for you was enough." It would have been enough for me, she thought.

"Who knows? But if that's what she believed, well, it sure as hell *wasn't* enough, as it turned out. What did all that love amount to, in the end? She stood there. She just stood there, while Papa kicked me out of the house. She wouldn't even hug me. Some way to show her love."

"She was too scared."

"Of course she was. But so were we."

She remembered: a flicker of candlelight dancing on the floor, just visible from there under the bed, Sadie's tiny thigh pressed against hers, her arm over her back hugging them close, until the noises would stop in the other room.

"What happened to you after you left?" Anna asked.

"I left the building and sat with my bag on the front stoop. I waited for Dora, but she never came back that day. I must have been crying there for a half hour, when Mr. Zussel, the old fish peddler, came across the street from his store.

"He sat down with me and asked me what was wrong. I didn't want to tell him at first, but he kept pressing me. So I broke down and told him I had been thrown out of the house and disowned, but I wouldn't talk about why. He took me into his big arms and squeezed my head to his shoulder." Sadie paused to imitate the movement, making a wide arc that closed in on herself in a hug.

"He said I could stay with him as long as I needed. When I asked him why he was being so nice to me, when we'd always been so terrible to him, he said, and I'll never forget this, Anna, he said, 'You know, my little Sadie,'" she wagged her finger like he had, "'I'm no fool. I know people they make fun of me, they think I'm a ridiculous old man. But you want to know a secret? I play it up. It's good for business. Many people they like it, and so I play it up a little, you know?'

"He said he'd known our family for more than thirty years, he even knew Mama when she was a little girl, and Bubbe and Zayde too. Then he said, 'It doesn't matter you're not my best customers. That's business, this is life. Life is more important than making a buck, you should never forget this,' he said.

"I told him my life was ruined — I'd lost my family, everything. But he wouldn't accept that. He told me not to be so quick to presume fate, and that sometimes families aren't who we expected them to be."

"Well, that's for sure," said Anna. Her words were a little more caustic than she had intended. Her own family, the one she'd created herself, hadn't been so bad, after all.

"Well, of course it's true, but at the time all I was thinking was there was no way he could understand what I was going through, and I told him so. He took my hands in his, like this, and said, 'Let me tell you a little something about old Zussel. I myself was disowned when I was your age. When life deals you a blow like that, you do what you need to so that it doesn't strike you again. You can even strike back.'

"I remember exactly what he said because of how his eyes bored into me. I have this vision of his bushy eyebrows coming together, like he was trying to tell me something more with them than he could say. It was one of those moments when you know that someone is telling you all they can and you don't dare ask for details. So you fixate on what's been said, on the exact words, trying to figure out if you missed some clue. He told me I should come with him and we'd figure out what to do."

"And did you go?"

"Well, at first I objected, of course. I told him I couldn't impose on him, but he wouldn't hear of it. He told me he didn't have a lot, but that he had a sofa to sleep on, and enough fish to feed me until I decided what to do next. He kept insisting until I said he couldn't tell anyone if I did. I made him promise absolutely to never say a word to Mama and Papa. He was reluctant about that, but in the end, he swore it would be our secret."

Anna shook her head in amazement. "So, Zussel took you in."

"For almost two months. He lived alone in a small apartment on West 4th Street. A simple place with some nice old pieces of furniture. A bedroom, a kitchen-living room, and a toilet, that was it. He let me use his bed, he stayed on the sofa.

"He had an old portrait on his bedside table, of a very handsome young man whom he told me was 'my David.' At the time I was so absorbed with my own problems that I never even thought to ask who exactly it was. I just assumed that it was his son, but a few years later when I was thinking back on it, I realized it might just as well have been his lover. Zussel must have been seventy already at the time. Who knows how long before then that the portrait was taken. I guess I'll never know for sure, but I'd bet money on it. It's the only thing that makes sense."

Anna chuckled softly. "I can't *believe* we never knew any of this! Well, I'll be damned if that man wasn't a guardian angel to all of us." She could see him winking at her, how he couldn't really do it without closing both eyes. It always made her smile.

"What do you mean?"

"After Papa died, Mama went to work for him. We were desperate — down to our last penny, and my job was barely supporting us. He gave Mama a job when nobody else would. And when he passed away, he left *everything* he had to us!"

"Everything?"

"His storefront, his business, everything. If he hadn't helped us, I don't know what we would've done. Mama ran Zussel's Fresh Fish until she retired. That store kept us alive. She moved it around the corner when they took the buildings down across the street, she opened a poultry section. In sixty-eight, she sold the storefront and invested the money to pay for her retirement. The place has changed hands a few times since then, but you can see where it was, it's where that Caribbean roti place is now, just around the corner."

Sadie's face showed her amazement. "I had no idea. I never kept in touch with him after I left New York. But you know what? It shouldn't surprise me. He had a heart bigger than a city block, that man, and we never appreciated it when we were growing up, did we? We just used to make fun of him, remember?"

"Yes, we were horrible. But then Mama set a bad example for us in that regard. She used to tease him mercilessly, especially when she was with one of her friends. Speaking of which, what ever happened to Dora? We never saw her after you left. Mama said they'd had a falling out."

"Well, while I was staying with Zussel, I got in touch with her to tell her what happened. Of course, she hadn't dared to contact Mama and Papa, and so she wondered what had happened to me."

"But where did she go that day? Why did she leave you alone in the apartment?"

"She went to do errands, she said. When she returned, she saw them coming toward the building and, like the coward that she was, she just ran off. Later, I think a few days after I contacted her, Mama went to her to demand to know where I'd gone. She figured out that Dora must have been involved with it all somehow, but I had made Dora promise not to say where I was, so she told Mama I was okay, but that was all she would tell her.

"You see, by then I knew I could call the shots, because she felt so guilty when I told her what happened that she agreed to everything I asked. She even convinced Shiny to give me some money. He gave me enough to pay for the abortion, and enough to pay for a train ticket to Toronto, where he had a business associate who would help me out. He promised there'd be money every month while I stayed with this guy, the deal being they would help me out until I could get a job and get back on my feet.

"I contacted the abortion doctor through Dora, and he came to Zussel's place to do it there. Zussel closed down his store for a few days and stayed home with me. You know how women used to die from botched jobs. This doctor was okay, but Zussel was there to make sure nothing happened to me. I was lucky — I didn't have any complications, but I honestly don't know what I would have done without Zussel.

"The day I left for Toronto, he packed me some smoked fish, bought me some sausage and a few pickles, and wrapped them up for me for the train ride. Then he pressed twenty dollars into my fist, which for him, back then, was a fortune. I told him I couldn't take it, and that I didn't need it anyway because Shiny had given me his guilt money.

"But he wouldn't hear of taking it back. He said to me, 'That other money is for you to survive. This is so that you can live,' and then I started bawling like a baby there on the train station platform."

Now Sadie needed a tissue for her eyes. Anna handed over her soggy handkerchief. She thought of her own goodbyes over the years — how many there had been, how robbed she felt, given how few people there were left.

"What a sweet, sweet old man," said Sadie. "More mitzvahs in two months than most people do in a lifetime. To think I'm as old now as he was then."

She sniffled, wiped her nose dry, and then cleared her throat to continue. "So, I went to Toronto and stayed with Shiny's business associate. It was one of his booze suppliers, a guy named Charlie Crenshaw. He lived in a big house with special quarters above the garage for his maid. Prohibition and the strange loopholes in Canadian law had made him a rich man. I moved into one of his many guest rooms, but it became clear really fast that he didn't just see me as a guest. He kept groping me any chance he could get, tried to invite himself into my bedroom, thank God there was a lock on that door. He never forced himself on me, but I had to do some fancy foot-work to keep him away."

"So you and he never ..."

"No, no. At least not then we didn't. He just let it be known he could make it worth my while and, in the meantime, gener-ally made things very uncomfortable. I put up with it because I didn't have anywhere else to go. To prove to me that he could help me, he used his contacts to get me a job in a garment fac-tory, and I have to tell you: that was no small miracle, since the Depression had hit Toronto just as hard as everywhere else.

"I earned enough money at that job that I had the means to move out of Crenshaw's place, if I could find a place to share with some girls from the factory. I wanted to start night school. Do all the things I couldn't do in New York."

"So Dora and Shiny must have cut you off, I guess."

"No. I still needed their money. The problem was, they were sending it through to Crenshaw, so I couldn't lie to them without his help. One night, before I moved out, after I had managed to fend off Crenshaw and was lying in bed crying, I thought of what Mr. Zussel said to me — about not letting life strike you twice. All those people — Dora, Shiny, Crenshaw — I don't know why it took me so long to admit to myself how awful they were. But once I did, I found there was an anger inside of me so fierce it was threatening to boil over and spoil everything. If I didn't do something with it, all my hopes for a better life would be drowned. I had to find a way to channel the anger. It seemed like I was trapped again — different city, different circumstances, but the same trap. So that night, I decided the only way to make things better was to stop feeling sorry for myself. And spring a trap of my own."

Chapter Nineteen

Miss Sadie Kalish
355 Palmerston Avenue
Toronto, Ontario

June 16th, 1932

Hand Delivered to:
Mr. & Mrs. Bud Parker
38 Grace Court,
Brooklyn Heights, New York

Dear Auntie Dora and Uncle Shiny,

Thank you, as always, for the money you sent through to Mr. Crenshaw. As you know, the economic situation here in Toronto continues to worsen, with job prospects even fewer and bread lines even longer. The depression has hit us hard, as I imagine it has done in New York.

I understand, from the long talks Mr. Crenshaw and I sometimes have, that the depression has affected demand and caused you all to focus your business, concentrating on a few special relationships to ensure the supply and demand stay carefully matched. How lucky it is that you and Mr. Crenshaw have one of these partnerships. But I understand your arrangement for transportation through Quebec is not working quite so well anymore.

You are probably surprised I know so much about the trade, since I have barely ever written about it before, but after living with Mr. Crenshaw for two years, one picks up things here and there. Why, just the other day, I overheard Mr. Crenshaw talking with you, Uncle Shiny, on the telephone, while you were arranging to shift your operations from the St. Lawrence River to St. Pierre-Miquelon. I understand that what with the busy customs activity along the St. Lawrence, St. Pierre-Miquelon is the place to be these days, even though it is more expensive.

How smart of the two of you! Well, what else could you do? I am constantly hearing Mr. Crenshaw talking of the "shrinking prospects of business that relies on the St. Lawrence corridor" and of having to make some difficult but necessary business decisions. I am assuming this is the combined effect of the depression's hitting New York customers hard and the effects of the Canadian government's having put an end, two years ago, to the granting of clearances to boats headed for New York State. Whatever the reason, you are smart to plan to shift your operations. Isn't Mr.

Crenshaw your only supplier here in Canada? If the St. Lawrence isn't working out, well then, by golly, you have to find another place to do business, and that's all there is to it.

I am sorry I did not say hello the other day. I asked Mr. Crenshaw to speak with you, but he was annoyed at me for interrupting his call and ushered me out of the room. I think he was cross that I was listening in. But how am I to know what is private? First he tells me all about his business, then the next moment he gets anxious. He should know I am not going to tell anyone. I'm very discreet and I understand what is at stake — am I not sending this letter via one of the shipments instead of through the mails?

Anyhow, enough business talk, you must tire of it even when it brings you money — you don't need me to chatter on about it at length, do you? Speaking of tiring, I am trying to remain cheerful here about the lack of job prospects, but it is difficult. I know I keep saying it, but I wouldn't be making it were it not for your help and Mr. Crenshaw's. I do hope you'll visit soon. It's been two years, and you haven't once come to Toronto. It's really quite a beautiful city, and Mr. Crenshaw's house is enormous. There is more than enough room for you to stay. I'm sure he would like it as much as I would, so please consider it. Toronto in July is hot, but not as hot as New York. It might be a welcome relief from the humidity.

Love,
Sadie

Mr. & Mrs. Bud Parker
38 Grace Court,
Brooklyn Heights, New York

July 6th, 1932

Miss Sadie Kalish
355 Palmerston Avenue
Toronto, Ontario

Dear Sadie,

We received your letter in good health and with great interest. I am sorry that things in Toronto continue to be so bleak, on the job front. Your Uncle Shiny says matters are bound to pick up one of these days, and you shouldn't lose heart.

We have decided you are right — it has been too long since we have seen one another. We have therefore decided to come to Toronto to visit on Tuesday the 19th, in two weeks time. But I must ask you a favor, my dear: Do not, under any circumstances, mention to Mr. Crenshaw that we are coming. But you could, if you're able dear, find some way to make sure he's home that morning. Shiny, who you know is fond of practical jokes, says he wants to give his old friend a start. Let's hope the man doesn't have a heart condition!

We'll be taking the overnight train and arriving at Union Station at nine o'clock. Don't come to pick us up or you'll ruin the surprise. We'll check into the hotel, and then take a taxi to the house and see you there at ten-thirty.

Won't it be nice to see each other again, dear?

Love,
Auntie Dora

It had taken Sadie the whole day to feign the onset of illness, beginning with her wearing an extra layer of clothing so that she would sweat more than usual in the summer heat. At ten o'clock in the morning, she began to mop her brow with a dazed and somewhat worried expression, until someone asked her what was the matter. She denied any problem until after lunch, when she admitted to her friend Julia that she was feel-ing a tad faint. But it was a staged confession for the benefit of others within earshot — Julia lived on the same floor of her Annex rooming house and was in on the ploy.

Her friend offered to switch places with her so that she would be facing the wall and could discreetly unbutton the top button of her shirt, but Sadie told her that she was a little chilled and wanted to keep her shirt done up. At three o'clock, she began closing her eyes frequently and holding them shut for a few seconds; of course, she stopped her sewing while she did so, breathing deeply to control the nausea.

Julia's performance that afternoon had been clever, strik-ing just the right balance between concern and skepticism. Her call the next morning, on the landlord's phone, to get Sadie excused from work, was less polished. She told their boss Sadie was running a fever of one hundred and two, but also mentioned that there was throwing up and greenish skin and foul breath, details Sadie had found unnecessarily vivid. No matter, their boss had agreed she could have the day off, and phase one was accomplished.

Now it was up to her alone to carry it through. She reread the letter from Dora for at least the fifth time that hour, just to make extra certain that she had the right time, and, more or less secure now that every last detail was taken care of, she stopped to look at herself in the shiny chrome siding of the hardware store on Bloor Street. The scarf on her face had shifted somewhat to the back; it needed to be pulled down a little more over her face. If she were spotted out on a day she had called in sick, she would surely lose her job, and then she would be nowhere. The job shortages had made people merciless, the prevailing attitude being: if you're not pulling your weight for the economy, there are ten others waiting to work harder.

She wiped the chrome wall of the hardware store to see better, scratched at the edge of her lip where some lipstick had bled slightly beyond the lipline, then retied the scarf tightly under her chin and moved on. Her walk was brisk and determined, but did little to quell her nervous stomach. Why did her nerves always travel straight to her stomach? Just for once she wished she could get a sore back or a headache or something.

On Palmerston Avenue, she leaned against one of the street lamps a block north of Mr. Crenshaw's house to catch her breath and compose herself one last time. Again, she reviewed the plan and all its contingencies, and then, satisfied as she knew she would ever be, she walked up to the door and rapped.

Crenshaw looked slightly annoyed when he answered. Their arrangement was weekly visits on Friday nights, not Tuesday mornings.

"Sadie. What's going on? I had to cancel all my morning meetings, so I hope this is important. You haven't been fired, have you?"

"No — I called in sick. I just need to talk to you. Can I come in?"

"Of course — come in. I'll have Bernice get you some tea if you'd like."

"Thank you. That would be nice."

She sat in the living room and waited for the maid to bring her a cup. She glanced anxiously at the clock on the mantel. It said ten-thirty. If they were prompt, she had arrived at just the right moment.

"So, are you going to tell me what's up?" he said, sitting down next to her.

"Can I use the washroom?" she asked, and she got up hastily, just as his arm was descending around her shoulders.

"You know where it is."

She ran up to the second floor and sat down on the toilet seat. Damn. Where were they? She had only been there a few moments, but she couldn't bring herself to make small talk, not today, and especially with Crenshaw irked at having cancelled his meetings. Just her luck, for the first time ever, he was more interested in her life than in his own needs, and now she needed to divert that line of questioning.

Mercifully, the doorbell rang a few moments later. She took a deep breath and went downstairs.

Crenshaw was moving to the door, muttering under his breath because he could see through the window who it was.

"Parker! What the hell are you doing in Toronto?"

"Aren't you going to invite us in?" Shiny asked. There was no handshake.

"Yes, yes. Come in. Sadie and I were just sitting down for some tea. I had some meetings this morning, but I cancelled them."

"Well, wasn't that a lucky coincidence." Shiny unbuttoned his navy blazer.

"Yes, a very lucky coincidence." He looked back at Sadie suspiciously. She smiled, but stayed back near the staircase.

"You should have called to tell me you were arriving, Parker."

"Oh, I thought a surprise would be appropriate, under the circumstances."

Dora was fidgety. She handed her handbag to Bernice and walked past Crenshaw towards Sadie.

"Sadie, my dear, you look just fantastic. Toronto's treating you well."

She leaned in to hug her, but Sadie kept her body tight and her arms at her side.

Dora seemed even more flustered by Sadie's aloofness.

Shiny said, "Dora dear, let's get on with this, shall we?"

"Get on with what?" Crenshaw asked.

"Drop the act, Crenshaw, you know why we're here."

"I don't know what you're talking about."

"You thought you could just cut me out without talking to me? Is that how you do business now? I'm a steady customer for fifteen years, and now you go and make a deal without even talking to me? Did you think I was just going to take it lying down? You know you're my only Canadian supplier."

Crenshaw took a cigar out of his pocket and snipped off the tip.

"Parker, there's been a misunderstanding. Surely we can discuss this like gentlemen. Let's go into the other room."

Shiny didn't budge. "I wanna know about St. Pierre-Miquelon." He pronounced it Saint Pee-air-Mikwa-lawn. "What, didn't you think I could get trucks to the Maine coast just as easy as I did for New York? Or Vermont? A transport's a transport, Crenshaw. It's a simple matter — St. Lawrence or Atlantic, it's all the same thing."

Crenshaw laughed and twirled the edges of his moustache into points. "It's not the same thing. And the fact that you don't know that means I've made the right decision. I'm not risking losing all my business — the Atlantic is a dangerous operation. It takes someone with just the right connections. And St. Pierre-Miquelon is too expensive for me to continue squabbling with some cheapskate over prices."

"What squabbling? We negotiate. Is that so unusual?"

"Ah c'mon, Parker. You've been gouging me for years now. You weren't this cheap before you met your girlfriend here. You might as well just throw in the towel and convert, already. You do business like them; why not go all the way."

Dora laughed, a desperate little noise.

Shiny's features narrowed and reddened. "The market speaks for itself, Crenshaw. You don't read the papers? People aren't paying what they used to."

Again, Dora projected a desperate laugh. "Sadie, dear, why don't we go into the other room while the men talk business? We have so much to catch up on!"

"Stay right here, Dora. We're not staying long." Shiny grabbed her arm and pulled her back.

"Darling, you and Mr. Crenshaw can work this out, I know you can. You both need to just take big, deep breaths and start discussing terms in a calm, reasonable manner."

"There are no terms to discuss," said Crenshaw, lighting his cigar with a beautiful silver lighter. "Sorry, Parker, but you're not part of this deal. I was going to call you in a few days to tell you." Then, speaking through a puff, he said, "I'm gonna have Tretheway's head for flapping his lips."

"Damn it! Tretheway?" Shiny turned around and punched the door frame. "Damn him! Damn that bastard! Jeez, I should've known. Ever since that thing with him in Albany in '28, Dora, he's had it..."

"Wait a minute." Crenshaw took his cigar out and pointed it at Shiny. "If you didn't know it was Tretheway, who told you?"

"Things get back to me, it's none of your business," he said, buttoning his coat up again.

"I told him," Sadie said. She said it quietly, but everyone heard.

Crenshaw turned to her, and she saw his eyes widen for just a moment. It was rare that he allowed his composure to break.

"You. Huh. Well, isn't that interesting."

"It wasn't her fault, Mr. Crenshaw," Dora said, moving between them. "She didn't know it was a secret — she overheard you on the phone making the deal, and she just wrote to us, innocently. It was an innocent thing. She thought you were talking to *us*. You can see how she would've made that mistake."

"No, Auntie Dora, it wasn't a mistake, and it wasn't innocent. I knew exactly what I was doing."

"No, you didn't, honey."

"What?" Shiny said, shaking his head. "Would someone tell me, for chrissake, what the hell is going on here?"

"Yes, Auntie Dora. I knew Charlie wasn't speaking to Uncle Shiny. And I knew if I wrote to you, you would come to Toronto."

"Wait a minute," Shiny said, a slight smile creeping past the confusion on his face. "Not that I don't appreciate it, Sadie, sweetheart, but why didn't you just say so in the letter?"

"Because this is more satisfying. Seeing the three of you sweat."

The smile dropped from Shiny's face. Dora looked ashen.

"Sadie, honey, what's come over you?" Her lilting voice had an edge. She put a hand up to her chest and waited, mouth agape, for a response.

"Nothing's come over me. Except maybe the exhilaration a person gets when she's finally free."

Crenshaw was shaking his head, but she could see he was amused. He'd figured it out. Sadie was surprised it had taken him this long — he was usually smarter than that.

"You didn't have anything to talk to me about today, did you," he said. "You set all this up. The call to me this morning was so I would cancel my appointments. You called in sick to work so you could watch us squirm. What — did you find yourself a new arrangement?"

"You have a job?!" Shiny slapped the wall behind him. "Jesus! Since when?"

"Since about a month after I got here. And you know something else? I don't live here with Mr. Crenshaw either. I have a place of my own. *And* I've been going to school. *And* I'm going to have a real life — surround myself with people who care about me. Who *really* care about me. Who are willing to do things for me if I need them, just because it's the right thing to do, not because there's something in it for them."

Dora walked up to Sadie and slapped her, hard.

"You ungrateful little tramp. After all we've done for you!"

But Sadie stood her ground, stared Dora in the eye.

Ungrateful. She wanted to scream at Dora, what should she be grateful for? But she didn't shout. She just took a deep breath and stared at Dora, until Dora's own stare began to dissolve, showing edges of fear.

Sadie said, "I have nothing to be grateful for, except that I'm not like you, Auntie Dora. I don't corrupt people because my life is hollow and I need a laugh. And I don't use people because I'm a coward and I'm afraid to look back at where I came from, lest I should slide back down into my pathetic past."

"What are you talking about, darling. Please, you're getting hysterical."

"I'm speaking quite calmly, Auntie Dora. Why don't you tell them, Charlie? About how when I came here, alone in a new city, a guest in your home, about how instead of just doing a nice thing for someone in trouble, instead you tried to take advantage of me? But then, I'm sure that's pretty much what they expected anyway. I'll bet you even talked about it before I got here."

"Listen, Sadie," Crenshaw said, "don't try to make it seem like you were some innocent little girl. I know all about what happened in New York. And besides, you'd be nowhere if it weren't for me."

"Am I supposed to thank you for that? For letting you help me when my alternative was to live here like someone's mistress? There isn't one thing you did for me that you didn't do without personal gain. You had a cut of Shiny's monthly cheque, and, don't forget, you had *me* — every Friday for two years. Sure, you kept your mouth shut and didn't tell them I moved out and got a job, but it sure as hell cost me. Just in case you're not getting the message, sleeping with you was not a pleasure. You're a goddamned pig is what you are, Charlie Crenshaw."

"Jesus, Crenshaw," said Shiny, "got any other knives you want to stick in my back? What the hell did I ever do to you? You weren't happy with our arrangement, you shoulda come talk to me. Instead, you double-cross me just so you can keep fucking some girl every week?"

"I'm a businessman, Parker. I see a good opportunity, I don't pass it up. It's nothing personal. The way I look at it, the cut I took after Sadie moved out almost made it worthwhile to do business with you. Almost. Obviously, you know now I'm looking elsewhere."

Shiny's fists were clenched at his side, shaking. "I've had just about enough of this." He turned to Sadie and pointed his finger. "And you! You conniving little bitch. If you think you can take advantage of me and get away with it, you got another think coming. You think Crenshaw's the only one I know in Toronto? You're gonna regret you did this."

Sadie didn't move, even though his finger was almost touching her nose.

"No, I'm not."

"Oh, you don't think so? You're finished here, Sadie. Finished."

"Yes, I am," she answered. "But before I go, I just want to mention one thing. You see, thanks to Charlie, I know pretty much everything about your operations, both of you. You know, pillow talk. So, if anything happens to me, the letters I've written — the three letters I've left with a trusted friend — they'll be put in the mail. One will go to the New York City Police, the second to the Canadian Customs Authority, and the third to the United States Coast Guard. So, I think you'll agree it's in your interest to walk away from this. 'Cause even if you think your fancy lawyers can keep you out of jail this time, Uncle Shiny — and I must say, with the information I've put in those letters, I'd be very impressed — but even if they do, Charlie here, and his Toronto friends, are gonna be real mad at you. Real mad. So why don't you just look at this as an opportunity. Sure, I tricked you into coming to Toronto, and I've taken some of your money, but it's babkas and you know it. I've given you a chance to save your business. When I walk out of here, you can work things out with Charlie, or you can leave, it's your choice."

And before waiting to see if they had anything else to say, she walked slowly past them and out the door. The three of them just stood there, Crenshaw chuckling softly to himself, and the other two just plain stunned that finally, she was striking back at life.

Chapter Twenty

1983

Anna took hold of her sister's hand and felt her firmly gripping back. The triumphant ending to Sadie's story seemed
more bitter than sweet in the weak illumination of the bedside lamp. Darkness seemed to push back at its weak rays,
reclaiming its territory in shadows on the wall. The shape of
their bodies was cast in one unrecognizable, free-form pool
of dark, low against the foot of the bed. It underscored the
loneliness that she had heard in Sadie's voice, a quality evi-
dent in its timbre and in the lassitude of her phrasing, even
when the events she recounted should have come out with
more satisfaction.

"What did you do after you left the house?" she asked.

"I took the money I had saved from Dora and Shiny's
cheques and used it to support myself. It lasted me the two years
I spent in teacher's college. The one before my practicum, and
the one after." She turned to her sister and smiled proudly. "I was

a math teacher for thirty-seven years, Anna. What do you think about that?"

"It's wonderful, Sadie. You did really well for yourself. That took a lot of guts what you did. It's much more than I would've had in the same situation, that's for sure."

"You never know what you're capable of until you're pushed into it."

"Maybe not." Anna tilted her head and stared at Sadie a few seconds, watched her lace her fingers together and work out some soreness. She let her sit for a while and let the story settle before she spoke. Then, when she felt there had been enough of an interval, when she was sure her question would come out right and she wouldn't drive her out the door again, she took her sister's hand.

"Okay," she said softly, "but I have one more thing I need to ask. I want to know how Mama and you came to be in touch. Okay, two more. I want to know what you were doing here in the apartment before the funeral."

Sadie raked her fingers back through her hair, pulling out the ponytail. She disengaged her hand from Anna's and sat up more stiffly.

"Well, like I said, she tracked me down about six months ago. It wasn't hard to find me once she set her mind to it. I'm listed in the phone book. She said she went to the library and looked at every directory for every major city in North America. She called a couple of wrong numbers, but she eventually found me. We've spoken every few weeks since then. It was awkward, to say the least."

"I'll bet."

"Believe it or not, it was even more awkward than it is talking to you."

Anna grunted. "Actually, I don't think we're doing too badly, given that we haven't said a word in over fifty years."

"Well, the point is it was difficult. Anyway, one day a few weeks ago, she called and she sounded different. She was very upset, and she didn't make any sense. I had to calm her down before I could understand a word she was saying. Then she says to me, 'I kept a diary, and I want you to read the part after your father died,' and something like 'I'm sewing it back into the bed and putting it in the box so that nobody can find it.' Does that make sense to you? She kept saying, 'It's very important that nobody finds it!'"

"Sewing a box into the bed? What box? Not that one over there surely?" Anna pointed to the empty cardboard box on the floor.

"I don't know. I asked her what she meant by putting it in the box, but she got upset at me and said, 'Don't ask me why!' I told her not to worry, that it would be okay, no one would find it. She was so... *grave* about the whole thing! Her voice had a terrible quality to it I hadn't heard before. It was so fragile. Like it would crack at any moment. It made me so uncomfortable that I laughed."

"You laughed at her? She's upset and incoherent, and you're laughing at her?"

Sadie pressed her fingertips against the bones around her eyes.

"I didn't really laugh, it was more of a chuckle. Look, I can't defend it, it was completely insensitive of me, I know. Of course she got upset again and started to cry. But I swear Anna, I didn't know what to do. She said this was serious. That she'd written things she'd never told anyone before. She made me promise that if she died I would go find the bed, get the diary, and read it. She said that I should read it and then *burn* it. I mean can you imagine? Burn it! As if throwing it out was too risky, like someone might be sifting through her trash and would give a damn what she wrote."

"Well, Mrs. Huang would."

"I don't believe it."

"I swear. I've caught her a few times. Anyway, who knows if Mama was even going to throw it out? Mrs. Huang has a key to the apartment. Maybe she was afraid she'd come in and find it before I had a chance to get there."

"Well, okay that makes more sense. Anyway, I looked in the beds and then I even tore open these God-awful mattresses. There was nothing there. No box, nothing. And then when we came here and found those diaries in the box in the closet, I thought she'd decided the closet was safe enough and had given up her crazy plan with the bed. But to tell you the truth, it did seem strange to me that there ended up being so many volumes. Obviously she couldn't have been thinking she'd bury that enormous box there in a bed, could she?"

"No, of course not."

Anna pondered the possibilities a moment. "Unless ... she was already a little bit demented from the stroke, which she was, I can tell you. Maybe after she put down the phone, she had a moment of clarity and realized the whole thing was nuts."

She got up off of the bed and went over to the box, pushed aside the pile of its dumped-out contents. "But look — come here, Sadie. You said she told you she'd written in the diary after Papa died. But I just finished reading the diaries that are here, and there's nothing at all written after Papa died. The last entry is in nineteen twelve. Papa died in thirty-one — it's not even close. I looked everywhere for another volume, but there isn't one."

Sadie cracked the small of her back and shifted impatiently. "Didn't Mrs. Huang say something about Mama's running up and down the stairs a few weeks ago?"

"Yeah, she did. She was pointing out how fit Mama was and how she was out in the backyard working in the garden. But I knew that, she always worked in the garden. She was just telling that story to point out that I'm in terrible shape. She never misses an opportunity."

"But what if she was actually going up and down the stairs, maybe not running. Come on, Anna, that *is* strange. The woman was ninety, for God's sake. I know Mrs. Huang says she was athletic, but she wasn't in training for the marathon. The only explanation is that she was confused. Maybe she already had suffered the stroke by then."

Anna looked stumped for a moment, but then sheer stubbornness took hold and she sloughed off the fog in her mind. "But it's *possible* something could've been up, isn't it?" She stood up again and started pacing. She chewed on a fingernail, tore off a strip, and then spit it out.

Sadie shrugged. "Yes, it's possible, I suppose, but it's not likely. She could have buried the volume of her diary in the backyard for all we know. Anything is possible. That annoying old Ida Gutstein said something yesterday about Mama burying something in the backyard years ago. Didn't she say she was burying the cutlery when she was nine months pregnant?"

"Oh my God, that's it!"

"What?"

"Don't you see? She wasn't burying cutlery at all. I just read the last entry in her diaries, and she wrote in it that she was burying her baby! She miscarried right after you were born. She lied to Ida to allay any suspicions because she decided to pretend you were hers. God! We should've known when Ida told that story that Mama was lying to her; she was never more than half-hearted — at best — about keeping kosher. She wrote in her diary that she buried her baby, wrapped up in Bubbe's featherbed, inside the old chest." She looked around the room. "Hold on a minute."

"What? What is it?"

"Something didn't seem right when I read that. I know that old chest she was writing about. It was here in the apartment long after you were born." Anna went to look in the closet, up on the shelf. "But it's not here now!"

"So?"

"So it says in the diary that Mama buried her baby in it. In 1911. I'm saying that she buried the chest once, and then dug it up again a long time ago. Who's to say she wouldn't bury the damned thing again? I know she must've dug it up, because the chest has been here in the apartment for ages. It was here before we were born, then she buried it, then it was here again, and it's not here now, so where did it go?"

She looked at Sadie, until her eyes were as wide as her own already were. "Come on, Sadie — let's go find it. Maybe we'll learn more about Sylvia too. Don't you want to know? Aren't you a little curious?"

But at the mention of it, Sadie seemed to sadden again, so she gave her a hug and, without saying a word, pulled her up from the bed and took her to the door to the hallway.

Sadie covered Anna's hand as it grasped the handle.

"You know that we're as nuts as she is, you *do* realize that, don't you? Here we are, two old women, it's past midnight, our mother's not cold in the ground, and we're going outside to dig a hole in her backyard. Does this strike you as normal?"

Anna smiled. "C'mon — there's a shovel outside the back door of the building."

Anna agreed that they should put something on more appropriate for an excavation and went immediately to get her mother's gardening pants and an old blouse. Then she found some gloves tucked up under a pottery casserole on top of the fridge. But Sadie's height and build posed more of a challenge. After combing through the dresser, she settled on stripping down and putting on their mother's floral robe.

Down in the garden, Anna snorted, putting her hands up over her eyes when her sister's bathrobe fell open as she lifted up the shovel. Already the robe was scandalously short on her, barely covering her hips. Now her bra and underwear showed completely.

Sadie shrugged. "So I look ridiculous," she whispered. "If someone should find a seventy-two-year-old woman shovelling dirt in the backyard at midnight, would it seem so much less strange to them if she were wearing coveralls?"

Thankfully, it had not been hard to find the place where their mother had dug. Except for the light shower the afternoon of the funeral, there had not been any rain in several weeks, and with the flashlight they could see easily that in among the tomatoes there was a spot where some plants had been pushed over to cover up an area of disturbed ground. A few seedlings were also planted there, but they were withered and dry from neglected thirst.

But the backyard was too quiet, away from the street, where there wasn't any traffic anyway, and Anna was worried. What if someone in one of the apartments above heard them and called the police?

"Try to shovel quietly, Sadie."

"How the hell am I supposed to do that?" Sadie answered, shaking her head.

"Just try."

Anna held the flashlight as Sadie bore down with the spade. The second slice sent tremors up Sadie's arm. "Ugn. I think I've hit something," she said.

"Here, let me help."

Anna got down on her knees and started scratching away with her gloved fingers. The top of the metal chest was only a few inches from the surface, and it took them about ten minutes to clear away enough dirt to pull it out of the hole in the ground.

It was lighter than they expected, made of extremely thin metal, probably of tin. Still, it was large. Their mother must have carried the contents separately, they decided, which would account for her many trips up and down. The catch on the chest was flimsy and held an old rusty combination lock that Sadie sheared off with two thrusts of the spade. They brushed the dirt away and pushed the lid up. A few bugs scurried away from the glare of the flashlight.

The chest was stuffed with a large black garbage bag. When they untied the knot in the bag, they pulled out what appeared to be an old down comforter. It was a little damp, rotted through in a few places, and stained dark brown, a deep uneven staining with lines on the edges of the patches like contours drawn with a makeup pencil.

Anna shook her head and smiled. "Of course." She touched the cotton gingerly, with the tips of her fingers. "It's the featherbed."

"What featherbed?"

"The one Bubbe gave to Mama. That's what she meant Sadie, when she was talking about the bed. She meant the featherbed, not those damned mattresses upstairs."

They pulled it over to the back stoop and sat down for a rest, their forearms tucked under the material. The featherbed lay out in a lumpy mass in front of them, still compacted from its confinement.

Sadie picked at it in a few places to try to let it air out, to get it to expand. But it didn't.

"What happened to it? What's this brown colour from? You don't think..."

"That it's blood? I'm sure of it."

"From?..."

"From your birth, I think, Sadie. From your mother. Or maybe from Mama's dead baby." She swallowed. The weight of the featherbed seemed to increase tenfold in their laps.

Sadie slumped forward into it and pressed her face into the material. "I ... I don't know how to deal with this ... Anna, how could she have expected I would react when I found this? And God, why? Why on earth would she *keep* such a thing?"

"I don't know." Anna started to move her hand to comfort her, hesitated a second, then lightly caressed Sadie's head and neck. "Let's find out." She looked along the seam and found a place where it had been sewn up. "Shall we?"

Sadie raised her head from the material and arched an eyebrow. That gesture, Anna thought, it was Mama through and through. She grasped a fistful of material, they pulled in opposite directions, and the seam easily gave way.

"Go ahead Anna, I've had enough of shoving my hands into things."

She winced as she reached in with both arms and felt around. Her fingers felt through the soft, clammy lumps of feathers and finally grazed a solid object, supple and smooth. She pulled it out, then retrieved the flashlight to illuminate what they had found. It took them a few seconds to see what it was; a clear plastic bag containing a roll of paper, closed with a twist-tie. She blew at some down stuck to the plastic and opened the bag.

"Let's take this upstairs, Sadie, and read the damned thing together like menschen, not here like animals in the dark."

They left a trail of down on their way up the stairs, and when they got into the apartment, they set the featherbed on the floor of their mother's bedroom, pulled off their dirty clothes, and pushed open the window for some air. They sat down in their underwear on the bed and had a good laugh when some stuffing tumbled out the side of the mattress, through the open slit.

Anna propped up some pillows, bobby-pinned her hair away from her face, and sat on the inside next to the window, nestled into the corner of the wall. Sadie sat down next to her, stretched out her legs under the covers, and reached over to turn on the bedside lamp.

The pages had been torn out of some other volume, lined sheets from a school notebook, stapled together. Anna leafed quickly through them and saw that they had been carefully selected — the whole entry was dated the same day in 1931. Their mother's handwriting was much more cramped and difficult to read than in her other diaries and, though still written with a fountain pen, in black ink instead of blue.

The last page of writing was different, not stapled, but attached to the rest by a paperclip and penned with a blue ball-point on expensive beige stationery. It was a letter, dated June 7th, 1983. A few weeks ago, the day before she went into hospital.

Anna started to pull out the letter, but stopped when she found the note attached to the top: *Please read this last.* At first, she was annoyed with her mother, still trying to control her from the grave. But then her gaze rested on the salutation. When she saw to whom it was addressed, her relief burst from behind closed lids and poured down her face, a release of pent-up hurt that her embarrassment could not contain.

"Look, Sadie — she *did* want me to read this — she did! I just knew she would. I knew it."

Sadie smiled. "Of course she did, Anna," and she patted her leg.

Anna settled into the pillow with her eyes closed and with a contented smile. She tilted her head back to listen and heard Sadie settle in too, taking a deep breath as she put on reading glasses.

This time Sadie can read, she decided. She can read out loud, for both of us.

December 6th, 1931

Dear Diary,

Years ago, when I started writing in a diary, I wrote "Personal and Private — do not read!!" on the cover page, stupidly thinking that would stop someone. Thank G–d, at last, I can write without care to that. It's been over a month now since Isaac's death. A month is nothing when you've been waiting over twenty years.

Twenty years? Now that's something. Can it really have been that long since I've picked up a pen to write down my thoughts? And what did I write back then? Lies, nothing but lies.

No, not all lies. It's difficult to say where the lies started, though. Even more difficult to decide where should they end. With the truth, I suppose. But what is Truth, really? Or *who* is she, and where did she go?

For two long decades, I've watched her from a distance, the estranged friend I pushed slowly away because she became too dangerous to have near. But she's always been just over there, patiently watching me as I watch her, reminding me with silent insistence that she'd be willing to speak whenever I'd have her back.

Well, I think I'm ready now that it's safe again. At least to write it down.

It's funny — I began to write the truth, with all my heart. I poured myself into those first pages, from the very first beautiful beige sheet of the very first smooth brown booklet that Hattie gave me all those years ago. For two whole years I wrote so freely. Then one day, he came into our room, holding my diary, and he struck me with it across my face.

He told me he'd been reading it — he had read all about how I thought Hattie was smarter than him, everything I had written about our intimate marital relations, all about my conversation with Sylvia when she admitted she thought he was a schmuck. Everything.

I was so angry that he had read my personal thoughts, but I was also embarrassed, and my cheek was stinging from the slap, and so I just sat there in shock as he yelled at me.

My first thought was to protect Sylvia — I tried to convince him she felt that way about all men, pointed out that she did say everything was relative, which meant that on the scale of men, he was pretty high up. I don't think he really believed me, especially since they had just had an argument that I had to patch up, but it did seem to calm him a little.

I asked him not to read my personal thoughts, that a diary was private, but he scoffed. He never promised a thing, only stormed out of the apartment to wander the streets for hours, coming back smelling of liquor.

After that, what sense of privacy could I have? I could hide my diary more carefully, but in a small apartment it's hard not to come upon things by accident. I suppose I could've stopped writing altogether, right then and there. Why didn't I? If I admit it to myself, I might have confided more in Hattie, but I suppose I felt she was too busy with her life to be burdened by what was happening to me. And besides, I wasn't ready to tell her everything.

So I decided from then on, if I was going to keep writing, it would be with two purposes in mind. I still wrote to put down my thoughts — that was the part of me that hoped I was successful in finding a good hiding spot, the part of me that needed a place to get things out. The suspicious and fearful side of me wrote more carefully. More deliberately. Well it sure didn't take long before careful and deliberate became a euphemism for lies.

Sometimes I wrote things about him that he couldn't deny, things that he probably knew already but that I couldn't say to his face. It was a dangerous game, choosing just how far I should go when I wrote about him, half of me hoping he would read my thoughts, maybe even gain some compassion from it. Sympathy for me, from Isaac. Looking at those words now on paper, I can almost hear his voice, telling me what a damned fool I was.

But eventually, my real life began to mirror the lies I was writing about, and when that happened, I hoped even more that he would be reading it. But for a different reason — because it made me feel safer about the risks I was taking.

I have to wonder, though: did the writing reinforce the lies, or vice versa? I'm not sure which anymore. It started as a purposeful exercise, but as with many games that one plays for too long, one tends to forget where reality begins and ends.

I've been waiting a long time to sift through, to blow away the husk of what I wrote and find its kernel of truth. After twenty years, the knowledge still burns or aches, depending on the day. Either way, it's a pain that has almost been too much to endure.

So now I want to catalogue all the lies. Maybe that will make it a little better.

There were lots of them, and the first big one was my pregnancy. I was never really pregnant at all. There, now I've said it. Not that first time at least. There was never any baby, and never any miscarriage. Only a big deception.

Sylvia and I planned it together. By the time she moved in, Isaac was already accusing me of being barren, and the reminders and the pressure only came on more strongly now that we had a pregnant woman living with us. Sylvia's growing body posed some kind of challenge to him. Maybe it was a visible reminder that his manhood could not be confirmed until his own wife was with child too.

But I didn't want to become pregnant yet, and I was not enjoying the trying. I'm not sure if intimate relations were really that bad. It was more that it always seemed like such an angry and determined act for him. He was clearly getting pleasure from it, but I always felt like after he was finished, his expression was saying to me, "There. That better do it." During it all, I would just lie there trying to relax, but I was stiffened by fear and disgust. I wanted it to be safe, and loving, not a bitter chore.

I began to talk to Sylvia about it. At first, I was embarrassed, but she was so used to talking about intimate things, being a prostitute and all, and so she put me at ease. She suggested different things to distract myself and make it more pleasant: perfume under my nose, thinking of a funny story, thinking of the shopping list. That helped a little, but she couldn't do anything to stop his blaming me for not conceiving.

One day, I said to Sylvia that if I could only get pregnant, even if I lost the damned child, it would at least convince him I wasn't barren, and it might ease the pressure a little bit. I felt terribly guilty for wishing it, but Sylvia's eyebrows furrowed, and she said, wait a minute, you might have something there.

So together, we conceived — not a baby, but a plan. We contrived to fake my pregnancy so that we could later fake a stillbirth. Sylvia and I knew that if we could carry through with it, we would ease the pressure on me, at least temporarily.

It was a completely crazy plan — I'm shocked, when I think of it now, that Sylvia was ever able to convince me it would work. Even more shocked that we did it without being discovered. But then that was twenty years ago, and men knew even less about women's bodies than they know now. And Isaac was, like most men, not very interested in female troubles. In fact, he was quite disgusted by them, and frankly, I don't think he was ever really that interested in me except as a potential mother for his children.

So, when I announced that I was pregnant, it was not difficult to convince him that I should move into Sylvia's room. He snored — it would disturb my sleep, and I needed to rest for the baby. It was not a good idea to have relations while a woman was pregnant, I told him — it could cause damage. These were just the excuses he was looking for anyway, so that he could stretch out in our bed and have it all to himself. So, I moved into Sylvia's room, and I took with me my mother's featherbed.

Sylvia's idea for faking the pregnancy came to her from a friend at the brothel who had used a similar trick to get herself out of the house and out of prostitution. The woman abruptly moved out of the brothel and in with a friend, announcing she was pregnant, but because she was still living nearby, she needed to give the appearance of still being with child.

Quite literally, she fabricated her pregnancy, fashioning padding for herself that she held in place under her dress with some straps tied across her back. She had started with a specially shaped, pillow-like design and had increased the stuffing very slowly until there was the need for a more bulbous superstructure.

The padding was made firm with two layers of leather — one hard inner layer to give the impression of muscle and one softer layer on the outside so that if felt like skin if you pressed against it accidentally. And of course, clothing smoothed things out quite nicely. Her friend had changed the basic structure twice — once at month five and once at month seven.

Sylvia contacted the woman, and she got the three differently sized pads along with the stuffing. It was everything we needed. All we had to do was make a few adjustments for my shorter height, and we had our baby.

He never saw me without my clothes on once I moved into the back bedroom — there was no reason for it. He became like my intended again, treating me more cordially, respecting my privacy — at least in terms of allowing me time alone behind a closed door. It brought out the best in Isaac. He picked things up for me and Sylvia on the way home from work. He laughed off his workaday troubles — something I had never heard him do before. He even organized a charity drive at the lodge he belongs to. I was never so happy as those months that I was never pregnant. But his kindness and good humor were not the reason. You see, my happiness had less to do with how I felt about him and more about how ambivalent I felt about being a wife. Now I had an occasional refuge from that. Seven months' refuge, I hoped, until we planned to lose the child.

And a refuge it was. When it was just me and Sylvia behind that door, we could be like schoolgirls again, whispering into the night about everything that mattered, and even more that didn't matter at all.

So our deception, and how we felt about it, grew with our bellies.

Sylvia's belly contained a real kicking baby, pushing her skin outward, hard and taut like an unripened fruit. And though the plan was her idea, she grew uneasy about the deception, nervous about being discovered. She said she felt like a hypocrite for suggesting we lie, when she had made such a strong point of not wanting to bring her baby into a house of lies.

But that lie didn't bother me at all. My belly was just rounded leather padding, but it calmed me, enveloping my body in a protective shield.

Meanwhile, Sylvia and I were spending more time together. It was so easy to do — we were sharing a room, and we had every opportunity to talk. She and I still fought often, but it was never like when I fought with Isaac. Our fights were between two people trying to impress one another, not the battle for dominance that my relationship with Isaac had become.

But I was still insecure around Sylvia. I was trying to prove myself to her, to prove that I wasn't some naive little greenhorn. To tell the truth, as long as I am doing so, when I argued with Sylvia, I was also trying to prove these things to myself. After all, if I were truly worldly, would I have been so embarrassed when I thought about what she did for a living? Would I really have felt the way I did about it? As much as I wanted to accept her free thinking, I couldn't help feeling that being a prostitute was wrong.

Sylvia's thinking posed a fiery challenge to my smugness, and I was drawn to the challenge like a moth.

No, that's too violent an image. That's not how I felt.

This is how I felt with Sylvia:

With her, I was like a butterfly, emerging from my cocoon and arching my wings toward her sunlight.

Chapter Twenty-one

1911

Rebecca's eyes darted left and right as she hurried along Allen Street. The rain had just lifted, and as she reached an inter-section, she winced at the stench of wet garbage and a sweat-ing horse, both of which were waiting there on the corner. Soon to be picked up by someone, she hoped. The horse stood in front of a shop that sold Sabbath items, the window dis-playing a careful arrangement of silver and pewter *kiddush* cups, a mahogany challah board with a silver knife, some candle-sticks, and a light blue and white ceramic *havdallah* set. A man was leaning in the door frame and called out to her.

"Why not stop and take a look at what nice craftsmanship I have here on display? How long have you been using the same old things? Come and look at this nice spice box I have here: made by Avram Dressler himself!"

The man started to say something else, but his voice was drowned out by a train thundering by overhead on the elevated tracks. The metal structure that supported the tracks shook dangerously as the train's wheels scraped and rolled on, overpowering all other noise for a good fifteen seconds.

Rebecca tipped her hat down further over her face and averted her eyes. She did not want anyone to recognize her. By the time the train passed, she was a few stores down, in front of one that advertised only holiday items: *menorahs, seder* sets, matzo trays, *shofars*, and dreidels. The store was dark, probably not even open, there being no major holiday until the fall. Beside that store, there was an open doorway to an apartment, and a few women stood outside leaning against the brick wall, necks craned to the sky to take in a little sun. One woman tried to cool herself vigorously with an oriental fan, arching her back so much that her white frilly blouse barely covered her breasts. Rebecca looked at the piece of paper she'd tucked into her sleeve to check the address, but this was not the right one.

The rest of the block housed a few more shops, one selling *tefillin* and *tallises*, and the last two simple grocery stands selling some wilted vegetables and pocked fruit. In each door frame, a man beckoned to her, and each time, she averted her eyes, pretending not to hear him or feigning distraction from some other noise coming from the other side of the street. Glad to reach the end of the block, she crossed under the tracks.

She thought again about what Sylvia had said, but she had no qualms about ignoring her wishes. Well, maybe a few. But if Sylvia wanted her to understand her life better, as she said she did, why wouldn't she let her see where she worked, just this once? Did she want her to understand, or was she just smoothing over their arguments?

It had been almost a month since Sylvia last went to work at Mrs. Fine's. The request had come a few days before and had been somewhat of a surprise, since she was beginning to show. But the girl who had delivered Mrs. Fine's message said that one of her regulars had asked for Sylvia specifically, that he wanted to see her once more before she got too big. Mrs. Fine would be too busy with her other houses to check up on her personally, but her message was clear: come now or don't come back later.

Rebecca had suggested this would be a perfect opportunity for Sylvia to leave the profession, but Sylvia would have nothing to do with that. This was a long-time client, someone she liked, and she would go. When Rebecca had asked if she could come with her to see where she worked, Sylvia had refused categorically.

"Just forget it, Rebecca," she said, and her hand waved the idea away. Of course, being silenced in that manner made Rebecca furious, so she set her mind up to go anyway. After all, they had grown close. Sylvia would be mad, but it wouldn't be so bad. She'd forgive her. And it wasn't as if she wanted to stand there in the room while Sylvia and her customer carried on. She just wanted to get some idea of where she would be going back to, after the baby came.

So Rebecca waited until Sylvia had been gone for half an hour, then she got dressed, put on her most conservative-looking shirtwaist and skirt, a navy blue waistcoat over top, and a large hat that she tipped to the side so that it partially covered her face. She set out across town to pay Mrs. Fine's little establishment a visit.

Now, stepping onto the curb on the west side of the street, she again pulled out the piece of paper to check the address. She had imagined it would be a little shabby, but nothing like this simple, dilapidated, narrow tenement. Again, she checked the street number; this was definitely the right place. She ducked in the door. The entranceway wasn't so different from her own. Perhaps the hallway was a little wider. Where was the big parlour with people drinking? Where was the large woman that she had imagined, with the red feather boas hanging from her neck?

There was no room, no woman. Gas lamps lit the faces of five men seated on a bench to the left of the staircase and another four standing in line. The men on the bench sat silently, most of them with their heads down and their hands in their laps, one looking up at the ceiling with his hands clasped behind his head, large circles of underarm sweat staining his brown shirt. When she stepped into the hallway, all eyes turned her way.

The man sitting second closest to the door jumped up from the bench and ran out. He tried to shield his face, but she recognized him, a man from the factory, married to one of the button-sewers. Rebecca had a moment of panic herself. What if he told someone he saw her there? But she shook the thought away. He'd never say anything, at least not to anyone she knew. He was clearly worried enough that someone might find out he came here himself.

The man closest to the exit slid down to fill the space, and the first one in the queue sat down in his place. Another man sat halfway up the stairs. He called out to her.

"Can I help you, miss?"

Rebecca felt her face flush.

"Are you the new girl?"

She tried to steady her voice. "No, I'm not. I'm waiting for a friend. She works here. If you don't mind, I'll just wait until she comes down."

"Who's your friend?" he inquired.

"Sylvia."

"I'm afraid there ain't no Sylvia here. You must have the wrong place. Try across the street a few doors down. Engel's house."

"No, this is it, I'm sure. Are you certain there isn't a Sylvia?"

"Look, miss, I been working here for two years. We only have eight inmates here. Seven since Sarah got — well, in the family way, if ya know what I mean. I think I know their names by now."

"Sarah! That's what I meant. I mean — that's her other name. I'm waiting for Sarah. She's here today, isn't she?"

"Sure, she just went upstairs about ten minutes ago. But you can't just wait there."

"Please, I'm not here to make trouble. Just forget I'm here." But as she looked at the faces of the men on the bench, it was clear that was a ridiculous request.

The man on the stairs looked at her and cocked his head. "You sure you ain't the new one? It's okay to be shy. They always come dressed like you the first day."

"I'm not the new girl," she said tersely, looking down at her clothes.

"Okay, suit yourself," he said. "She should be down soon." The man looked like he was going to say something else, but then shook his head and stared down between his knees at the step.

Moans could be heard coming from directly above them, through the creaking floorboards. Rebecca leaned sideways against the wall, turning away from the men so that she would-n't have to see them. She wished someone would start talking.

A few excruciating minutes later, a man staggered down the stairs. He combed his hair back as he hurried by. The sentry on

the stairs shouted "Next!" and the first man on the bench got
up. He was told to go to number two. The other four slid down,
and the empty spot was filled by the next man standing.

Rebecca thought she would scream and run out the front
door if Sylvia didn't hurry up. But then, how could she be expected to hurry when she didn't even know Rebecca was waiting?

After a five-minute eternity, she appeared around the corner of the stairs dressed in a cream robe. A man had his arm
around her. He looked to be in his fifties and was wearing grey
pants, a white shirt with a bow tie, blue suspenders, and a jacket. His face was deeply creased and his complexion ruddy, and
he had a salt-and-pepper, handlebar moustache. He gave
Sylvia a chuck under the chin, and she smiled and leaned in to
kiss him sensuously on the lips.

Rebecca just stared up at her, unable to look away. Sylvia's
smile followed the man down the stairs, but it deflated when
she saw Rebecca standing there at the door, her mouth agape.

"What are you doing here?!" she asked, her arms
crossed stiffly.

Rebecca started up the stairs. "Don't be mad. I just came to
see where you worked."

Sylvia's body tensed. She stomped her foot.

"Dammit — I told you not to come!"

"I know. But I wanted to see for myself."

"I don't know what to do with you. Come up here while I
get ready," she commanded.

Rebecca followed her up the stairs into an apartment.
Standing in the doorway, she saw a large room divided by a
sheet hung from the ceiling. She saw a small bed, a dresser, and
a chair next to a window. Also, on the other side of the room,
there was a wash basin, a countertop with a lace doily on it, a

small table, and a few chairs. The window opened onto a narrow and dim airshaft that formed the sliver-shaped core of the building. It looked as though one could reach across and touch the windowsill on the other side.

Sylvia removed her robe and sat on the bed.

"Well, it's just as I thought," Rebecca said. "It's disgusting. And now I know why you didn't want me to come here."

Sylvia looked a little surprised Rebecca was fighting back. "It's not so bad. You're just not used to it."

"Sylvia, now that I've seen it, you can let up on the act. I mean, look at this room."

Sylvia looked around. "Yeah, and?"

"And look at those men, lurking about downstairs! And what is this?" She had picked up a bottle on the dresser, unscrewed the cap, and sniffed the foul-smelling liquid inside.

Sylvia grabbed the bottle from her and started screwing the top back on. "Rebecca, please, try to keep your voice down. This is for cleaning off ... It's for cleaning them off beforehand."

Rebecca's face scrunched up. "Eeeeww! Cleaning them off?"

"Yeah. You take his putz, and you squeeze it. Really hard, like this...," Sylvia clenched her fist tight and pumped a little., "...to see if anything comes out. You know, to see if he has the clap. Then, if he's okay, you wipe him off with the stuff. All over."

Rebecca put her hand up to her mouth. "That's disgusting. There's nothing else to say about it. It's just disgusting."

"Oh, come on, Rebecca. It would be much more disgusting if I didn't use that stuff, let me tell you. You're such a prig sometimes."

Rebecca stared at her, open-mouthed with indignation, her hand to her chest.

"Look, I do what I have to do. I'm not saying I have a rip-roaring time at it, but I get by, and someday I'm gonna have a place like this of my own — be a business woman like Mrs. Fine."

"Why on earth would you want to do that?"

"Why not? Mrs. Fine is the only woman I know who runs her own business and doesn't have some man telling her what to do. She mixes with all the important people in society, and they respect her. Plus she isn't so tied down by society's rules."

"Sylvia, how can you be so naive? The whole city is trying to shut her down. I read about her in the paper last week. She's notorious — she owns twenty houses like this. "

Sylvia shook her head as she pulled up her skirt. "Read between the lines, Rebecca. They may say in public that they want to shut her down, but privately, they all come to her houses. So it's not in their interest to shut her down. Think about it: don't you think they would've done it by now? They've been making speeches about her for ten years!" She did up the last few buttons on her shirtwaist.

Rebecca's voice dropped almost to a whisper. "Well, you sure looked happy enough back there on the stairs, the way you said goodbye to that man." She shifted uneasily on her feet.

Sylvia's head tilted. "What's going on here, Rebecca? Why did you really come here?" She walked toward her, but Rebecca turned away.

"Nothing's going on! ... I don't know!"

"That's what's going on, isn't it? You didn't like the way I kissed him!"

Rebecca turned her back. "Leave me alone!" The air seemed thinner in the room. She took shorter, shallow breaths.

"Rebecca's, he's nothing! He's harmless! I've been seeing him for years. He's just a little sweetheart. We actually have a lot of fun together, and he gives me really big tips."

Rebecca put her hand on the wall. She heard Sylvia move up behind her and felt her touch her shoulder.

"Rebecca, that's it, isn't it? You think that I might have had a good time with him, isn't it? It's okay. It's okay to admit it. I would probably feel ..."

With a jerk, Rebecca pulled away from Sylvia's hand and bolted out the door. She needed air. She swallowed the lump hard and bounded down the stairs. She bumped into the sentry, rushed past the men on the bench. Through the blur of her tears she thought she saw them stand up, but she was out the door too fast to be sure.

The street was thick with people, and she felt caught in their soupy mass. Her legs were moving, but they felt twice her body weight. She pushed her way through, ran halfway down the block, knocking into people as she wove in and around them. An alley caught the corner of her eye, and she ducked into it. Away from the noise of the street, beside a pile of broken crates, she leaned against the brick wall and sucked in oxygen.

Her heart was pounding in her neck.

Her chest heaved in and out. She felt nauseated.

She wiped the dusty ledge at the foot of the wall with her hand and sat down. Sylvia was right! Oh God, she was right, she was right, she was right! She shook her head, buried her face in the curves of her palms. It *was* the kiss. She was upset about it. She was upset to see Sylvia kiss that man. Another wave of nausea overcame her, and she started gasping again.

Back in that room, hearing Sylvia's words, there had been a flash of clarity, and what she saw had mirrored her worst fears.

She could pretend that it was something else — pretend that it was concern for Sylvia's state of mind, pretend that she was concerned about her emotions being too clouded by her job to distinguish pleasure from professional make-believe. She could pretend that it was about Sylvia, but it would be no use. Denying an emotion was easy, but this was different. The emotion came charging at her brandishing insight at its side. Once it cut her open, she could not close the wound.

No. There was no use denying it; this wasn't about Sylvia at all.

And yet it was.

In that moment, in that room, Sylvia's hand clasped on her shoulder released a flood, the last few months pouring back in images brought into focus through a lengthening telescope. The images moved back through time with each extension of the lens, further and further back with each adjustment.

She saw last night, the pulsing vein on Sylvia's neck, thump-thump, thump-thump, as she slept quietly at her side. Then she saw back further, and there was Sylvia's arm, flying up with her smile, her empty shopping bag flopping upside down. Back to her red face, her brow furrowed with anger, her corded neck long and proud as she stood up to defend her from Isaac.

She saw back to the tendons in Sylvia's hands, rippling as they smoothed out and cut material at the sewing machine. To her eyebrow as it pooled sweat from her red curls, as a trickle ran down the side of her face, dripping from her jawbone when she lifted her head up, introducing herself that very first time.

Back further still, back to before they met, to Sylvia's hand as it mopped blood from her forehead on the cold floor of Cooper Union, to her fiery eyes on the podium and her fists pounding the air to punctuate her speech. And then ...

Then even more quickly, Rebecca's feelings for Sylvia had rushed forward, and like a sock being pulled inside out, they wrenched her back to the present. All the ambivalence, the confusion, the frustration she had felt about Sylvia blurred.

Now there was admiration, which grew into compassion. And companionship, which spread itself out into friendship, and friendship, which matured into intimacy. And then, when she had pulled all the way back and out of those feelings, when everything vaporized and she was left there with jealousy choking her in that airless room, she had to get out.

She had to. Because suddenly, she saw something else. It moved out from behind jealousy, it stepped unbidden into her conscience and swallowed it whole.

It was love. Unexpectedly, undeniably, it was love.

She scraped her feet angrily over the dirty ground in the alley. An abomination — she was no more than an abomination. What had her night school teacher called them? Inverts, that was it. She was an invert, perverted, deviant, and sick.

Oh God, what would she do now? How could she have let this happen, this ... sin? *God Almighty*, what would she do now?

A shadow cloaked her legs. She looked up from the dust to see that Sylvia was standing over her, blocking the few rays of sun from the street.

She turned her eyes quickly away. She couldn't face her. Not now.

"Rebecca, I'm sorry."

She felt Sylvia's hip press against hers as she sat down beside her on the ledge.

"How did you find me?"

"You practically left a trail of knocked-over people on the street."

Rebecca turned even further the other way, covered her face with her folded arms.

Sylvia leaned against her. "Hey, hey. It's okay." Her fingers touched the back of her neck.

Rebecca flinched and sat up straight. "It's not okay! I'm such a baby. You were right, I'm just a stupid, naive little child who can't control her horrible emotions!"

"Rebecca, look at me." She felt Sylvia's arm on her shoulder pulling her around to face her, her hand pulling her chin up toward her face. She kept her eyes closed. There was no way she could look at her. No way.

She felt Sylvia wipe away a tear running down her cheeks. Then she felt her hands glide into hers.

"You need to know something, Rebecca."

"What's that." Her words came out raspy.

"I have never thought you were stupid. Not once. I've never ever thought you were naive. And I *certainly* don't think of you as a child."

"Well, I am."

"No." Sylvia held their hands side by side, and her thumbs gently stroked Rebecca's fingers. "You're most definitely a woman. And you're the smartest woman I've ever known. The smartest, the most interesting, and...," she heard Sylvia swallow, "...and you're the most beautiful."

Rebecca allowed her eyes to open, and she carefully raised them to look into Sylvia's. Her lashes curved up to catch the light, but her amber irises seemed to shine on their own. Were they what was making her face hot? She felt helpless in their hold, but slipped one hand free, held it to her chest to temper the hollow ache. Her throat was suddenly dry. Sylvia leaned in closer, almost filling the space between them.

She hovered there a moment.

Rebecca felt her breath's caress on her cheek.

Then she closed her eyes again and drew expectation gently in through her mouth. Tentatively, slowly, she exhaled her fears. Her lips eased effortlessly into place, comfortable and deep and warm. And soft, Sylvia's mouth was so soft. It was the smoothest butter folded into the richest cream.

Chapter Twenty-two

November 8th, 1911. 12:30 A.M.

"What time is it?" Rebecca yawned and rubbed her eyes. Sylvia had her finger over her mouth to shush her. Rebecca felt her other arm draped over her stomach.

"It's past midnight. I can't sleep."

"Oy, Sylvia. I just got to sleep myself. It's so uncomfortable having this damned thing strapped to me all night. I wish I didn't have to."

"I know. I just don't trust your husband. What if something happened, like he got up to pee at the same time you did, and he saw you?"

She sighed. "Remind me again why I couldn't put it on before peeing."

"Because if there was a fire or something …"

"Okay, okay. I know. I'm just grumpy."

"Well, try having a real baby inside you, dancing on your kishkes every five minutes."

Rebecca laughed noiselessly. "I know. I shouldn't complain. And I should remember this will all be over soon."

"Don't bring it up — that means you'll have to go back to his room."

"What difference does it make — you keep saying you're leaving soon after anyway."

"I have to — Rebecca, let's not get into this again. We can still see each other. In a way it will be a lot easier."

"Yes, but we won't be able to spend the night together anymore. You're right, I shouldn't have brought it up. It's just that I *like* sleeping next to you. I sleep better. At least when you don't wake me up, I do."

"Me too." Sylvia pulled her tight against her body.

Rebecca slipped her hand under Sylvia's nightgown and tucked it into the space between her breasts and her belly.

"Mostly I'm gonna miss this. My own personal hand-warmer."

Sylvia swatted her playfully, and then pulled her even tighter for a kiss.

"You know you always ..."

She stopped talking and picked up her head.

"What? What is it?"

Sylvia disentangled their arms, jerked sharply away from her.

"I thought I heard ..."

The door swung open.

Isaac was standing there with a crumpled sheet of paper in his hand. Rebecca pulled the covers up with her as she struggled to sit upright.

"Isaac!"

His face was unsteady, shifting.

"Get out of bed, Rebecca. Get away from her. You're not safe next to that woman."

"Isaac, calm down and tell me what you're talking about."

"This!" He waved the crumpled sheet.

"What? What is it?"

"She's sick. A pervert. It's so disgusting I can't even say it. Get your stuff and get out of the room."

"Mr. Kalish, please, let me explain."

"Explain what? That you lured my wife into your bed?" He approached the bed, stood next to it, close to Rebecca.

"No, I didn't ..."

"Is this what you do? Is this how you people do it?" He waved his finger back and forth over the bed.

"Isaac! What does it say on the paper?"

"Ask her! Ask *her* what this is."

She looked into Sylvia's eyes for some information, but any strategy she might have been trying to communicate was clouded by an expression of anguish. Sylvia shook her head in desolation.

"I'm sorry, Rebecca. I shouldn't have written it. I'm so sorry."

"Sylvia, I'm sure it's okay. Just tell me what it is."

"It's a love letter," Isaac said. "To you. I found it under a pile of material on the sewing machine."

Fear spread over Rebecca's face. "Oh my God."

She pulled the sheets even tighter to her body. What did she write in the letter? How much did she say? Why was Isaac snooping around the sewing machine?

"You *should* be afraid, Rebecca. You've been sharing a bed with her for months. Just be grateful you're so unappealing these days, otherwise you don't know what she might have done." He waved the letter close to her face.

So he didn't suspect her. But how could Sylvia write such a letter in the first place? Had she just left it lying there under the material so that she would find it? Such a sweet thing to do, but so imprudent!

Before she had time to consider her actions, she snatched the letter from his hand.

"Rebecca, give that back to me."

"Isaac, I only want to see what it says."

"Rebecca, don't. You should never read such filth. I should have just torn it up. And *you*, you disgusting, filthy whore. You have ten minutes to get out of this house."

"No, Isaac, please. She could have her baby any day now. Have a heart."

"You're defending her? You actually want her to stay? Why would you want such a thing? Unless you and she — oh my God!" He brought his hand to his mouth.

"No! It's not like that Isaac!" She dragged herself out of bed. "I don't need to read the letter. It's disgusting. She's obviously sick. We should take pity on her." She turned to look at Sylvia as she said this.

Rebecca searched in vain for some sign from her. Some hidden message that Sylvia thought her words were part of some kind of strategy. But Sylvia's face was coarse and hard, like unglazed clay.

And there was no strategy anyway. All Rebecca felt was terror, cold and naked, and her words were just plain treachery. She was unworthy of Sylvia's love. She had betrayed her in order to save herself. She was a spineless coward, unworthy of Sylvia's letter, whatever it said.

A tear jumped its way down Rebecca's cheek. She wished she could seep through the floorboards. She was unfit for love. She took the crumpled letter and reached out to give it back to her.

Sylvia's face remained quite controlled, but as she took the letter from Rebecca, her eyebrow showed she was surprised.

"It's okay, Rebecca. I don't need pity, I just need a safe home for my baby." She looked at Isaac coldly. "This place isn't safe. I'll leave."

"No, wait, Sylvia. Let me talk about this with my husband. Isaac, can we please talk about this in private for a second?"

But Sylvia said, "No, Rebecca," and she got out of bed and went to the small dresser near to the door. "I don't need charity from him."

"Why, you little two-bit, cheap, sick," Isaac swung his arm out, and his hand struck Sylvia's face, the knuckles against her nose, the rest of his hand against her cheek. Her head snapped to the side, and she lost her balance.

Rebecca gasped.

As Sylvia fell, she tried to reach out to soften the impact, but her arm was not quick enough. Her hip cracked against the floorboards. She lay beside the bed, trying to prop herself up on one elbow. The fingers of her other hand dabbed at some blood beginning to trickle down the side of her face.

Isaac was lifting his hand up again. "Don't you dare talk to me like that, you little tramp."

Rebecca went to restrain his blow. "No!" She grabbed tight around his arm, almost hanging from it as he pulled to get it free of her grasp.

"Rebecca, get away from me!" He pulled his leg back, and it seemed to stop for a moment before propelling forward. The toe of his boot hit Sylvia squarely at the most prominent part of her stomach. The skin and muscle indented, almost swallowing half of his boot before her back arched, pulling her stomach backwards and away, her shoulders forward to cradle the area of impact. She brought her knees up as far as they would go. A moan escaped her lips.

"Isaac!" Rebecca cried.

But he had stepped forward and was already pulling his leg back again. This time it scraped along the floor, to scoop under Sylvia's arms, where they tried to form a shield. His boot connected again, a weaker blow, but Rebecca heard the blunt, squishy impact.

"Please, Isaac, you'll kill her! You're crazy, this is crazy! Please leave the room, we'll deal with this later!" She pushed him toward the door.

"I don't know why you're defending her, Rebecca. She's not worth it."

He spit into Sylvia's face, paused to look back at the two of them, then stomped out. The door to the front bedroom slammed shut, and Rebecca heard him shout, "She has ten minutes!"

She fell to her knees at Sylvia's side. The blood from her nose made a red gash where Sylvia had smeared it across her cheek.

"I'm so sorry, Rebecca. I'm so sorry."

Rebecca took the sleeve of her nightgown and wiped up her blood.

"Shhh. Shhh. Please don't apologize to me."

Sylvia was lying on her side, and she suddenly she groaned, doubled up again, folded herself as much as her swollen body would allow. "Rebecca, I think something's wrong."

Rebecca saw a pool of wetness flooding out from between her legs.

"Sylvia, I think your water broke. Oh my God. We need to get someone fast. You're going to have your baby."

"Don't leave me."

"I have to get someone, Sylvia! I have to." She turned to the door. "Isaac!"

"No, please. Don't call him."

"I'm just going to tell him to get the doctor."

Isaac was back at the door of the room.

"What is it now? Why isn't she getting ready?" Then he saw the water on the floor. "Oh God." His mouth twisted up in disgust.

"Isaac. I need you to go get the doctor. I think when you kicked her something went wrong."

"I'm not getting anyone for that woman. She can have her baby alone in the street where she belongs."

"She can't even move. If you want her to have it in the street, you'll have to carry her down there yourself. Are you going to do that?"

He didn't answer.

"At least let me call for a midwife."

"No. You can do it yourself, if you care so much. I don't need people coming in here and asking questions about why she has blood on her face."

"But Isaac! Nobody will fault you! If they blamed you, the letter would surely explain why..." A thought flashed in her mind: where was the letter? Where had it fallen?

"You think I want people knowing about that letter? Knowing that I was stupid enough to let my own wife share a bed with a sick pervert? No. You deal with the baby. You said you learned how from your mother."

"Isaac, I was fourteen years old. I don't remember exactly how. My mother did everything, I just brought her things that she needed. Please, let me go."

"I will not have my home become a spectacle. A source of gossip for the whole neighbourhood. 'You know Isaac Kalish?'" he said, his face scrunching up and his voice rising an octave. "'The one with the two women, both with child? I heard one of them gave birth! Was it his wife? No, not his wife, but that whore that they have living with them. Is it his child too, I wonder? Probably!'"

"Isaac, that's crazy talk," Rebecca said. "Everyone already knows Sylvia is expecting. How could this make any difference? We haven't even told anyone what Sylvia does. It doesn't make sense. And anyway, people talk — you can't help people talking. Are you such a small man that your opinion of yourself comes from what other people say when they're gossiping?"

She went to move past him to go to the door.

His open palm hit her hard, not only slapping her cheek but propelling it, and her, backwards. The room blurred as her body twisted around from the shock of the blow. She tumbled and hit her head against the table.

"That woman has been nothing but poison," he said. "You will not talk to me like that anymore, Rebecca — you'll do as I say, or that woman and her baby will be out on the street in ten minutes," he said.

She sat on the floor looking up at him. The back of his hand was still raised, his elbow pointed at her. She felt the metallic taste of blood on her tongue, and wiped a little bit from the corner of her mouth. She picked herself up, moving backwards crab-like toward the bedroom.

A knock at the door.

"Rebecca, it's me, Ida. I couldn't sleep and I heard a commotion. Is it Sylvia? Is the child coming?"

Rebecca got up to go to the door, but she felt Sylvia's hand on her arm tugging her back down. She heard Isaac open the door and tell Ida to go away, that she would be taking care of things. Ida tried to convince him to let her in, but Isaac firmly refused. Sylvia cried out when one of her contractions came, and then she heard Ida become more insistent; it sounded like she was trying to push her way past Isaac.

"I want to hear from Rebecca that everything's okay. Rebecca?" she called out past him.

Isaac came into the bedroom and pulled Rebecca up from the side of the bed where she was attending to Sylvia.

"You'll tell her to go away," he hissed. His hand hurt her forearm.

She came to the front door with him and saw Ida standing there. Ida's eyes tried to search for some real information from her. She saw Ida's eyes rest for a moment on her forearm, where Isaac's grasp was holding firm. Rebecca mustered as calm an expression as she could.

"It's okay, Ida. Thanks for coming by, but we're okay."

Isaac released his hold, and she retreated to the other room. Then she heard Isaac say, "You see? I told you everything was fine. If you're looking for something to do this late at night, why don't you pay our landlord, your friend Mr. Gutstein, a visit? I'm sure he'd be pleased to see you. More pleased than your husband would be if I told him how you've been spending your afternoons for the last year."

There was a long silence. Then she heard Ida say, "All right. I'll go, Isaac. But you promise to call me if there's the least sign of trouble."

She heard the door click shut. Rebecca looked at Sylvia. She was wincing through another contraction. She expelled air from her lungs after it was over, sucked in another breath, and then opened her eyes and looked up. Rebecca took her sleeve and mopped Sylvia's brow.

"Sylvia, let me help you up onto the bed. It's softer on the bed. This may take a while."

They struggled together, and then laid her down on the softness of the featherbed. They felt the air in the quilted pockets rush out from the sudden weight of her.

Once they had settled her in, Rebecca looked away to hide her tears. Sylvia pulled her chin right back to her face.

"You can do this Rebecca. I know you can. Just remember — I trust you."

"I don't deserve to be trusted."

"Yes, you do. You're the best friend I have. The best friend I'll ever have. You're my brave, sweet Rebecca. And I love you."

"Please, Sylvia, lower your voice. We don't want him to hear."

"I don't care anymore. He read the letter. He knows it's how I feel."

"But I don't know if I can ..."

"It's okay. I understand. I've been discovered, you haven't. It's better that way. You were smart to act the way you did. That was quick thinking."

"No, it wasn't quick thinking. You don't understand. It was nothing but ..."

"Shhh. Don't say anything. It's not necessary."

John Miller

"I do love you. You know I love you, don't you?"

"I know you do." She kissed her palm. "Now let's think together what we need to get through this together."

They started to make a list of things to gather but were interrupted by a contraction. Rebecca couldn't remember when the last one had come. Closing her eyes, she tried to recall what her mother had done at this point. She gathered her fingers into a wet brush-tip and inserted them into Sylvia's folds. Once her hand was in, she used her thumb and forefinger to measure the second opening, up inside. Fixing them in position, she gently slid her hand out to see how far apart they were. The opening was not that wide yet, maybe an inch, which meant they had some time yet. At least she hoped that was what it meant. If only she had been given some time to recall more accurately.

But there was more time between contractions than she had expected. She was able to go to get what she needed in the apartment, moving wordlessly around Isaac, who was not asleep, but sitting up in bed and staring at the wall. He moved his eyes only to watch her movements as she gathered an extra blanket here, some old cloths there, the ceramic bowl on their dresser. In between the next two contractions, she went to the stove and put on some water, grabbed a knife to boil for the cord when it came time.

Why had she never once considered that things might turn out this way? Lying in bed late at night, constructing scenarios together, even in the most pessimistic one, delivering a baby had never been considered. Perhaps it was too banal a part of the equation when compared with more threatening factors like the sin of their relationship, the potential loss of shelter and food, the possible devastation of their lives.

306

"He'd murder us both right away," Sylvia told her. Rebecca, on the other hand, was certain Isaac did not have it in him. Perhaps she had been right, although she never imagined a circumstance such as this one, where he would suspect only one of them. No, her worst scenario, when Sylvia prodded her morbidly to come up with one during her bouts of insomnia, was to end up cast out on the streets with nothing.

She pictured little tableaus that represented their misfortune. The Scorn: the two of them huddled under a blanket trying to walk down the street as people cast vegetables as judgement upon them. The Shunning: the merchant turned the other way as she tried to pay for a sack of potatoes. The Informant: the spiteful neighbour poised with a fountain pen over a desktop, grimly determined in her duty to inform the parents of their daughter's disgrace. The Shame: Her mother standing by a Russian wheat field, the crumpled letter at her side, her other hand covering her sobbing mouth.

The pregnancy had never figured into it. Perhaps she knew they would at least have been able to find a midwife through the help of Sylvia's colleagues. If she and Sylvia had focussed at all on the child-bearing, it had only been her own phoney cloth-and-leather protuberance that had preoccupied their thoughts, and how would they pretend to have a miscarriage.

This real delivery of this live baby, the most obvious and probable outcome of all, had entirely escaped their night-time agonizing.

And now, as they waited out the contractions, they were paying the price of their foolishness. The night took on an oceanic presence, as vast and as bottomless as fear itself. The hours of the early morning squeezed by painfully, through the narrow confines of the apartment. Time only occasionally became unstuck, leaping forward suddenly, but never very much, maybe five, ten minutes.

It seemed the baby would never arrive, not only because the contractions were not quickening at any significant rate, but also because they were aware of Isaac's presence in the other room, brooding and impatient. Not like an expectant father of course, but impatient for the thing to be done with so that he could throw Sylvia and the baby onto the street.

At six in the morning, Sylvia's contractions began to come more quickly, more powerfully. Isaac came to the door.

"What's taking so long?" he asked gruffly.

"You can't quicken these things, Isaac," Rebecca told him, even though she realized it would be soon. Sylvia had her eyes closed the whole time he was at the door.

"They take their own time. If you can't wait for it, perhaps you'd be better off going out."

"Fine then, that's what I'll do." He moved away from the bedroom, and they listened for his footsteps as he gathered his things and left. As the door shut, another contraction came.

"Ugnnn. Rebecca. I don't know if I can take this much more," Sylvia said weakly.

"Let's wait a few minutes until I'm sure he's gone. Then I'll go see if I can fetch someone."

"No, please, Rebecca, if he finds out you disobeyed him, there's no telling what he'll do to you."

"At least I can try to find Ida. Let me go see."

"Okay, but come right back, please."

"I promise."

She waited ten minutes to be sure that Isaac had left the building and then ran out the front door. She descended the stairs as quickly as she could and knocked on Ida's door, tapping her toe impatiently in her slipper. There was no answer.

Sidney would already have left for work, but where was Ida? God, not at Gutstein's, surely. Was this when they had their time together, early in the morning, just after her husband left, when people were still moving about groggily beginning their days? She thought it was the afternoons. Well, it didn't matter. She didn't care if she had to disturb them, embarrass them both, this was important.

She began to go down the next flight of stairs but heard a faint moaning coming from above, perhaps her name being called? She turned on her toe and ran back up to the apartment. As soon as she entered the bedroom, Sylvia begged her not to leave her again.

"I'm afraid, Rebecca, something doesn't feel right."

Rebecca looked between her legs. There was blood. And also the crown of the baby's head was right there.

"Sylvia, sweetheart, this is it. It's gonna have to be just the two of us, because the baby's coming. I can see its head. You have to push really hard next time."

"Oh my God." Sylvia cried out, then clamped her face into a wrinkled ball of blotchy red and white patches. Rebecca pulled her chair up to the end of the bed and, with her finger, drew circles around the baby's head where it was stretching the labia. She remembered her mother told her this might gently help things along.

Sylvia's next contraction pushed the baby out enough that it seemed half of the head was in and half was out. But when she took another look, she realized this was only the beginning, that the head was actually much bigger, that this was only the soft skull doing what it had to in order to get out any way it could. Blood seeped over the skull all around, and Rebecca couldn't tell where it was coming from. Sylvia had torn a bit, but the blood also seemed to be coming from inside.

Two more pushes sent the head out, and then, with Rebecca slipping her fingers inside to help the shoulders by, the rest of the baby came slithering out into her arms. The baby's toes wriggled. Its face was scrunched up, and it let out a sharp little bleating noise.

"A little girl," Rebecca said. "It's a little girl."

She took the knife she had boiled and cut through the cord, then tied off the end at the baby's belly. Then she picked the child up and gave her to Sylvia to hold in her arms. Sylvia's face relaxed when she felt the tiny body, and she smiled.

Rebecca noticed that there was blood still flowing from her vagina. She gathered some clean cloths together and held them firm against her. Sylvia winced a little, but breathed in and out. The blood soaked through the cloth quickly, and Rebecca changed it. She squeezed out the cloth into the bowl beside the bed.

The cloth was not stopping the bleeding. Rebecca's breathing quickened, but she tried not to show that anything was wrong. Besides, she couldn't be sure this was not a normal thing to happen after a birth.

Sylvia had placed the baby on her breast, and it was beginning to suckle. She was stroking her finger over the baby's lips.

"Rebecca, come look at her face." Every word seemed an enormous effort. "It's the funniest little thing, I could just eat her up. And her head — all lumpy ..."

Rebecca shifted up to her side, never taking her hand off the cloth. "She's adorable." She leaned in and gave the baby a kiss on the back of the head. Then she leaned over Sylvia and kissed her on the lips. "You were incredible, my love. I don't know how you did it."

Sylvia smiled. "With your help. That's how."

Rebecca felt the blood running over her hand, soaking again through the cloth. Why wasn't it stopping? Maybe it was because she needed to pull on the cord. When she had watched her mother, this was another part of the birth to which she had not paid much attention, so distracted had she been by the little boy that had emerged and been placed on the woman's stomach. She remembered only that her mother had somehow tugged on the cord, and there had been some more contractions to expel the piece of flesh at the end of the cord.

"Sylvia, I think we need to help the afterbirth to come out. Are you ready to push a little again? I'll help by pulling the cord."

"Okay. But I don't ... think I have left ... I'll try." Her words were beginning to slur, and Rebecca saw her eyes droop a little.

"I need you to stay awake, sweetheart. Please concentrate. Later you can sleep."

Rebecca counted to three, and then Sylvia made an effort to push. Rebecca tugged a little, but nothing was giving way. She tugged harder. Still no give. The blood seemed to be seeping out more quickly now, in little waves, pushed along by the persistence of Sylvia's heart.

"One more time, Sylvia," Rebecca said, and then she tensed her arm muscle for a strong tug. This time something gave, and Sylvia screamed. Rebecca pulled the cord out more, and saw at the end of it a lumpy object shaped like a great swollen tongue emerge partway from the opening. The cord was attached to the tip of it, and it had a bluish-purple translucent coating. It appeared to be still attached to her body, at the back of the tongue, just inside the vaginal opening.

Sylvia's cry became a soft whimper. Something was wrong. It wasn't coming out. She pulled hard, and the cord detached from the protrusion. She gasped, and looked up at Sylvia. She hadn't noticed.

She looked at the afterbirth, slick and sticking out and enormous. The one that her mother had pulled out didn't look like this. It was much smaller, and it was all red, like a nice flank steak. She looked again and realized what it was. This was Sylvia's womb. She had pulled too hard, turned it inside out, pulled it out of her body. And now she had pulled the cord right off.

"Oh my God. Oh my God." She muffled her words with her hand over her mouth. Sylvia did not seem to hear her. She was rocking her head back and forth, holding onto the baby. Quickly, Rebecca pushed the womb back in with her fingers, stuffed it back in any way that seemed possible. The folds of Sylvia's vagina closed back tightly over it as the shells of a clam would do to shut itself in protection, but they could not hold back the blood.

Rebecca stepped back from the bed, holding her bloody hands at her side. Her mouth hung open to say something, and she stared between Sylvia's legs. She stood for what seemed an eternity, the sucking sound of the nursing baby a distant noise. A soft voice cut through her daze.

"...becca?"

She fell beside Sylvia, draping her arm over Sylvia's body, convulsing, enfolding her and the baby.

"I'm so sorry. I'm so sorry. I've done something terrible. I don't know what to do."

"Shhh. 's okay ...'s okay now."

"Sylvia, what'll I do? What are we going to do?" She rubbed tears from Sylvia's eyes, mixing them with the blood from her hands so that her face was a streaky patch of red, more blood on her skin, Rebecca thought, than under it. But Sylvia's tears flowed over the patches, washing deltas down her cheeks.

"Shhh. Look who's here," Sylvia whispered, and she closed her eyes as she said it, and stroked the baby's lips again with her finger. The movement was so strained Rebecca wondered if she was trying to caress her child or merely point to her.

"Sylvia, please stay awake. We need to get you a doctor. I need you to hold on."

Sylvia mumbled something barely audible. She had stopped crying.

"Sylvia!"

"Shh, Elsie." Her lips tried to pucker, and her eyes squinted half open. "Will be safe with Sadie. Sadie'll take care'v us."

"No, Sylvia, please no. Don't give up, Sylvia." She pressed her face into her side. "...please, oh please..." One of the baby's hands had latched onto Sylvia's thumb; it was asleep now and had let go of the nipple. Rebecca felt Sylvia's arm relax at her side. She clung to her lover, crying, feeling with her ear for a heartbeat.

She waited to hear something, anything at all.

She waited, wishing this felt less real, wishing it had the quality of a true nightmare, the kind from which one could waken.

She waited, until waiting was futile, remained there until time became agony itself, each second a stabbing cut, each minute an evisceration.

She stayed still, not even moving to attend to the baby, until she no longer knew what pain meant, until its meaning was irrelevant for its abundance.

She was slumped, crumpled, motionless, waiting for her insides to be completely torn out, inverted and bloodied on the floor.

She remained there, time creeping by, her body becoming a shroud, until she felt nothing more than a cavernous hollow, echoing faintly of something far away.

Until the bleating sound of the baby waking up, and the feel of her as she wriggled a little under her outstretched arms, jogged her out of her paralysis.

And then she got up.

And wiped her face.

And looked about the room.

The clock said eleven-thirty. She had been there four and a half hours.

Purposefully, she set about to do what she had to do.

She took the baby into her arms, gently prying her tiny fingers free from Sylvia's thumb, and wrapped her in a cloth to set her on the bed beside her mother. She gathered up the bowl and knife and placed them on the bed. Then she took the bloodied cloths, not quite fully dry, and wiped her undergarments with them, holding them firm to ensure that they sufficiently stained.

She would put them on again later to complete the deception when Isaac returned, but for now, she removed her nightdress and untied the straps from her back, straining to reach the ties in their awkward location, and freed herself of the padding. She took the knife, cut away a large square of soft leather from the exterior, and placed it on the bed beside the bowl.

She washed her hands and face and changed into new clothes, a clean shirt and a skirt, and tied a scarf over her head, covering her eyes enough so as not to be recognized. She took the padding, bundled it up in a blanket, and, listening for the sound of Isaac returning, she quietly left the apartment to go out to the street. Around two corners, and behind a building, she ducked into an alley and stuffed the padding in amongst some garbage.

Then she returned to the apartment. She went into the bedroom again and looked around. She felt under the bed and found what she was looking for. She smoothed it out. Some drops of blood had soaked through in a few places, slightly smudging the ink.

Dear Sweet Rebecca,

I don't know how to write like you, but I told you I would try if I felt inspired, and I do. Also, I can't sleep again, and I'm watching you lie there and I'm thinking I might explode if I don't say how I feel. I shouldn't even do this, but I need to write it down, just to see it myself once on paper so that I can make it more real. Maybe I'll get rid of this afterwards. Maybe I'll swallow it to keep it with me. If you ever read this, I'm sure you'd be horrified.

I keep wondering, do you even know? Do you know how in love with you I am? You're breathing so softly now, and your eyelids are sort of fluttering in your sleep. I wonder what you dream about. I hope it's about me.

If I could, I would shower you with letters a hundred times better, but I don't think I could even show you this one. I've never written a love letter before, and certainly never to a woman.

Sometimes when I see you in the kitchen, when your husband is just there reading at the table, I want to touch you so bad it hurts. I have to hold myself back from coming up beside you, wrapping my arms around your huge belly and squeezing you tight. I wish I could kiss you all over. I have to think of something else or I'll go crazy.

When I wake up in the middle of the night and see you beside me, I thank God you came into my life. Maybe it's His way of making up for taking away my sister. It makes me think maybe I'm not such a bad person after all.

Rebecca, you deserve so much better than this. I love you so much, I think I would do anything for you. No, I know it. I'd do anything. But even that wouldn't be enough.

That's all I really wanted to write down. How much I love you, Rebecca.

For ever and ever, with all my heart,

Sylvia

She read it through three times, memorizing the words, and then, acting quickly so as not to lose her resolve, she folded it carefully and wrapped it in the leather from the padding, tying it into a neat square envelope with some string.

Then she tugged gently at the featherbed, carefully rolling Sylvia's body to the side until it pulled free. The blood was beginning to form a dry crust. The mortician would need to be called. Later. She would make Isaac do it.

She placed the leather envelope on top in the centre and then rolled it up inside the featherbed. Into a burlap bag from the kitchen she stuffed it, binding it closed with some more string, and pushing out as much air as possible to compact it to its tiniest possible size.

Finally, she pulled out the tin chest from the closet, emptied its contents, replaced them with the burlap bundle, and allowed just one sharp sob to escape her lips as she sealed the vestiges of her happiness inside their small metal coffin. Were it not for the baby crying behind her, she might have tried to crawl in there with them.

Chapter Twenty-three

1983

When Sadie finished reading, Anna settled herself into her mother's bed, while her sister took the back room. She tried to find sleep, shifting and stretching under the sheet, but it eluded her. There was no sound coming from the other room. Could Sadie have dozed off so easily?

She took a sleeping pill, and eventually her erratic thoughts settled under a fog. But her sleep became fitful, stirred up by visitations from babies and rusted metal trunks and the blurred faces of people from distant memory and recent imagination. Most of the people who plagued her subconscious were dead or disappeared, making it all the more distressing. There was nothing coherent about the dreams, they were tangential and surreal, but every tortuous image made perfect sense to her. At one point she started crying, a wrenching wail more pitiful than she had ever produced while awake, and then jerked her eyes open a moment later, surprised to find she had not uttered a sound or shed even a single tear. Then she was pulled back down again, drawn into a dark undertow against which her conscious mind was too weak to swim.

At seven o'clock, Anna got up and slipped past the streak of sun sneaking its way across the floor. The kitchen was still dark when she put on the kettle, striking a match to start the flame on the old gas stove. The light from the element flickered against the cloudy walls.

She went to use the toilet and saw that the tiny mirror over the sink was still covered with a towel. She washed her face and brushed her hair, resisting the temptation to look at herself in the chrome reflection of the towel rack. She felt her part with her fingers to try to ensure that the comb had done its job.

She knew she was not supposed to be vain when in mourning, but didn't God give some allowance for a person's dignity? After last night, she could only imagine how hideous her eyes must be. Probably with lines as wide as the New Jersey Turnpike.

Was all of that her mother? The person who insisted she have the most traditional wedding, the woman who played Mah Jong with the old ladies from the neighbourhood every week and wore pink nail polish like there was a state decree? Was this the same woman who risked her life in an elaborate deception, for a passionate affair with a woman, to fake a pregnancy? The same woman who watched her lover die?

She felt a bit sickened when she thought of her mother with another woman. There, she admitted it to herself. She knew she couldn't say anything about it to her sister. She was ashamed to discover she was not as liberal-minded as she had thought, and furthermore Sadie seemed not to be bothered by it at all. It irked her that her own reaction was exactly why her mother had kept this secret for so long. She was annoyed at her mother for knowing her so well, for being right — again.

At least the woman took a risk, for once in her life.

She thought about that for a moment, stepped back to observe the unexpected flash of anger with which her mind had spit out that conclusion. She squeezed some hand lotion through her fingers and sat back down on the toilet seat. No, that wasn't really fair at all. That was most definitely not the only time she took a risk. There was another.

The whistle of the kettle signalled to her that she should end her ablutions. She wiped the excess lotion on her arms and came out of the bathroom. Sadie was at the table pouring water into the teapot.

"I'm sorry, Sadie, I didn't mean to wake you up."

Sadie yawned and waved away her apology. "No, no, I always get up early. It's the curse of getting older: less to do and more hours in the day to fill."

"I know, it's terrible. Mama was the only exception to the rule. She used to go to bed at ten o'clock and sleep until ten every morning. I used to tell her because she'd been asleep half of her life, she was really only forty-five."

"Well, it's too bad she had to die so young, but she was lucky she got some sleep."

Anna grinned. She'd forgotten her sister shared her sense of humour; it was nice to know they could still laugh together after all these years.

"Yeah, a real shame. Cut down in the prime of her youth."

They laughed a bit at that, then looked away from one another. The intimacy of last night seemed more elusive in the emerging daylight.

Anna went to pull some plates out of the cupboard. "Unfortunately, being a sound sleeper was the only way she was lucky."

"That's for sure. God, we knew she had it tough with Papa, but it never occurred to me it was worse before we were born."

"Me neither."

"You know, we're just as self-absorbed as any other children. You always think your birth is the most exciting thing that ever happened to them. You never think your parents did anything of importance before you came along." Sadie fumbled through the cupboards for a tea bag until Anna directed her to the second shelf on the right. She picked out a box of Salada, grabbed two Sweet 'N Low's. Anna pulled two ceramic mugs out of the cupboard, and some bread from the fridge. She turned on the oven and put the toast on the upper rack. They sat down at the table and picked at the corners of the tea bags, letting the aroma rouse them.

"My Allan used to be like that," said Anna. "He never imagined that his own mother could've been young once. I remember when I published my first young adult novel. He was twelve years old, and I dedicated it something like, 'For Allan, for showing me how my youth might have been.'" She laid out the typesetting in the air. "I can't tell you the conversations that one sentence provoked. He couldn't get his mind around the fact that his own mother was once his age."

"You're a good writer, Anna."

"You read my books?"

"I've followed your career ever since your first book came out. The author's notes didn't tell me a lot about you — they never even printed your picture — but at least it was something. I have to tell you, it's a strange thing waiting for a newspaper article or a book jacket so you can find out about your own sister. I only found out that your husband died about five years after the fact. I didn't even know you lost Allan until something like '73, when they did that story about you in the *New York Times*."

"I wish you'd called at some point."

"So do I. I wish I'd had the guts."

Anna stirred some sugar into her cup, wondering how to begin this. "It was hard for me after you left, Sadie," she said, letting her sister's eyes flicker for a moment with curiosity.

"It sounds like you've had more than your share of loss in your life, Anna. I'm sorry."

"I'm not talking about losing Mel and Allan. You're forgetting that Mama and I had another two years of *Papa* before he died."

"I know. It must have been awful."

"The worst part was when she would beg him to stop. She wouldn't beg him for her own sake, no. She begged him for his heart condition. I couldn't bear it, I just kept thinking, shut up, Mama! Say something else if you want to protect yourself, but let him drop dead!" Sadie reached over and grabbed her sister's forearm. Anna had been absent-mindedly spreading some jam on a piece of bread, reducing it to pieces.

"Meanwhile, Mama barely paid attention to me, except to pressure me to study harder at school. The only time there was any closeness was when I was helping her to ice down her bruises. Isn't that sick? Oh, and of course when she would invite her friend Hattie over. Then all of a sudden we were best friends."

"What ever happened to that woman?"

"I don't know. We lost touch with her shortly after Papa died. She moved out west, and she and Mama fell out of touch.

We actually saw her the day Papa died. She came over. She and Mama had their regular weekly outing planned. It was the first Sunday in November. Your birthday, actually."

"Hmph. Hattie came by the day Papa threw me out too. She was like the harbinger of doom."

"No she wasn't. She was just Mama's only friend."

"Ah c'mon. Mama had other friends."

"No she didn't. Nobody *she* would have considered a friend. Her friends had either died, or she cut them out. She cut Dora out when you left home. That left Hattie. Of course, there were others right there in front of her eyes, but until that day, she never looked hard enough to see them."

Chapter Twenty-four

1931

The afternoon crawled by, until it felt like if they went into one more shop to do nothing but pick at merchandise, Anna would explode. Because it was Sunday and she was off work, she had joined her mother on her weekly outing with her friend Hattie. But her mother was not herself today. Usually she charged about, leading them this way and that, at such a brisk pace that they had to practically run after her to keep up. Today, she dawdled behind, shuffled her feet on the ground, and barely engaged in the conversation.

Whereas she normally had a precise list of groceries, from which she rarely deviated, today she forgot it. Anna had to keep reminding her, didn't they need some flour, or weren't they running out of potatoes, or didn't she want some vegetables for a salad. Her mother seemed to be shopping for nothing in particular, lingering in a trance over a pile of apples or sifting her fingers back and forth through a bin of lentils, making

furrows on top until the shopkeeper tactfully asked her if he
could help in any way. Thankfully, her Auntie Hattie was
engaged in collecting things of her own and did not seem to
notice that anything was wrong.

But the conversational topics were running out. They had
discussed world affairs, city politics, the ever rising price of
produce, the growing depression, Hattie's son, her newly completed short story, Anna's job, and the latest fashions. They
had even talked about the baseball scores. That was how desperate she was.

After a lengthy and increasingly uncomfortable silence,
Anna was almost ready to give up. But not before she had one
last go at it.

"So what else is new, Auntie Hattie?"

She tried not to sigh too obviously; she had clearly reached
the dregs. Mercifully, before Hattie could answer, her mother
dragged them into yet another shop. The room was lined on
both sides with enormous columns of fabric, in a rainbow of
colours, stretching from floor to ceiling. The air smelled slightly of vinegar — in the right aisle, a woman was washing the
floors with a rag mop. Dividing the room in two, long narrow
tables were piled with various odds and ends, red pincushions
lying among spools of thread and yarn, plucked tomatoes in a
field of cylindrical flowers. At the back of the shop, a few
derelict sewing machines were covered with leather pattern
cut-outs. A wooden mannequin was dismembered and draped
over one of them, its armless torso arching back dramatically
over the fly wheel.

Her mother went to a bolt of cloth near the end of the left
aisle and examined the material intently, holding it up to the
light to see the thread count. She and Hattie slowly followed

---

her, perusing the items on the table. Anna hoped her question had been forgotten — it would be just as well. Better to let it die the peaceful death it deserved.

But Hattie suddenly picked up her head and said, "Well, I'll tell you what's new, Anna, I have some great news. But I want your mother to hear this too."

"I'm listening," her mother said, not lifting her eyes from the cloth.

"I'm leaving Marty."

Her mother looked at Hattie and squinted, like she had spoken a foreign language.

"That's the news. I'm finally leaving."

"No you're not." She went back to examining her cloth.

"I am so. I'm serious this time. I've packed my things. I have a place to stay in Los Angeles with a cousin on my mother's side. I'm going to stay with her. I'm taking Bobby with. There's a good school near them. Emma Goldman convinced me to do it."

"What nonsense are you talking now, Emma Goldman convinced you? You and Miss Goldman chat regularly?"

"No, don't be silly, she's not even in New York. I've been reading her memoirs. Haven't you, Rebecca? They're being published in the *Forward*."

"I haven't paid much attention to them," her mother said. "Frankly, it's mostly foolish idealism."

"It's not idealism, Rebecca. She not only has ideals, she lives by her ideals. She made a decision not to marry, because she knew it would change everything. She knew that being married would mean an end to her independent thinking. Even though she has truly loved several men. And isn't that what I've been complaining about all these years?"

"You certainly have. And as I've always told you, it's nonsense."

Her mother's voice had developed an edge.

"It's not nonsense," Hattie continued. "It makes perfect sense. Here is this woman, this famous, world-renowned person, and she's expressing exactly how I feel. I love Marty, but it's not enough. Don't you see? Emma Goldman acted on her feelings, and look at how successful she's been. Maybe I could be too. I just have to have the courage."

Anna looked to her mother, expecting a rebuttal, but she didn't even turn around.

Getting no reaction from her friend, Hattie turned back to Anna. "What do you think, darling?"

"I hate to admit it, Auntie Hattie, but I think I agree with Mama. Emma Goldman's just too radical. I admire her, but she lets principles get in the way of her happiness. It depends on who you're married to, whether or not you can be an independent woman."

"What makes you so sure of that?"

Anna disregarded her condescending tone. "Well, for instance, it doesn't make sense why she couldn't marry Alexander Berkman or Ben Reitman. They sounded like exactly the kind of men who would support her to be whoever she wanted to be, and do whatever she wanted to do. Like Uncle Marty does with you."

"But don't you see? That's not enough. It's how *other* people see you once you're married that matters. Other people hold you back, even if your husband doesn't. No offence dear, but if you were married, you'd notice that right away."

"I don't want to talk about this anymore," Rebecca said. "Can't we just have a nice day together?"

She closed the door behind her, and Anna could see her through the window, standing outside, arms crossed.

"What's the matter with her?" Hattie asked, gesturing towards the exit.

"It's Sadie's birthday today," she mumbled.

"Oh, heck."

"That's okay, she doesn't talk much about it."

"You mean, she doesn't talk about it at all. Still, I should've remembered. I'm such a fool. Well, I've gotta go say something to her. Wait here for a second," she said.

"No, please, Auntie Hattie, don't mention Sadie, it'll just upset her more."

"I won't. I'll just tell her I'm gonna miss her."

She went outside, and through the pane of glass, Anna watched her lips move. Hattie held her mother by the shoulders and was trying unsuccessfully to meet her eyes.

Their tradition of celebrating Sadie's birthday had started long ago, and they'd never missed a year until this one. Even last year, the year after Sadie had run away, they followed the same strange and comforting routine that Anna had never really questioned. First they would go to Seward Park for a picnic, nearly freezing to death in the cold, wrapped in huge shawls over their winter coats and spreading their food out on a frosty picnic table. Then, when the cold was beginning to numb their fingers through their thin wool gloves, they would walk over to Allen Street. There, they poked into the shops, warmed up, looked at shiny, expensive, silver items they could not afford. It was not to find a birthday present for Sadie — they always got their presents first thing in the morning, wrapped up and sitting in a bowl on the table.

Though her mother had not uttered Sadie's name since the day she left, Anna knew she still thought about her. Last year, on Sadie's birthday, her father had barely left the apartment when her mother said to her simply, "It's November eighth." Without another word, they set about to prepare the picnic basket, and then they followed the route, like two figures on a board game, being moved through the city by an unseen player.

Why didn't they go this year? She didn't dare ask. Perhaps it was that Sadie's birthday fell on a Sunday, and Hattie came by that day. But it would have been easy enough for her mother to reschedule her friend's visit. There had to be some other reason, not that she would ever find out.

She saw through the window that Hattie and her mother were hugging, and then Hattie squinted through the glass, waved to her and blew a kiss, and walked off. Anna joined her mother outside, and they headed towards home. But her mother pulled her into three more shops on the way, despite Anna's warnings that it was getting late and they hadn't started dinner. Something wasn't right. Even though she knew why her mother was upset, it wasn't like her to dawdle so much near the end of the day. It wasn't worth it to risk Papa's wrath.

They were walking along Henry Street when they passed Zussel's Fresh Fish, up the block from their building. Normally, she would have quickened her pace as she passed it by. But this time, it was no surprise that her mother motioned to her that they should go into the store. As they approached the window, Ida Weiss could be seen inside talking to Mr. Zussel. She had her newborn, Danielle, cradled in her arm.

"Hell," her mother mumbled, and she tried to pull them away from the door, but it was too late. Ida saw them too, and was waving them in.

"Rebecca, Anna!" they heard her muffled voice through the window.

Anna led her mother into the shop. Colourful rows of fish were packed on crushed ice in front of the window. On some other shelves along the side of the store there were jars of pickled fish, boxes of salt and pickling spices, some bins of onions and garlic. Two women poked and prodded the fish in the window display, lifting up the gills to see the colour underneath, turning them over to see if the scales looked healthy. A long counter at the back had some fish heads in piles next to a bloody cleaver.

At the end of the counter, Mr. Zussel stood behind the cash register, spectacles on the tip of his nose, squinting at the display. He wore a white apron smeared with guts and scales, and brown fingerless gloves. He glanced up at them and smiled, but returned his gaze quickly to study the figures on the register. Wisps of hair snuck out over the collar of shirt, through the holes near his cuffs, and out of his ears. Like hay poking out of a scarecrow. The hair on his head stuck out to the sides in great tufts.

Ida pulled them over to the cash.

"Rebecca, I can't believe you came by. I was about to come tell you. You'll never believe it. Mr. Zussel's offered me a job. He needs some help because his store has been doing so well. Who else could make money these days except our Mr. Zussel?"

"No thanks to you two, I should say," he snorted, pointing to Anna and her mother.

"Ida, that's wonderful," her mother said, ignoring him. "This couldn't come at a better time for you."

"You can say that again." She began speaking in hushed tones, so that the other women in the shop wouldn't hear.

"Sidney only left me a few weeks ago, but I'm already down to almost nothing. And Danielle here is turning out to be quite the chazer. She's sucking me dry." She tickled her baby's chin.

"Ida, I'm so sorry about what's happened. You know my husband, sometimes, he doesn't always consider the consequences of what he says."

Mr. Zussel had a coughing fit that stopped the conversation dead, a little conspicuous in its timing, Anna thought.

"Rebecca, I don't blame you," Ida said. "But what he did, it wasn't necessary. You don't need to apologize for him. I know I was never a good wife, but what reason was there for him to tell Sidney now? For the last two years, I've been completely faithful since Arthur and I decided to just be good friends. Your husband was dredging up old news. And it was none of his business."

"I know. I agree it was horrible."

"It wasn't just that. He'd already driven Arthur away, what did he need to go bothering himself with my marriage?"

"Are you sure about that? How can we know that Mr. Gutstein wouldn't have taken that job anyway? I really don't think he meant for him to leave. I'm not saying what my husband did there was right either, but I think he was just trying to get him to lower our rent."

"By blackmailing him, Rebecca?"

Mr. Zussel coughed again, even more loudly than the first time. Her mother looked at Mr. Zussel and sighed. He was pretending to ignore them, writing some figures down on a paper bag.

"I'm sorry, Ida."

"Rebecca, it's like I said, it's not your fault. And besides, what's done is done. All that's behind us now. My husband's gone, and even if he weren't, there's nobody around I can even cheat on him with!" She let out a short little cackle, and then they all stood and waited quietly while a woman came up to have Mr. Zussel wrap up a large carp.

When the woman had paid and left, Ida said, "Maybe your husband did me a favour, Rebecca. I have a newborn to look after now. What do I need with all these men, distracting me? Of course I don't mean you, Mr. Zussel — you've done me such a mitzvah."

She smiled weakly, and Anna found she had to look away.

"If you think this is a mitzvah, that is because you have not started working yet. A fish store is not as much fun as everyone thinks, Mrs. Weiss."

"I'm prepared to work hard, don't worry."

"And how about you, Mrs. Kalish? Will you think about working a few hours for me too?"

"Don't be silly. What would I do here?"

"Tell funny stories, what do you think? Sell fish, of course. Unless you want to cut off their heads and pull out their kishkes. Then I could be out with the customers more. Mrs. Weiss is helping me with my books."

"I don't think so. But thank you very much for the offer. It's very generous."

"Well, maybe you will think about it. You two have known each other since you were no bigger than two scrawny legs of chicken, and that's good. When people know each other, it makes it easier. I cannot have two people working side by side here, pretending to be nice all of the time, making me want to throw myself into the East River, because they are afraid to say what is on their minds."

"I'll think about it," she said, but Anna thought her mother didn't make much of an effort to be convincing. She had already taken hold of her hand and was tugging them on their way. She waved back at Mr. Zussel, thanking him again, then they both waved goodbye and left the store.

When they carried on straight to their building, Anna was surprised. She thought they would never get home. As they made their way up the stairs, she gripped the banister harder and harder with every flight. She knew her father would be home, stewing. It was already seven o'clock, and they had not even begun dinner.

When they got in the door, as she predicted, her father glowered at them from his chair. Her mother greeted him casually, a weariness in her voice. With Anna urging them silently on, they threw together a simple meal: some barley soup, boiled broccoli, and fried chicken livers with onions.

They sat down at the table. There was no conversation at all, making all sounds louder, more conspicuous. Their chewing seemed grotesque and slobbering, the clacking of cutlery against tin plates was like small thunderclaps. Her father's chair scraping along the floor reminded her of nails on a chalkboard.

What made it all the worse was that her mother didn't seem to care. The more obvious her father's annoyance, the more abrupt his movements, the more slowly her mother moved. Lazily she ladled out soup, blowing on it to cool it down before pouring it into their bowls. Instead of gathering plates up efficiently after each course, she cleared them one by one, prolonging the agony with every trip to the counter.

Anna had never seen her mother behave so provocatively. The slower she moved, the madder he got. His face reddened, his fists tightened, the muscles in his jaw rippled. When the dishes were done, Anna fled to her room. Because she knew what was coming next. Or at least she thought she did.

She jumped into bed and pulled the pillow over her head to try to block out the sound of the shouting. To distract herself, she pictured that she was flying. Sadie always used to say that she was a strange girl, not because she wanted to fly, but because most people who dreamt that they were flying did so when they were asleep. Anna only had waking dreams of flight, and never of her own body swooping and hovering of its own propulsion, but only of flying a real aeroplane, like Miss Earhart did.

She shut her eyes tight and tried to imagine she was with Amelia in the cockpit of her Lockheed Vega. How would they look? They would have their aviator goggles pulled down over their eyes, to keep them from tearing as they cut a straight line across the Atlantic. She might say, "Pull up the nose" just for the heck of it, and Amelia would pull back on the steering column, sending the tip of the plane soaring upwards and backwards into a loop-the-loop. She could feel the plane righting itself again, could hear Amelia laugh with exhilaration, and could see her point straight ahead at some cotton-batten clouds. The plane shot ahead, bored a hole in the first one they could reach, until they were soaked in the mist, bathed in milk, surrounded by the heavens.

But as they pulled out of the clouds, her father's voice disturbed her reverie. It was futile trying to ignore it.

She couldn't hear the full conversation, but enough words filtered through to figure it out through abstraction. It penetrated the walls most when his shouting crescendoed.

"... many *times* have I ... *never* can depend ... will *not be* made to ..."

Her mother's voice was harder to hear, taking on that calming tone that she hated so much, the one that never worked anyway.

"... happen again ... please ... agitate yourself ..."

The shouting went on for another minute, and she couldn't make out any more words.

Then, she heard a slight change in her mother's tone. It was taking on a hint of frustrated anger and she was crying as she spoke.

"... only wanted to ... my only friend had something important to tell me ..."

And her father's voice, "*And what was so important that ....*"

And then she heard her mother much more clearly, shouting every word.

"*She has had the sense to leave her husband! That's what!*"

Anna sat up in bed, gripping the blanket. Her mother had never raised her voice before during an argument. Not like this, never.

Oh my God.

She closed her eyes and braced herself. She heard a thud, and then a crash. Her mother started crying, louder than she usually did, almost a rasping, howling sound, interrupted by small thuds, but getting louder each time. Then, suddenly, that was cut off and replaced by a muffled scream, the force of it clearly dampened by something covering her mouth.

Anna got up from her bed. The smothered noises were getting more desperate, and she heard her mother's body thrashing about.

She ran to her parents' bedroom. When she flung open the door, she saw her mother on the floor beside the bed, her father sitting on top of her, his hand over her mouth. Her face was red, and her eyes were bugging out. The noise she was making was getting weaker.

"Papa! Get off her! She can't breathe!"

"Go away, Anna." He did not look up.

"I said get *off* her!"

She threw herself at him, her weight knocking him off of her mother and onto his side. His head cracked loudly against the wooden bed frame, and he fell on his side, stunned. She quickly scrambled to her feet and stepped backwards over her parents. Her mother was still lying on the ground, coughing to regain her breath.

Anna looked at her father. His eyes were closed, but his head moved slightly. Her first instinct was to try to pin him down with her body so that he wouldn't be able to retaliate, but she realized that her weight and strength would be insufficient.

She looked quickly about and realized there was nothing she could use to pin him down. Then she saw his prayer shawl hanging on the back of the door. She took the tallis and quickly grabbed her father's arms. She didn't have very much time if she wanted to do this. Surprising herself with her deftness, she grabbed hold of his wrists and wrapped the shawl around them several times very tightly, tying a few knots. Then she pulled his arms over his head and tied the tallis ends firmly to the bedpost.

Her mother was just beginning to recover and was standing up. "Anna, what are you doing?"

"I'm protecting us, Mama."

Her father was now fully conscious, and he had quickly assessed his predicament. "Anna! You'll untie me now if you know what's good for you."

She sat up, but did nothing.

"Untie me, I said."

Her mother looked nervous. "Anna dear, please. This isn't a solution. He'll only get more angry."

Anna started to cry. "I don't care, Mama! I'm tired of it, and you should be too!"

"Rebecca, get these off of me now and control your daughter, for God's sake."

"Shut up, Papa! Shut up! I can't stand it anymore! Don't talk to us like that!"

"Don't you tell me how I can talk to my own family! I'll talk any way ..."

"Stop it!" She reached for the pillow on the bed and pressed it onto her father's face. "Just stop it!" She knelt down on his chest. "Now how do you like it? How does it feel, Papa, to be pinned down and not breathing? Not too big and strong anymore, are you?"

Her father's smothered shouts came angrily from under the pillow. He bucked up against her to try to throw her off, but she kept the pillow pinned firmly. Her mother ran to her and pulled at her arms.

"Stop it, Anneleh, please!"

Anna resisted her.

"Anneleh, I'm begging you. Please, darling!"

For a few seconds longer, she stood her ground. And then abruptly, she gave up. She pulled her arms off of the pillow and sat there. Her father stopped bucking, but shook his head to get the pillow off of his face.

Her mother took the pillow away, and her father wheezed and coughed once. His face was red and puffy.

"Please, darling, get off of your father, I don't want you involved in this." She put her arm on Anna's shoulder.

Anna shook her head. "Oh, Mama," she said, and she got up slowly. "I thought this time would be different. I heard you shouting, and ... and I came because I thought ... He almost killed you, Mama. What is it gonna take?"

She walked toward the door. In the shadow outside the bedroom, she saw Ida standing there, holding her baby in her arms. She must have let herself in.

Ida looked frightened, unsure whether or not she should come into the bedroom. She and Anna looked at one another, but since Anna said nothing, neither seemed surprised to see her nor asked for help, Ida stayed where she was.

Anna turned back to look at her mother. She had not yet noticed there was anyone else in the apartment, and was going to untie her father. He jerked his hands free once the tallis was unwrapped, and her mother stepped away from him.

"Stupid woman. I could've been killed."

Her mother stepped backwards again until she bumped into Anna. She turned around and saw her neighbour standing there.

"Ida! What are you doing here?"

"I heard the noise. I came to see if you were okay."

"Ida, you shouldn't be here."

Her father propped himself against the side of the bed, his legs stretched out and coughing into his hands.

He spoke hoarsely. "This is none of your business, Mrs. Weiss. My God, is the whole building to be involved in my relationship with my wife?"

"I was in the hallway, and I heard noises," she said.

"Perhaps you have too much time on your hands now that your lover has moved away and your husband is gone."

"They didn't just leave, Mr. Kalish. You drove them away."

"I think I only beat you to it." He winced and started coughing again, started clenching and unclenching his left fist.

Anna placed her hand on Ida's shoulder to show sympathy, but she barely noticed, for at that moment the baby started crying, and so Ida fumbled with her nightdress to pull her breast out. Her mother helped Ida to adjust the baby in the crook of her left arm, and Anna went to the other room to get her a small pillow.

When she came back, she noticed that her father had started to push himself off the floor. The baby calmed down when her lips cleaved themselves to her mother's nipple, but now a different cry pulled their attention back the other way.

Her father had managed to pull himself halfway up to the bed, but he was clutching at his chest. He cried out again and slid back down to the floor. Anna and Ida both jerked forward instinctively as he fell, but her mother grabbed their wrists.

"Rebecca, my medicine," he said. "I ... uhnn ... my ... medicine."

Her mother looked at him and squinted her eyes, cocked her head a little to the side. Her grasp on their arms did not relent. Anna wondered what she was looking at. Then she saw the tiniest smile creep across her face.

Ida looked puzzled. "Rebecca? Don't you want me to get the medicine?"

There was no response. She tried again.

"Rebecca, shouldn't we help him?"

Again, her mother didn't answer. Her father wheezed, slumped a little bit.

Then, after a few seconds, her mother turned slowly to Ida and said, "After all he's done to us both Ida, I don't believe we should." She turned to Anna. "What do you think, Anna, darling?"

Anna looked at her mother, astonished. Her mouth dropped open slightly. "Mama?"

"What do you think, sweetheart? Should we help your papa, or should we just stand here wondering what the best course of action would be?"

She looked into her mother's eyes, and she saw in them a quality that she had never before found. It was a flicker of something. Something like fire.

Anna smiled, because she finally understood.

"Oh, absolutely. I think you're right, Mama. We're far too brainless and upset to be thinking clearly right now."

"And you, Ida?"

Ida brought her eyes to meet Rebecca's and said simply, "It's hard for me to think straight, what with a newborn and everything."

Her mother released their wrists, and the three of them just stood there, watching her father's chest heave up and down. His eyes were getting droopy.

"Please, Rebecca, I'm begging you. My medicine."

They stood firm.

Her mother said, "Go to hell, Isaac."

A look of panic blanched his face. His body was now stretched out fully, his neck bent forward by his head's being propped against the side of the bed. He moaned, and slid even further down.

"You'll never ... get away with this ... Rebecca. People will know ... what happened."

"No, I don't think they will."

He wheezed.

Anna reached out and took her mother's hand.

Ida put her arm around her mother's waist.

And they stood there, the three of them, exhaling, inhaling, and then, just as her father's face tightened one last time, Anna held her breath.

Only once he was as still as the air, a lifeless mass on the wooden floor, only then did she breathe again.

Chapter Twenty-five

Please read this last!
June 7th, 1983

To my beloved girls,

Read first what I have attached to this letter. If you choose not to, don't blame me if you're confused. That entry from my diary was written long ago, but it is the truth about a very important part of my life. As much as I dared to tell, or could bear to write down. So read it.

Of all my ninety years, the early ones passed like the blink of an eye. Or maybe like the blink of an eye while you're staring straight at the sun. What I mean to say is that I don't think those years shaped everything that I am, but the people and events did affect me profoundly, leaving a lasting imprint.

When I was sixteen, I began keeping a diary. With more than my share of youthful arrogance, I wrote that

I believed a person's history should be separated from what lies in her heart. I believed this very strongly then because it was a way for me to show that I could think freely, differently from my mother. In truth, I was angry that she was treating me as a child, that she would not tell me about her past. I saw no reason why she would keep those things from me, believing myself to be oh-so mature.

But as I grew older, just as my mother warned, I lived a history of my own.

I realized that I could not find a way to separate my history from a heavy, unbearable pain that settled in and never left. I could find no way to tell the story without reigniting my most secret grief, my most terrible guilt, and so I never told you the story at all.

Even later, when I admitted to myself that my juvenile notion was more rebellion than wisdom, even then this did not help. Here was my own history, my own life burning a hole in my breast, and yet I still could not bring myself to tell you the truth. So I told you bits and pieces over the years, but very little, and I wrote a lot more down on paper, but not all. And though I fully intended to share everything with you at some point or another, I never fixed that point in my head, and so I never did share much of anything at all.

Not only could I not tell *you* the truth, I couldn't even write it down. But I shouldn't mix the two things up, I think. Those written lies were constructed for a different purpose, and I'm sure you understand now what that was. What matters is that you forgive me, late as my apology comes, for my omissions and for my deceit.

You might have guessed that I am feeling the need to unburden myself — a brick in the face would be less obvious. Perhaps it is because I am afraid I won't live another year, and won't get the chance. Perhaps it is because today is the anniversary of the day I discovered love. Or, perhaps I have simply waited too long, and it's time.

I don't know what you will think of me for having loved a woman. In truth, I'm not sure what I think of it myself. You'll pardon me if I don't use the L-word. I suppose that's what people like Sylvia and me call themselves these days. It's just that we never knew that word, so it doesn't feel right. We never used it when we were together, and I haven't been with anyone since. What happened with Sylvia is just part of who I am. I guess it's part of who I've always been.

So enough, already. Anna, my dear, let me begin with you.

You've made me a lucky mother, you should know that. You have given me immeasurable joy over the years, and I am sorry if I didn't say so sooner. There is a bright spark in you, a creativity that I wish I had. If I didn't say so more often, maybe it's because I was a little jealous, I'll admit it. You and I are more similar than you might think. But the difference between us is that if I ever once had a gift, it was lost somewhere along the way. Or maybe I just ignored it, I don't know. You, on the other hand, seized yours, held it tight, and never let it go.

I have always been so very proud to be your mother, dearest Anneleh. And I shouldn't forget grateful! For your protection of me, for your fierce and steadfast devotion. You welcomed me in your house, always came to spend time with me. No matter how badly I treated you, you were always there. Not just on that one day, but always.

And now you, dear Sadie. How can you ever forgive me? I know you say that you do, but I don't know whether or not I believe it. In the last few months I have been blessed once again by your presence in my life, something that I thought I had lost forever. I only hope that I will get to look at your sweet face again before I die.

Hearing your voice on the phone, talking to you, you remind me so much of my Sylvia that it is agony. But it is a sweet agony, believe me, darling. And even though what you just read may not seem as terrible to you as my many years of silence, I hope you will forgive me for it also.

The two of you are so different, and yet I see pieces of me in both of you. I hope that instead of feeling horror that you couldn't escape my influence, you can find some comfort in the continuity of generations. What more could a selfish old woman want than to know that she has wormed her way into a child's gestures, into the inflection in her voice, into the very sensibilities that enrich her life. Maybe you'll keep my memory alive, together.

And after reading all of this, if you feel you were robbed of your past, I hope you will not dwell on it. Instead, I hope you can accept this wisdom:

My mother was right. Our history and our heart are inseparable, bound together like the sun and the earth, or like paint hugs a canvas. Together, they are compelling, a beautiful and sad duet that serenades our soul.

So reach back over time, spreading out the dark cloak that has obscured our lives. Feel beneath it, to where truth is a needle waiting for courage to guide her way through. Help her to repair the harm I've done.

The needle will prick as it mends, and leave bunches in the cloth where you stitch together holes. The folds of our past will not easily be smoothed out. But none of that matters. Lumpy and uneven, there is comfort in an old blanket. It can warm a numb and aching heart.

My darling girls, be good to one another.

Love,
Your Mama

Chapter Twenty-six

June 27th 1983, 8:00 P.M.

The third day of the shivah seemed longer than the first two. Anna listened intently to people as they shared memories of her mother, but there was no glimpse of the new Rebecca, the mother she seemed barely to have known. Story after story amounted to little more than the false treasure planted by a woman who had fiercely protected her true wealth. Her mother had carefully drawn her own caricature, and the one friend who might have known her true form was not having a good day.

Ida spent the afternoon sitting in the armchair in Rebecca's room, attended to solicitously by her daughter. When she was spoken to, her answers were brief. She smiled uncharacteristically. Danielle explained that this was her mother's way of feigning lucidity when she felt confused.

As the afternoon drew to a close and dusk settled in, the guests shuffled out slowly, either escaping before the prayers or making their excuses shortly after. By nine o'clock, only the

Gutsteins were left. On her way out the door, Ida pressed into their hands two envelopes.

"A little something for after the shivah," she winked, hinting at possible indecency. Anna and Sadie exchanged embraces with them, then closed the door and listened to them trundling down the hall. They opened the envelopes immediately and smiled at their contents, a crisp new twenty-dollar bill each.

The air had cooled off some since the late afternoon, the July humidity breaking slightly and allowing a soft breeze to ruffle the curtains in the front room. Anna went in and opened the window wider, breathed in the air and looked down at the street. She heard her sister come up behind her and felt her arm around her shoulder. They looked down below and watched as Ida was helped into her daughter's car, parked across the street with the permission of a handi-capped sticker.

Sadie asked, "Do you think Ida ever told anyone about Papa?"

"Probably," said Anna. "She could never keep her mouth shut."

"Seriously."

"At the very least I imagine she told her husband."

"Well, very few must've known, otherwise you can be sure someone would've ratted on you, Anna."

"I don't know. When a man hits his wife, people almost never interfere. But it doesn't mean they aren't glad when he gets his comeuppance."

"That's only because it soothes their guilty consciences."

"Maybe so, but just because people are cowards, that doesn't make them evil."

"I don't agree. I think when people stand by and watch that and do nothing, it *is* evil."

Anna shrugged it off, she was too tired to start an argument. They set about to tidy the apartment a little, putting some food back in the fridge and wiping down the kitchen table. Most of the guests had cleaned up after themselves, so there was little to do. She put some tinfoil over a coffee cake while her sister did a few dishes, then sat down for a minute and listened to Sadie slosh some water around in the sink.

"I wanted to ask you," she said, the apprehension making her voice unsteady.

"Yes?"

"Will you come back soon and visit? I've got lots of room at my place. You could stay as long as you like."

"I'd love to."

They smiled, neither looking at the other, and Anna stood up to continue straightening things up. She worked her way along the side counter with a cloth, making her way to the refrigerator, where she rearranged some plastic containers. She would have to take all this stuff home eventually. Or have a garage sale. She couldn't think of it now.

She closed the refrigerator door and looked up. "You know," she said, putting her hand on her chin, "you really do look a bit like Barbara Stanwyck."

"Look, Little Orphan Annie, don't start with me."

Anna tapped her sister lightly on the arm, and Sadie stuck out her tongue. The gesture made Anna laugh.

"Remember when we were kids and we used to do that? We could go on for five minutes calling each other names if Mama wasn't there to break it up."

"Yeah, what did I used to call you?"

"Fig-face. It was a terrible nickname."

"Right. How could I forget? And you used to call me Sadie String-bean. It wasn't much kinder."

"Boy, we must have been two pains in the butt to have around."

They went into the bedroom and began to straighten out the bed. The mood seemed a lot lighter, and Anna wondered if nostalgia had obscured the past for a moment so that their childhood actually seemed comforting and happy. Or was it that their relationship as children was a light peeking out from the darkness? Whatever it was, it lingered on their faces, kept them smiling as they tucked in the corners of the bottom sheet.

Weariness sent Anna to the edge of the bed to sit down.

"I'm glad Mama knew some happiness in her life. Even if it was only for a short while," she said, folding her hands in her lap. "Even if it was with a woman. I'm just glad she knew what love was."

Sadie smiled, and Anna looked past her face and saw the photograph of their mother on the wall. It was a head and shoulders shot, and she looked to be in her twenties. There was an awkward smile on her face, and her shirt collar looked too tight. The picture was taken in a professional studio, the matching one of their father long since discarded, no doubt. Anna felt her smile fading, and sadness coloured what remained of it.

Sadie followed her eyes to the photograph.

"What's wrong?"

"I was just thinking ... that there's nobody to break up our fights anymore."

Sadie nodded her head. "That's true. But from my point of view, until a few months ago I didn't have either of you. It was just me. At least it's nice that there's us again. You and me."

"Yes, it is."

But that wasn't how Anna was feeling. She considered what Sadie said, about how it should probably comfort her more than it did, about how the comment was probably meant to make them feel more close. It was not that she couldn't under-stand how Sadie would feel; after all, Anna had been the one to set the tone by asking her sister to come back and stay. It was just that, unfortunately, Sadie's remark only underscored how much their years of separation had given them different per-spectives. It didn't make her feel closer to her at all. In fact, she missed her mother more than ever, and that was all that there was. It was a primal emotion, and she just wanted to let it be.

But Sadie was oblivious.

"C'mere, I want to see something," she said, and she took Anna's hand, leading her out of the bedroom to the wall beside the door.

The hall mirror was still covered with a scarf. Anna stared at it, puzzled, and a little irked at being distracted from her grief.

"What? What is it?"

Sadie went over to the mirror and picked at the corners of the material. "I know we're not supposed to," she said, "but I don't care." Carefully, she removed the veil, put it around her neck, then stepped back and put her arm over her sister's shoulder.

Side by side, they contemplated their reflection. At first, the light from the lamp on the side table seemed inadequate. One could not see anything properly, and Anna noted only a dim profile, an odd silhouette that merely accentuated their distinct shapes, their differences once again.

She looked more intently — perhaps she was missing what Sadie was trying to show her. But when her eyes adjusted to the light, though the image became more complex and she was able to see the detail more clearly, this truer likeness of them offered no more comfort. Their features seemed so heavy, so burdened with thick, ugly strokes of time.

But then Sadie smiled.

And then, by contagion, so did Anna.

And when they smiled, it illuminated their reflection, and the harshest of their traits was suddenly adorned by expectation. By a strange trick of the light, for a moment, their years apart and the secrets that tainted their past no longer mattered, barely even showed.

And, though she saw the image in that strange way that mirrors echo reality, the essence of it was not at all distorted. In fact, its clarity caught her off guard, and it showed on her face. It was a disarmingly honest reflection, at once appealing in its warmth and comforting in its strength. It was as if their wrinkles and lines, pressed and squashed together by their smiles, joined past and future in every direction that they ran. Their skin was like that old blanket her mama talked about — one skin, covering both of their bodies. Comforting.

And yet, what stood out most was something else, just as powerful, but far more surprising. There in that mirror, above all, she saw a portrait. It was imperfect, and it was unfinished, but there it was nonetheless.

A portrait, looking something close to family.